D0032390

SEDUCTION GAME

PAMELA CLARE

BERKLEY SENSATION, NEW YORK

BERKLEY
SENSATION

An imprint of Penguin Random House LLC
375 Hudson Street, New York, New York 10014

SEDUCTION GAME

A Berkley Sensation Book / published by arrangement with the author

ISBN: 978-0-425-25495-0

PUBLISHING HISTORY
InterMix eBook edition / October 2015
Berkley Sensation mass-market edition / January 2016

PRINTED IN THE UNITED STATES OF AMERICA

10   9   8   7   6   5   4   3   2   1

Cover design by Rita Frangie.
Photo of couple by Claudio Marinesco.
Photo of "Downtown Denver, Colorado" by photo.ua/shutterstock(image #215314255)

Penguin
Random
House

This book is dedicated to Rachel Bavaro Patarino, my friend and former mother-in-law, who died suddenly following a tragic car accident as I was writing the first chapter of this book.

Thank you for reading my stories, Rachel, and for encouraging me in the pursuit of my dreams. Thank you most of all for loving my children, your grandsons, Alec and Benjamin. You are not forgotten.

ACKNOWLEDGMENTS

I started writing this story in January 2014. As it turns out, my former mother-in-law's death that month was not the only tragedy the year had in store for my family. In April, I was diagnosed with Stage 1C breast cancer and, soon thereafter, a parathyroid adenoma, a benign kind of tumor.

Writing on this story came to a halt as I endured three surgeries, twelve weeks of chemotherapy, and twenty-five sessions of daily radiation in an effort to beat the disease. I forgot the plot. I forgot what I'd written. Between doses of painkillers and antinausea meds, I felt I would never be able to write again.

A few weeks after finishing radiation and a little more than three months after finishing chemotherapy, I opened the story again, and the words poured out. I finished the book in three months and three weeks—a record for me. Whether the story had been gestating that entire time or whether I simply had a rush of creative energy after feeling so terrible and suffering so much pain for so long, I can't say.

But my arriving at that moment came as the result of a thousand acts of kindness from family, friends, fellow authors, and readers. I was able to write this book because I survived cancer and treatment and had the opportunity to write it.

It would be impossible to list the names of all the people who sent cards and gifts. I wish we'd kept some kind of gift registry, but keeping track of it all was truly overwhelming for someone who was healing from repeated surgeries and in treatment. Still, I read every card, every email, every Facebook post, and I kept everything you all sent me. Your gifts and cards are in a special box. I kept it all so that I could remember the love you poured into me during those dark and terrible months.

Still, there are those whose kindness and generosity were so stunning and constant that I must single them out.

Many thanks to my mother, Mary, my beautiful sister, Michelle, and my son Benjamin for their support and care day in and day out after my surgeries and during treatment. Thanks to my brother David for the impromptu trip to Mount Rushmore. It's a rare bright spot in a very dark year.

Heartfelt thanks to: Grace Burrowes, Jackie Turner, Marie Force, Thea Harrison, Hestelle Bonthuys, Jenn Le-Blanc, Courtney Milan, Libby Murphy, Robin Covington, Kimberly Kincaid, Kaylea Cross, Marliss Melton, Kristin Daniels, Jane Porter, Norah Wilson, Joyce Lamb, Roxanne St. Claire, Julie James, and the clergy and parishioners at St. John's Episcopal Church in Boulder for their generosity and their compassion. Your kindness, your messages, your emails, and your prayers were a lifeline.

Thank you to the more than twelve hundred members of the Facebook I-Team group, who gathered in a virtual waiting room each time I had chemo, who let me vent, who encouraged me every day during the course of my treatment. I am so lucky to know all of you and to be able to hang out with you every day. You are such special people, and I am blessed by your friendship. Plus, ducklings.

Thank you to every one of the many dozens of authors and readers who donated to the Good Food Fund that delivered meals to the house during chemo so that I didn't have to cook, and to those who donated to my medical expense fund. Not being able to write is devastating for an author's finances, and without your help, this time would have been so much more difficult.

Thank you to Brian Grable and Dana Lightsey, two childhood friends who came back into my life, bringing understanding and emotional support at a time when I needed it most. I'm so happy to be back in touch with both of you. The older I get, the more I value the misspent days of my youth.

Many thanks to Oakland Childers for visiting me at home when I was on reverse isolation and so many other friends had simply disappeared.

Thank you to my dear friends and family in Denmark, whose love and friendship is with me every day despite the distance.

Thank you to my precious cousin Kymber for the cards she sent from everywhere on her exciting travels, and my talented cousin Madison Daniel, who treated me like a heroine in some mythic battle rather than a sick person. CousinFest?

Additional thanks to all my friends at RBL Romantica. You put together a box of cards and gifts and treats that lifted my spirits at the most difficult point of this journey. I cried while I read each card, held each gift. I didn't cry when I ate the treats, however.

Thank you to the authors who put together a boxed set as a fund-raiser for me, helping me to end the year without overwhelming medical debt: Dianna Love, Norah Wilson, Bonnie Vanak, Joan Swan, Elisabeth Naughton, Cynthia Eden, Mary Buckham, Adrienne Giordano, Stephanie Rowe, and Tracey Devlyn. What a crazy-kind thing to do.

A very special thank you to the people who helped me get back into writing by helping in one way or another with this book: Benjamin Alexander, Norah Wilson, Heather Doherty, Joyce Lamb, Michelle White, Jackie Turner, Shell Ryan, Sue Zimmerman, Kristi Ross, and Amy McBurnie.

Special thanks to Russ Shumway and Terry Gudaitis for sharing their expertise with me on all things decryption

and CIA. Any mistakes in this work are my doing and not
theirs.

I hope to repay the kindness I received with acts of generosity to those in need. If last year taught me anything, it's
that kindness truly matters. It can lift up hearts, lessen pain,
and even save a life.

Thank you, all!

Pamela Clare

May 3, 2015

CHAPTER 1

Trust no one.

What the hell was Kramer trying to tell him?

Nick Andris rubbed his closed eyes with the heels of his hands, then looked up at the clock. Almost midnight.

Shit.

This was a waste of time.

For almost three weeks, he'd been keeping Holly Elise Bradshaw under round-the-clock surveillance. He'd turned her life inside out, but had found nothing. He'd tapped her cell phone and landline, sifted through her laptop, searched her condo, memorized the details of her childhood, learned about her friends, pored over her financial records, scrutinized her posts on social media for hints of tradecraft, and tracked every move she'd made via GPS. He'd found nothing remotely suspicious.

He'd even gone behind Bauer's back and contacted Rich Lagerman, an old buddy from Delta Force who was now working for the FBI, and asked whether Bradshaw was one of theirs. Every federal agency in the country now had undercover officers, and it wouldn't be the first time operatives from different agencies had tripped over one another while pursuing a suspect.

"Nope. Not one of ours," Lagerman had said. "But if you need any help with her, maybe some late night, under-the-covers work, let me know."

"Right."

Nick now knew more about this woman than she knew about herself. If Holly Bradshaw were some kind of underworld operative, a foreign agent, a traitor who sold US secrets, then he was Elvis fucking Presley.

Someone at Langley had screwed up.

Bauer had recalled Nick from assignment in Tbilisi amid whispers that a handful of officers were missing or dead and that the Agency was conducting an internal investigation of its Special Activities Division, or SAD, the top-secret branch of the CIA that had recruited Nick out of Delta Force nine years ago. He'd never been assigned to operate within US borders, so he'd arrived in Langley expecting to find himself in the middle of an inquisition.

Instead, Bauer, his supervisor, had given him a file with the latest intel on Sasha Dudayev, aka Sachino Dudaev, the Georgian arms smuggler who'd killed the only woman Nick had ever loved.

"He killed an officer and stole a flash drive containing classified information vital to US operations outside the homeland," Bauer had said. "Holly Elise Bradshaw is his contact for the deal. Keep Bradshaw under surveillance, recover the data, and neutralize them both using any force necessary."

As a rule, the Agency left affairs within the homeland to the NSA and FBI, but they sometimes broke that rule when it came to high-value international targets and US citizens who'd crossed the line to work with those targets. It was unusual for Nick to run surveillance on a fellow American in her home, but apart from that element of his current mission, Bauer had given him exactly what he'd wanted for two long years now—a chance to make Dudaev pay.

Dudaev had played the Agency and brought the Batumi op down on their heads. Nick had been there that night. He'd watched, wounded and pinned down by AK fire, as the son of a bitch had emptied his Makarov into Dani's chest, then made off with the cache of AKs the Agency had wrested away from Chechen terrorists. Nick had crawled over to Dani and held her body afterward, held her until he'd passed out from blood loss.

His sole task that night had been to protect her, and he'd failed.

But now things were about to come full circle.

There was only one problem.

The suits at Langley had clearly made a mistake when they'd fingered Ms. Bradshaw as Dudaev's contact. Okay, so it was an understandable error. The bastard's last lover had been an Italian journalist who'd acted as his mole and messenger—until he'd killed her. Analysts must have assumed he'd recruited Ms. Bradshaw when she'd interviewed him about his new art gallery and then begun dating him.

As understandable as the error might be, nothing changed the fact that Nick had now wasted *three weeks* discovering that Holly Bradshaw was exactly what she seemed to be—an entertainment writer; a smart but shallow blonde; a woman who loved sex, expensive clothes, and good times with her friends. He'd explained all of this to Bauer, sharing every bit of intel he'd gathered on her. If Dudaev was about to sell the flash drive, the deal would go down without Bradshaw's knowledge or participation.

Bauer had blown him off. "Stick with her. I swear she's the one."

Some people just hated to be wrong.

Nick's time would be better spent trailing Dudaev and hunting down the real contact—or sorting truth from rumor on the internal investigation and the missing and dead officers.

Trust no one.

Kramer had contacted him this afternoon, insisting they speak face-to-face. He'd be passing through Denver tomorrow and had asked Nick to meet him for lunch. Nick hadn't needed to ask what was on Kramer's mind. It wasn't unusual for an officer to be killed in the line of duty, but it *was* strange that Nick and Kramer had worked with all of them. Then Kramer had ended the call with those three words—and Nick's imagination had taken over.

"They're ombré crystal pumps in royal blue with four-inch heels."

Nick took another swig of cold coffee. In his earpiece, Bradshaw and her friend Kara McMillan were *still* talking.

"I love them," Bradshaw said, "but my shoe budget is blown for the next ten years."

Nick doubted that. Bradshaw's daddy was a retired brigadier general who had served with US Army Intelligence—another reason analysts believed Dudaev had chosen her—and Daddy had created a nice little trust fund for his baby girl.

"How much do a pair of Christian Louboutins cost?" McMillan asked.

Nick ran through the key facts on McMillan, more to help himself stay awake than because he'd forgotten anything.

McMillan, Kara. 40. Journalist, author, journalism instructor at Metro State University. Wife of Sheridan, Reece, lieutenant governor of the state of Colorado. No arrests. No suspected criminal associations. Three children. Formerly employed by the Denver Independent *on its Investigative Team, aka the I-Team. Met Bradshaw through work. Close personal friend.*

"Well, it depends on where you buy them, whether they're on sale, which shoe you choose—that sort of thing."

"Holly," McMillan said in a stern voice. "How much?"

Bradshaw hesitated. "These were just over three thousand."

Nick had just taken another swig of coffee and nearly choked.

Three thousand dollars? For a fucking pair of shoes?

"Wow!" McMillan laughed. "Reece would divorce me."

Damn straight!

"Did you get them for your big date with Sasha tomorrow?"

"I needed something to go with my new dress."

Nick rolled his eyes. The woman's closet was full of shoes. The last thing she needed was one more pair—especially one that cost *three fucking grand*.

"I read in the paper that he's a billionaire—gas and oil money," McMillan said.

Nick's jaw clenched.

Dudaev had built his fortune on human lives, including Dani's. Killing her had been nothing more than a business transaction to him. He could change his name, wear designer suits, and open a dozen art galleries to make himself seem respectable, but nothing could wash the blood off his hands.

"You should see the sapphire necklace he gave me last week. The chain isn't actually a chain. It's a strand of diamonds."

Nick already knew from another conversation—this time with Sophie Alton-Hunter, another friend from the newspaper—that Bradshaw had bought the dress to match the necklace. Now she'd gotten the shoes to go with the dress. And at last Nick understood what a woman like Holly Bradshaw would see in Dudaev.

Well, greed was blind.

She had no idea what kind of man he truly was. If she wasn't careful, he'd strangle her with that necklace.

"Sophie told me. It sounds like he's serious about you. Do you think this will be it—the big night?"

Nick frowned.

What did McMillan mean by that?

"I don't know. I mean, he's good-looking enough."

"Good-looking enough?" McMillan laughed. "He's a lot better looking than that banker you went out with last year. Where was he from?"

"South Africa."

"He's better looking than that Saudi prince, too, whatever his name was. In the news photos, he looks a lot like George Clooney. Sure, he's got some gray, but I'll bet he's fully functional."

Ah, yes. They were talking about Ms. Bradshaw's love life. Again.

Nick glanced for a moment at the photos of her he'd pinned to the wall above his desk. He could see why men were eager to sleep with her. She *was* hot.

Okay, she was incredibly hot. Platinum blond hair. A delicate, heart-shaped face. Big brown eyes. A full mouth, and a body that . . .

Get your mind off her body.

What good were looks if they got you into trouble? There were men who preyed on beautiful women, and Dudaev was one of them.

"Yeah, but he's . . . I don't know . . . self-absorbed. He's probably the kind of man who makes you wish you had a magazine to read when you're in bed with him. You know—the kind who acts like he's doing you a big favor when he rams into you for two minutes."

McMillan was laughing now.

But Bradshaw hadn't finished. "A lot of guys are oblivious like that. 'Don't worry about getting me off, babe. I just want to go down on you all night long'—said no man ever."

Nick shook his head. *Is that truly what she expected?*

A dude would have to have a motorized tongue to pull that off.

Did all women talk like this about sex? Nick couldn't imagine his sister sharing details about her sex life with her friends or using this kind of language. His mother, a devout Georgian Orthodox Christian, would have had a coronary if she'd caught her daughter or even one of her five sons talking like this.

Not that it offended Nick. He found it kind of sexy, actually. But then, given the things he'd seen and the things he'd had to do, a conversation about oral sex was pretty damned tame.

"Not all men are selfish."

You tell her, McMillan.

"No, I suppose not. But lots of them are. It makes me want to take out a full-page ad in the paper just to help out womankind. 'It's the clit, stupid.'"

Nick let out a laugh—then caught himself.

Keep your shit together, Andris.

HOLLY BRADSHAW GLANCED over her shoulder at her living room wall. "Mr. Creeper must be watching something funny on TV. I just heard him laugh. I never hear him."

"You still haven't met him?" Kara asked through a yawn.

"He's lived there for almost a month now and hasn't once come over to say hello. He stays indoors and keeps the shades drawn. I've seen him outside once. He was taking out the trash, but he was wearing a hoodie. I couldn't see his face."

Kara's voice dropped to a whisper. "Maybe he's a serial killer."

"You're *not* helping."

"Who cares about him anyway? If I were you, I'd be so excited about tomorrow night. You lead such a glamorous life. I'm so jealous."

But Holly knew that wasn't true. "You and Sophie and the others—you spend every evening with your kids and men who love you, while I watch TV by myself or go out to the clubs. I think you're the lucky ones."

Like the rest of Holly's friends, Kara was happily married to a man who cherished her. Reece was one of the kindest, most decent, and sexiest men Holly had ever met—which was really strange, given that he was a politician. He'd bent over backward to prove to Kara that he loved her. Now, they had three kids and lived what seemed to Holly to be a perfect life.

The fact that all of her friends were now married and most had children had changed her life, too. She spent a lot less time out on the town with them and a lot more time alone while they took on new roles and responsibilities. As much as she loved excitement and enjoyed the city's nightlife, some secret part of her had begun to long for what they had—a family, a sense of roots, the certainty of belonging with someone. If she hated anything more than boredom, it was loneliness.

But Kara didn't seem to believe her. "Are you saying you'd be willing to trade places with me?"

"And sleep with Reece?" Holly smiled to herself, stretched out on her sofa, and wiggled her toes.

"That's not what I meant."

But the question, however intended, had Holly's imagination going.

Reece was sexy with dark blond hair, blue eyes, and muscles he hid beneath tailored suits. How fun it would be to peel one of those suits away from his skin.

Then there was Julian Darcangelo, Tessa's husband. He was the city's top vice cop and a former FBI agent who'd worked deep cover. Tall with shoulder-length dark hair, a ripped body, and a strikingly handsome face, he was sex on a stick—and crazy in love with his wife.

Then again, Marc Hunter, Sophie's husband, had served six years in prison and had that badass vibe Holly loved. A former Special Forces sniper, he was also devoted to his family—and sexier than any man had a right to be.

Gabe Rossiter, Kat James's husband, had a rock climber's lean, muscular build and a daredevil attitude. He had all but given his life for the woman he loved. Kat was lucky.

Zach McBride, a former Navy SEAL and Medal of Honor recipient, had saved Natalie from being murdered by the leader of a Mexican drug cartel. All lean muscle and confidence, he had the hard look of a man who was used to taking action.

Nate West, Megan's husband, had been badly burned in combat, his face and much of his body disfigured. The part of him that wasn't scarred was extremely handsome—and he had a cowboy charm that brought the song "Save a Horse (Ride a Cowboy)" to Holly's mind.

Javier Corbray had rescued his wife, Laura Nilsson, from captivity in a terrorist stronghold in Pakistan, sacrificing his career as a SEAL. With a sexy Puerto Rican accent, dreamy dark eyes, and a mouth that—

"Are you fantasizing about my husband?" Kara's accusing voice jerked Holly out of her reverie.

"No, of course not. Not really. Okay, a little," Holly confessed. "I was just deciding which one of you I'd most like to trade places with."

It was just a game. Holly had never so much as flirted with a married man. She didn't poach on other women's territory. But that didn't mean she couldn't fantasize.

"Holly!" Kara laughed. "I'm sorry I phrased it the way I did. Let me try again."

Tessa, Holly decided.

She'd trade places with Tessa. She'd always had a secret crush on Julian.

But Kara went on. "If you want to meet good men, maybe you should quit going to the clubs. Most of the guys there are just looking for someone to hook up with."

It wasn't the first time Kara had suggested this, but she didn't understand.

How could she?

Holly fired back. "You met Reece at a bar."

Okay, so it had been a restaurant. Still, Kara had consumed three margaritas, so it might as well have been a bar.

"Only because *someone* interfered," Kara replied.

Holly smiled to herself. It had been *so* easy.

"Where else can a woman meet men? If I don't go out, I'll never meet anyone. It's not like Mr. Right is going to walk up and knock on my front door."

"You never know." Kara changed the subject. "Hey, did you hear that Tom is converting to Buddhism?"

Holly sat upright. "Tom? The same Tom Trent I know? The one who spends his day shouting at everyone? He's converting to *Buddhism*?"

"That's what my mother says."

Kara's mother, Lily, lived with Tom.

"She would know. But Tom—a Buddhist? He and the Dalai Lama have *so* much in common, like, for example . . . nothing."

Tom was the editor-in-chief of the *Denver Independent*, where his temper was as much of a legend as his journalistic brilliance. As an entertainment writer, Holly didn't work directly beneath him like her I-Team friends did. Beth Dailey, the entertainment editor, was her boss. Beth never yelled, never insulted people—and she appreciated Holly's shoes.

"I think it's perfect," Kara said. "If anyone needs to meditate, it's Tom. Gosh, it's after midnight. I need to get to bed—and so do you if you want to be rested for tomorrow night."

The two said good night and ended the call.

Holly got up from the sofa and went through her nightly routine, undressing, brushing her teeth, and washing and moisturizing her face, a sinking feeling stealing over her. Naked, she walked over to her dresser and carefully took her new Louboutins out of their red silk bag, moving them so that the light made the crystals sparkle.

She didn't want to spend another moment with Sasha Dudayev, but she'd already accepted and had the shoes . . .

Just one more date and that would be it.

She tucked the shoes carefully back in the bag, turned out her light, and crawled between her soft cotton sheets.

NICK FELL TO *the concrete, pain knocking the breath from him. He looked down, saw that the round had penetrated his right side. He pressed his hand against the wound to staunch the blood loss.*

He glanced over his left shoulder, caught sight of Dani. She lay flat on the ground behind a forklift, her gaze on him, her eyes wide.

She was safe.

Thank God!

She got to her knees, clearly about to run to him.

Nick shook his head in warning. "Stay there!"

But their attackers had already spotted her and opened fire again.

Rat-at-at-at-at!

AK rounds struck the forklift, ricocheting wildly.

Dani fell flat again, panic in her eyes.

Then Dudaev appeared, gliding down the center of the warehouse like an apparition.

The bastard walked over to Dani.

"No!" Nick shouted.

Dudaev glanced his way, looked back down at Dani, and said something. Then he drew a Makarov from a shoulder holster inside his jacket.

"Dani! No!" Nick fought to reach her, bullets raining from above, pain and blood loss making it impossible to move.

He was too late.

God, no!

"Dani!"

Bam! Bam! Bam!

Nick awoke with a gasp, sweat beaded on his forehead, a hand pressed to his side. There was no blood, pain only a memory.

Around him, the room was silent.

Another nightmare.

He rose, walked to the bathroom, splashed cold water on his face, his sense of terror slowly receding, grief taking its place.

Dani.

Every damned time he had one of these, it was like losing her again, the pain as real and new as it had been when he'd lain there holding her body, her lifeless eyes looking up at him, her blood and his mingling on that warehouse floor.

God, how he wished it had been him.

How he wished Dudaev had killed him instead.

* * *

"THEY SAY THEY'VE got more leg room, but that's bullshit. I'm six feet. You just can't get leg room in economy."

Nick nodded, took a swig of Tsingtao, his gaze on Kramer as he typed a message onto the Notes app of Nick's phone with one finger. Nick had known Kramer since the beginning. He'd been working under Bauer when Nick had joined the Agency and had taken Nick under his wing, acted as his mentor, showed him the ropes.

Kramer had always seemed indestructible to Nick, but today he was looking rough around the edges—older, pale, worn. There were thick bags under his eyes and a couple days' growth of whiskers on his jaw. His hair was more gray than brown now and looked as if it hadn't been combed in a few days. Then again, he'd just flown in from South Korea. But it was more than that.

For the first time since Nick had known him, Kramer seemed shaken, worried.

Kramer turned the phone so Nick could read it.

We've got big trouble.

As soon as he'd read the message, Nick deleted it and typed his own.

An internal investigation. Who? Why?

"I'm six-three, man," he said aloud. "You're preaching to the choir."

On his plate, an order of kung pao beef was growing cold, the food and conversation nothing more than cover.

Kramer frowned, took the phone, typed.

Daly, Carver, both dead.

"I sat there for the last three hours of the flight wishing I could stash my legs in the overhead compartment," Kramer went on, the tone of his voice casual, his Brooklyn accent standing out in this crowd of Coloradans and California imports.

"I've had that same fantasy." Nick deleted the words, typed his own message.

I heard. Were they outed?

Kramer shrugged, deleted Nick's message, and began to type again. "They're going to have to decrease their fares or take out a couple of rows of seats if I'm ever going to climb into one of their rust buckets again. I felt like a goddamn sardine."

McGowen's dead, too.

"Too bad you've still got four hours of flying time to go, old buddy." Nick's mouth formed words that barely registered with his mind as he did the mental math, a sense of foreboding growing in his gut.

He typed out his reply.

They were all part of the Batumi op. What the hell is going on?

"Yeah, too damned bad about that, for sure." Kramer looked Nick straight in the eyes, typed one last message, then finished his beer and stood.

Nick turned the phone so that he could read it.

Watch your six.

That was it? Kramer had met with him just to tell him to watch his back?

Nick had every intention of doing just that, of course. He erased the message, stood. "Want a ride to the airport?"

Kramer tossed a couple bucks onto the table. "I'll grab a cab."

As he watched Kramer leave the little Chinese joint, Nick felt certain that Kramer knew more about all of this than he'd just shared.

CHAPTER 2

NICK ADJUSTED HIS platinum-and-diamond cufflinks, his gaze focused on the crowd, a knot in his stomach, the same knot that had been there since he'd gotten the news.

Kramer hadn't made it to DC. He'd stepped out of that restaurant, climbed into a cab—and disappeared. His luggage had been found in an alley in Aurora beside a couple of spent 9mm shell casings and a pool of blood that would probably test as his. But so far police hadn't found his body.

What the *fuck* was going on?

A dozen possibilities had been running through Nick's mind all evening, but one stood out among the rest: Dudaev must have known Kramer was in Denver and had gone after him. That meant Nick was in danger. If Dudaev had been able to identify and track down Kramer, Nick had to assume the bastard could do the same with him.

That thought had prompted Nick to switch his cover at the last minute. Rather than showing up at the gallery opening as a member of the catering staff, he had come as a wealthy art collector, the glasses, graying hair, and mustache an attempt at a last-minute disguise.

You look like something out of a 1970s Stasi manual, Andris.

Maybe so. But Nick didn't need to win a beauty contest. He just needed to get Dudaev before the bastard got him.

He hadn't cleared the change of cover with Bauer. If there was a leak somewhere in the chain of command, someone within the Agency who was handing officers over to the enemy, he didn't want to give himself away. As far as everyone in DC knew, he was currently walking around the gallery dressed in black and wearing a fine apron.

He shifted his attention back to the crowd, mental discipline pushing other thoughts aside. He had a job to do.

It was already past nine and Gallery Dudayev was packed. Denver's glitterati had turned out in force to see and be seen at the grand opening—and to meet the city's newest billionaire. By Nick's estimate, there were almost two hundred people here, all of them dressed to kill. He had no difficulty picking Dudaev's men out of the crowd. He'd counted five. They stood along the edges of the room, their gazes moving over the sea of faces. Compared to the gallery's guests, they looked sullen and stiff, their suits not quite enough to camouflage the thugs within.

Meanwhile, Dudaev was still at the restaurant with Ms. Bradshaw. He was probably planning on making a late entrance. The bastard loved drama.

Nick accepted a glass of champagne from a young server and feigned interest in a sculpture, his gaze shifting to the other side of the room. He was here tonight to see if he could spot Dudaev's real contact, the person who'd come to act as Dudaev's courier and deliver the stolen intel to its buyer. He couldn't be certain the contact would show tonight. Still, the gallery's grand opening was guaranteed to draw some of Dudaev's underworld contacts.

Near the buffet table, Denver's new mayor was talking with a city councilman about tighter regulations for the city's private marijuana clubs. In the corner, an older man and his wife argued about whether he'd been ogling younger women. A hipster in skinny jeans kept circling back to the buffet as if he hadn't eaten in a week. A gay couple moved from painting to painting, discussing the merit of each and holding hands.

"What he's trying for here is modern art with a classical aesthetic, a contemporary reinterpretation of the canon," said one.

Nick drew out his cell phone, thumbed in his passcode. If

Ms. Bradshaw hadn't forgotten her cell phone at home, he would be listening in on every word of her dinner conversation. Instead, he was stuck looking at the location of Dudaev's limo on a special GPS app on his cell phone. The blip on the screen, fed to his phone by a small GPS transmitter he'd fixed to the underside of the limo, told him they were still at the restaurant. *How long did it take to eat a damned meal?*

What Dudaev had in mind for Ms. Bradshaw, Nick wasn't certain. The son of a bitch wanted to fuck her, of course. That went without saying. But if he tried to recruit her, and she had the strength of character to refuse . . .

What's it to you, Andris? The woman isn't your problem.

If she had the bad taste to get mixed up with a killer like Sachino Dudaev, that was her mistake. The Agency wasn't there to bail her out. Then again, Dudaev wouldn't get far, regardless of his plans for her.

Soon, he'd be dead.

Nick felt a sense of anticipation at the thought. Hell, no, he didn't enjoy killing—most of the time. He was willing to make an exception in this case. The Agency wanted to terminate Dudaev because he and his organization posed a serious threat to US security. But Nick's reasons were far more personal.

He felt his cell phone buzz, glanced down. The green blip was moving.

It's about damned time.

A few minutes later, the limo pulled up to the curb. A uniformed driver hurried around to the rear driver's-side door and opened it. Dudaev stepped out like a conquering hero and walked behind the vehicle to the rear passenger door, where he stood, smiling, waiting for the driver to open it.

The knot in Nick's stomach became a ball of rage.

It had been a little more than two years since he'd seen the son of a bitch. Dudaev had done well for himself. Dressed entirely in black—Italian shoes, Armani suit, diamond ring—he waved to his guests, acknowledging their applause, then turned and reached back to help Ms. Bradshaw.

She emerged one long, silky, slender leg at a time.

Holy . . . *hell.*

Nick's mouth went dry.

He'd spent three weeks listening to her and had looked at dozens of photographs, but he hadn't really *seen* her, not like this.

Shit.

She wore a strapless dress of beaded royal blue, its hem barely low enough to cover her ass. A sapphire the size of a robin's egg hung from a necklace of glittering diamonds, more diamonds hanging from the end of the stone in a tassel that just touched the dark cleft of her breasts. Dudaev's gift. She looked up at the bastard as he helped her out of the vehicle, her brown eyes warm, her red lips curving in a smile, her shoulder-length platinum blond hair arranged in tousled waves.

A whisper moved through the crowd.

"Those boobs have to be as fake as that necklace."

Fake or real, her tits were in serious danger of becoming another gallery exhibit. How the hell did that dress stay on?

"I think she's an actress."

She was certainly beautiful enough to make it in Hollywood, but an actress wouldn't have shied away from the cameras the way Ms. Bradshaw did.

"It figures the rich old goat would get to sleep with a chick like that."

Yeah. That thought sickened Nick, too.

He tore his gaze from Bradshaw and moved casually on to the next sculpture, trying to fade into the background.

THEY REACHED SASHA'S hotel just after one in the morning.

Holly watched while Kirill, Sasha's chief bodyguard, searched her clutch, examining her cell phone, looking inside her compact, checking inside her emergency box of tampons, and opening her lipstick. "The color is called Heat Wave. I can pick some up for you if you like it."

Kirill glowered at her.

"For your wife, I mean." Holly met Sasha's gaze. "It was a joke."

Sasha chuckled. "Kirill is not one for the jokes, I think."

Kirill motioned her forward. "Put your hands behind your head."

She looked up at Sasha, putting a pout on her face. "Do I have to do this?"

"I am sorry, but Kirill is most particular about security," Sasha answered. "I am a very powerful man. There are some who would do anything, even send a beautiful woman, to get to me."

"Fine, but if there's going to be a pat down, I want *you* to do it." She smoothed her hands down Sasha's chest.

"He won't touch you, my sweet. I promise." There was a hint of steel in Sasha's voice—a warning for Kirill.

Holly turned toward the grumpy security guard and did as he asked, giving him a little smile. "Do I look like I'm carrying a gun? Where would I hide it?"

Two spots of red appeared on the dour man's cheeks as he ran a metal detector over her. It beeped as it passed over her breasts.

"It must be the underwire in my bra," she said. "Should I take it off?"

Kirill looked like he was about to demand that she do just that, when Sasha muttered something to him in Russian.

"Your shoes, please, miss." Kirill pointed to her feet.

Holly stepped out of one pump and then the other, handing them over. "Okay, but be careful. These are Christian Loubou-tins. They're very expensive."

Sasha settled a big hand on the nape of her neck. "If he makes so much as a single scratch, I will buy you new pair."

Kirill examined the shoes, then handed them back to Holly.

She slipped them on one at a time, holding on to Sasha's arm for balance. "I didn't realize being an art collector could be so dangerous."

"Money attracts danger, and art is money." Sasha turned to the door of his hotel suite, swiped his key card. "Ladies first."

Holly stepped inside and glanced around. She'd stayed in the Roosevelt Suite once before when she'd gone out with that South African banker, but she wouldn't tell Sasha that. "This is amazing!"

He gave her a grand tour, his arm around her shoulders. The furniture was masculine and had a historical feel, with dark leather sofa and wing chairs, walnut cabinets, and pol-ished wood floors. A portrait of Teddy Roosevelt from his

Rough Rider days graced one wall. A four-poster bed stood in the spacious bedroom.

Sasha guided her to the windows that gave them a view of the city lights. He caught her chin, pressed his lips to hers in a soft kiss. "You have only tasted a little of what could be your life with me. I can fly you around the world, show you places you have never seen. Paris? Rome? I will buy them for you. I can take you sailing on my yacht—*Star of the Black Sea*. It is a beautiful ship."

"That all sounds so romantic." She'd heard it all before. He'd even shown her photos of the yacht.

He smiled. "Shall we have some champagne?"

On a sideboard just inside the door, a bottle sat chilling in a crystal ice bucket.

"You're such a gentleman, Sasha."

He'd been a perfect gentleman all evening—if being a gentleman were measured in grand gestures, spending money, and bad kissing. He'd reserved an entire restaurant for the two of them, their table set with old English roses. The chef had served course after course of delicacies, each with its own wine. Everything had been delicious, from the prosciutto appetizer to the coconut sorbet dessert.

Sasha had asked her about her job and what she wanted out of life, making it clear that he had much to offer her— excitement, glamour, even work if she wanted it. When she'd asked him what kind of work, he'd told her that he sometimes had need of someone he could trust to deliver packages and that he paid handsomely for such service. Holly had told him that she was happy with her job at the paper and had steered the conversation back toward art.

After dinner, they'd taken the limo back to the gallery, kissing in the privacy of the back seat. He had no skill as a kisser, going with too much tongue too fast. She'd been relieved when they'd arrived at the gallery and he'd had to put that clumsy oral appendage back in his own mouth.

The gallery opening had been fun, with lots of people Holly knew from Denver's cultural scene and tasty little hors d'oeuvres she'd been desperately tempted to eat. She knew Denver's art scene well and had brushed up on art history just for the occasion. Not that she could hope to match Sasha's knowledge on the subject—he truly was an expert—but at least she'd held her own.

He drew her closer and kissed her, again leading with his tongue. "Can you feel it? You belong with me."

Oh, please!

Beneath the glitz and the whiff of danger, Sasha was . . . *boring.*

His cell phone buzzed.

He drew it out of his pocket, frowned at the display. "I apologize. I must take this call. Please, make yourself comfortable."

She gave his tie a tug. "Don't take too long."

"I promise." He smiled down at her, then put the phone to his ear and answered in his native tongue, disappearing into the small office and closing the door behind him.

Holly slipped out of her heels and glanced around. Behind the closed door, Sasha began to shout, clearly angry and in the midst of a serious conversation.

She saw her chance—and she took it.

She opened her clutch, took out the box of tampons, and retrieved the nitrile gloves hidden inside one of the plastic applicator tubes. Slipping the gloves on as she went, she hurried to the bedroom and opened the closet door, searching behind his suits for the room's safe, listening as Sasha continued to argue. She punched the hotel's default password into the safe's keypad and opened the door, memorizing the placement of the contents at a glance. Makarov PM pistol. Two loaded magazines. Cash. Files. Passport. Red aluminum RFID-safe case.

She opened the RFID-safe case and found it—the stolen USB drive.

Sasha's voice boomed from the office beyond, making her pulse spike, and not for the first time she wished she understood Georgian. She spoke French, Russian, and some Arabic, but not a word of Georgian, which was a bummer because she had no idea what was making him so angry. Had someone outed her?

Focus!

If he were to come out and discover her, she would die.

She took the special adapted smartphone from her

handbag, popped it out of its case, and plugged the flash drive into the concealed USB port. A log-in prompt appeared on her screen, and she entered the password. The retrieval program kicked on and asked her if she wanted to download the data and upload the virus. She pressed "Yes," her gaze drawn toward the bedroom door and the living area beyond.

While the data was downloading, she tucked the phone and disk drive back into the open safe and hurried into the living area, reaching into her bra. Careful not to break the slender wires, she loosened the tiny listening device, its compact body made to look like a button, and pulled it free. She knew exactly where she wanted to place it. Her gaze fell on the portrait of Roosevelt with its thick gilded frame. She hurried over, lifted the portrait away from the wall, then affixed the device to the back edge of the frame and activated it.

"Bully!" she whispered to Roosevelt, sure he would approve.

Knowing she was running out of time, she opened the copy of the *New York Times* that sat on the coffee table and turned to the entertainment section so that Dudaev would think she'd been reading this entire time.

Behind the closed door, Sasha fell silent.

She froze.

Oh, hell!

When he began shouting again, she ran to the bedroom and pulled the phone and flash drive out of the safe, looking back toward the office as the seconds ticked by and the phone finished uploading the virus. Ninety-four percent. Ninety-eight percent.

Done.

She tucked the flash drive carefully away, closed the safe, and smoothed the suits back into place, then ran for the bathroom, locking the door behind her.

She took a deep breath, willing her heartbeat to slow. She peeled off the gloves and flushed them down the toilet, her gaze landing on her own reflection. Her cheeks were too pink, and there was a sheen of perspiration on her forehead. She dabbed it away with a tissue.

He'd quit shouting now. Was he finished? If so, she had only seconds.

With practiced calm, she left the bathroom, looking

quickly for anything she might have missed, and found her clutch gaping, the box of tampons open. She closed the box and snapped the clutch shut.

As they'd taught her in training, death was in the details.

She slipped her pumps back on and sat on the sofa, and had just picked up the newspaper and rubbed newsprint onto her fingertips when he opened the door and stepped out. Willing herself to relax—a predator like Sachino Dudaev would sense her adrenaline—she put a concerned frown on her face. "Is everything okay?"

He moved toward her, a heavy scowl on his face, fury in his brown eyes.

Holly felt her pulse spike.

Had the call been someone warning him about her? Had she been exposed?

"I apologize." He bent down, pressed a kiss to her forehead, then walked over to the sideboard, his back toward her.

She closed her eyes, exhaled.

He went on. "The art world spans the globe, and that sometimes means calls come at strange hours. I promise—no more business tonight."

He seemed tense as he opened the champagne and poured them each a glass. "Veuve Clicquot 1996 Grande Dame. It was the best they had."

What had he been shouting about? She wished she knew, though she seriously doubted it had anything to do with art.

She got to her feet and joined him. "I'm sure it will be wonderful."

Though she'd recovered the stolen intel, her task wouldn't be complete until she'd uploaded the virus to his computer to destroy any files he might have copied. Unless he went to the bathroom in the next few minutes, she would have no choice but to let the night take its course, even if that meant having sex with him. If she got lucky, maybe he had a bad case of erectile dysfunction and was out of Viagra.

Hey, a girl could dream.

Sasha turned to her and offered her a glass, looking into her eyes in a way that was no doubt supposed to be sexy but made her want to laugh. "To beauty."

Holly clinked her glass with his and sipped, the bright

taste dancing across her tongue, bubbles tickling her nose. "Mmm!"

Sasha drew her down on the sofa beside him, the fingers of his free hand possessing hers. "You were tonight the most stunning exhibit in the gallery. Every man in the room wanted you. Every woman wanted to be you."

"What a sweet thing to say." Holly resisted the urge to pull away.

What was her problem tonight?

She'd always gotten a thrill out of playing with dangerous men, manipulating them, turning their own lust and stupidity against them. They looked at her and saw a sexual plaything, a pretty toy they wanted to claim and control. They took her to dinner or to their beds, never knowing that *she* controlled them. The fact that her job was extremely risky—and would have both shocked and horrified her father—had only added to her sense of excitement. But tonight . . .

Tonight was no different. The only thing that mattered was doing her job.

You are the spider. He is the fly.

She took another sip of champagne, looked up at him from beneath her lashes. "Thank you for a magical evening."

He leaned down until his forehead almost touched hers, his gaze on her boobs. "The night isn't yet over. I had hoped you would stay."

She let her lips curve in a slow smile. "If . . . if it's not too soon. I wouldn't want you to think I'm the kind—"

He kissed her, a hard kiss, again leading with the tongue. She worked with it, trying to turn off her mind and just react with her body.

He drew back, reached for the champagne bottle, and refilled their glasses. "Let's go to the bedroom."

Feeling a little light-headed, she rose to her feet and followed him, her heart beating erratically. She took another sip of the golden liquid to calm herself.

"I want to see you wearing nothing but my necklace." He turned her to face away from him, and she felt his fingers take hold of the concealed side zipper. He drew it down, letting her dress fall to her feet, exposing her black lace bra and thong. His hands stroked the bare skin of her buttocks, cupping her, his body pressing close enough to prove that he, unfortunately, did not suffer from erectile dysfunction.

The fingers of one of his hands took hold of her bra strap. "May I?"

"Yes." She felt a strange rush of breathlessness.

Was she aroused by him? No! She couldn't be.

Then why was her heart beating so strangely?

Though she'd enjoyed sex with one or two of the handful of men she'd had to sleep with as part of her job, she didn't find Dudaev attractive in the least. For starters, he was old enough to be her grandfather. Second, there was that mustache. But mostly there was that bit about him being a murderer and a thief and a . . .

She needed to stop drinking. It was getting hard to think.

His fingers released the clasp, and he pulled her bra away, tossing it aside.

Wearing only his sapphire necklace, her black lace thong, and her Christian Louboutin pumps, she stood still before him, a shiver sliding through her as his gaze moved over her.

He reached out, cupped one of her breasts. "Oh, you are beautiful."

But something was wrong. The room was spinning.

Oh, damn!

"Sasha?"

He stared at her, a strange look on his face. He seemed angry, and he was stammering, some of his words coming out in a language she didn't understand. And then he was holding a gun.

"What . . . ?" A burst of adrenaline hit her bloodstream—and dissipated.

Drugged.

She'd been drugged.

Dudaev was going to kill her.

This is so *going to suck.*

She took a step away from him, felt herself begin to fall, and then . . .

Nothing.

CHAPTER 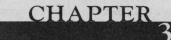 3

NICK STEPPED OUT of the elevator wearing the room service uniform he'd liberated from the laundry and pushed a cart laden with strawberries and more champagne down the hall toward Dudaev's room. The same thug stood sentry outside the door as before, watching Nick through dull, angry eyes.

Nick rolled up to the door, lifted the cover off the serving dish with a white-gloved hand, picked up a strawberry, and popped it into his mouth, speaking as he chewed. "Want one?"

The big Russian glowered at him and slammed the lid back into place, swearing in his native tongue. "Those are *not* for you."

The man reacted as Nick had hoped he would, not questioning whether his boss had placed another order, but turning toward the door to alert Dudaev that his strawberries and champagne had arrived—and were being poached by the help.

Nick struck him at the base of his skull with the butt of his Ruger MK III, rendering him unconscious. The man fell against the door and slid to the floor in a heap.

Nick searched him, confiscating his Makarov, his cell phone, and the key card to his room—and Dudaev's. He glanced up at the security camera, uncertain how long it would take for the hotel's security staff to realize the footage on this floor had been hacked and was set on a ten-minute feedback loop.

With a swipe, he opened the door to Dudaev's room, dragged two hundred pounds of bodyguard inside with him, then quietly closed the door. From the bedroom, he could hear Dudaev swearing, his speech slurred.

The son of a bitch was still conscious.

So much the better.

Unable to leave witnesses behind, Nick aimed the suppressed pistol at the bodyguard's forehead and pulled the trigger twice, ending the man's life in a single, painless second with a double-tap.

Pop. Pop.

Too bad Nick didn't have one of those magic Hollywood suppressors that turned pistol shots into whispers. Even with integrated suppression and .22 subsonic rounds, the shots weren't silent.

Still wearing gloves, he picked up the two shell casings, popped them into his pocket, and walked back to the bedroom, taking it all in at a glance.

Ms. Bradshaw passed out on the bed, wearing nothing but a lace thong and those sparkling shoes, the sapphire nestled between her breasts. Dudaev still dressed and slumped half on the bed and half off, trying to raise his head, a small pistol on the floor near his feet. He must have realized something was wrong when the drug began to take effect and had gone for his weapon.

At least Nick had managed to stop him from getting his hands on Ms. Bradshaw and enjoying one last fuck. He could feel good about that.

Dudaev spotted Nick, saw the weapon in Nick's hands, and his pupils dilated.

Pulse ratcheting up a notch, Nick moved toward him, speaking in Georgian. "Remember that night in Batumi?"

Dudaev seemed confused, mouthed unintelligible words.

"I'm here to settle the score."

Dudaev made a clumsy effort to sit up, his gaze on his pistol.

"You want that, don't you?" Nick bent down, retrieved it, and stuck it in the waistband of his trousers. "It's mine now."

He looked into the face of the man who'd killed Dani and who was almost certainly to blame for the disappearances and deaths of the other officers. There were lines around his eyes, his skin dull from tobacco use and tanning. His mustache and the gold chains around his neck made him look like a low-rent hustler. But it was the hatred in his eyes that revealed what he truly was.

A ruthless killer.

Nick hadn't planned on taking out Dudaev tonight. Then he'd overheard one of Dudaev's men telling him in Georgian at the gallery that Ms. Bradshaw was under Agency surveillance. While Dudaev had insisted that Holly wasn't a risk to him and was only being watched because she'd been seen fraternizing with him, the other man had urged him to kill her—just to make certain.

Nick felt he'd had no choice but to move early. Clearly, he'd been made. He needed to retrieve the stolen flash drive and eliminate Dudaev before they could move against him— or harm Ms. Bradshaw. The best way to do that here, where a firefight would draw all kinds of attention and perhaps get bystanders killed, was to render both Dudaev and Bradshaw unresponsive before Nick moved in.

"It's over, you son of a whore." Nick took a pillow from the bed, pressed it over Dudaev's face. The bastard struggled and moaned beneath him. Nick pushed the barrel of his pistol deep into the down to muffle the sound further.

"For Kramer. For Dani."

Another double-tap.

Pop. Pop.

An explosion of feathers and blood.

Beneath Dudaev, a pool of crimson began to soak into the sheets.

For two long years, Nick had thought of this moment, imagining the sense of triumph he would feel as he glared into Dudaev's eyes, spoke Dani's name, and pulled the trigger. He waited for the elation to come. But nothing inside him seemed to have changed. And it occurred to him as he stared down at Dudaev's corpse that the fucker had suffered a much less painful death than Dani.

It's better than you deserved, you son of a bitch.

He picked up the shell casings, glanced at Ms. Bradshaw, lying unconscious and all but naked on the other side of the bed, and immediately felt a tug of regret. He quashed it. Why should he care if she woke up next to a corpse, blood spatter on her skin? It hadn't been his idea for her to go to bed with the guy. Besides, he had probably saved her life. There was nothing he could do about the mess anyway.

Shit.

He slipped the pistol back into his shoulder holster, then took Ms. Bradshaw's wrist and felt for a pulse. It was slow, but steady, her breathing even. He hadn't been sure who would drink from which glass, so he'd dusted each with enough drug to subdue a two-hundred-pound male. Relative to her weight, Bradshaw had ingested a dangerously high dose.

Nick found his gaze traveling along her legs to the apex of her thighs, and over the curve of her hip to the fullness of her very real breasts, the tassel of diamonds draped over one pale pink nipple, cold, glittering ice against soft, warm skin.

He jerked his gaze away.

You're an asshole, Andris.

He needed to knock this shit off and get to work. He'd already compromised part of his mission to save her life. He wasn't being paid to stare at her tits. And, no, looking her up and down did *not* constitute a search.

He grabbed a throw blanket from a nearby chair and draped it over her to keep her body temp up, then went to work, searching for the missing flash drive.

Dudaev was cocky and not terribly smart, so Nick went straight to the safe, punched in the hotel's override code, and opened it. There, next to a mean-looking Makarov PM and thirty grand, sat an RFID-safe case. Inside was the USB drive.

Gotcha.

Nick put it back inside the case and pocketed it, leaving the pistol and the jack.

He had the most important thing he'd come for, but there was more.

He walked out into the living area. A copy of the open *New York Times* sat on the coffee table beside Ms. Bradshaw's clutch, which held exactly what he'd expected it would—makeup, house keys, cell phone, a couple of credit cards, and tampons. Careful not to step in the dead body-guard's blood, he searched the chairs, the couch cushions, the cabinets, and shelves, just being thorough.

He found a listening device on the back of the frame of the portrait of Teddy Roosevelt, one he didn't recognize.

Who the hell put you there?

He deactivated it and examined it, turning it over in his gloved palm. It closely resembled a black button and appeared to be similar to technology used by the Agency. He pocketed it as well, knowing the experts at Langley would want to examine it.

In the office area, he found a laptop sitting open on the desk, a leather briefcase beside it. Dudaev had left the computer running.

Nick tapped the track pad to awaken the display.

Images flashed across the screen.

They were all there—Kramer, Daly, Carver, McGowen, even Bauer and Nick's old buddy Lee Nguyen.

And Dani.

What the . . . ?

Then the laptop seemed to realize it had drifted off. The images on the screen disappeared, and a small white box popped up, prompting him to enter the password.

So Dudaev *did* have intel on all the missing and dead officers. That's probably what was on the stolen flash drive. Somehow, Dudaev had managed to decrypt the files.

But something didn't feel right.

Why did Dudaev have intel on Dani? She'd been dead for two years now. The Agency would have purged any files it had on her long ago.

The Batumi op.

Dudaev had been there. All of the officers who'd disap-peared or been killed in the past six months had been there. Now Dudaev had files about them on his computer, files he'd most likely taken from the stolen Agency flash drive.

The internal investigation.

Was the Agency investigating that operation?

Nick had always had questions about that night. He'd

handled the security personally, prepared for every contingency. Or so he'd thought.

Kramer's words echoed through his mind.

Trust no one.

Something was wrong.

It's above your pay grade, Andris.

The best he could do was get these files back to Langley and let the people who got paid the six-figure salaries sort it out.

He picked up the computer then left the room, concealing the laptop on the room service cart. He made his way down the service elevator, through the kitchen, and out into the alley, an image of Ms. Bradshaw lying helpless and all but naked beside Dudaev's corpse trapped in his mind.

It was pain and bright light that roused Holly.

"She's alive. We called for an ambulance."

She tried to open her eyes, but couldn't, pain ricocheting through her skull. She tried to sit up, but couldn't move, her body limp. She heard herself whimper, her head throbbing so hard she thought it might shatter.

"The cops are on their way, too."

"You ever seen anything like this before?"

"No, man, never."

Men's voices.

An ambulance? The cops? What had happened?

A car accident? A migraine?

Thirsty. She was so thirsty. And her head . . .

Oh, God!

Holly willed herself to open her eyes, and found herself in a hotel room, two men in hotel security uniforms standing over her.

"Where . . . ?" She tried to ask the question, but couldn't muster the strength.

A wave of nausea rolled through her, a strange chemical taste in the back of her throat. Moaning, she turned onto her side, something cool and heavy brushing against her breast. She glanced down at it through half-closed lids.

A diamond necklace with a sapphire.

What . . . ?

If only her head didn't hurt so much. If only she could think clearly.

Was she hungover? That would explain the headache and her thirst.

She opened her eyes. When had she closed them again?

She heard shouting in the distance, two men, their voices angry.

"You'll stay out here till the police say it's okay for you to enter. That's hotel policy, and that's my policy."

Two men were still standing there, but they weren't looking at Holly. They were staring at the bed beside her, a look of stunned revulsion on their faces.

Holly followed their line of vision.

She heard a strangled cry and realized she was screaming, her heart thrashing in her chest as adrenaline hit her bloodstream.

A man lay dead beside her, two holes in his forehead, blood everywhere.

In that moment, she knew only that she needed to get out of the bed, away from him, away from the stench of blood, and . . .

Oh, my God!

It was on *her.*

Blood had soaked into the sheets, spattered the right side of her face and body, bits of brains on the sheet like curds of cottage cheese.

On a burst of adrenaline, she sat bolt upright—and then her training kicked in, clearing her mind, overcoming for a moment the pain in her skull.

Sachino Dudaev.

The dead man was Sachino Dudaev.

The necklace was a gift from him.

She'd been on a job. She'd found the USB drive Dudaev had stolen and had downloaded the info into her cell phone. They'd had some champagne, and he'd undressed her. And then . . .

She couldn't remember anything after that.

Dudaev must have drugged her.

And then someone had killed him.

Someone had been here in this room. Someone had killed Dudaev and left her all but naked in bed with his corpse.

Perfect. Just flipping perfect.

For a moment she thought she might throw up—which would be gross.

Then her heart gave a hard knock.

The cell phone!

It held extremely important classified information, stolen intel she'd been sent by the Agency to retrieve. Had the killer taken it? She tried to remember where she'd put it. If only the throbbing inside her skull would stop.

Damn it!

"Please." She pointed toward the living area, struggling to piece words together, her mouth dry, her mind sluggish. "My clutch. In the other room. My cell phone. I . . . I want to call my mother."

One man looked to the other, who nodded, then hurried off to get it for her.

It was then Holly realized she was covered to the waist by a throw blanket. It had probably slipped down when she'd tried to sit up. She took hold of the end and covered her bare breasts, just as the man returned with her clutch.

"Thank you." She took it and fumbled with the clasp.

The cell phone fell out, landing on her lap.

Thank God!

She closed her eyes, drew a slow breath of relief.

Aware the men were watching her, she typed in her password and activated the emergency retrieval beacon, assuring that no matter what happened to her or where the cell phone went, her case officer would be able to find it.

But what about the computer? She still needed to plant that virus before the police arrived. The moment they got here, this would become a crime scene. She could already hear sirens down the street.

"My computer. It's in the office. On the desk. Can you bring it to me?"

One of the men left the room only to return a few moments later. "There's no computer anywhere. The office is empty."

Oh, God! Damn! Damn!

Whoever had murdered Dudaev had probably been after the same information as she. She'd bet the USB drive was gone, too. Well, they wouldn't be able to retrieve anything from it. She had destroyed that data. But the computer . . .

For the first time in almost a decade, she had failed.

And then it hit her.

The listening device she'd planted.

Wouldn't her team have realized already that something had gone terribly wrong? Wouldn't whoever had been monitoring the audio feed have heard the gunshots? Even if the killer had used a suppressor, which he almost certainly had, there was no way to silence the sound of a pistol firing completely. If they'd left her here . . .

Had she been discarded?

The thought brought with it a wave of panic, her head spinning.

No. No! They wouldn't abandon her unless her connection to the Agency had somehow been exposed. If the killer had known *why* she was really there, wouldn't he—or she—have killed Holly, too? The situation was probably too hot for anyone to get in and get her out without making things worse.

The thought gave her some comfort.

You're supposed to be calling your mother.

She remembered what she'd told the security guards, but the last person in the world she wanted to call was her mother. Still, Holly *did* need help. She needed help here and now, in the real world, where, apparently, her case officer and team couldn't reach her. But she knew someone who would help.

She tapped his cell number into her keypad, certain he was still asleep. It wasn't daylight yet, and it was a Saturday. She hated to bother him but she had no choice.

"Darcangelo." Julian's voice sent a surge of relief through her.

With relief came a rush of tears, words spilling out of her in senseless babble. "It's H-Holly. Someone killed my date last night. Someone drugged me. Maybe *he* drugged me. I don't know. But someone murdered him while I was next to him in his bed. I woke up, and he was dead. There are blood and bits of brains and—"

"Are the police there? Is medical there?"

"N-not yet. I can hear sirens. Hotel security guards are with me."

"Hang tight. Don't talk to anyone. Don't answer any questions. Don't touch anything. Where are you?"

"The Roosevelt Suite at the Palace."

"I'm on my way."

CHAPTER 4

THE ROOM AROUND Holly seemed to explode into questions and camera clicks as first the police arrived and then EMTs and the medical examiner.

"What's your name?"

"How did you get here, Holly?"

"What do you remember?"

Holly had done the so-called Walk of Shame before, heading home in the morning wearing a cocktail dress and heels after a night of fun and sex. She'd never once felt the way she felt now—raw, humiliated, exposed.

Holding a blanket against her chest to cover herself, she deflected the barrage of questions as best she could, the noise and light making her headache worse, until she truly feared she would throw up or pass out.

Then Julian walked in.

Wearing a white T-shirt and jeans, his dark hair pulled back into a short ponytail, he flashed his badge, then slipped his hands into nitrile gloves and his shoes into blue booties before approaching her. His gaze moved from her to what was left of Dudaev and back again, and she saw his expression darken.

"What was your relationship with . . . ?" a detective asked her, his words trailing off when he saw Julian. "Hey, Darcangelo. What're you doing here?"

Julian shook the man's hand. "Holly's a friend of mine.

Can you cut her a break, man? She needs medical attention. Let's move her out of your way so the EMTs can do their job. You can question her later."

He stood back and held up a blanket to shield her from view while the EMTs lifted her to a gurney and covered her with a sheet. They wheeled her into the spacious bathroom, where it was quieter.

Julian stood beside her while an EMT took her vitals. "How do you feel?"

"Like I have the world's worst hangover."

"I bet." He gave her hand a squeeze. "Do you remember anything?"

"We were talking, sipping champagne. We went to the bedroom. He . . ." This was harder to talk about than she'd imagined. "He undressed me, and then . . . that's it."

"BP is eighty-eight over sixty. Oxygen saturation is ninety-two."

One of the EMTs produced an oxygen mask. "We need to give you some oxygen, okay? We also need to start an IV."

"Really? Do you have to do the IV? Can't we just skip that? I hate needles."

Julian held her hand and tried to distract her while they jabbed the biggest needle Holly had ever seen into her arm and got the IV going. "Police are probably going to take your clothes and shoes into evidence. They will likely also request a forensic exam once you get to the ER. You can refuse, of course. I know it won't be easy, but it might turn up evidence that will help police catch this killer."

"You mean . . . *Ouch!* A rape kit?"

There was nothing like a vaginal exam to make a horrid day better.

"You were drugged and unconscious and alone with a killer, Holly. You can't be certain he didn't do other things while he was there. Even if all he did was touch you, he might have left a fingerprint or DNA. There could be evidence on your body that might help us catch him."

She started to tell Julian that a man who hadn't had time to steal a gazillion-carat diamond-and-sapphire necklace probably hadn't had time to whip out his weenie and rape her, but thought the better of it. Instead, she nodded and closed her eyes, her tears returning, sliding down her temples. "This sucks."

He gave her hand another squeeze. "Yeah, sweetheart, it really does."

Outside the bathroom door, detectives compared notes with the ME, telling one another what Holly already knew. "It looks like a professional hit to me. We got a DB by the sofa, a DB in here. Both were killed by a double tap to the head from a twenty-two at point-blank range. She could have killed them, then drugged herself, but the blood spatter on her skin shows she was lying on her back right there when the victim was killed. Unless her reach is longer than a fucking orang-utan's, there's no way she could have fired those shots."

Holly must have drifted off because the next thing she knew they were in the elevator. Julian stood next to the gurney, talking to dispatch on his radio. "Eight-twenty-five. We're heading to the hotel's rear entrance. I want a wall of uniforms between the public sidewalk and the alley. Over."

"Copy, eight-twenty-five."

He noticed her watching him. "They've moved the ambulance to the rear entrance, and we've got units in place to hold the press and gawkers back."

"Thank you." Holly's voice was muffled by the oxygen mask. "For everything."

He looked down at her, smiled, his blue eyes full of concern. "You just rest."

Guilt niggled at her. If Julian knew the whole truth . . .

She fought to put the guilt aside. These were her friends, the closest friends she'd ever had. They cared about her, even if they didn't know everything about her. She did what she did in part for them. She did it for her country. If that meant the occasional lie or letting them believe things about her that weren't true, that's just how it was.

But this felt different. She had crossed a line.

She'd gotten into trouble on the job and she'd called Julian, knowing he would come. She hadn't thought for a moment that she would be exposing him to the horror that was in that hotel room. "I'm sorry."

"For what?"

"For dragging you out of bed on a Saturday. For taking

you away from Tessa and the kids. For making you see . . . *that*."

"I'm just glad I was able to be here." He gave her a rueful grin. "Believe it or not, I've seen much worse."

"Really?" She felt tears sting her eyes again, her voice breaking. "I haven't."

She'd never seen a dead person, much less one with holes in his head. Her job entailed serious risk, but it was well managed. It wasn't like the work done by other operatives. She didn't even own a firearm. She was only called up a handful of times a year, and when she was, it usually just entailed going on a few dates with someone so she could slip a GPS tracking device or listening devices into his car, condo, or hotel room. Last night had been unusual in that she'd also been tasked with recovering the intel on the USB drive. Most of the time, however, she set up people of interest—mostly foreign visitors who posed a potential security threat to the country—for surveillance.

It wasn't supposed to involve blood and corpses.

Yes, she'd had a few close calls. She'd been roughed up more than once. She'd had to do things in bed she hadn't wanted to do with men she hadn't wanted to touch. She'd even had to eat escargot. But this particular mission had turned out to be a whole lot more than she'd bargained for.

She closed her eyes against the pain in her head—and the images in her mind. "God, I'm glad I don't have your job."

Julian gave her hand another squeeze. "It's going to be okay."

They pushed out the back door into early morning light. From a distance of about twenty feet to her right, cameras began to whir, reporters shouting out questions.

Just freaking great.

Dudaev's murder would be front page, above the fold.

Then came a shout. "Holly?"

Holly recognized that voice.

Joaquin.

Of course he would be here. Joaquin Ramirez was the paper's best photographer, the shooter all the editors wanted to assign to stories that were likely to appear on the front page.

"Hey, you got to let me through, man. She's my friend."

"I'm sorry, but you need to stay behind the line."

"Hey, Darcangelo!" Joaquin called. "Tell these guys to let me through."

The gurney was lifted into the back of the ambulance.

"You can see her at the hospital, Ramirez," Julian called back, climbing into the ambulance beside Holly.

Then the doors were closed and they were off.

NICK SAT OUTSIDE Bauer's office waiting to be debriefed, his stomach empty apart from coffee. He looked down at the small photo of Dani he carried in his wallet when he wasn't on assignment. She was smiling at the camera, her dark hair caught in a breeze, a smile on her beautiful face as she posed in front of St. Basil's Cathedral in Moscow, enjoying just being a tourist.

They'd been on vacation—one of the few times they'd been able to get away together. She'd just come off a long mission in Ukraine, so they'd spent most of their week in Moscow in their hotel room, making up for weeks of being apart. They'd talked about leaving the Agency, getting married, having a couple of kids.

Three months later, she was gone.

Nick hadn't been able to tell his family how she died or how he'd been wounded. They didn't know what he did for a living. He'd told them only that she'd been killed in a robbery. His mother, who'd been pushing for a big Georgian Orthodox wedding since the day she'd met Dani, had lit a candle for her at church. And though Nick saw the worried glances they shared with one another when they thought he wasn't looking, they hadn't mentioned her again.

But Nick hadn't been able to let it go.

He hadn't been able to let *her* go.

He wanted to tell her that he'd killed the man who'd ended her life, but he couldn't. There was nothing he could ever say to her or do for her again.

People said the pain would lessen with time but Nick had begun to think a person just got used to living with it.

Dani.

He kissed the photo, tucked it back in his wallet, pushing aside the ache that always lingered in his chest. He glanced at his watch.

He'd left Denver immediately, catching a special military flight from Buckley Air Force Base back to DC. The USB drive, laptop, and the listening device he'd found were now in Bauer's hands.

He'd accomplished his mission—for the most part. He'd eliminated Ms. Bradshaw as a suspect, retrieved the stolen data, and terminated Dudaev, but he'd failed to identify Dudaev's contact. Bauer would be disappointed about that last part.

Dudaev was dead.

The thought struck Nick again, some part of him struggling to grasp that the son of a bitch who'd killed Dani was truly gone. Two years of wondering what had gone wrong. Two years of grief and rage. Two years of waiting for Dudaev to step into his crosshairs. Now it was over.

Or was it?

He'd had a long time to think on the flight back from Denver. He'd thought about his visit with Kramer and Kramer's warning. He'd thought about Dudaev and what he'd seen on the bastard's computer screen. He'd thought about Dani and the night she'd died. He'd thought about the internal investigation. He'd thought about the dead and missing operatives. He'd turned it all over in his mind like pieces of a puzzle.

And then the pieces had come together with a *click*.

The Agency was investigating the Batumi op, trying to answer the questions that had haunted Nick for two long years, and the operatives who'd been a part of that mission were being permanently silenced.

Someone didn't want the truth to come out.

Had that someone been Dudaev, or was there a traitor inside the Agency?

Driven by that question, Nick had done something he would never have imagined himself doing. He'd cloned the laptop to an external hard drive before turning it in and had hidden the external hard drive in his rental car.

You must be out of your fucking mind.

Nine years of service to the Agency, a spotless record, several commendations. One stupid move and he would throw all of that away—not to mention land himself in prison or find himself with a bullet in the brain. He'd known this when he'd cloned the drive, but he'd done it anyway.

If someone other than Dudaev was gunning for him, he wanted to know who they were—and be able to see them coming.

He stood, glanced at his watch, caffeine, lack of sleep, and too many unanswered questions making him restless. It wasn't like Bauer to keep him waiting. He wanted to get this over with and check into a hotel so that he could get some sleep, buy a bunch of equipment—CPUs, monitors, keyboards—and then take a crack at decrypting those cloned files.

"More coffee?" Cheryl, who'd worked as Bauer's executive assistant for as long as Nick had been with the Agency, pointed toward the almost empty pot on the counter near her desk. "I need you to drink the old stuff so I can make a fresh pot."

Nick grinned. "It's my fault you're all here on a Saturday, so I'll take one for the team."

He crossed the room and refilled his cup.

The door behind him opened and Bauer stepped out. "You're up, Andris. Catch any sleep on the plane?"

"Not really." Nick walked over to his boss and gave his hand a firm shake, nodding to Lee Nguyen, who stood inside the doorway. "Good to see you, man."

Nguyen grinned and reached out to shake Nick's hand. "You're looking good, staying fit."

"If you didn't sit on your ass all day, you would be, too."

It was a running joke between the two of them. Nguyen had put on a few pounds after giving up fieldwork for a desk job, but he was still capable of kicking ass. Like Nick, Nguyen had been recruited by the Agency out of Delta Force, where the two had served together. It was partly because of him—and partly because he'd grown up speaking both Russian and Georgian—that Nick had landed this job.

Bauer ushered Nick into his office, closed the door. "Let's get down to it."

Martin Bauer had been with the SAD all of his professional career. Recruited out of college, he'd made a name for himself during Operation Desert Storm working with a team of paramilitary operators and Green Berets behind enemy lines prior to the US attack. He'd served as Nick's supervisor for the past three years.

Bauer's father had worked for the Agency in the early days right after World War II and was something of a Cold War legend. He'd played hide-and-seek with the KGB and the Stasi in Berlin before the Wall went up. If even half the stories they told about him were true, the man had been a certified badass.

Bauer resembled his father, whose portrait hung on the wall behind his desk. He was tall with light brown hair, brown eyes, and a face that was ordinary in every way. He'd used that plain, nondescript face for his nation's benefit.

Nick took a seat across from Bauer, who sank into his executive chair behind his desk, while Nguyen stood off to the side, looking out the window onto the street below.

Bauer spoke first. "You changed your cover without notifying us."

"After I learned of Kramer's disappearance, I felt it prudent to assume that I would be next. I couldn't be certain my cover was intact, nor could I be sure who was responsible for what happened to Kramer or how they'd gotten the drop on him. I didn't feel like walking into a trap, so I changed my play at the last minute."

"It may interest you to know that one of the catering staff was kidnapped and assaulted that night. He was about your height with your coloring." Bauer let that news sink in. "Good move on your part."

So Dudaev *had* tried to eliminate him.

Nguyen glanced away from the window long enough to give him an approving nod. "Way to stay on your toes out there, man."

Nick looked from Bauer, who was looking at his desk, to Nguyen, who was staring out the window again, a strange silence stretching between them.

"About Kramer . . ." Bauer shifted in his chair. "You met with him?"

So they knew about that.

Of course they did.

Nick nodded. "We took advantage of his passing through Denver to grab a couple of beers and some Chinese. We're rarely in the same hemisphere."

"What did you discuss?" Bauer asked.

Nick pushed to the back of his mind the fact that he was about to lie to his boss, a man he admired. "Mostly we talked about how much it sucks to sit on a plane when you're tall. He didn't have much time. I offered him a ride to the airport, but he insisted on taking a cab."

"You didn't discuss business?" Bauer's gaze fixed on Nick's and held it.

Nick shook his head. "Not really. He looked worried, rough around the edges. I asked him if anything was wrong. He told me to watch my back."

"What do you think he meant by that?"

"He didn't say. That's when he got up and left."

Nguyen turned away from the window. "You were the last person to see him before his disappearance."

It took Nick a moment to catch the hint of accusation, and when he did, he almost laughed. "You think *I*—?"

"We don't think anything," Bauer said. "We're just trying to put the pieces together. What time did Kramer leave the restaurant?"

Bauer and Nguyen questioned Nick about his meeting with Kramer for the better part of an hour. What had they eaten? What, exactly, had they said to each other? Had Kramer mentioned going any place other than the airport? What time had they arrived at the restaurant? Had they left together? Did Nick see Kramer get into the cab?

It was beginning to feel like an interrogation when Bauer shifted gears. "We weren't expecting you till tomorrow. You moved on Dudaev early."

Nick nodded. "I overheard one of Dudaev's men at the gallery telling him that Ms. Bradshaw was under Agency surveillance and urging him to get rid of her. I took that as confirmation that I'd been made. I felt I needed to finish the mission before Dudaev got the chance to finish me."

Bauer raised an eyebrow. "Your decision to move wasn't influenced at all by a perceived threat against that pretty blonde?"

"Not entirely." Was Nick that fucking transparent? "Last I heard, the Agency's mission includes protecting the lives of US citizens."

"You horny, Andris?" Bauer looked over at Nguyen. "I think he has a hard-on for this woman. She must really be hot."

After the grilling about Kramer, Nick wasn't in the mood for bullshit.

He turned the tables. "The intel Dudaev stole—it has something to do with the Batumi op and the disappearing officers, doesn't it? That's the focus of the internal investigation everyone's whispering about."

Nguyen's brows drew together in a frown, a hint of warning in his voice. "Nick—"

Bauer cut across him. "What makes you say that?"

"Dudaev's computer was going into sleep mode when I found it. I caught a glimpse of images before the screen went blank—photos of me, of you two, of Kramer and the others. He had a file on Dani, too. Dani ought to have been purged from the system two years ago. If the intel he stole from us was new, it wouldn't have contained data on her—unless someone is looking into how and why she died."

He let that hang in the air for a moment. "As for the rest, it's a strange coincidence that photos of Dani surface on Dudaev's computer while operatives who were part of the Batumi op keep disappearing and turning up dead, don't you think?"

Nick had worked for the CIA too long to believe in coincidences.

Bauer leaned back in his chair, clearly trying to make up his mind how much to tell Nick. He drew a deep breath, as if about to take a plunge. "Dudaev was working on behalf of the Georgian Mafia to expose US intelligence officers and assets in Eastern Europe to their criminal and terrorist buddies. As for an internal investigation, if there is one, that's something I can't discuss."

It was a simple answer. It made sense. It fit most of the evidence.

But it didn't explain everything—Dani's file, for example.

For the first time in his career, Nick wondered whether Bauer was lying to him.

Nguyen glanced at his watch. "We need to get back to the debriefing and what went wrong with this mission."

Nick felt compelled to defend his actions. "The contact may have gotten away but the files have been recovered and Dudaev is no longer a danger to the United States or its operatives. I completed the most important elements of this mission."

"No, you didn't." Bauer drew something out of his top drawer and dropped it on the desk—the USB drive Nick had recovered. "The drive has been erased. The classified files it contained were downloaded and then overwritten by a virus. You didn't retrieve the data. Bradshaw did."

CHAPTER 5

DROWSY FROM THE most recent dose of morphine, Holly repeated what the doctor had told her, her hair still damp from the shower they'd let her take once they'd completed the forensic exam. "It was some kind of anesthetic—a derivative of fentanyl. She said they'd never seen anything like it. They want to keep me overnight."

"Fentanyl?" Kara stood next to Holly's bed, together with her husband, Reece Sheridan, who looked as good in a T-shirt and jeans as he did in a three-piece suit.

"Is that like GHB or Rohypnol?" Tessa Darcangelo sat next to the bed. Tessa was a former I-Team member who now worked as a freelancer. She'd also written a couple of award-winning books about human trafficking.

"The doctor said it acted in a similar way to drugs they use to knock patients out for surgery. My headache and nausea are a side effect."

"That could have been lethal," Reece said. Then he asked the question that had been running through Holly's mind. "Who could have had access to something like that?"

"I don't know." Russian agents had used a fentanyl-based gas to knock out a room full of people during the Moscow theater hostage crisis some years ago, but Holly didn't tell Reece this. "The doctor said I came close to cardiac and respiratory arrest."

"Well, that's a reassuring thought." Tessa's words were laden with equal parts Southern sweetness and sarcasm.

In less than an hour after Holly had arrived in the ER, most of the gang had gathered in the waiting room, their presence more comforting than Holly could have imagined. She'd lived most of her thirty-three years without close friends and wasn't used to needing anyone. But right now, she needed them, and they were here for her.

Unlike her case officer. Where *was* he?

Holly told herself that he would approach her only when he knew it was safe. She'd spoken to him face-to-face only a few times over the years, and each time had been carefully managed. He would come. But when?

She felt for her clutch beneath the blankets, closed her fingers around it, afraid that in her drugged stupor she might lose it.

"I'm so sorry, Holly." Kara's long, brown hair was still wet from her shower. She and Reece had just gotten out of bed when Julian called them. "It must have been terrifying to wake up like that."

An image of Dudaev's corpse, with the two bloody holes in his forehead, crashed through Holly's mind. She took a deep breath, fighting a wave of nausea. "Thanks."

"I'm just glad you're all right." Reece pressed his hand on top of hers and Kara's and held them both. "Chief Irving will get to the bottom of this."

Holly didn't say so, but Dudaev's murder would soon be taken away from Chief Irving and the Denver Police and transferred, together with all the evidence, into federal hands. "I hope you're right."

Whoever the killer was, he hadn't taken Dudaev's money or the necklace. He'd been after only Dudaev and the files.

That alone meant he—or she—was all kinds of dangerous.

Watch what you say. You're drugged. Don't get sloppy.

Julian walked in. "Look what I found at the rifle range."

Marc Hunter, Sophie's husband, followed behind him, wearing butter-soft faded jeans and a dark green Fat Tire T-shirt. "Looks like you've had a rough night."

"Just the worst date *ever*." His sympathy had Holly fighting tears again.

"Hell, yeah, it was." Julian went to stand beside Tessa, one big hand coming to rest on his wife's shoulder. "That was a damned awful thing to wake up to."

She looked up at both men. "Thanks for coming."

Marc walked up to her bedside and gave her a hug, a worried frown on his face. "Hey, we take care of our own. You know that."

Warmth blossomed behind her breastbone.

Marc glanced around. "Where's Sophie?"

"She, Kat, and Natalie are running a few errands," Tessa answered.

"Oh." For a moment, Marc looked confused. "*Errands.* Right."

It didn't take advanced training in HUMINT techniques— human intelligence collection—to know that they were up to something. But, lulled by the morphine, Holly quickly forgot what they'd said, drifting in and out of sleep while her friends talked quietly around her.

Then it was time for Kara and Reece to get back to their kids, who had swimming lessons. They each gave her a hug, Reece bending down to press a kiss against her cheek. "Feel better. We're just a phone call away if you need us."

The conversation turned to Marc's shooting practice.

"How'd it go?" Tessa asked.

Marc grinned. "One-inch groups at three hundred yards."

"What Hunter here means to say is that he did all right. I bet I could kick his *ass* in tactical handguns."

Holly had listened to the guys banter about firearms more times than she could count and had always found it amusing. But it wasn't funny now, the words filling her head with images she wanted to forget.

"Please," she said, interrupting them. "Can we *not* talk about guns today? I just saw a man who was shot in the head."

"You don't need to explain." Marc shared a glance with Julian. "Sorry."

Someone knocked on the door, and Sophie peeked inside. "Can we come in?"

"Please do," said Tessa, in her sweet Georgia accent. "I was about to throw our husbands out of the room for being insensitive louts."

48   PAMELA CLARE

"Insensitive? Our husbands? Never." Sophie walked over, gave Marc a kiss, then bent down and hugged Holly. "How are you feeling?"

"Like I'm never going to date a billionaire again."

Another knock, and Kat James entered, holding the hand of her toddler, Nakai. She spoke quietly to him in Navajo, her native language, then scooped him into her arms and gestured to Holly with a nod of her head. "Can you say hello to Auntie Holly?"

Nakai buried his little face in Kat's chest. She laughed and brushed a dark strand of hair off his forehead. "He fell asleep in the car and isn't quite awake yet. Gabe would have come, too, but Alissa is running a fever, so he stayed home with her."

Then Natalie and Zach McBride walked in. Natalie had once worked for the I-Team but had left journalism after she and Zach had gotten married. Now she had taken up fiction writing and was almost finished with her first romance novel. She was also seven months pregnant.

They all exchanged hellos and hugs.

Natalie had brought a bouquet of pink and yellow roses. "It's from Javier and Laura. They send their love. They're up at the Cimarron with Nate and Megan, giving those friends of theirs from Sweden a tour of the Rockies and helping Nate manage things while Jack and Janet settle in with the new baby."

The Cimarron was a mountain ranch owned by Nate's family. The Wests ran cattle and bred horses—and hosted the world's best barbecues.

"That's so sweet of them." Holly sniffed the roses, then accepted Natalie's help settling the vase on the nearby stand. "I bet they're having a great time."

Holly knew how much Laura looked forward to visiting with those particular Swedish friends, and she knew why. She'd helped pull some strings behind the scenes, though Laura and Javier didn't know that. They never would.

The phone rang—not for the first time—and Tessa answered.

"No, I'm sorry. She's not taking calls from the press. No, not even from you, Alex. Bye-bye, now." Tessa hung up. "Well, bless his heart."

Alex Carmichael, the jerk who covered cops and courts for the I-Team, would do anything for a scoop or quote—including harass a coworker in the hospital, apparently.

"Is the media giving you trouble?" Marc asked.

Holly nodded, reciting a possible front-page headline. "'Naked woman found in bed with murdered billionaire.'"

"Yeah." Marc nodded in comprehension. "That will move a lot of newspapers."

"She's had five requests for interviews in the past hour," Tessa said. "The hospital switchboard is stopping most of them."

There was a lull in the conversation.

Zach broke the silence.

"Any time you want me to start running background checks on the men you date, just let me know." There was a teasing note in his voice but she could see the steel in his gray eyes and knew he meant what he said. He looked over to Julian and Marc, motioning toward the hallway with a jerk of his head. "Can I talk to you two?"

He knows something.

He must know that Dudaev wasn't what he'd appeared to be. As chief deputy US marshal for the Colorado territory, he'd have access to intel not readily available to the police. That didn't include Agency files, however.

Marc and Julian followed him out the door.

Natalie rubbed her lower back and sat with a relieved sigh. "I'm so glad you're going to be all right."

"So am I—and thanks." It was then Holly noticed that Sophie, Kat, and Natalie were all holding bags. "You've been shopping?"

The idea lifted Holly's spirits a notch.

Shopping was, after all, her native habitat.

Sophie sat at the foot of the bed. "Do you remember what you did when I was arrested and spent the night in jail? You charmed my attorney into letting you pretend to be his assistant, then smuggled in makeup and a brush so you could do my face and hair before my arraignment in court."

Despite the morphine fog, Holly remembered. "I couldn't let you walk into court looking guilty. First impressions matter."

Sophie smiled. "You made me feel human again. In that moment, it was everything to me."

"Remember when those bastards attacked Zach and me and I was waiting at the hospital, not sure he was going to make it?" Natalie asked.

Holly nodded, an image of Natalie's tear-stained face coming to mind.

"I was soaked through to the skin from that thunderstorm and out of my mind with worry. You and Kara showed up with a change of clothes and makeup. I've never forgotten that."

Holly felt tears prick her eyes. "You're going to make me cry again."

Then Tessa spoke. "When I witnessed María Ruiz's murder and broke down in the women's room at work, you gave me a little emergency makeup kit and helped me put myself back together. Now it's our turn to help you. We thought you might want to go home wearing, you know, clothes—or at least lipstick."

Natalie stood, and she and Sophie and Kat laid the bags on the bed.

Sophie looked inside them. "We don't have your talent with fashion and makeup, but we hope you at least like what we got you."

But Holly knew she would love it all, even if the clothes were burlap and the makeup was nothing but finger paints. It had come from her friends.

ZACH McBRIDE WAITED for Hunter and Darcangelo to join him in the hallway. He kept his voice quiet. "This Sasha Dudayev was no art dealer. He's got a long criminal history that includes everything—robbery, assault, murder, human trafficking, drug smuggling, and arms trafficking. From what I could gather, he was some kind of leader in the Georgian Mafia."

Hunter gave a low whistle. "Jesus!"

Darcangelo shook his head. "Holly is damned lucky to be alive."

"You don't know the half of it." They weren't going to like this. "Last year, he struck up a relationship with a young

Italian journalist—a real beauty. She became his lover and served as his courier for a while. Eventually she got tired of him and wanted out. They found her in pieces. Dudaev hacked her to bits while she was still alive."

Both men winced.

"Shit. Well, I guess I'm glad he's dead," Hunter said.

"Saves me the trouble." Darcangelo had made a reputation for himself in the FBI fighting human trafficking and had a hard grudge against criminals who preyed on women. "He must have been hoping to recruit Holly."

"That's what we're thinking." Zach felt his cell phone buzz, pulled it out of his pocket. He had a text from Corbray.

We're on it.

"The art gallery would have been a nice way of bringing his operations to Colorado," Hunter said.

Zach tucked the phone back into his pocket. "DEA already found a shipment of heroin in a crate at his warehouse."

"Any idea who might have killed him?" Darcangelo asked.

"I'm getting to that." Zach knew both men wanted answers. He did, too. They all cared about Holly. "The moment I started looking into his background, everything on him disappeared. The files just vanished."

Hunter and Darcangelo glanced at each other, then looked at him.

"Are you thinking this might be federal?" Hunter asked.

Darcangelo nailed it. "You're thinking CIA."

"I called Corbray and asked him to look into it. Derek Tower has all kinds of connections with the CIA that might prove useful—if that's what's happening here. He just texted me back to say they're on it. I'll keep you posted."

NICK ARRIVED BACK in Denver early that evening as Nick Andrews, combat veteran turned writer. The lair he'd used for the past three weeks had been converted into a home. It looked like the Agency had bought out IKEA. The décor was Tasteful Single Guy with a few houseplants meant to show his sensitive side. Hell, did they have a decorator on the payroll, too?

He wouldn't be surprised.

A dark yellow sofa sat in the living room, throw pillows in gray and black artfully arranged at its corners. There was a coffee table, a bookshelf, and an entertainment center in matching high-gloss black, as well as a tripod floor lamp with a black shade and a blocky armchair in black leather. There were curtains now instead of blinds. They'd even thought of magazines. He reached for one to find out what he was supposed to be reading. *SKI*, *Men's Health*, *Atlantic Monthly*. So he was active, but intellectual and not afraid of poetry. Good to know.

Nick walked into the kitchen and found it equipped and stocked—matching black plates and bowls, coffee cups, silverware. There wasn't much food in the fridge—a steak, some eggs, basic condiments—but there was a bottle of wine on the counter. There was even an espresso machine. What the hell was he supposed to do with that?

He found his desk and surveillance gear in the extra bedroom together with a set of weights and a treadmill. Well, thank God for the last two things. More time cooped up in this place was likely to drive him insane.

On the desk was a folder with his social media info—passwords and printouts of Nick Andrews's website, Facebook page, Twitter account. He glanced at the printout of his website's home page, saw his own face smiling up at him. What a charming guy he was. The site even had excerpts from the book he was writing—all part of the cover.

He walked to the master bedroom, dropped his gear on the bed—a high platform bed with a dark wooden headboard, a yellow and gray comforter, and way too many little pillows. Then he opened the closet.

You've got to be kidding me.

Whoever had put this all together must have read in his report about Bradshaw's love of designer clothing and decided she'd like a man who dressed the same way. But Nick knew what really turned her on.

Hard bodies. Jeans. A badass vibe.

And that's what Nick was going to give her—whether he wanted to or not.

The little bitch.

She had stolen that intel right from under his nose. Analysts had decided that Bradshaw must have downloaded the contents of the USB drive to a special cell phone then uploaded a virus that rendered the files unreadable. That way there was no drive for her to smuggle out and no chance that Dudaev would discover that the drive was missing and kill her.

Nick had known she'd left her smartphone at home. That's why he hadn't been able to listen in on her dinner conversation with Dudaev. Why hadn't it clicked that the phone he'd found in her purse couldn't have been hers?

You got sloppy, Andris, and she got away.

Or so she thought.

Bauer and Nguyen had played back the audio from the room that night, filtering out the argument Dudaev was having with one of his goons about the waiter they'd mistaken for Nick so that Nick could hear the digital beeps of the room safe as Bradshaw punched in the hotel's override code. The time index on the audio feed had left no doubt that Bradshaw had played Dudaev and made off with the files.

Either she *had* been the contact and had double-crossed Dudaev and simply stolen the files, or she was working for some unknown third party. Nick's job was to use any means necessary to find out who pulled her strings.

Fuck.

This wasn't his scene. He hadn't trained for this kind of operation. There were men who had, but for some reason Bauer had insisted on sending him.

Nick also had misgivings about moving against a US citizen in the homeland. "You have the evidence. Just arrest and interrogate her."

"That's not an option," Bauer had said, without explaining.

Nick had laid down his boundaries. "I won't terminate her."

Bauer had shrugged. "I don't like the thought any more than you do, but she's a traitor to her country. She might not give you any choice."

What had Nick overlooked in those three long weeks he'd spent surveilling her?

He walked into the bathroom, took a leak, and washed his hands and face, marveling at the way the toothbrush holder matched the soap dispenser. In a cupboard, he found a selection of fluffy black towels. He reached for one, dried his face, his gaze landing on his own reflection.

You look like a damned shaggy dog.

He hadn't had time for a haircut before leaving Tbilisi, and he hadn't had time while he'd been here keeping track of Bradshaw, either. His dark hair got wavy when it had any length to it, and it was almost touching his collar. He needed to shave, too, but he'd decided to wait. Bradshaw would like a bit of stubble on men.

As he unpacked his gear, Nick thought through everything he knew about her.

She'd been an Army brat, moving around the country. Her father was a career officer with Army intelligence, her mother a former model. Her parents had divorced when she was fourteen after her mother had had an affair with one of her husband's staff, and Holly had gone to live with her mother. She'd gotten good test scores and had won both Air Force and Army ROTC scholarships. She'd chosen Air Force but had dropped out in her first year for reasons that weren't clear. She'd earned a 4.0 GPA in college and graduated summa cum laude with a double degree—journalism and political science.

What would make a good girl like Holly Bradshaw turn to the Dark Side?

Growing up with a father in the Army probably meant that she hadn't had many close friendships. Her father hadn't been around a lot. Maybe she hadn't gotten enough of Daddy's attention. That could explain why she'd chosen Air Force over Army—a bit of rebellion to get the old man's goat. And when he hadn't given a damn, she'd dropped out and turned to her mother for approval, taking up expensive shoes and clothes.

It was a theory, anyway.

One thing was certain. Holly Bradshaw was smart.

Her Air Force aptitude test had put her IQ at 154.

Why with brains like that did she put so much emphasis on her appearance?

Blame Daddy again. Her father had been gone a lot and had probably felt guilty. When he'd been home, he'd told his daughter how pretty she was and bought her pretty things, because deep down he had no clue how to relate to a daughter, especially not one who reminded him of his faithless ex.

Nick had no idea whether he was hitting the target or just making shit up now. Yeah, he'd had HUMINT training, but Nick was a paramilitary operator, not a profiler or analyst. He was used to being the muscle that backed up the Agency's play. When they needed security or demolition, they brought him in. They had to have better men for this job, men whose Agency experience included using their cocks for counterintelligence.

"Seduce her if you have to. You've kept her under surveillance for weeks now. You must know what makes her tick. How hard could it be to get into her pants?"

Nguyen had seemed to get a kick out of Nick's reluctance, hinting that his Georgian Orthodox upbringing was to blame.

"Lighten up, Andris. You just might enjoy this. Most men would."

Stupid bastard.

Nick had waited until he was away at college before he'd started bringing girls home, and he hadn't fucked around as much as some of his friends had. But it wasn't because he had some kind of guilt-based sexual hang-up. His mother had drummed it into him and his brothers not to treat women like disposable goods. Hell, he had every bit as much sexual drive as the next man. He just had more self-control.

Getting sexual with a stranger wasn't his style. Then again, Holly didn't feel like a stranger. He already knew so much about her. Still, he hadn't been with anyone since Dani, and he wasn't sure he'd be able to get into another woman— so to speak—especially one capable of sleeping with men for secrets and betraying her country. How was he supposed to kiss her, touch her, give her pleasure?

Okay, so she *was* incredibly hot. She had a body that could stop traffic.

Yeah, he could definitely see what Nguyen was saying.

And yet his first impulse wasn't to fuck her. It was to cuff her and haul her in for interrogation. She was a traitor, and she'd bested him.

But Nick had more to think about than Holly Bradshaw. The missing and dead officers. Kramer's warning and subsequent disappearance. The Batumi op. The internal investigation. The encrypted files on the cloned hard drive. The nagging feeling that Kramer, Bauer, and Nguyen had kept something from him.

He stowed the rest of his gear, shoving socks, T-shirts, and underwear into the chest of drawers. That left his two semi-autos, the ammo, and the rest of the shit in his go-bag—thirty grand in cash, fake IDs, credit cards, a medic's field kit, batteries, duct tape, a radio, and a whole bunch of other crap. Where the hell was he going to put these? The equipment didn't go with his cover.

He was supposed to be a writer working on a story about his years in Delta Force. It was an attempt to explain his scars, why he never left the house, and why he spent so much time on the computer.

He opened the drawer of the nightstand.

Condoms.

The Agency really *did* think of everything.

He would need to install a gun safe. In the meantime, he'd stow the go-bag high in the closet, keep the Ruger MK III close by in the nightstand, and carry the SIG concealed. He couldn't be certain trouble wasn't headed his way—word was the Georgian Mafia was looking for payback for Dudaev's death—and he didn't want to get caught with his pants down. Especially if his pants *were* down.

As he unpacked two bricks each of .22 long rifle subsonic and .380 ACP anti-personnel rounds, he found himself hoping he didn't have to plant one of them in Holly Bradshaw's pretty skull.

HOLLY AWOKE TO find a man sitting in a chair beside the bed. For a second, she thought it was her case officer, but then she saw. "Joaquin."

There was a worried look on his sweet face, his camera bag resting on the floor near his feet.

"Hey." He smiled and took her hand, lacing his fingers

through hers. "How do you feel? I hear they're giving you the good stuff."

"You came." Holly was happy to see him. "They quit giving me morphine a little while ago. I'm just taking pain pills."

She still felt queasy and exhausted but her headache was better.

"I'd have been here sooner but it was a busy news day." His expression grew serious. "I got a hell of a shock when they wheeled you out on that gurney."

"I got a hell of a shock when I woke up next to a dead guy."

"I heard some of the hotel staff talking about it. They say someone shot this dude point blank in the head while you were unconscious in the bed naked beside him. You're lucky the killer decided not to kill you, too—or to take advantage of your situation."

Holly thought she knew where this conversation was going.

Joaquin released her hand and leaned forward in the chair, resting his elbows on his knees, his gaze fixed on hers. "The way I see it, this was a wake-up call."

Here we go.

Holly knew her friends thought she was a bit of a slut. They didn't know that it wasn't quite what it seemed. There were men she dated as part of her personal life and men she dated for the Agency. She slept with some of them. Others she didn't. But she couldn't settle down, not until she'd left the Agency. How would she be able to explain to a potential boyfriend that she moonlighted for the CIA and that he would have to share her in the name of national security?

"Joaquin, I—"

"Hey, let me finish, okay? I've got something I've been meaning to say for a while now." His brow bent in a thoughtful frown, and he seemed to hesitate. "How you live your life is your business, but as your friend I got to say that these men—they're not good for you. They don't care about you. You are worth so much more than they know."

He took her hand again. "You're so beautiful on the outside that a lot of guys don't look beyond that. They have no idea how funny you are or how much you do for your friends or what an amazing reporter you are. You're smart, too. Oh, *chula*, I know you're smart. Your mind runs a million miles a minute so that sometimes you have no idea what's going on around you and you say things . . ."

He laughed, smiling as if he were remembering something funny.

But Holly didn't laugh. There was a rock-hard lump in her throat, his words cutting too close to something soft and sore inside her.

His laughter faded, and his smile disappeared. "That man who got popped last night, the one cops say might have drugged you, the one who's going to be stuck in your memory for the rest of your life—all he saw, all he wanted, was the package. He didn't care about who you are beneath your skin. You got to stop wasting time with these *cabrones* and find the man who does."

Holly blinked back the tears that were forming in her eyes. She swallowed—hard—and gave Joaquin's fingers a squeeze. "I wish it were that easy."

After a moment, she asked the question she'd always wanted to ask him. "Why have you and I never gotten together?"

There'd always been an intense and mutual attraction. They both knew it. They'd never acted on it or even talked about it.

Joaquin gave her a sad smile. "Because, *chula*, I'm looking for happily ever after, and you're just looking for your next adrenaline rush."

CHAPTER 6

NICK SPOKE INTO the listening device, chuckling. "Hey, Nguyen, fuck you."

The device was one of five he'd found in the place—a hazard of the profession. He, like all SAD officers, had to assume he was under Agency surveillance much of the time. But that didn't mean he had to like it.

He deactivated the bug, tossed it into a small biometric safe with the others. This was his form of protest. They put in the devices, and he removed them. He couldn't be certain he'd gotten them all, of course, but at least Langley had no doubts about his point of view on the subject.

He went into the kitchen and tried out the espresso maker, getting three shots out of the thing. He drank it straight, not bothering with steamed milk, then tossed the cake of grounds into the sink and left it there, adding to the mess he'd made this morning. Thanks to some dirty dishes, pizza boxes, dirty clothes, old newspapers, and full trash bins, the condo now looked less like an IKEA floor display and more like someone's home.

The espresso cleared the fog from his brain, got his pulse going. He'd put in far too many hours last night getting the computers set up and installing the special software. Now he had six CPUs running at once, all trying to recover Dudaev's password and open the encrypted drive. Once the password was cracked, Nick was pretty certain he'd find the key for decrypting the encoded files on the hard drive. But cracking the password wouldn't be easy.

Dudaev's mother tongue was Georgian, but he also spoke English, French, and Russian. He could have chosen a password in any of those languages. He could have used the Georgian or Cyrillic alphabets, or he could have used the standardized US keyboard to spell out transliterations of Georgian or Russian words. In case that wasn't challenging enough, there was more than one way of translating the characters of the Cyrillic alphabet into data streams—ASCII, Code Page 855, Code Page 866—and Nick had no idea which one applied in this case.

It made him want to break open a bottle of tequila.

Cryptography wasn't his strength. While he'd sat there fucking around with something that could earn him a quiet cell in federal prison or a nice bullet to the brain, he'd found himself wondering once more whether he'd gone out of his mind.

He glanced at his watch.

Zero-nine-twenty.

Bradshaw would be discharged from the hospital soon.

He needed to get moving.

Wearing nitrile gloves, he used the key he'd created to open the deadbolt on Bradshaw's back door, stepped inside, and disarmed her security system, taking advantage of her absence to have another look around. True, he'd put her in the hospital, but given what she'd done, she was lucky to be alive.

Had he known that night what he knew now . . .

Bauer had insisted Bradshaw was a professional, but Nick was holding out hope that Dudaev represented her first foray into espionage and treason. Maybe someone had heard she was dating him and had paid her to double-cross Dudaev. Maybe the person who'd hired her had given her only part of the truth and had made her believe she'd be doing something good for the country by getting sensitive data away from Dudaev.

Regardless, her life was about to get ugly.

Nick had searched her condo the day he'd arrived in Denver three weeks ago and had been back a few times since to check her mail and to go through her trash and her recycling. The first time through, he'd been looking for evidence that she was involved in Dudaev's underworld dealings. He hadn't found anything to tie her to any covert activity, and he wasn't expecting to find anything like that today. He had to assume that she still had the special cell phone with her and that the Agency was holding eyes on her in case someone tried to make contact with her. This time he was searching for clues about Ms. Bradshaw herself—clues that would help him break her.

She'd left the air conditioning on, so the place was cool despite near triple-digit temps outside, the blinds still drawn. He started in the kitchen, working his way systematically through the room, which clearly doubled as an office. She had pens, paper, and a laptop on the kitchen table, and even a paper shredder, but the cupboards held few pots and pans or even silverware. That meant she probably ate out a lot or brought home carryout—something he would remember.

He opened the shredder and found nothing more than junk mail and shopping receipts—exactly what he'd found every time he'd searched her house.

After searching the bathroom, where he'd taken in the soft floral scent of her shampoo, he started in the bedroom, sniffing the contents of perfume bottles, then going through her drawers. Soft silk and sexy lace. And . . .

Holy shit.

He held up a pair of what looked like crotchless panties, the back side done up with tiny laces. He'd gone through these three weeks ago, but that was before he'd seen her lying on that bed wearing only a thong. An image of her came to his mind—breasts bare, that fat sapphire lying against a rosy nipple, diamonds glittering against the skin of her throat, those long silky legs. He dropped the panties, slammed the drawer shut.

Get your mind on the job!

How was he supposed to stay in control and get the better of her when just being alone with her panties gave him wood?

Her bed was neatly made, shams resting on top of a coverlet of blue cotton. The sheets were made of white cotton

and fringed with lace. Fluffy flokati area rugs dotted the
wooden floor, perfect for her polished toes and soft, pedi-
cured feet.

On her dresser sat a photo of a sweet little towheaded girl
holding the hand of a man in a US Army uniform. It was Holly
and her father. Interesting that it was the only family photo in
the house—and that she was so little.

The book on her nightstand had changed. He picked it up,
glanced at the title. *Theories of Modern Art.*

She'd been boning up for her "date" with Dudaev.

She had a vibrator in the top drawer, along with a box of
condoms. Because Nick had been running surveillance, he
knew she used the vibrator, coming with a quick inhale and
a long slow exhale that, truth be told, had turned him on. But
the point was that she had enough libido left over from her
nights on the town to do herself. Then he remembered what
she'd said to McMillan about too many men not caring what
their partners needed.

It's the clit, stupid.

Maybe she didn't find her nights out all that satisfying. It
was hard for him to say, given that she hadn't had sex with
anyone but herself in the three weeks he'd been keeping a
watch on her. Then again, she'd been dating Dudaev that
entire time, and he knew she hadn't had sex with him.

That was revealing, too.

He moved into the living room, searching in and around
the cream-colored sofa with its pastel blue pillows and throw
blanket, noticing for the first time how soft the colors and
fabrics were. He searched the cabinet of distressed white
wood where she kept her DVDs and saw that the shelves held
lots of popular romantic comedies, as well as some documen-
taries, art films, and Hollywood classics. He checked the
framed prints on the walls, this time looking at the content of
the art—black and white photographs of landscapes, old
French theater posters, prints of Impressionist paintings. He
flipped through her books one by one, a mix of nonfiction,
literary fiction, and popular fiction. She'd obviously read Jane
Austen to death—and Dickens. Then his gaze was drawn to
a dog-eared romance novel with a man's chest on the cover.

It was bookmarked at an explicit scene of some guy going down on a woman.

He'd remember that as well.

He turned on the light and entered the massive walk-in closet that had once been a second bedroom. A chaise lounge in dark blue velvet sat in the middle of the room, one wall entirely of mirrors, more flokati rugs on the floor. He ran his hand over the velvet of the chaise, inhaled the hint of perfume that lingered in the air.

The woman was a sensualist to the core. That might be the most important thing for Nick to know about her. She wouldn't like discomfort.

He glanced around, but he knew what he'd find here. She had easily two hundred pairs of shoes, all neatly organized. Her clothes were organized, too, arranged on racks according to length and from casual to formal—blouses; skirts; pants; dresses; long, glittery gowns.

He stepped out, glanced around.

This was Bradshaw's home, her sanctuary, and everything about it was soft, feminine, tasteful, even sweet. It was easier for him to believe that she'd been deceived into helping someone steal those files than it was to believe she enjoyed playing dangerous games with dangerous men for a living.

And that was another mystery.

How was she being paid for this? There'd been no suspicious activity in any of her accounts before she met Dudaev or since, no fat deposits from offshore . . .

An engine. A car door.

He glanced outside and saw a black SUV roll up, an unmarked police car behind it. Julian Darcangelo got out of the car and motioned for Bradshaw, who sat in the passenger seat of the SUV, to stay in the vehicle. Nick recognized Darcangelo from the files he'd made on her friends and acquaintances. Nick was certain the man, who was former FBI, would clear the condo before he let Bradshaw enter.

Time for you to go home and get pretty, Andris.

He already had his chance encounter with Bradshaw worked out, the accidental meeting that he would make certain turned into something more. He activated the alarm and slipped out the back, making it inside his own condo just in time to avoid an unnecessary and painful confrontation with Darcangelo.

Mr. Creeper she'd called him.

She had no idea how creepy he could be.

HOLLY SET ASIDE the note the florist had left on her door—they'd left a bouquet of flowers from Beth Dailey, her boss, with Mr. Creeper—and made a pot of coffee. She set mugs on the table for Chief Irving and Julian, trying to stay focused on the conversation, her mind fixed on the classified files that were still in her possession.

Why hadn't her CO contacted her yet?

She fought back a trill of panic. The situation must be hotter than she'd imagined. Even if they felt she was compromised, the Agency would want to retrieve the intel she'd recovered. They wouldn't leave the cell phone and its precious contents in her hands any longer than they had to.

She realized that both men were silent and looking at her expectantly. "I'm sorry. I got lost in my own world."

Pull yourself together!

Julian stood, pulled out one of the chairs. "Sit."

"I was going to get you sugar."

"Tell me where it is, and I'll get it."

Holly sat. "There—next to the toaster."

Chief Stephen Irving had been at the helm of the Denver Police Department for as long as Holly had lived in Denver and had been sleep-deprived for that entire time, judging by the bags beneath his blue eyes. "I asked you whether your laptop was stolen from the hotel room. One of the security guards said you asked for your laptop. If it was stolen, I'd like to include it in the report."

"My laptop?" Holly feigned confusion. It wasn't hard. "I don't even remember asking for it. I must have been really out of it. My laptop is right there."

She pointed, hoping they would buy it.

Chief Irving nodded—and that seemed to be the end of it.

"Whoever did this was a professional," he said. "The security system was hacked. It took more than five hours for the security desk to realize they weren't getting live feed. By the time we arrived to investigate, the hotel's footage from that night had been destroyed. The killer left no prints. There were no witnesses, no one who heard the gunshots, which means he probably used a suppressor."

"That's a silencer?" Holly knew perfectly well what a suppressor was.

"Yes." Chief Irving reached for the sugar, dumped a teaspoon into his coffee, then stirred with the same spoon. "Whoever it was didn't steal your necklace or touch you. He also didn't touch the money Dudayev had in his safe. Put all of that together and it looks like a professional hit. The rounds he used were designed to . . ."

Julian frowned and Chief Irving let that thought trail off with a cough.

Holly was touched by the effort that Irving, Julian, and the others were making to shield her from the ugliness of this. Some part of her wished she were that innocent, but she knew more about what had happened that night than they ever would.

"Why would someone hire an assassin to kill an art dealer?" she asked, but the questions running through her mind were altogether different.

Who was the killer? Had Dudayev been betrayed by a prospective buyer? Had someone in Dudayev's organization turned on him and decided to take the files and the profits? Had a foreign government penetrated US security, learned about the files, and taken advantage of Dudayev's theft to grab them and run?

Julian answered. "McBride was looking into that, but the moment he reached out to the federal boys, they swooped in and took over the investigation. The case is now in the hands of the FBI. I've got some contacts there, but they're being tight-lipped about this one."

Holly had been expecting this. Soon, the investigation would be in Agency hands—and then it would quietly disappear.

Then it dawned on her.

"Does that mean I can have my pumps, dress, and necklace back? Not that I'll ever want to wear *that* dress again, but the shoes . . ."

"That's our Holly." Julian grinned. "You'll get them back."

He drew out his cell phone, glanced down at a text message. "You've got company. McBride and Corbray."

Holly walked to the door to find a whole lot of sexy walking up her sidewalk, Zach in front, Javier behind him, and Derek Tower in the rear.

Derek had been the head of a private security company until his biggest client—Laura Nilsson—was abducted by al Qaeda while doing a live news broadcast from Pakistan. Taller than Javier, he was as golden as Javier was dark. He and Javier had hated each other's guts until the truth about Laura's abduction had come out and Derek had turned his own life inside out to help Javier make things right for her. Now they owned a private security company together— Cobra International Solutions, or CIS.

Despite the heat, Zach and Derek wore suits, as if they'd just come from a meeting. Javier, on the other hand, was wearing jeans and a white T-shirt. But all three had grave expressions on their faces, their eyes hidden behind sunglasses, and Holly felt a little jab of warning. Derek had been a Green Beret and had done classified work for the government. He had deep connections in the State Department and the Agency. If he discovered the truth . . .

Get a grip! You're jumping at shadows.

There were few people in the country who had a high enough security clearance to access her Agency file, and Derek Tower wasn't one of them.

She opened the door and stepped back as they entered. "I've got coffee in the kitchen. I can make iced tea, too, if you're thirsty."

"Nah, I think we're fine, thanks," Javier said, touching Holly lightly on the arm as he passed. "How you holding up?"

"I'm okay."

Julian and Chief Irving had come out of the kitchen and the men exchanged greetings, then waited for Holly to sit on the sofa, Julian taking a seat on one side of her while Chief Irving settled his girth on the other.

"Okay, spill it," Chief Irving said.

Zach spoke first. "Sasha Dudayev wasn't a Russian art

dealer, Holly, he was an arms dealer from Georgia—the country, not the state."

God, did he think she was that stupid? It almost hurt her feelings. Apparently, she'd done her job a little too well.

"An . . . an arms dealer?"

Zach nodded. "Unfortunately, as soon as I started digging, every bit of intel I had on him disappeared."

"We tried to work our contacts at all of the alphabet soup agencies and the State Department," Javier said. "No one is talking but Tower has a buddy at Langley who had something interesting to tell us off the record."

Holly's pulse skipped. "Langley? The Air Force base?"

"CIA headquarters," Zach clarified.

He and Javier turned to Derek, who seemed reluctant to share anything.

Derek's gaze fixed on Holly's, his eyes so hard that she didn't even notice their color. "This is off the record, do you understand? Deep background. Don't tell anyone."

Holly held up one hand, palm out, to stop him. "I don't want to know anything that is going to get me killed."

Javier glared at him. "See, man? That's what I'm talking about. Why do you do shit like that? Now she's scared. That's not why we came here, bro."

"I can't afford to fry my contacts over this," Derek fired back. "She's a reporter. What's to keep her from printing whatever I tell her?"

"She's our friend." Julian didn't shout the words, exactly, but they filled the living room. "She won't print a word of it or speak about it with anyone who isn't in this room. You've got *my* word on that."

Holly wanted to hug Julian, his faith in her putting an ache in her chest. "I won't tell anyone. My lips are zipped."

She made a lip-zipping motion and turned the imaginary key.

Derek pinned her with his gaze, seeming to measure Julian's words. "Two years ago, Dudaev murdered an officer during an operation in Batumi, Georgia, and stole a cache of firearms, which he sold for more than a million on the black market. The Agency has had it in for Dudaev since."

Holly already knew this. It had been part of her pre-mission briefing on Dudaev. "Sasha did that?"

"There are also rumors that there's some kind of internal investigation in the top-secret Special Activities Division related to that operation and that has everyone in the SAD running scared. Word is that the hit on Dudaev was an Agency job, possibly carried out by a rogue officer who is trying to silence everyone who was involved in that op in Batumi. It certainly has all the marks of an Agency hit."

"Do you understand what that means?" Julian asked.

"It means I really suck when it comes to picking men." Holly's response was almost automatic, her mind racing.

If the killer really *had* come from the Agency, it could mean only one of two things: the Agency had gotten its wires crossed and had sent *two* officers with two conflicting missions—or someone truly had gone rogue.

Either way, she was lucky to be alive.

She looked from Julian to Chief Irving to Zach to Javier, trying to gather her thoughts, knowing they were waiting for her to respond. "Wait. Are you saying someone from *our* government killed him?"

No wonder her CO hadn't contacted her. In either scenario, he would be doing all he could to protect her identity, to keep her ties to the SAD secret—not an easy thing to do if another operative from the SAD had seen her naked in Dudaev's bed. He'd keep his distance, find a time when it would be safe for him to move in. Otherwise, she'd be compromised and worthless to them—and possibly a target. If the rogue officer found out she was an officer, too, and thought that she knew anything she shouldn't . . .

"That's what it looks like to me," Derek said.

"If it's true, it helps explain why both you and Dudaev were drugged," Zach said.

Holly hadn't known that. "Dudaev was drugged, too?"

"The ME got the results of the toxicology tests this morning," Chief Irving said.

"The shooter incapacitated both of you before moving in, probably so that he could avoid having to put a bullet through your head, too," Derek said.

"Nice." Javier shook his head.

"Just telling it like it is, Corbray."

Holly could have sworn she saw Zach roll his eyes.

"If it's true this was a CIA hit, you can feel pretty certain he won't come after you," he said. "Whoever it was took steps to keep you out of the crossfire."

"I'd like to kick his ass," Julian said. "The drug he used almost killed her. At least it's over."

"Not necessarily." Javier's gaze shifted from Julian to Chief Irving. "Word is that Dudaev's boys want payback. They saw their boss go into a room with Holly and come out dead. ICE has revoked their passports and is searching for them, but we need to put some serious security on Holly until the danger passes."

BY THE TIME the men left a half hour later, after arguing about how to handle the security detail, Holly's headache was back in full force. She took a shower, her mind busy sorting out the pieces as she shampooed and conditioned her hair, washed the hospital off her skin, and shaved her legs.

If Dudaev's death *had* been an authorized Agency hit, it meant the computer with all its files were now back in Agency hands. It also meant that something had gone terribly wrong at the SAD. But if the hit had been carried out by an officer with a personal agenda, there was no telling where this might end.

Under normal circumstances, this kind of speculation held no interest for her. She operated independently, blessedly cut off from the Langley rumor mill. But this time, a job had put her in the center of it. And then there was Javier's news about the Georgian Mafia. If they blamed her, if they came after her . . .

An image of Dudaev lying dead beside her flashed through her mind, almost making her knees buckle.

She sagged against the tile, her heart thrumming.

A gun.

She needed a handgun. She needed a way to defend herself in case someone broke through CIS security. Javier's men were good, but no one was infallible. Though she knew how to use firearms, she'd never owned one. She'd never felt the need before.

She'd get something simple—a Glock 19 maybe—then she'd ask Julian or Marc to get her into the police range for some practice. At least then she'd have some way of protecting herself.

She turned off the water, dried off, stepped into her silk robe—and nearly jumped out of her skin when the doorbell rang.

Still in her bathrobe, she hurried to the door, hoping with everything she had that she'd find a brown box with a new pair of shoes waiting for her. She looked outside and instead saw a man holding a bouquet of flowers, his head turned away from her.

She glanced across the street and saw an unmarked police unit was already keeping watch on the place, Chief Irving's men watching over her until Javier could put together a protection detail. She opened the door.

The man turned his face toward her, smiled. "Hey, I'm Nick, your new neighbor. I hope I'm not catching you at a bad time. The delivery guy left these with me."

CHAPTER 7

HOLLY FELT THE breath leave her lungs. She knew she was supposed to say something like hello, thank you, nice to meet you, come in—but the words weren't there. Instead, she stood there staring up at him.

This was Mr. Creeper?

She'd seen handsome men before, hot men, sexy men, but looking up at him, she couldn't remember any of them.

He stood well over six feet, with thick, dark hair, deep-set blue eyes, and his face . . .

Absurd cheek bones. Dark, brooding brows and long lashes. Strong jaw. Full lower lip.

He frowned, his gaze dropping to her wrist. "Are you okay?"

The hospital bracelet.

She'd forgotten to cut it off.

"I . . . Yes, I'm fine." *Snap out of it!* "Sorry. I'll take those."

She reached out to take the bouquet but he held it back. "They're pretty heavy. Why don't you just show me where you want them?"

"The coffee table is fine, next to the other ones." Holly stepped aside, making room for him, and caught the scent of clean skin as he passed.

He bent down, set the bouquet of roses and waxflower on the table, faded Levi's 511s moving over a perfect ass.

She shifted her gaze upward just in time to find herself looking into his eyes. She held out her hand. "Thank you. Nick, was it?"

"Nick Andrews." His shake was firm, his hand warm.

"Holly Bradshaw."

"I saw on the card." He smiled, glanced around, his hands coming to rest on his hips, a gray T-shirt that read "Get Belayed" stretching over the muscles of his chest. "Nice place. Sorry I haven't been over to introduce myself before today. I'm slamming on a book deadline, and I've just been holed up alone in my cave."

A book deadline?

"You're a writer."

That explained a few things.

He shrugged. "My agent thinks so."

"I'm the senior entertainment writer with the *Denver Independent*. What kind of book is it—fiction, nonfiction?"

His gaze slid over her from her face to her bare feet before he jerked it back to her face. Holly remembered she was wearing only her silk robe, her hair a damp rat's nest, her face bare of makeup.

"My book? It's supposed to be a fictionalized account of my time serving with Delta Force in Afghanistan and Iraq, but I'm having a hard time figuring out how to take classified facts and make them fiction."

Delta Force.

Something inside Holly purred—then went soft. She'd always had a great respect for the men and women who put their lives on the line.

"If you give me a second to get dressed, I'd love to hear more—if you feel comfortable talking about it, that is, which not all writers do, of course. I understand that. Can I get you a glass of iced tea or water or coffee or something?"

You're babbling like an idiot.

Since when had a man affected her enough to make her babble?

"No. Thanks. I had some espresso that I made with my espresso maker."

She realized he was nervous, too, and *that* made her relax.

She smiled up at him. "Thanks for bringing over the flowers. Sorry for whatever disruption they caused you."

"It was no problem, really. It was about time I came over to say hello." His eyes narrowed, then recognition dawned on his face. "You're the woman from the hotel, the one who woke up next to . . ."

"Yeah." All the warmth seemed to leave the room.

"Sorry. That was wrong. I shouldn't have said anything."

Holly ought to have expected this. The news had been all over the papers, together with photos of her walking into the gallery on Dudaev's arm. They were great photos, but they brought unwanted attention her way.

"That's okay. I'm sure you won't be the only one who recognizes me."

"That must have been pretty terrifying." The shadows in his eyes told Holly he'd seen more than his share of death.

"I will definitely think twice before I date another billionaire."

Her joke didn't make him laugh, didn't make him so much as quirk a smile. "On second thought, a glass of water might be nice."

"Okay. Make yourself at home. I'll be right back. Ice?"

"Yes. Thanks."

She hurried to her bedroom and slipped into underclothes and a short, pale-pink sundress, stopping at her mirror only long enough to work the tangles from her hair with her fingers, apply some tinted lip gloss, and remove the silly hospital bracelet. She wished she had time to do something about the circles beneath her eyes but how long could a guy expect to wait for a glass of ice water?

She found him standing in front of her old Théâtre de l'Opéra poster.

He took the glass from her, his gaze sliding over her again. "Thanks. Have you been to Paris?"

"A few times."

"I passed through once on my way back to the US. It's a beautiful city. Full of tourists, but beautiful."

"That's Paris." She took a seat on the sofa, her head still aching. "I was about ten the first time I went there. My dad was stationed in Germany. I remember not liking the long lines at the museums, but I really loved the fountains—and the Eiffel Tower."

"An Army brat." He sat in the chair across from her. "How did you end up here?"

She told him the truth. "I came to Denver when the *Indy* hired me, and fell in love with Colorado. How about you?"

"I came for the mountains."

She pointed to the message on his T-shirt. "You're a climber?"

He nodded. "I love to ski, too. Camp, hike."

"I've got some friends you ought to meet, guys who live for that."

"I'd like that—after I meet this deadline." He glanced at his watch.

She knew he was thinking about leaving, and she didn't want that—not yet. "Tell me about your book."

"Oh, no." He shook his head, grinning. "Once I start talking, I won't shut up."

Holly couldn't help but smile. "Take that as a good sign. All the authors I've ever interviewed are like that."

He set the water glass down on the coffee table. "I need to get back to work—and you need to rest and get rid of that headache."

How did he know she had a headache?

Her surprise must have shown on her face.

"You keep rubbing your temple," he explained, getting to his feet. "Do you have your cell phone handy or something I can write on?"

"Yeah. In the kitchen." She stood and walked down the hallway.

He followed, took the pen she handed him, and wrote his phone number down on her notepad. "If you need anything, just call. If anyone bothers you, I can be here in a second."

"Thanks." Holly was genuinely touched. On impulse she wrote her number on the lower half of the page, tore off the piece of paper, and gave it to him. "Here's mine. If anyone bothers you, I can, um . . . call the police."

He laughed, a broad smile lighting up his face. "Fair enough."

She walked him to the door, the two of them talking about how hot it was.

He stopped on her front step. "You're sure you'll be alright?"

After the news she'd gotten today, she wasn't sure of anything.

"Yeah." She willed herself to smile. "Whoever killed him didn't kill me when he had the chance, so I doubt he's after me now."

He cupped her shoulder, his touch warm. "Get some rest."

As Holly shut and locked her door, she knew it was only a matter of time before she and Nick ended up in bed together.

NICK DROPPED ONTO his sofa, let out a breath, shaking his head at his own stupidity.

I had some espresso that I made with my espresso maker.

"That wasn't lame at all, buddy."

Jesus!

Still, it had gone better than it might have. She'd swallowed every bit of bait he'd laid out for her—his military record, his life as a struggling writer, his athletic interests—and he knew she was attracted to him.

And you're not attracted to her at all.

No, he wasn't. He couldn't afford to be.

What's the last thing Bauer had said to Nick?

Watch your back, Andris. She's good.

Hell, yeah, she was.

Nick had listened to her play her so-called friends. She knew what a suppressor was, and she sure as hell had understood that they'd been talking about Georgia the nation and not the state. But she'd come off as vulnerable, even fragile. She'd had every man in that room tripping over himself to make her feel safe.

Nick didn't blame them. She'd fooled him, too. If he hadn't seen proof that she'd downloaded the files from that USB drive, he would *still* believe she was innocent. Well, God hadn't done men any favors when he'd given them balls instead of brains.

An image of her filled his mind—the curves of her body

outlined by the thin silk of her bathrobe, her hair damp and tousled, her flawless face free of makeup. She'd looked vulnerable, shaken. She was still suffering from the side effects of the drug he'd given her, and he'd had to fight a nagging sense of guilt to remember that he was not here to help her, but to expose her.

What a waste!

She was beautiful, smart, talented—and well on her way to life in prison.

If someone doesn't kill her first.

She'd seemed genuinely surprised and a little relieved to hear that Dudaev's death might be a CIA hit. Interesting that she still trusted the government—given that she apparently had no problem betraying that same government. Her response might have been an act, or it might mean that she believed she was working for the good guys.

Or maybe she thinks the CIA is run by monkeys and is no threat to her.

He could certainly understand why someone might get that impression—especially lately.

He'd found it interesting that she'd asked for "her" laptop at the hotel—proof she'd been after the same intel as he. At least he'd kept her from getting her hands on that piece of it. She'd covered nicely with the police chief, pretending confusion. She was smooth and quick on her feet.

But Holly Bradshaw wasn't the only thing Nick needed to think about.

The Batumi op *was* the focus of the internal investigation.

Derek Tower must have sources high up in the Agency if he could get that kind of information. Nick hadn't been able to get anyone to tell him about the investigation, not even when he'd asked Bauer directly. Did Bauer not trust him?

As for the threat of a rogue officer, that was something to take seriously. Nick had had a gut feeling that someone from the inside might be responsible for the missing and dead officers. After hearing what Tower's connections had to say, Nick was certain his gut had been right. But that wasn't the most interesting thing Tower had shared.

Word is that the hit on Dudaev was an Agency job, possibly carried out by a rogue officer.

Nick had been authorized to take Dudaev's life, but then the whole SAD had become a clusterfuck of rumors and crossed wires. It was probably nothing more than someone talking out of his ass. But whoever had told Tower this had known more about the internal investigation than Nick. Was it possible that someone in the Agency was getting ready to burn him—and let him take the blame not just for Dudaev's death, but for the whole damned mess?

He thought about this for a moment, turning the pieces over in his mind. His unanswered questions about that night in Batumi. The disappearances and deaths of the other officers. The way Bauer and Nguyen had drilled him about Kramer's disappearance. And Nick didn't like the way the pieces were coming together.

Trust no one.

He'd known Nguyen since his days in Delta Force. They'd fought and bled together, watched friends die, worked together in the Agency. The man had always had his back. Always. As for Bauer, Nick had looked up to him, counted on him, trusted him with his life more times than he could count. He had to be out of his mind even to entertain the idea that either of them could betray him.

You're getting paranoid, man.

And yet something was terribly wrong, and Nick kept seeing himself—and the lovely Holly Bradshaw—in the middle of it all.

He stood, some thought of letting Bauer know that someone was leaking intel to Derek Tower and Cobra International Solutions half-formed in his mind. He stopped, mid-stride. On second thought . . .

THE SHOES ARRIVED first thing Monday morning when Holly was rushing to get to the newspaper on time. This time, the mailing label said it had come from Neiman Marcus. On a surge of relief, she ripped the box open, grabbed the packing slip, retrieved the key from her CO's Twitter account, and began decoding the ciphertext, barely noticing the Prada platform sandals inside.

SITUATION CRITICAL. BELIEVE YOU ARE IN DANGER AND
UNDER SURVEILLANCE. CANNOT RISK MEETING. TAKE
PACKAGE TO YOUR OFFICE IN BROWN PAPER BAG. AT
09:30, DROP BAG INTO TRASH CAN ON WEST SIDE OF
PAPER'S REAR ENTRANCE. KEEP LOW PROFILE. RECOM-
MEND YOU TURN TO LOCAL LAW ENFORCEMENT. WILL
CONTACT YOU AGAIN WHEN POSSIBLE. I'M SORRY.

Holly read her CO's instructions, her mind on the message as she ran the packing slip through her shredder, then
took the bits of paper, flushed the toilet, and sprinkled the
remnants into swirling water until they were gone.

She wished he'd taken the time to tell her, oh, maybe *why*
he believed she was in danger. That could be helpful to
know. Or maybe he could give her just a teensy hint as to
who might be after her. The message was encoded, after all.
Why not tell her everything?

That would make too much sense. You know that.

Was he referring to the Georgian Mafia? The rogue officer? Or was there some other threat?

But that wasn't the part of the message that worried her
most. She'd known she might be in danger from the moment
she'd woken up in that hotel room. The corpse beside her had
been her first clue. No, that wasn't what scared her.

What scared her was the apology at the end.

I'm sorry.

In the years she'd worked for him, her CO had never gotten personal, never used the word "I" in a message, never
talked about feelings—his or hers. What did he mean by "I'm
sorry"?

Was he apologizing for what she'd been through? Was he
sorry that he couldn't do more to help her right now? Or was
that his way of letting her know that she was on her own?

Mystery was half of the fun of working for the Confused
Idiots of America—except that Holly wasn't finding much
fun in this.

As for being under surveillance, she'd come to grips with
the fact that working for the Agency meant some loss of
privacy. It would do more harm than good to dry-clean her
apartment and get rid of any listening devices. What enter-

tainment journalist would even think about searching her place for bugs? Whoever was holding eyes on her would realize she'd been tipped off—and that might escalate the situation. No, it was better to leave the devices in place. There was nothing for them to hear anyway. It's not like she sang about her missions in the shower.

She glanced at her watch, realized she didn't have much time. She hurried to the kitchen and grabbed a small brown paper bag. She tucked the cell phone inside the paper bag and placed it in her handbag. Making sure she had her real cell phone with her, she took one last sip of green tea, then stepped outside.

Javier was waiting for her. "Ready?"

"Yeah." She *so* owed Javier for this. "I can't thank you enough, Javi—well, you and Derek both, though I don't think he really wants to help me."

Javier grinned. "He's not as much of an asshole as he seems."

Just then, Nick stepped outside wearing a pair of gym shorts and nothing else. When he saw her, the right side of his mouth curved in a lazy grin. "Morning."

Holly's heart gave a thud, and she suddenly felt much more awake, the hit of pheromone stronger than caffeine. "Good morning."

He was all lean muscle, his shoulders broad, his well-defined pecs sprinkled with dark curls, his abs bisected by a happy trail that disappeared behind his waistband. She caught just a glimpse of a scar on his abdomen before he turned and walked down his sidewalk to fetch his newspaper.

"Check out that dude," Javier muttered. "He's out here, working it, making sure you get a good look at what he's got. *Pendejo.*"

Holly pulled her gaze away from Nick's amazing body and followed Javier as he escorted her toward the second of two black, bulletproof SUVs that waited at the curb. "We'll take a different route to the office every day. Some days you'll ride in the first vehicle, other days in the second."

But Holly wasn't really listening.

How surreal it all seemed. Dudaev's murder. The possibility of a rogue operator. An internal investigation. And now her CO's message.

At least the contents of that USB drive would finally be out of her hands and back in the Agency's. She'd be done with this mission—and hopefully free to explore her neighbor.

HOLLY ARRIVED AT the office ten minutes late. Javier and his men had taken her on a route that had snaked through most of downtown Denver, then dropped her off in the underground parking lot, away from any TV cameras and news crews that might be waiting for her near the paper's front entrance. The security team had staked out the building, and they would remain in place until it was time for her to head home again.

"Hey!" Beth, her boss, came up behind her. "I wasn't sure you'd be back today. How are you feeling?"

"Better," Holly answered, turning on her computer, one eye on the clock. "Thanks for the flowers. They're beautiful."

"Do the police know who did it?"

Holly shook her head. "I'm not supposed to talk about it."

"Can you at least tell me what it was like waking up like that, seeing that he had been murdered?"

How was Holly supposed to answer that question?

It was a blast. Thanks for asking.

Holly liked Beth, but sometimes she could be irritating.

"It was terrifying," Holly said at last.

By the time Beth had finished asking questions that Holly really couldn't answer, it was time. Holly took the brown paper bag from her purse, double checked to make sure the correct cell phone was inside, and slipped out of the newsroom, making her way down the back stairway to the rear entrance. At precisely zero-nine-thirty, she stepped outside and tossed the bag into the trash can. As she went inside again, she caught just a glimpse of a van turning into the alleyway.

She leaned back against the closed door and let out a long exhale, listening as the van stopped to retrieve the package and moved on again.

Feeling a little lighter, she made her way back upstairs in time to see the I-Team staff leave the conference room after their morning meeting. The I-Team reporters were the rock stars of the newspaper as far as Holly was concerned. Investigative journalism was a disappearing art but they kept it alive, edition by edition, exposing wrongs that wouldn't have been exposed otherwise. Though she wasn't a part of the team, most of her friends were.

She walked to their corner of the newsroom to find Laura Nilsson on the phone and Sophie at her desk, tying her strawberry blond hair back in a ponytail.

Sophie stood when she spotted Holly and gave her a hug. "How are you feeling?"

"I still have a headache off and on. Thanks for everything."

"Marc says it looks like Dudayev's death is connected to some pretty serious stuff, but he won't tell me anything," Sophie said.

"I can't talk about it." Holly hoped Sophie would leave it at that.

"Fine. Keep me in the dark. Just do what Javier says and stay safe, okay?"

"I promise. No more dates with shifty foreign billionaires."

"Oh, hey, did you hear that Tom is converting to Buddhism?"

From his office came the sound of Tom shouting.

"Kara told me Friday." It still struck Holly as absurd. "Who's he yelling at?"

"Alex, I think."

Matt Harker, the city reporter, walked past them. Holly's consistent choice for Worst Dressed Journalist, he looked more rumpled than usual, dark circles beneath his eyes, his reddish hair uncombed.

It didn't take HUMINT training to see that something was wrong.

"Matt?"

He looked up, saw her. "Hey. How are you doing?"

"I'm fine. How are *you*?"

"Sorry about Saturday." He seemed distant. "I would have come to visit you in the hospital, but I spent the day with a divorce lawyer. My wife packed up and left."

"Oh, Matt, I'm so sorry." Sophie's words seemed to slide off him, unnoticed, as he walked to his desk, set down his coffee, and sank into his chair.

Holly lowered her voice to a whisper. "Wait . . . Matt was married?"

Sophie glowered at her. "For more than ten years. I've never met her. She never came to newspaper functions."

The door to Tom's office opened, and Alex stepped out.

His gaze fixed on Holly. "Hey. Glad to see you back. Do you have a few minutes?"

He flipped to a clean page in his reporter's notebook.

Holly shook her head. "I can't answer any questions, Alex. The investigation—"

"The cops aren't talking but my sources say it's been taken over by federals." He stood there, pen to paper, as if waiting for an answer.

"I can't talk about it."

"I saw the crime scene photos, including the photos of you from the ER—the blood spatter on your skin."

Heat rushed into Holly's face. "How did you get those?"

She'd been nude in those photos, pictures meant to show the pattern of blood spatter on her body should a suspect be arrested and the case come to trial. She hadn't worried about being photographed because she knew there would be no case. It wasn't the fact that she was naked in the images that bothered her. It was the possibility of the photos one day being used to expose her.

If they'd been leaked to Alex, who else might have them?

"That's confidential," Alex said. "Word is your date was a lot more than just an art dealer and maybe had some underworld connections. Do you know anything about that? Did you ever hear anything that made you suspicious?"

"I can't answer your questions."

"Here's one you can answer: Your date was murdered while you were drugged and unconscious. How did you feel when—"

"You deaf, man? She already said she doesn't want to talk." Joaquin.

He came up to stand beside her.

Alex glanced from Joaquin to Holly, then turned toward

Tom, who now stood in his office doorway. "I joined the I-Team because I thought it would give me the chance to do some hard-hitting investigative work. But this team you have here—it's compromised. One reporter hooked up with the SWAT captain. Rather than giving us the inside scoop, she protects her husband's interests. Same thing with Laura and her husband. He lands in the middle of a murder investigation, and we can't get a word out of either of them. To make it worse, they're all friends. When something happens, they circle the wagons."

The newsroom had gone silent.

Alex looked around, pointed at Holly. "What's the problem with me doing my job and asking her questions? What kind of ethical standard do we have if our staff get the kid-glove treatment?"

Laura stood. "It's not the fact that you ask questions, Alex. It's the complete lack of compassion and tact you demonstrate when you do."

Tom clapped his hands together. "We've got a paper to make and six hours till deadline, people. Carmichael, you asked your questions and got your answers. Bradshaw, I think your desk is in the entertainment department."

As Holly turned to go, Sophie whispered, "The Zen of journalism."

Holly realized as she made her way across the newsroom that she'd completely forgotten to tell Sophie and Laura that Mr. Creeper had turned out to be Mr. Sexy.

CHAPTER 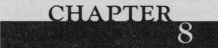8

"HE SAID HE was writing a book about his time in Delta Force." Holly took a sip of her coffee, watched the lack of reaction on her friends' faces.

They'd surprised her by showing up on her doorstep with brunch. Among them, Sophie, Kara, Tessa, Laura, and Kat had brought a breakfast quiche, shrimp and cocktail sauce, lots of fresh cut fruit, home-squeezed orange juice, amazing Puerto Rican coffee, and champagne for mimosas. Natalie had brought beignets, evil little French pastries that Holly was finding impossible to resist.

Now, the seven of them sat on Holly's deck in the back, sharing a feast, shielded from the morning sun by a tall umbrella.

A week had already gone by since that terrible morning when she'd woken up next to Dudaev's corpse, and life was beginning to feel normal again—apart from the CIS security team that still sat out front, keeping watch on her place.

"He claims to be ex-military?" Kara asked. "He could be lying."

Holly didn't think so. "He's got a scar on his abdomen that looks like a gunshot wound. Is he lying about that?"

She shouldn't have said that. How would she know what a bullet scar looked like?

"He's not lying." Laura took a sip of her mimosa. "Javi ran a basic background check on him a few days ago. He served in Delta Force and saw combat in both Afghanistan and Iraq, just like he said, but parts of his service record were vague or missing. Javier wasn't able to find anything about the nature of his discharge, but he had no arrests, no FBI file."

Holly let out an exasperated breath. "Your husbands—they're sweet and sexy and I love them, and they've done so much for me this past week. But they can be *so* overprotective. It's like having a bunch of aggressive, armed big brothers."

Sophie dabbed powdered sugar off her lips with her napkin. "They just worry about you. They want to see you with someone who cares about you."

"I know, and I'm grateful. I get it. I really do. It's been a week since the date that almost got me killed, and you all think it's too soon for me to be thinking about another man." Of course, Dudaev didn't really count, but she couldn't say that. "If you all could just *see* him . . ."

Holly let their advice roll off her. They didn't know—and she couldn't tell them—that a long-term relationship was impossible at this point in her life. What was wrong with having a little fun in the meantime? It had been a long time since she'd spent more than a weekend with someone of her own choosing. She would take all the happiness she could steal for herself, even if it lasted just a few weeks.

"Hot men are a dime a dozen," Tessa said over the rim of her coffee mug. "It's not about appearance, anyway. It's about what's inside."

"Easy for you to say." Holly glared at Tessa. "Look who you married."

Tessa smiled sweetly and took a sip of her coffee.

"If you're not going to eat your beignet, I will," Natalie said. "Now that I'm not feeling sick all the time, I'm *starving.*"

"Take half." Holly cut her beignet down the middle and gave a piece to Natalie, then took a bite for herself, savoring the fried pastry taste and the sweetness, her gaze traveling to Nick's sliding patio door. "He came over last night after I got home from work and asked to borrow a cup of laundry detergent. It was a ploy, I know, just an excuse, but I thought it was cute."

"That's something to consider." Kat got up from the table

with a plate that held a bite of everything they'd eaten and set it down in the shade—part of a Native spiritual tradition that Kat, who was Navajo, observed. "He's your neighbor. Wouldn't it be awkward if the two of you hooked up and it didn't work out? You'd have to see him almost every day. You'd have to watch as he brought other women home."

"That's a great point," Kara said.

Everyone nodded, agreeing that Kat had just said a very wise thing that Holly would do well to consider.

Then Nick's sliding glass door opened—and all conversation at the table stopped.

He stepped outside wearing nothing but pajama bottoms, a cup of coffee in one hand, his newspaper in the other. His hair was uncombed, his face unshaven. He looked like he'd just crawled out of bed after a night of wild sex—or so Holly imagined.

He saw them, did a double take. "Morning, ladies. Looks like a party."

"Oh!" Kat whispered, resuming her seat at the table.

"You're welcome to join us if you want," Tessa called. "We've got lots of food."

"And beignets," Natalie offered.

"And mimosas," added Sophie, lifting the bottle of champagne.

"There's an extra chair here." Laura pointed.

Kat scooted over to create a place for him.

He flashed them a smile. "Thanks. Maybe next time."

With that, he sat at a slatted wooden table, his back facing them, and began to read his paper.

Kara leaned in, rested her hand on Holly's arm, lowered her voice to a whisper, a conspiratorial gleam in her eyes. "Go for it."

NICK BIT HIS lower lip, fought not to laugh. There wasn't anything funny about this situation—except that he'd heard every word they'd said and could still hear them whispering about him.

Okay, it *was* funny.

It didn't hurt his ego, either.

He'd worked most of the night dealing with a program that kept crashing. He'd had to drag his butt out of bed when Holly's friends had arrived so that he could make sure the surveillance was running. He'd been on his second cup of coffee before he'd realized Holly was hoping he'd make an appearance. He'd obligingly stripped off his T-shirt—who knew women were such horndogs?—and come outside to be ogled.

You're just a piece of meat, Andris; beefcake, to be exact.

Somewhere, Nguyen was laughing his ass off.

Now that Holly had the approval of her friends and had had some time to move beyond Dudaev's murder, perhaps she'd warm up to him a little.

He needed her to respond—and soon. Bauer wanted results yesterday, and it was Nick's job to procure them. If she didn't open up to him in the next week or so, he'd be forced to drop all pretext and resort to rougher methods.

The thought wiped the stupid grin off his face.

Just how far was he willing to go to make Holly Bradshaw talk?

NICK POURED THE last of the wine into their crystal glasses and set the empty bottle on his coffee table. "Can I ask you something?"

Piano music drifted from his speakers, part of a Pandora channel he'd seeded with songs from the "Romantic" playlist on Holly's MP3 player.

"Sure." Holly's lips curved in a smile. "I have no secrets."

"Oh, babe, I'd bet my life that's not true. All women have secrets."

"We don't have to talk. If you want to kiss me, just kiss me."

The woman knew how to cut to the chase, but he couldn't let her take control of the moment. "How can a woman as beautiful and smart as you still be single?"

He hoped she'd talk about her job—the one at the newspaper and then the other one, the one no one else knew about.

"Have we reached the 'probing questions stage' already?"

"Shouldn't that come before kissing?"

"That depends on what you really want."

"Answer the question. I really want to know."

They'd finished dinner an hour ago. Although they'd moved from the dining room to his sofa, neither of them had so much as mentioned turning on the TV or watching the DVD she'd brought over. Dinner and a movie was turning into dinner and something else, as he'd hoped it would.

But Nick wasn't sure which one of them was in bigger trouble, him or Holly. The woman was a sensual onslaught. Every move she made, every glance, every touch, even the way she breathed, was feminine in a way he hadn't been prepared for. He wasn't even certain it was deliberate. It's just who she was—or who she'd been trained to be.

He'd been afraid he'd hate her too much for his body to respond to her. But his half-hard cock told him this was a non-issue—and he hadn't so much as kissed her yet.

She took a sip of her wine, seemed to consider his question. "I guess I'm waiting for the right man to come into my life at the right time. How about you?"

"I thought I'd found the right woman once."

"What happened?"

"She died."

Holly's brown eyes went wide. "I'm so sorry. I . . . I can't imagine. What happened? I mean . . . if you don't want to tell—"

"She was shot and killed during a robbery." That was the truth.

"Oh, God. How horrid. I'm so sorry."

"That was two years ago."

She's the one who's supposed to be talking, Andris, not you.

He locked away his grief. "So tell me about this Mr. Right of yours."

She watched him for a moment, then shifted against the couch cushion so that she was facing him, bare feet tucked beneath her. "He's tall, dark, handsome."

Nick gave a nod. "That's a given."

"He's got a strong appetite for adventure, a sense of purpose about his life, and he loves me to distraction." She was smiling again. "Oh, and he has to be a good lover, a man who can match or beat my libido."

Those last words hit Nick in the solar plexus. "So, once a week?"

She laughed, looked up at him through dark lashes. "Sure—when I'm eighty."

"Which is more important—quantity or quality?"

She raised a blond eyebrow. "Can't a woman get both?"

"That depends on the man, I suppose."

She smiled again, touched his hand. "Exactly."

"Sorry, but I have to ask. If that's what you want, how in the world did you end up with that old guy? If you tell me it was his money, I'm going to be disappointed. He was old enough to be your father. He couldn't have had it going on between the sheets."

Her smile disappeared, and she looked away. "I didn't sleep with him. I didn't even want to sleep with him."

There it was—the first bit of intel he'd gotten from her. It didn't tell him much but at least he knew she was being genuine with him.

He waited to see if she'd say anything else, and when she didn't, he pushed a little harder. "Then why bother going out with him? It's not like anyone forced you."

"It wouldn't be the first time my curiosity has gotten me into trouble." She played with one of the buttons on his shirt.

She'd turned the subject away from Dudaev to sex so deftly and subtly that it took Nick a moment to catch up. He decided to go with it. He was too distracted for much else anyway.

He took her wineglass, set it on the coffee table together with his own. "How curious are you feeling right now, tonight, with me?"

"Curious enough to get us both into a lot of trouble."

"Good." He slid his hand through the hair at her nape and drew her to him, brushing his lips over hers.

At first contact, she gave a little gasp, but he'd felt it, too—a jolt of heat arcing between them, shooting straight to his groin.

He drew back just enough to see her face, found himself staring into surprised brown eyes. "*Holly.*"

And then instinct took over.

Their lips met in a kiss that set him on fire—and made his

brain go blank. He forgot he didn't really want to kiss her, because, oh, hell, yes, he did. He forgot his mission, the entire reason he was here. He forgot everything but the feel and taste and scent of her—her warm lips, her soft body, the sweetness of her skin.

She gave a hungry little whimper, her tongue teasing his, the fingers of one hand fisting in his hair, the other clenching in the fabric of his shirt. He responded with teasing of his own, taking control of the kiss as he lifted her to straddle him, bringing the two of them even closer, her breasts crushed against his chest.

This isn't real, Andris. Don't get lost in it.

But the warning was drowned out by the pounding of his heart as she wrapped those long, silky legs around his waist and let her head fall back, exposing her throat.

He took what she offered, pressing his lips to her pulse, licking her silken skin, nibbling her ear, the faint scent of her perfume leaving him intoxicated. He found himself lifting the cloth of her dress in fistfuls, drawing her upright to pull it over her head. She stretched up her arms to help him, watching him as he tossed it aside, her blond hair tousled, her lips wet and swollen. For a moment her gaze met his, and he saw that her pupils were dilated, black against deep brown.

She wasn't acting.

Neither was he.

He rested his hands on her slender shoulders, ran them down her arms, let his gaze rake over her as they each caught their breath—the swells of her breasts, the tight buds of her nipples beneath the red lace of her bra, the rapid rise and fall of her chest.

With a little smile, she reached behind her, unfastened her bra, and dropped it over the back of the sofa.

The breath left Nick's lungs as he drank in the sight of her. He cupped her breasts, stroked her pebbled pink nipples with his thumbs, and felt her body tense in response. With a groan, he splayed one hand across her back, lifting her to his mouth, suckling first one nipple and then the other, tugging them to tight peaks with his lips.

Little tremors shuddered through her, her fingers twisting and curling through the hair at his nape, her breathing ragged.

Soon, she began to squirm, her hips restless, her thighs tightening around his waist.

And that was it.

He slid both hands beneath her panties, gripped the firm flesh of her bare ass, then rose to his feet and carried her to the bedroom.

THIS WAS WHAT Holly had needed, this crazy rush of sexual arousal. It made her forget everything else, the world around her fading until there was nothing but breath and lips and skin—his and hers.

And, God, he was good.

She felt small and feminine in his arms—out of control, overwhelmed, on the edge. When was the last time a man had made her feel like this?

He lowered her to the bed, peeling off her panties in the process, his gaze fixing on her bare labia, his pupils going wide. She got onto her hands and knees and crawled up toward the pillows, giving him a more enticing view, playing with him.

"Jesus!"

She heard clothing hit the floor and looked back over her shoulder—just as strong hands grasped her ankles and dragged her toward the foot of the bed again, flipping her onto her back. Her breath caught—and then seemed to stop.

He stood over her, gloriously naked, his cock jutting upward from a thick patch of dark curls, the masculine sight of him flooding her with heat.

His weight came down on her, his hot mouth reclaiming hers, while she explored his beautiful body with her hands— satin skin, ridges of muscle, sensitive valleys. Then his mouth strayed to her nipples again, his lips, tongue, and teeth making them painfully hard, the ache between her thighs both sweet and agonizing, his erection just inches away from where she most wanted it.

She took hold of him, stroked him, pleased by the way he more than filled her hand, hot and hard.

He groaned, one big hand reaching down to cup her, his finger teasing first her clit and then the entrance to her vagina. "You are *so* wet."

She was dying. That's what she was. *Dying.*

Had she just said that aloud?

He blew hot breath over one wet nipple, chuckled.

Yes, she had.

"Let's take care of that."

She expected him to grab a condom and put it on. Instead, he began to kiss and nip his way down her ribcage and over her belly.

Her pulse skipped.

He was like a lover from a girl's wet dream, someone conjured out of her fantasies. He licked and nibbled his way to her inner thighs, her skin now so sensitive that she jerked as if burned at the contact. She tried to relax, but her hands clenched in his hair in expectation, anticipation coiling inside her.

She didn't have long to wait.

He tasted her with a few bold strokes, then, with a groan took her with his mouth, suckling her clit, teasing her with his tongue, penetrating her with his fingers.

"Oh, God, yes!" She gave herself over to it, her hips arching upward, her fingers still clenched in his hair.

The combined sensations of lips and tongue and fingers were part bliss, part torment, the craving for completion at odds with the need to make it last. But he was just *too good* at this. The tension inside her drew to a shimmering crest— and then exploded, flooding her body with pleasure.

He stayed with her, sucking and licking and stroking her until the tremors inside her subsided and she was too sensitive to take more. Then he kissed his way back up her body and gazed down at her, grinning. "Don't tell me that's all you've got."

She smiled, her body floating. "Not on your life."

"Good." He reached into the drawer of his nightstand and took out a condom.

Holly liked a man who didn't have to be asked.

She took the little package from him and opened it, bending down to lubricate his cock with a few slow licks that made the muscles of his belly jerk before sliding the condom down his length. Already, she could feel it—the stirrings of renewed desire.

He grasped her hips and drew her beneath him, his hands sliding down her thighs to wrap her legs around his waist. Then with a single slow thrust, he filled her.

Their gazes locked, and for a moment he held himself still inside her. "Think you can come again?"

She was really starting to like this guy. "Think you can last?"

He grinned—and began to move.

His slow, silky thrusts felt incredible, but what turned her on even more was the intensity on his handsome face, his brow furrowed, his jaw tight, his gaze still fixed on hers. Then he grinned—and shifted his weight so that the base of his cock and his pubic bone put pressure on her clit.

She sucked in a breath. "That's cheating."

"Hey, I do whatever I need to do to get the job done."

But Holly wasn't really complaining. What he was doing to her felt so incredibly good, stretching her, satisfying the emptiness inside her, bringing her to the edge. She couldn't keep her hands off him, her palms taking in the feel of him, of his muscular back, of his biceps, of the hard mounds of his buttocks, which contracted and released as he fucked her.

She came fast and hard, crying out as he drove her climax home with strong thrusts. Then his rhythm and angle shifted, and he pushed into her again and again, faster and harder than before. His breath caught, his body seeming to shake apart in her arms as climax claimed him.

They lay in the bed in a tangle of limbs, her head resting on his chest, both of them breathless. She tilted her head back, looked up at him. "Don't tell me that's all you've got."

"Just give me . . . a little while . . . to reload."

NICK AWOKE THE next morning to the sound of someone pounding on his door.

"Holly, are you there?"

What the hell?

A man's voice. More pounding.

He came fully alert, found Holly still asleep in his arms, lashes dark on her cheeks. "Hey, honey, I think we've got company."

"Holly, it's Julian!"

Her eyes flew open, and she sat bolt upright. "What time is it?"

Nick glanced at his alarm clock. "A little after nine."

"Nine? Oh, no!" She tried to get out of bed, but they were tangled together with the sheet and she would have pitched headlong onto the floor if he hadn't caught her.

"Holly! Open up!" a second male voice demanded.

Nick kicked away the sheet, steadied Holly as she got to her feet, then rose and went in search of a means to cover his bare ass. He found his jeans at the foot of the bed where he'd dropped them. "Don't they know it's Sunday morning? People sleep in on Sunday morning."

Especially people who'd been fucking all night Saturday.

"They're taking me to the police range to teach me how to shoot my new handgun, and I forgot," she said, darting naked around his room as if searching for something—her clothes. "Well, I didn't forget, exactly. I just didn't think I'd still be here. I was supposed to be dressed and ready to go."

Nick ought to have remembered this himself. Thanks to the tap on her cell phone, he knew about the Glock 19 she'd bought, knew her cop friends had agreed to take her to the police range this morning to teach her to shoot.

You're slipping, Andris—in more ways than one.

He didn't want to think about that just now.

He stepped into his jeans, found her panties, and tossed them to her.

"Where's my bra?" She glanced around.

He tried to remember. "I think it's back in the living room."

"Oh. Right." She darted out of the bedroom, putting on her panties as she went, a sight that was both amusing and arousing.

He didn't know a person could do that while running.

She found her bra and quickly put it on, then retrieved her dress, which was now wrinkled from a night on his floor. She drew it over her head then went in search of her shoes and purse.

He bit his lower lip. "Holly, honey, your dress is inside out."

More pounding on the door.

"Holly, it's Marc! Open up!"

Nick shouted back. "Shut the hell up! We're coming!"

Poor choice of words.

They both laughed.

"It's not funny." Holly struggled out of her dress, turned it right side out and shimmied back into it. "They're going to *know*."

"I hate to break it to you, but I bet they already know, given that they're knocking on my door and not yours."

A look of comprehension dawned on her face, followed by one of resignation. "That's freaking fantastic. I'm going to get lectured. You don't know these guys."

Actually, he knew a lot about these guys—probably more than she did.

"Hey, you're over eighteen. It's your life." He walked to the door, hoping to open it before the two men beat it down with their fists. "You ready?"

She grabbed her purse, slipped her feet into her sandals, and nodded.

Nick didn't have the heart to tell her that her hair was a tousled mess—or that she smelled like sex.

He opened the door to find Darcangelo and Hunter on his doorstep. They glared at him, their gazes softening when Holly stepped into view.

"Sorry! I—"

"I kept her up all night watching old movies," Nick said.

He knew neither man would buy it but if it saved Holly embarrassment and kept them from beating his face in . . .

"How fast can you get ready to go?" Darcangelo said. "We don't want to lose our range time."

"Just give me five minutes." Holly dug in her purse for her keys, then turned back to Nick, lowering her voice to a whisper. "Thanks for everything. Tonight?"

"Yeah." He caught her and kissed her, nice and slow, just to piss off the two men.

Then she unlocked her door and disappeared inside her own home, and Nick found himself, alone and shirtless, facing two big guys who looked like they really wanted to beat his ass.

"Nick Andrews." He held out a hand, and they shook.

"Marc Hunter."

"Julian Darcangelo."

"So . . . you guys part of Holly's security team?"

Hunter nodded yes.

Darcangelo shook his head no.

Then the two of them looked at each other.

It was Hunter who finally spoke. "We're the guys you'll get to know *really* well if you do anything to hurt her."

Five minutes later, when three SUVs pulled away from the curb, Nick found himself wondering what these guys would do when they found out the truth about the woman they were trying so hard to protect.

CHAPTER 9

HOLLY SAT IN the backseat of the SUV, fighting to keep the smile off her face, her body still singing. No one spoke as they made their way toward I-70 and the DPD's private shooting range on the edge of Denver. The silence gave her time to think, her mind filled with memories of last night.

Nick carrying her to the bedroom. Nick catching her and flipping her onto her back. Nick going down on her—not once but twice. Nick shaking apart in her arms as he came, all that muscle tensing beneath her hands.

Don't tell me that's all you've got.

She inhaled, his scent still on her skin, the taste of him still on her tongue.

She couldn't remember the last time a man had challenged her in bed. He'd put her through her paces, but he hadn't been selfish. He'd given every bit as much as he'd taken—and then demanded and given more. He was *fun*, had a sense of humor, and an incredible amount of self-control.

And, oh, how the man kissed! He knew how to tease her lips, knew when to deepen the kiss, when to back off, when and how to use his teeth, his tongue. He was a five-alarm-fire sexual fantasy of a man—and he was her next-door neighbor.

She loved how he'd stood up to Julian and Marc, not an easy thing for any man to do. He'd kissed her in front of them, more to goad them than anything else. But there'd been a possessive edge to that kiss, too, and it had her looking forward to tonight.

But right now, she needed to focus on other things.

She ran her hand over the rough black plastic case of her Glock, the weapon and its magazines locked securely inside. "I really appreciate this."

Julian glanced back over his shoulder. "You're welcome."

"How much do you know about that guy?" Marc asked.

Now came the lecture.

"Javier ran a background check on him, so I know he's clean. He served with Delta Force in Afghanistan and Iraq, was injured in combat, and now he's writing a book about that. He's funny and intelligent and amazing in the . . . kitchen."

They wouldn't want to hear the rest of it.

For a moment, there was silence.

Marc looked over a Julian. "What did you mean by saying 'no'? You made us look like idiots."

Julian turned to look at Marc over the top of his sunglasses. "You did that all by yourself. You're the one who started making shit up. I answered truthfully."

"I just figured the dude would have a little more respect if he thought we were strapped and part of the CIS team."

Julian shrugged. "If he doesn't take us seriously, that's his grave mistake."

"Guys, it's okay," Holly said, interrupting them. "He's not a threat, and I'm not sixteen. You don't need to worry. I'm sure he found you both very intimidating."

Men!

They arrived at the DPD shooting range fifteen minutes later—not a moment too soon—and Holly followed them inside. They led her down a hallway, past vending machines offering soda and junk food, around a corner, stopping at a counter beside a heavy set of double doors.

"It's the Dynamic Duo," said an older man behind the counter. He caught sight of Holly and smiled. "Well, hello there. Who are you?"

"She's with us," Marc answered.

"Right." The smile left the man's face. "You're in lane seven. What're you firing?"

"Let's start with a hundred rounds of nine mil," Julian said.

Marc and Julian signed in while Holly filled out a visitor's registration form on a computer screen. From the other side of the thick bulletproof wall came the muffled sound of high-caliber weapons fire. There was a large sign on the door that read, "Eye and ear protection required beyond this point."

Holly wondered if she should tell Marc and Julian, then decided against it.

This was going to be fun.

She pulled out the shooting glasses and hearing-enhanced earmuffs she'd picked up when she'd bought the Glock— both flaming pink—and slipped them on.

"You're going to need ear and eye pro . . ." Julian said, his words dying off when he turned toward her and found her ready to go. "Oh. You brought some. Great."

Both men had custom ear protection, their shooting glasses tinted yellow.

She followed them through one set of doors, and then another, onto the range. It was a low-light range with twenty lanes, the firing line divided into stalls with adjustable lighting and what looked like a sophisticated target carrier system.

They settled in and she listened while Marc and Julian went over basic gun safety. She'd been taught all of this, of course, but it never hurt to hear it all again. A mistake with a handgun could be deadly and no one was so expert a shooter as to be above a refresher.

"Above all, never put your finger on the trigger unless you're willing to destroy whatever is in front of that barrel. Got that?"

She nodded.

They explained all the features—a simple thing on a Glock—then showed her how to load a magazine.

She inserted five rounds, slid the mag into place, and racked the slide.

"That's great," Julian said. "You're doing great."

Marc set the target for a distance of seven yards. "Let's start simple."

Julian showed her the stance. "Stand with your feet about hip-width apart, and lean slightly forward, supporting the pistol with . . . Yeah. Perfect. Just like that."

Marc, a decorated sniper who'd once held the US record for confirmed kills, talked her through sighting on her target. "It's good to keep both eyes open if you can. You want to focus on the front sight. It should line up with your target, but the target should be a blur. Go ahead and fire a few shots when you're ready. Just squeeze the trigger nice and—"

BAM! BAM! BAM! BAM! BAM!

Holly squeezed off five quick shots, found herself staring at a two-inch group at the center of the target. Not bad, but far from her best at only seven yards.

For a moment, there was silence.

Marc looked over at Julian, then down at her. "I think you've done this before."

Holly smiled. "It's been ages since I've held or fired a gun. My dad was a brigadier general. He made sure his little girl knew how to shoot."

It was a lie. Holly had learned to shoot during her training at Langley. She'd rarely seen her father, and when she had, he'd told her how pretty she was—and barely listened to a word she said. Except when he'd been drunk.

Then he'd said things she wished she could forget.

Julian grinned. "Let's see what you can do."

They moved the target back to ten yards, then twenty-five, then put her through a series of tactical drills, eventually joining in and finishing with moving targets as Holly worked out the rust and got used to shooting with the Glock. By the end of their hour, she felt confident, prepared, and was shooting almost as well as the two of them.

"You've got fantastic trigger control," Marc said, a wide grin on his face, as they made their way back to his SUV. "If we worked a little on your grasp, I think you'd manage the recoil better and get back on target faster."

"Thanks for letting me get in some practice. I had a lot of fun."

Julian opened the vehicle's door for her. "Hey, any time you want to come shooting with us, just let us know."

* * *

NICK STOOD BACK and looked at the whiteboard, unanswered questions running through his mind. How had Dudaev known when the guns were set to ship and where to find them? How had he gotten the drop on Nick's team? Why had Dudaev made a special effort to go after Dani? The bastard hadn't just shot her, after all. He'd entered the warehouse, exposing himself to enemy fire, in order to shoot her at point-blank range, while walking past Carver and McGowen, both badly wounded, and leaving them alive. Clearly, he'd wanted to make certain Dani was dead.

The analysts had answers to these questions, answers that had been part of his original debriefing two years ago. The official record of the event stated that one of the men in the Georgian police, known to be infiltrated by Dudaev's men, had betrayed them, and Dudaev had made a point of killing Dani because she was the officer in charge. It was his way of sending a message to Langley. But those answers had never sat well with Nick. Now that he knew an internal investigation was underway, he knew they didn't sit well with someone high up in the Agency, either.

If Nick could figure out what had happened that night, he might be able to uncover what was really going on. He'd hoped the encrypted files would tell him what he needed to know but that was taking too long. He had half a dozen CPUs running twenty-four-seven and he still hadn't cracked the password.

Somewhere, a clock was ticking. He could feel it.

So he'd spent the past few hours shut in his office doing his best to re-create the events of the night Dani had died down to the smallest details. He'd listed all the players, drawn the warehouse and pier, noted everyone's positions. He'd written down the chronology of the orders he'd received and those he'd given.

And he'd come to one conclusion.

His entire world was a goatfuck.

The SAD was turning itself inside out. Most of the officers who'd been involved in the op that night were either missing or dead, forever silenced. Of those who'd had boots on the ground that night, only he and Nguyen remained. Rumors were making him out to be some kind of rogue operator. And he was starting to have serious doubts about his chain of command—and his mission.

Meanwhile, he was here in Denver, trying to decrypt classified files he'd stolen—certainly the actions of a rogue operator—and running an op against a US citizen, yet making little progress on either front, apart from developing an emotional connection to the very person he'd been assigned to bring down, which was not only counterproductive but extremely dangerous and fantastically stupid.

Did that about cover it?

Sucks to be you, Andris.

He needed to clear his mind, get a fresh perspective.

He hit the weights, pushing it until he'd maxed out, then did a quick five-mile run on the treadmill, endorphins easing some of the tension. He paused the treadmill at the five-mile mark, stepped off, and headed through his bedroom toward the master bath, his body sweaty, his mind on a hot shower.

The sight of his rumpled sheets stopped him. He found himself standing next to the bed, the pillow she'd slept on in his hands. He held it to his nose, breathed in, the lingering scent of her perfume filling his head.

Holly.

She was everything he could want in bed—playful, intensely erotic, feminine. From the tips of her manicured toes to her bare pussy to her full breasts with their soft, pink nipples to her angelic face, she was good enough to eat. But more than that, she was fun. She'd made him laugh, and it was a long time since he'd laughed with a woman.

Last night had blown his mind. *She* had blown his mind.

Strange that he hadn't thought of Dani once.

What the hell was he doing? What was he thinking?

He ripped off the pillow case, tore the sheets off the bed, then carried them to the laundry room, tossing them into the machine with detergent and starting the wash cycle. For a moment, he stood there, watching water pour into the washer. Then he dropped the lid and turned away.

He shouldn't waste time thinking about last night. Holly

was nothing but a job he had to do. Fucking her had been part of a covert operation. Yeah, he'd enjoyed it. Any red-blooded heterosexual man would have. But it didn't go beyond that. He could not allow himself to lose his objectivity and develop feelings for her.

And, hell, no, it wasn't too late.

He was in control of his feelings and there was no room in this for emotion—especially not the tenderness he'd felt for her when she'd been asleep beside him.

He headed back through the bedroom without looking at the bed and hit the shower, hot water washing away sweat and the scent of sex. He soaped up, tried to focus on the sensation of water on his skin.

But one thought wouldn't leave him—and it had nothing to do with the Batumi op or the Agency or decryption.

Holly didn't act like a woman with a guilty conscience.

Nick had met plenty of traitors in his time—men and women who would do anything for a buck, including sell out their governments, their leaders, their families. Whether Russian, Ukrainian, Georgian, Chechen, or American, they were unhappy people, sociopaths and misfits twisted by bitterness and driven by agendas that were written on every choice they made. A five-minute conversation was enough to reveal the rottenness inside them.

Holly was nothing like that. She also had none of the red flags that indicated someone ripe for coercion. She wasn't in debt. She didn't need money. She never expressed a single political opinion. More than that, she had the untroubled eyes and the bright smile of someone whose conscience was clean.

In Nick's experience, not even the best sociopath could fake that for long.

The only time Holly's smile had wavered was when he'd asked her about Dudaev. She'd said she hadn't really wanted to go out with the man, and Nick believed she'd been telling the truth. But then why had she done it?

Why the hell was he spending so much time worrying about it?

Whatever doubts he might have about the Agency, his mission, or Holly, he knew for certain that she'd broken into that safe and downloaded those files with Dudaev in the next room—a demonstration of tradecraft. He knew from repeated searches of her place that she no longer had the special cell phone or the stolen files, which meant she'd somehow managed to make a drop under everyone's noses. That was also tradecraft. Add to that her skill with firearms. Yeah, he'd been listening in via her hacked cell phone and hadn't been surprised at all when she'd shot like a pro.

Nick wasn't thinking clearly when it came to Holly. She'd already bested him once. He needed to trust Bauer on this. And yet the pieces of her didn't add up somehow, leaving him with misgivings he couldn't seem to shake.

It was time Nick quit fucking around and took a more direct route to getting answers from her. Bauer had chewed Nick's ass off once already this week and Nick had the encoded files and his own survival to worry about. He needed to wrap this mission. He'd have to be careful. Once Holly knew what he was after, all she'd have to do to bring those armed CIS men through the door was scream. And now that she was armed . . .

Well, that certainly made the game more interesting, didn't it?

He needed a way to remove her from her condo without the CIS team noticing. He'd already spent some time considering this, building blueprints in hand, and he had a good idea how to go about it.

He stepped out of the shower and toweled off.

It was time for a trip to the hardware store and the start of a little home improvement project.

CHAPTER 10

"HAVE YOU EVER done anything in bed with a man you didn't want to do?"

They sat on Holly's back deck, having just finished a dinner of Thai carryout with pinot grigio that was chilled to perfection.

Holly smiled at Nick's question. "Yeah, a few times, when I was younger and stupid and didn't know how to stand up for myself."

That was the truth, though not the whole truth.

"I'm sorry to hear that." Then he nudged her elbow with his. "Like what?"

"Pressing for the dirty details are you?"

"You know it." A smile lit up his face.

And, God, what a face. She'd come to appreciate the finer points of his features over the past couple of days—the scar high on his cheek by his right eye, the slight deviation of his nose as if it had once been broken, the perfect cupid's bow of his lips, the dark brows that gave him a brooding look.

He had the face of a fallen angel.

"Let's just say I don't do anal or anything involving real pain."

He watched her over the rim of his wineglass. "Ever been with a woman?"

That question caught her off guard.

Only once in her career had she been sent on a mission

where the quarry had been a female. She'd had real misgivings about the assignment, but in the end it hadn't been much different than going on a date with a man in whom she had no interest. The woman—a tall, blond Dutch banker—hadn't been as self-absorbed as most of the men of her social status and had gone out of her way to make Holly feel at ease when she'd learned it was Holly's first time.

"I tried it—once." She saw Nick's pupils dilate and knew the idea turned him on.

He nodded, still grinning. "Would you do it again?"

She smiled, finished her wine, ignored his question. "I have a surprise for you."

She scooted her chair away from the table, lifted her dress high up her thighs to reveal the garters, and then did The Leg Cross.

He gave a long, slow exhale, his brow furrowing when he saw that she wasn't wearing panties. "Please tell me that's dessert."

"You're still hungry?" She stood, picked up her wineglass, and walked slowly toward the door, leaving the plates and silverware for later.

A strong arm shot out, caught her around the waist, and drew her back. "Where do you think you're going?"

She lowered her voice. "Somewhere the neighbors and CIS guys won't see us."

He took the wineglass from her hand and set it on the table. "I am the neighbors, and fuck the CIS guys."

He drew her into his lap so that they sat face-to-face, her legs straddling him, then drew down his zipper and freed his erect cock from his boxers. "I want you now."

A shiver ran through her.

"But people—"

"People will be jealous." He grinned. "Just try not to give us away."

He reached down with one hand to tease her inner thighs with light brushes of his fingertips that made her skin tingle.

She felt herself grow wet, already wanting him inside her. She took his cock in hand and began to stroke him, felt his hips jerk, heard his breath catch.

But his gaze never wavered.

He caught her clit between his fingers, gave it a little tug, then explored her fully, the tip of one finger making delicious circles over the opening to her vagina before sliding inside her.

"See, that right there is what's going to give us away. Don't let your head fall back all sexy like that. Keep your eyes open. Look at me. We're just having a conversation here."

And what a conversation.

His fingers caressed her deep inside, taking their time, asking her if she wanted more. Her body answered *yes*.

He withdrew his fingers and began to tease her clit with his thumb, asking it to join in the game. It swelled beneath his touch—another *yes*.

Oh, God, she was melting, coming to pieces in his lap, the gliding pressure of his thumb making the ache inside her worse.

He reached into his pocket with his free hand, drew out a condom, and handed it to her. She opened it, rolled it over his erection while his hands reached beneath her dress to grasp her buttocks. When the condom was in place, he shifted in his seat, lifted her up, and let her guide him inside her.

She couldn't help but moan, her eyes drifting shut.

He felt so good, as he thrust into her from below, stretching her, filling her, the slick friction already carrying her home.

"Keep it together, honey."

She opened her eyes, smiled at him.

Two could *so* play at this game.

She put her inner muscles to work, clenching them as he withdrew and entered her, contracting around his length.

He fought back a moan, his eyes closing, his body going tense, the muscles of his neck and his jaw drawing tight.

"Keep quiet," she teased, a bit breathless, her fingers toying with his hair.

He picked up the pace, bucking into her, only his hips moving, one thumb still teasing her clit, giving her everything she needed.

She clenched her inner muscles tight, one hand now fisted

in his hair, the fingernails of the other digging into the cloth of his shirt at his shoulder, her breathing every bit as rapid as his. But using her vagina like this came at a price, arousing her even more, ensuring that his cock hit every sweet spot inside her.

"You're so close. I can tell." His voice was strained. "Don't lose it and scream."

Holly fought to control her response as he drove her head-long to a shattering orgasm, the tight knot of heat inside her exploding into bliss. She bit back a cry, her body arching in his arms. He stayed with her, keeping up the rhythm, making her pleasure last with deep strokes, until she sagged against him.

"That was a dead giveaway," he teased.

"At least I didn't scream." Holly drew herself upright. "Let's see if you handle it any better."

"Piece of cake." His hands grasped her hips, and his rhythm changed, his breath coming hard and fast.

But Holly wasn't about to let him off easy.

She began to rotate her hips to match his rhythm, until he was pounding into her hard enough to lift her with each thrust, his control hanging by a single, fraying thread.

She saw on his face the moment that thread broke, the intensity of his climax making his eyes go wide for a moment before he squeezed them shut, then buried his face in her neck, moaning out his pleasure against her skin, his body shaking.

He stayed that way for a while, holding her against him, his cock still inside her, while she kissed his forehead, caressed his nape, her heart swelling with an unfamiliar emotion. She couldn't go there.

Not yet. Not now.

These past few days with him had been like a dream. It wasn't just the fact that they had great sex together, freaking amazing, mind-blowing sex. It was that he truly seemed to care about what she thought, how she felt, what she did with her life. Not that she could be honest with him.

She could never be completely honest with him.

And that's why she shouldn't be feeling what she thought she might be feeling. There was no room in her life for a real relationship. Besides, she barely knew him. They'd had sex for the first time Friday night, and it was only Monday. A week from now, they might not want to have anything to do with each other. He might once again be the creep who lived next door to her.

She felt his body relax.

He raised his head and looked at her, his gaze soft.

She smiled. "Dead giveaway."

THEY CLEARED THE dishes together, put them into the dishwasher, Holly's blood as warm as honey. They talked about everything and nothing—the demise of journalism, reality TV, seventies versus eighties music—which somehow led first to kissing and then to sex in the shower, Nick fucking Holly slow and deep from behind while hot water sluiced over their skin.

They had just turned off the water when the doorbell rang.

Holly reached for her towel, wrapped it around her body. "Why are people always coming to the door when we're naked?"

"Maybe because we're always naked." Nick took a towel and began to dry off.

Holly traded her towel for her bathrobe and hurried through the house toward her front door. She glanced through the peephole—and froze.

A FedEx delivery truck.

It was nine at night.

Damn!

She took a breath, let the tension slide away, and opened the door to find a frightened FedEx driver sandwiched between two armed CIS men. "Oh, great! It's finally here! I've been wondering if you'd make it."

She signed for the package—this time from Saks—thanked the driver and the CIS guys, and closed and locked the door.

Nick appeared, towel wrapped around his hips. "I didn't know FedEx delivered this late."

"Custom delivery," Holly said. "It's my package from Saks."

"What is it?"

She smiled at Nick. "Give me a moment, and I'll model it for you."

He grinned. "I like that idea."

Holly couldn't tell him what was in the box because she had no idea. It might be anything—a bra with micro listening devices worked into the underwire or a special cell phone inside a designer handbag or shoes or clothes. Regardless of what it was, it included a message that she needed to decode as soon as possible.

She tossed him the TV remote. "I'll be right back."

She carried the package toward her bedroom, glancing back down the hallway to make sure Nick wasn't following. She picked up her cell phone and letter opener in the kitchen and took them with her, closing her bedroom door behind her. Quickly, she opened the box to find a studded Valentino tote in pastel yellow, blue, and pink.

She moved the purse aside, reached for the packing slip . . .

Her heart gave a hard knock then began to race, adrenaline hitting her bloodstream in an ice-cold rush.

Looking up at her was a printed image of Nick's face.

Beneath it was the encoded packing slip.

Fighting to master the autonomic effects of panic, she used her cell phone to retrieve the key off Twitter, picked up the packing slip with a trembling hand, and began to decode the ciphertext.

Nikolai Andris, aka Nick Andris, aka Nick Andrews is a CIA officer operating without the authorization of the Agency. He is a CI threat and believed to be responsible for the unauthorized termination of foreign national Sachino Dudaev. Last sighted in Denver. May have an interest in you due to incident with Dudaev. If sighted, proceed with extreme caution and contact authorities. Andris is armed and extremely dangerous. Suggest you leave town immediately. Tickets, ID, cash enclosed.

The words formed before her eyes, some part of her mind rejecting them, even as their meaning became terribly, horribly clear.

Nick was the rogue officer.

No. No, he couldn't be. He couldn't.

She'd had sex with him a half dozen times, stayed overnight at his house twice, slept beside him, and he hadn't hurt her. She hadn't seen any sign of tradecraft, any hint that he wasn't who he said he was. He'd been living there since before . . .

Oh, God!

He'd moved in a few days *after* she'd started dating Dudaev.

And the day he'd finally introduced himself—that had been the day she'd come home from the hospital, the day after someone had drugged her and left her alive in Dudaev's bed.

Had that someone been Nick?

Holly felt sick, her pulse pounding, a sense of rage warring with hurt as her mind flashed back through the hours she'd spent with him, not just having sex but sharing meals, talking, and sleeping together. All of his thoughtfulness, all of the questions he'd asked about her life—she'd thought he was interested in her. But he'd done to her what she'd done to dozens of men.

And she—*she* of all people—had fallen for it.

It figured that the one man she'd *really* liked, the one who'd seemed interested in her life, turned out to be a murdering rogue officer.

Fan-freaking-tastic.

She couldn't waste time feeling hurt now, not when a man who might be out to kill her sat in her living room. No, killing her wasn't his primary plan. If it had been, she'd be dead already.

So what *did* he want with her?

She heard the door creak behind her. Strong arms grabbed her and she found herself hauled backward against him, one of his hands holding a cloth over her mouth and nose. She recognized the sickly sweet scent.

Ether.

"Don't fight me, Holly. That's it. Just breathe. Let's do this the easy way."

Fighting true panic, Holly held her breath, pretended to struggle, and then slowly went limp. As she slumped down, her hand brushed soft terry cloth, and she realized he was still wearing nothing but a towel.

She grabbed his balls, squeezed *hard*—and felt him crumple.

"Fuck!"

Holly leaped over him and ran for her life.

GODDAMN!

Almost blinded by pain, Nick dragged himself to his hands and knees, driven by the need to stop her before she could retrieve her Glock or alert the CIS team. He grabbed the end of the flokati rug she was running across—and jerked it out from under her feet.

She fell to the hall floor, hit her forehead hard, and lay there for a moment, dazed, the wind knocked out of her.

He grabbed the ether-soaked cloth he'd dropped and fought his way to his feet, pain leaving him nauseated and making it damned hard to walk, the towel falling from his hips. He stumbled over to her, let his full weight come down on her, driving the air from her lungs, pinning her to the floor with a knee to her ribs.

She gave a muffled cry, then tried to roll out of it, clearly familiar with ground fighting tactics. But he outweighed her by eighty pounds and was a lot stronger and more experienced with close-quarters combat. He wouldn't let her get the best of him again.

He lay on top of her, careful to protect his nuts, and clamped the cloth hard over her nose and mouth. "Stop fighting. You can't win. If you play rough with me, you're going to get hurt."

Blood on the floor told him she was already hurt.

Still, she struggled, holding her breath, trying to twist away from him. But she couldn't hold her breath forever, especially not with her heart beating as hard as it was and no air in her lungs.

In the end, all it took was a single shuddering breath.

Her eyes drifted shut on a whimper and her body went limp, this time for real, one whispered word on her lips as she lost consciousness. *"Creeper."*

* * *

NICK WAITED UNTIL he was reasonably certain he wouldn't puke from the lingering pain in his crotch, gut, and thighs, then pulled Holly after him through the little access door in her laundry room and into her crawl space, where he'd hidden a bag with ether, duct tape, a flashlight, and his Ruger MK III earlier this afternoon when she'd been at work. He bound her hands and feet with the tape, trying not to notice the bruise on her forehead or the blood on her lip. Then, holding her head and neck against his chest with one arm, he crawled through the darkness, pulling her along with him to the opening he'd cut in the sheathing plywood that separated her crawl space from his.

It took less than five minutes to move her into his condo. Still naked, dirt on his hands and knees, he stopped only to make sure she was breathing before crawling back into the darkness.

He made two trips back to her place. The first time, he retrieved his bag, the photo of himself and the encoded message, as well as clothes and a few other basics for Holly. He found five grand inside the purse, along with a fake ID and plane tickets, and took that, too.

Whatever organization Holly worked for, they were professionals.

The second time, he went back so that he could clean himself up, get dressed, and make a proper exit that the CIS team could witness.

He paused before he opened the front door, looking around Holly's condo one last time, a strange feeling in his chest as he realized this life was now over for her.

Stop feeling guilty.

Okay. Right. Well, that was easier said than done.

He hadn't planned to have sex with her again. The intimacy messed up his emotions, made it hard for him to do his job. Besides, he felt like some kind of predator, having sex with her when he knew full well what he had in store for her. But she was too much, and he'd gotten lost in her again. He'd found himself putting off his plans for taking her into custody, unable to bring himself to move against her so soon after holding her, kissing her, being inside her. If the package hadn't arrived, if he hadn't peeked through her bedroom door and seen the image of his own face . . .

This is her own damned fault.

Nick was only doing what he had to do to protect himself. He had to know what was in that message and who had sent it. It wasn't just a matter of stolen files and national security now. His own survival might well be at stake.

He turned and walked out her front door and in through his own to make sure the CIS guys saw him going home—alone.

His rental vehicle—a gray Ford Explorer—was already packed, his gear, the whiteboard, all of his surveillance and computer equipment, as well as food and water stowed in the back and the third row. He picked up Holly, carried her through the door to his garage, and laid her down in the second row, fastening seatbelts around her. Then he climbed into the driver's seat, raised the garage door, and backed down the driveway and into the street, waving to the CIS guys as he drove away.

CHAPTER 11

NICK DROVE HER to an isolated cabin that belonged to the Agency. Sitting at about ten-thousand-feet elevation above the old ghost town of Caribou, it was rustic to say the least, with two rooms, an old iron hand pump that served up bad well water, and a ramshackle outhouse. Its primary virtue lay in the fact that it was surrounded by miles of pine forest and deserted mining claims left over from the gold rush— not a soul in sight. Bauer had told him that officers sometimes came here to evade law enforcement when an operation went bad, but Nick was certain it had been used a time or two for interrogations.

Holly was just starting to come around, semiconscious and moaning from what Nick was certain was a rotten headache and nausea.

He grabbed his SIG P229 and flashlight, climbed out of the vehicle, and glanced around, the only sound her soft whimpers and the whispering of the wind through the tops of the trees. He cleared the cabin, carried her inside, trying not to notice how helpless she felt in his arms. He laid her on the bed in the back room, cuffing her to the iron bedframe by an ankle. Then he unloaded his gear—go-bag, firearms and ammo, medic kit—leaving the surveillance gear, computers, and whiteboard locked in the vehicle. He couldn't allow her to see any of that. Besides, the cabin had no electricity, so it would be impossible to continue running the decryption programs—for now.

He found an old camping lantern, a bit of fuel left inside. He lit it, set it on the table, then drew a chair up against the wall and allowed himself to doze.

He knew she was awake when he heard the clinking of the cuffs followed by a hard thud as she fell to the rough wooden floor. He picked up the lantern, carried it to the bedroom, and hung it from a small hook in the ceiling that must have been put there for that purpose. He found her lying on her side, her bathrobe open to reveal a slender shoulder, her gaze fixed on him, her eyes wide.

Some part of him couldn't believe what he was about to do to her but seeing his face on that piece of paper had changed everything. She'd received an encrypted message about *him*. There was no room in this for compassion or chivalry.

Holly Bradshaw was the enemy. He needed to know what she knew.

"What are you going to do with me?" There was fear in her eyes, her lower lip swollen, the bruise on her forehead looking almost black in the semidarkness.

He knelt down so that she could see his face. "I'm going to ask you questions, and you are going to answer them. We're far away from CIS and your cop friends, somewhere no one can hear you scream. I'm the only person who can help you now."

She shook her head as if in disbelief. "You must be crazy."

"Don't waste my time with denials, Ms. Bradshaw." He picked her up, tossed her onto her back on the bed, her bathrobe falling open, revealing her body from her breasts to the tips of her toes, bruises and dirt on her creamy skin.

A few hours ago, he'd been inside that body, holding her, kissing her.

It didn't mean anything. Forget about it.

She quickly covered herself, crossing her arms protectively over her chest.

He laid out what he knew, as much to harden his own resolve as to show her how serious her situation was. "I know you were in Dudaev's hotel room the night he died. I know you downloaded stolen government files from a USB drive you found in his hotel safe. I've listened to the surveillance. I saw the time index. You were the only one with him at the time. *You* took those files, and *you* passed them on to some unknown entity."

He reached into his pocket, pulled out the folded sheets with the image of himself and the encoded message, then unfolded them in the lantern light so she could see them clearly. "I also know you received these tonight."

She glanced at them, not a flicker of emotion on her face.

"You have until dawn to answer three questions: Who pulls your strings? What do you know about me? What does this message say?"

"What happens at dawn?"

"Your life becomes a lot more . . . uncomfortable."

She closed her eyes, turned her head away from him, said nothing.

HOLLY TRIED TO sleep, knowing she needed to be as rested and clearheaded as she could be, no matter what lay ahead. It wasn't easy. She was terribly thirsty. Her ribs ached where his knee had bruised them. Her head throbbed.

Plus, there was that whole thing about being held prisoner and facing torture at dawn—or whatever he had in mind.

For the first time in her career, Holly felt truly afraid.

The Bastard—formerly known as her neighbor Nick, aka Mr. Creeper—slept in a nearby chair, his long legs stretched out in front of him, his arms crossed over his chest. He had a loaded SIG P229 in a belt holster. She wasn't sure how willing he was to use it on her, but he'd made a point of chambering a round in front of her.

Something inside Holly seemed to shatter, the sharp edges cutting at her heart as the full weight of Nick's betrayal hit her.

How could she have been so blind?

He'd showed up on her doorstep, the embodiment of everything she wanted in a man—a sense of humor, brains, skill in bed, a genuine interest in her thoughts and feelings, good looks—and some part of her had been so lonely, so desperate for a man who cared just for her, that she'd let herself believe he was real.

Pathetic, Bradshaw!

He'd known what he was going to do with her, but still he'd kissed her, slept with her, had sex with her. Now he wanted more. When the sun came up, he would do God only knew what to her body so that he could get into her mind and steal secrets she'd vowed to keep.

Well, to hell with that.

She wouldn't let him. She couldn't let him.

How had he managed this? How had he kidnapped her right under the noses of Javier's men? Would he tell her if she asked?

She ran his three questions through her mind. He knew she'd been with Dudaev. He'd seen her there. But he didn't know she worked for the same organization as he. He seemed to think she was an operative for some foreign interest. Or maybe he didn't believe that at all and that was just his way of trying to force her to say she worked for the Agency, too. If she admitted that, would he be relieved, or would he kill her? How would he react if she told him she knew he'd killed Dudaev without authorization and was now a fugitive?

She needed to stall him with half-truths, partial truths, pieces of the truth, give him enough so that he wouldn't hurt her, but not enough that she compromised herself or the Agency in any way.

What will he do to you when he doesn't get what he wants?

Would he kill her?

That's what she needed to know.

Outside the window, the sun was beginning to rise.

Butterflies filled Holly's stomach, the fear she'd spent the night trying to ignore creeping up on her again.

She hadn't been kidding when she'd told him she didn't like pain. Her idea of suffering was being forced to sleep on cheap, low-thread-count sheets. Never had she faced a situation that involved prolonged pain and suffering. She'd undergone R2I and SERE training, and although she'd passed, she'd hated it. Now that training, together with her advanced HUMINT experience, was all she had to keep her alive.

No matter how afraid she was, no matter what he did to her, she would have to keep her head. She would have to make herself vulnerable, test how far he was willing to go to get what he wanted from her. And if it became clear that he was willing to kill her?

She'd rather die with her secrets intact than die after giving them up.

That decision made, she felt some of her fear leave her.

At least today won't be boring.

She closed her eyes, dozed.

"Wake up." He kicked the bed.

She jolted awake, drew back from him, wincing at the pain in her ribs.

He bent down and unlocked the cuffs, then cut the duct tape from her ankles and wrists and stepped back, the SIG P229 appearing in his right hand. "There's an outhouse about twenty yards south of here. I'll be right behind you."

She drew her robe around her, sat up slowly, then carefully got to her feet, clutching an arm to her left side. She looked up at him. "You broke my ribs."

It wasn't true, but The Bastard didn't know that.

She gauged his reaction.

A slight furrowing of his brows, a tightening of his jaw.

"All is fair in love and war. You nearly broke my balls, and you don't hear me whining. By the way, go for my nuts again, and I'll drop you. Move."

She walked outside to find that they were surrounded by forest, not even the distant murmur of traffic to announce the presence of a nearby highway. Treading gingerly over the pine needles and moss that covered the forest floor—this was going to destroy her pedicure—she made her way back to the outhouse, opened the slatted wooden door, and shrank back.

Spiderwebs—big ones with equally big spiders.

She shook her head. "I'd rather go in the bushes."

"Suit yourself. If you try to run, you'll spend all night locked in the outhouse. Understand?"

Five minutes later, she was back in the cabin. Morning light revealed how filthy the place truly was—rodent droppings on the floor, spiderwebs, dead flies and wasps on the windowsills. But what held her gaze was the iron bar that ran from one side of the back room to the other. Set into the wooden walls just below the ceiling, it didn't look like it had been put there for architectural support.

A chill ran through her.

Who owned this awful place? How had Nick—The Bastard—known about it?

He entered the bedroom, tossed something into her lap.

Clothes. Her clothes.

"Get dressed."

She waited, but he didn't turn his back.

"It's nothing I haven't seen before."

She stood, let her bathrobe fall to the bed, then slipped into the panties and jeans, wincing as she bent down to put her feet through the legs. She let every bit of discomfort she felt show and then some, stopping when she went to fasten the bra around her bruised ribcage. "I can't. It hurts too much."

Again his brow furrowed, that telltale muscle tensing in his jaw.

She dropped the bra onto the bed, picked up the tank top, got her head and right arm into it, then stopped again, whimpering in exaggerated pain.

He swore under his breath, closed the distance between them, and helped her get her arm through the sleeve, his touch gentle, his gaze dropping to the purple bruise his knee had made. "I never wanted to hurt you, Holly. You left me no choice."

And Holly knew she had a powerful weapon against him.

Her pain bothered him. It hurt him to see her suffer.

Whatever else he might have done, he still had a conscience.

If she were smart, if she were careful, she could use that to bend him, to break him—and find a way out of this.

"What are you going to do now—waterboard me?"

"Do you want me to waterboard you?" Nick carried the cuffs to the iron restraining bar and draped them over, making his intent clear. "This is where you're going to spend every moment of the day and night until I find out what I need to know. You'll be on your feet, no food, no water, no sleep. I don't want to do this. I don't want you to suffer. But you've made choices that have put you outside the law and—"

"That's not true!"

"And it's my job to get answers. Make it easy on both of us, and start talking."

He watched as she backed away from him, keeping her distance, her gaze flitting to the bottled water.

"You must be thirsty. Tell me what I need to know, answer even one question, and I'll let you drink your fill. Answer two questions fully and truthfully, and you can eat and maybe even wash. This place is filthy. Your skin must feel grimy."

"If I answer three, do I get to go home—or is that when you kill me?" She glared defiantly up at him, but there were tearstains on her cheeks and dark circles beneath her eyes—proof she hadn't really slept.

He stepped closer, looked straight into her eyes. "Tell me what I need to know, and I promise I won't touch you."

She sat on the bed, scooted back against the wall. "I know you murdered Dudaev. I figured that out for myself. You drugged both of us, and you shot him."

He sat in the chair across from her. "Keep going."

"You said I could have water if I answered a question. I just told you what I know about you."

That wasn't all she knew about him—he'd bet his life on it.

"That was a partial answer. Until you tell me everything you know about me, you haven't fully answered the question."

"I know you're an ass. I know you lied to me. I know that all of your questions, all your affection, all of *that* . . . was just a ploy to get me to open up."

He shrugged. "Isn't that what you do for a living, Holly? You set men up, seduce them, steal secrets. How many men have you fucked?"

"How many have you murdered?"

"Answer the question."

"I thought we were talking about *you*."

"All right, Ms. Smartass." He grabbed her right wrist and dragged her onto her feet and toward the restraining bar.

"No!" She tried to pull away, then all but collapsed when

the strain hit her ribcage, sagging against him, teeth biting her swollen bottom lip, her left arm clutched against her side, her right hand fisted in his shirt.

He fought the impulse to help her and slipped her wrist through the handcuff, tightening it with a series of clicks.

"No, please don't!" She regained her balance, turned her left side away from him.

He reached out, took her left wrist, the rage he felt at being forced to cause her pain making his voice rough. "Tell me what you know about me. Have you been tasked with terminating me?"

"You really are crazy. I've never killed anyone. That's your job."

Slowly, he stretched her left arm over her head, and, ignoring her pain, closed the cuff around her wrist.

He stepped back, far enough away that he couldn't smell the scent of her skin, his gut knotting at the sight of fresh tears on her cheeks. "I'm not playing games."

"Really?" She glared at him. "Because this has to be a joke."

He tried to see nothing but the enemy when he looked at her, but he was familiar with that body. He'd kissed and sucked the nipples that stood out like pebbles beneath her T-shirt, held those breasts in his hands. He'd felt those slender arms encircling him, holding him when he'd been inside her. He'd kissed those lips, the ones that were swollen and bruised. She looked delicate, helpless, fragile.

She's dangerous, Andris.

"I'm the best friend you have right now, Holly."

"I think it's time I started seeing other people." She glared at him, fury on her face. "Did you plan to kidnap and torture me all along? What was last night—just another chance to get off before you broke out the guns and chains? Were you thinking of *this* when you came? Does hurting women turn you on?"

Her words hit home and hit hard, fueling his own rage.

"I can help you, or I can end you. What happens next is entirely up to you. Spare yourself a lot of needless suffering and answer the questions."

"You repulse me." She spat the words at him, loathing on her face.

Nick sat in the chair, steeled himself against her distress, against her tears. "What do you know about me? What did that message say? Who sent you to get those files?"

ZACH STEPPED THROUGH the front door of Holly's condo and made his way over to Corbray, who stood in her living room looking ten years older than he had the last time Zach had seen him. "How the hell could this have happened?"

"We don't know. Her escort arrived to pick her up and take her to work, but she wasn't here. They knocked on the neighbor's door, thinking maybe the guys had missed her heading over to spend the night with him, but no one answered. Her neighbor hasn't come home yet. He's our number one suspect, but we can't be sure it was him. DPD is waiting for a search warrant for his place."

This was DPD's crime scene, of course, and neither Zach nor Corbray nor Darcangelo nor Hunter, whose cars Zach had seen out front, had any real right to be here. Zach was a deputy US marshal. Corbray was a private contractor. Darcangelo and Hunter worked for the DPD, but on vice and SWAT, not crime scene investigations. But Holly was one of theirs, and they couldn't sit by and do nothing. If Chief Irving wanted them to leave, he'd have to throw them out.

"What *do* we know?"

"We know that she didn't leave voluntarily." Corbray motioned for Zach to follow him. "The forensic team found blood on the floor in the hallway outside Holly's bedroom. One of the rugs near the bed was out of place and crumpled. Her cell phone was found on the floor near the bed."

"She struggled with him." Zach took it in—the chalk marks on the floor that circled a small amount of dried blood, the rumpled rug. "She couldn't weigh more than one-ten, one-fifteen. She wouldn't present much of a challenge to an adult male."

"Especially if the bastard drugged her first." Darcangelo, who was wearing forensic overalls, walked out of the kitchen and held up an evidence bag containing a rumpled piece of cloth. "Ether."

"*Puñeta*," Corbray muttered under his breath.

Son of a bitch.

He opened the bag, took a quick whiff, closed it.

Zach did his best to lock down his rage. He wouldn't be any good to Holly if he didn't focus on the job. "So the bastard—whoever he is—surprises her near her bedroom with an ether-soaked rag. She struggles with him, and one of them trips over the rug and falls. Do we know whose blood that is?"

Corbray shook his head. "Not yet."

"How the hell could anyone get her out of here without being seen?"

"I wish I knew, man." Corbray looked down at a notepad. "The neighbor guy—Andrews—came over shortly after six. The two had dinner and a little al fresco action on the deck, then came inside. FedEx delivered a package at twenty-one-hundred hours. She was home then, and Andrews, her neighbor, was still here at that time. The neighbor guy walked out of Holly's front door and into his own condo at twenty-two-oh-seven, then pulled out of his garage five minutes later and drove off down the street. He hasn't been seen since. No one else approached the condo, and Holly was never seen leaving."

"What about the back yard?"

"We've got a unit covering the back. They never saw anyone come near the place. Once Holly and lover boy went back inside after dinner, that was it."

"Hey, guys, I think we found the answer." Hunter came up behind them, holding a flashlight, the knees of his forensic overalls brown with dirt. "You've got to see this."

They followed Hunter into the laundry room, where he opened the access door to the crawl space.

"I don't think I'm going to like this," Darcangelo muttered.

"I guarantee you won't." Hunter crouched down and crawled into the darkness.

One by one, Zach, Darcangelo, and Corbray followed.

"Be careful not to destroy the evidence. You can see where he dragged her." Hunter pointed the flashlight at the ground.

There in the earth were marks that might have been made by someone's heels dragging in the dirt.

They crawled a bit farther, then Hunter held up the flashlight to reveal a hole in the plywood wall that separated Holly's crawlspace from her neighbor's.

Javier let loose with a string of swear words in Puerto Rican Spanish, only a few of which Zach recognized. "That *mamabicho*. It *was* her neighbor. I hated that dude from the first moment I saw him."

"You and me both," said Hunter.

They moved closer, found piles of sawdust in the dirt—proof that the hole wasn't a part of the building's original structure but had been cut recently.

They passed through the opening, made their way to the door, and found themselves in her neighbor's laundry room. They drew their weapons, quickly and silently clearing the condo.

There was no sign of Holly or her neighbor.

Zach holstered his weapon. "What was the fucker's name?"

"Nicholas Andrews," Javier said. "We ran background on him. He came up clean. I'll call Tower, get him to dig deeper."

"You don't need to do that." Chief Irving walked out of the laundry room, dusting the dirt off his slacks, apparently having followed them through the crawl space. "I just got a call from Langley. Andrews is actually Nikolai Andris. He's one of theirs."

"He's CIA?" Corbray looked over at Zach, disbelief on his face.

Irving nodded. "They say he's the one who killed Sachino Dudaev, without their authorization, of course. Apparently, he's the rogue officer we've been hearing about. He's armed and considered extremely dangerous."

Zach didn't like that. "What interest does he have in Holly?"

"I asked that question, and they said that perhaps he wants to make certain she didn't see him that night. The officer who spoke with me said they've been trying to bring Andris in and have been in touch with him. I'm sorry to say this because I know she's your friend, but they believe he intends to kill her."

It felt like a physical blow, the anguish Zach felt visible on the faces of the others.

Corbray shook his head. "No fucking way. We're going to find her first."

"Why would he spare her life the night he murdered Dudaev only to kill her now?" Darcangelo asked.

It was a good question.

Irving shrugged. "I don't know, but it's no longer our problem."

Hunter took a step forward. "What the hell does that mean?"

"They're taking over this case, just like they did Dudaev's murder," Irving said. "We've been ordered to stand down and turn over all evidence to them. That's my way of telling you that you need to get the hell out of their crime scene."

"Fuck that." Zach pulled out his cell phone, dialed the DC office. "As of this moment, I am claiming jurisdiction over the abduction of Holly Elise Bradshaw and the manhunt for Andris on behalf of the US Marshal Service. We outrank the Agency here in the homeland. If they want a dick fight, we'll give them one."

CHAPTER 12

HOLLY WAS LOSING all sense of the passage of time, her pain now very real as she forced herself to hang by her wrists from the bar, her weight making the steel cuffs bite into her already bruised and blistered skin, her shoulders and bruised ribs aching, her body screaming for water. A day and a night had passed, and now it was almost evening again, wasn't it?

If she could just hold out, if she could just stay strong . . .

He was going easy on her, she knew. So far he hadn't hit her or threatened to hurt or kill her. There were so many horrible things he could do to her if he wanted to. But he didn't want to do this, and slowly he was losing his resolve. She could see it in his eyes. She could hear it in his voice—the strain, the anger at himself, the frustration.

"What did the message say?"

She struggled to stand upright, needing to give her wrists, shoulders, and ribs a break, but that only made her numb fingers start to tingle. Her throat was parched, her mouth dry. "I told you already! It said your name . . . was Nick Andris. And that you were . . . a danger to me. Well, that was true . . . wasn't it? Here I am."

She had decided it was safe to tell him things they both knew were true, ladling it out bit by bit, making him pay for every word in emotional distress over her suffering.

"What else did it say?"

"It said . . . I should leave town . . . They sent money,

tickets. That's all it said . . . That's all. *Look* at it . . . It's not that long. Please, can I have water? You said . . . you said if I answered . . ."

"Have you been tasked with terminating me?"

"No! I'm not . . . the killer. *You* are."

"That's right. You just seduce men for money. I guess that makes you a whore. Why do you do it? To hurt your father?"

That brought her head up.

"I know you joined Air Force ROTC instead of Army ROTC. Was that a way of trying to piss off the old man? When that wasn't enough to catch his attention, you dropped out of ROTC altogether."

Holly felt an old, familiar pain well up inside her. "My father never . . ."

She stopped herself, tried to lock that part of herself away.

"Your father never cared about you, did he? That photo in your bedroom—that's one of the few good memories you have of him. Daddy never gave you the attention you needed." Nick paused, watching her like a predator watches its prey. "Or maybe he gave you too much attention. That's it, isn't it? After you sprouted tits, your relationship changed. Maybe he even wanted you, his own daughter. Maybe he got physical with you. Or maybe he fought that unnatural impulse by ignoring you."

Holly felt her pulse pound as The Bastard's guesses struck terribly close to home. "My father . . . never touched me."

But he'd said things, things that had made her feel dirty.

You are a hot piece of ass, baby girl. I bet there isn't a man on base who doesn't want to fuck you.

Holly found herself in tears, whether from physical pain or stress or sheer exhaustion, she didn't know.

"But you got back at Daddy, didn't you? You took that beautiful body of yours, you took that beautiful face, you took the tits he wished he could touch, and you put it all to work for the very elements your father spent his career fighting."

"That's not true!" She lunged for Nick. Pain screamed through her wrists, shoulders, ribs, the room spinning. When her knees gave out this time, she wasn't pretending. "I am . . . a patriotic American. I never . . . betrayed my country. *You* did."

"What do you mean by that?" He took her chin between his fingertips, forced her to meet his gaze. "Goddamn it, Holly, answer me!"

"The message . . . says you're a rogue officer . . . a CI threat."

What had she just said? Had she slipped? Had she compromised herself?

He stepped back as if she'd struck him. "That's what it said?"

"Now . . . you're going to kill me." The sweet oblivion of unconsciousness called to her, and for a moment the world faded away.

She heard something click, felt herself falling.

He caught her, carried her to the bed, and held her as he trickled water between her parched lips. "Drink, Holly. That's it. Not too fast. Don't choke."

The water felt so good, sliding down her dry throat.

She opened her eyes, looked up at him, played her last card. "When you kill me . . . shoot me in the heart . . . not the forehead. I want my face . . . for my funeral."

But she saw in his eyes that he wasn't going to kill her. He wasn't going to hurt her anymore, either. He couldn't. He was finished.

She'd done it. She'd held out.

It was over.

"ONE MORE SWALLOW. There you go."

Nick coaxed more water down Holly's throat, then laid her head gently back onto the bed, watching as her lids closed and her body slowly relaxed. He retrieved the medic kit from his go-bag and did what he could to make her more comfortable, putting ointment on her bruised and blistered wrists, wiping dried blood away from the corner of her mouth, pressing an instant cold pack against the deep purple bruise on her ribs.

She whimpered in her sleep as the cold pack touched her skin, pain etched into her sweet face, her cheeks stained and still damp with her tears.

He took an auto-injector of morphine out of the kit and set it aside with an alcohol wipe in case she needed pain relief when she came to again.

He had done this to her.

Bauer had *ordered* him to do this to her, and Nick had followed those orders, even when his gut had warned him that something was wrong.

Goddamn it!

"Forgive me, Holly. I didn't know."

Jesus!

Why hadn't he figured it out sooner?

Not that Holly had outright admitted that she worked for the CIA, but Nick knew it just the same. Her use of the term "CI threat" had given her away. The moment he'd heard those words it had all come together for him. Her mastery of R2I techniques. The quality of the fake ID he'd found in that purse. The tradecraft involved in sending ciphertext via catalogue shipments.

A pang of regret sheared through him.

He'd just spent the past thirty-six hours interrogating an innocent woman, a fellow Agency officer no less. He couldn't undo it. He couldn't take it back. All he could do was take care of her now—and hope she didn't kill him or knock his balls off when she regained consciousness.

As for his own situation, the writing had been on the wall. The internal investigation. The way Bauer and Nguyen had questioned him about Kramer's disappearance. Rumors that Dudaev had been killed by someone operating without Agency authorization. The fact that he was one of only two men left who'd had boots on the ground in Batumi that night.

Taken together, it was a giant "Kick Me" sign taped to his back.

Now Holly had confirmed it for him.

He'd been set up.

Bauer.

It had to be Bauer.

He'd been the one to recall Nick to the US. He'd assigned him to take out Dudaev and run surveillance on Holly, insisting she was Dudaev's contact. He must have known all along that Holly was with the Agency, must have known she'd been sent to retrieve the stolen files and had wanted to stop her.

What role she had to play beyond that Nick couldn't say, nor did he understand why Bauer wanted her dead. And he *did* want her dead. He'd called to authorize her termination less than an hour ago, tasking Nick with an illegal act that he would never have been able to carry out. The entire operation had reeked of bullshit from the beginning, but Nick had been too fucking blinded by his desire to even the score with Dudaev—and his loyalty to Bauer—to admit it to himself.

And what about Nguyen?

Nick felt something twist in his chest. Nguyen had been there when Bauer had given him his assignment. He knew what Nick had been ordered to do. He must be in on it, too. But why?

From where Nick now stood, only one thing was certain.

He and Holly needed to get the hell out of here. They needed to find a safe place, hole up, crack the password, decrypt the files, and figure out what was really going on. The moment Bauer realized Nick was no longer playing his game—

Something sharp bit into Nick's thigh, and he looked down to find the morphine auto-injector buried in his quadriceps, Holly's fist wrapped around it.

"What the . . . ?" A sickening wave of euphoria surged through him as ten milligrams of morphine hit his system all at once.

Shit!

"You bastard!" Holly scrambled past him out of the bed and stood just beyond his reach, glaring at him with undisguised hatred. "How do you like being drugged?"

"You aren't . . . as hurt . . . as you let me believe."

"*Never* underestimate the strength of a truly pissed-off woman."

Nguyen had been wrong. She wasn't good. She was *amazing*.

And it struck Nick suddenly as funny.

He now knew she worked for the CIA just like he did, but she still believed he was a CI threat, a fugitive, one of the bad guys. Given that he'd just spent the past thirty-six hours interrogating her, what else could she think?

"Holly, honey, we're on the same side." He tried to stand, but sank to the floor in a boneless heap.

She watched him drop. "*Don't* call me that."

He lay there chuckling to himself about the absurdity of it all while she disarmed him, using no more force than if he'd been a child.

"Shit. Holly, listen. I work for the CIA, too, see? I'm not really a fugitive. I've been set up."

Except that maybe he *was* a fugitive.

Was he?

If Bauer and Nguyen had burned him and turned the Agency against him, if officers had been sent to bring him in or terminate him, then he *was* a fugitive.

Well, fuck.

Not exactly a promotion, now, is it?

But Holly was glaring at him. "I never said I was CIA."

"I put it . . . together." He fought to clear his mind, to keep his eyes open, but felt himself going under as the drug took full effect. "I've . . . been set up. We . . . need to leave here . . . They *know*."

"They know what? And who are 'they'?" She tore into an MRE and began to eat.

"My boss from Langley . . . set me up. Sent me after you. Authorized your termination . . . Didn't tell me . . . you were CIA, too." He tried to focus, fought to get the stupid smile off his face. "He knows we're here. If he finds out I didn't kill you . . . he'll send people here after us. He may have . . ."

The world was going black.

He may have people on the way already.

HOLLY ATE THE rest of the MRE trail mix and washed it down with more water, her gaze fixed on Nick, who lay semiconscious on the floor. It wouldn't take long for his body to metabolize enough of the morphine for him to get back on his feet. She likely didn't have time to dry-clean the vehicle to make sure it was free of listening devices and GPS tracking. That meant she would have to hike out—and fast.

There were only a couple hours of daylight left. She didn't want to find herself benighted in the mountains.

She'd heard what he'd said—that his boss at Langley had set him up, authorized her termination, and hadn't told Nick she was with the Agency, too.

Could he be telling the truth?

Not likely. He'd done nothing but lie to her and deceive her from the moment she'd met him.

Would it change her plan of action if he was?

No, it wouldn't. She needed to get away from him, contact Javier to let him know where she was, and call Beth to ask for some time off from work.

Then she needed to disappear until this sorted itself out.

But first things first.

She fished the encoded message and the image of his face out of his pocket, tossed them into the fireplace, and poured a little lantern oil on them. Using matches she found next to his gear bag, she set the paper on fire and watched it burn until it was reduced to unreadable ash. When that was done, she rummaged through his gear and was relieved to find her running shoes and a pair of socks that he'd brought for her, along with the five thousand dollars her CO had sent. The false ID and plane tickets were there, too, though the tickets were no longer of any use. She put on the socks and shoes, then tucked the money and ID, the matches, several bottles of water, a flashlight, and two MREs into a little folding daypack she found.

Nick tried to raise his head, muttered something. "Decrypt the files."

She knelt beside him, took the watch off his wrist, strapped it to hers. "Decrypt what files?"

"Outside. In the back."

"The back of the vehicle?" Another reason to leave the SUV.

She didn't want to be caught with files she wasn't authorized to see.

He opened his eyes, a troubled look on his face. "Got to go . . . *now*."

"That's my plan." She took the medic kit, dug through it, and almost jumped for joy when she found a packet of ibuprofen.

She popped two, washed them down with water, then begin searching for anything else she might be able to use. She took a light jacket, a baseball cap, and ammo for the SIG, but left twenty grand in cash—who knows where he'd gotten that—and a custom-made Ruger MK III, probably the weapon he'd used to kill Dudaev. She zipped the little daypack and strapped it on to her back, wincing at the pain that shot through her ribs. Then she put on the baseball cap to keep the sun off her skin.

But what should she do about The Bastard?

She should cuff him to the bed and report his location to law enforcement. What happened to him after that was *not* her problem. He was a fugitive, wanted by the Agency. He'd deceived her, humiliated her, hurt her.

He'd hated it. He'd hated every minute of it. But he'd still done it.

And what if he'd been telling her the truth about the rest of it—his boss authorizing her termination, setting Nick up, sending men after them?

In the end, Holly couldn't bring herself to cuff him. Nor could she leave him without a weapon and defenseless. If he was lucky, he'd be gone before anyone arrived.

"All's fair in love and war." She turned her back, leaving him on the floor.

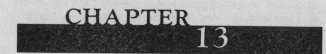

CHAPTER 13

HOLLY FOLLOWED THE SUV's tire tracks uphill through a glade of aspen to a dirt access road, then followed the road downhill. Adrenaline quickly gave way to exhaustion as she walked on, her body aching, her emotions raw, every ugly thing The Bastard had said to her like a laceration.

You just seduce men for money. I guess that makes you a whore. Why do you do it? To hurt your father?

She had to give him credit. He'd certainly done his homework.

Daddy never gave you the attention you needed. Or maybe he gave you too much attention. That's it, isn't it? After you sprouted tits, your relationship changed.

She felt tears on her cheeks, dashed them away with the back of her hand. She couldn't let herself go there—not now.

Right now, she needed to survive.

She was lucky to be alive, and she knew it. Nick had slipped in under her radar, under everyone's radar. If he had followed orders, she'd be dead now. As it was, she was likely compromised and out of a job, given that he knew she was a CIA officer. In the end, she supposed it didn't matter. Somehow Nick had figured it out.

Maybe nothing mattered anymore. The life she'd known was probably over. Even if the Agency didn't fire her, they'd most likely relocate her, and she'd have to pack up and say good-bye to everyone and everything she knew like she'd done so many times before, moving wherever her dad's job had taken them, never being able to keep friends. Only this time it would be so much worse. This time she'd be leaving behind a city she called home and friends that had become her family.

And her friends—how would they react if they learned the truth?

Would they stand by her? Would they hate her?

No, they wouldn't hate her. They cared about her. They might not understand, but they would forgive her.

They were surely terrified for her. And poor Javier! He would blame himself. Her disappearance would be a big blow to the reputation of his company. She would call him from a pay phone, tell him where she was, let him be the one to bring her back. She would ask him to hide her, pay him to help her disappear. It didn't matter where she went, as long as it was secret and safe.

A beach wouldn't hurt, either. A beach with little umbrella drinks. And maybe a spa where she could get a good massage and a mani/pedi. A Jacuzzi would be nice, too. And a big, soft bed with fluffy pillows.

It was almost dark by the time she came to a paved highway, the hard press of the SIG P229 against her back reassuring as the last rays of the sun disappeared behind the mountains. She looked at the sign—"CO HWY 72."

She must be just outside Nederland.

She stopped to put on the jacket so that the firearm and the bruises and sores on her wrists wouldn't show. Feeling a kind of weariness she'd never known, she followed the road until she came to a gas station.

Stepping through the door was like stepping into another world, a world of normal everyday things far from murder and rogue officers and chaos. A little boy was trying to talk his mother into buying potato chips. A teenager was paying for gas at the counter. An older couple in matching Colorado T-shirts—tourists—were looking at postcards.

Suddenly aware of how dirty and battered she looked, Holly glanced around for a pay phone or restroom. She found both in the back corner off to the right. She lowered her head and made straight for them.

She picked up the receiver, dialed Javier's cell, reversing

the charges and speaking her name at the prompt. "Holly Bradshaw."

He answered almost immediately. "Holly? Are you okay? Where are you?"

"I'm . . . fine." The sound of his voice brought tears to her eyes, but she blinked them back. She could fall apart later. "I'm at a gas station off Highway 72 just north of Nederland. I tricked him and got away. I need someone to come get me before he catches up with me, and I need a place to hide."

"We're tracing the call. I'll send the Nederland police to get you as soon as we get your location, and I'll meet you up there with a team. Do you need an ambulance? Did he hurt you?"

God, yes, he'd hurt her, and in ways she hadn't imagined a man *could* hurt her, manipulating her, using her, humiliating her.

"I'm kind of dehydrated and bruised up, but . . . it's not bad."

"We'll take care of that, too. Where is he?"

Holly felt herself hesitate. "He's . . . he's in a cabin above Ned somewhere. I've been walking for a couple of hours and—"

From behind her, Holly heard two men talking. The language wasn't English. She strained to listen, the cadence of it somehow familiar. With a sinking feeling, she glanced over her shoulder and saw two big men in gray sports jackets walking toward her. She recognized one of them from the gallery opening.

Oh, no way!

They were Dudaev's men.

You are so screwed!

She lowered her voice to a whisper. "Javi, they're *here*! Sasha's men."

"Are you sure?"

"Yes. I recognize one of them. They're walking this way. I have to go."

"Holly—"

She hung up the phone and took the first way out that didn't involve walking past them. She stepped into the restroom and locked the door behind her, realizing too late that it was the only restroom.

Damn it!

The two men stood just on the other side of the door, probably waiting for their turn. Even bad guys had to pee.

Now what?

Holly took care of her own needs, flushed the toilet, and washed her hands and face, using the time to think. She couldn't climb out the window because there wasn't one. She could open the door and shoot both of them before they had time to recognize her, but that would put the lives of everyone in the gas station at risk and lead to lots of thorny questions. Or she could wait right where she was until Javier and the Nederland police arrived.

That seemed like the best choice—until about five minutes later when they started pounding on the door.

"Hurry up in there!"

This wasn't good.

After another few minutes, and more pounding, she heard the attendant's voice. "Are you sure someone's in there? Maybe the door accidentally locked itself. It does that sometimes. Let me get the key."

Unless she wanted to be cornered in here and start a firefight that might cost civilian lives, there was only one thing Holly could do.

She tucked her hair under the baseball cap, zipped the jacket up to her chin, and took a deep breath. Then she opened the door and stepped out, turning her back to them as she passed them in the narrow hallway. She headed directly for the door, hoping she could find a place outside to hide until Dudaev's men left and the cavalry arrived.

Careful to keep her head down, she stepped outside and glanced around the parking lot, then turned to her left, making her way toward the rear of the building. A man with a big belly stood nearby, cleaning the windows of a black Cadillac. She'd almost reached the corner of the building when he started shouting—in Georgian.

Stay cool. He's probably not shouting about you.

She looked over her shoulder, saw that he was pointing right at her.

Okay, so he's totally shouting about you.

Holly ran, heading for the highway and the shelter of the forest.

A familiar gray SUV cut her off in a spray of gravel, the passenger door opening to reveal Nick. "Looks like it's them or me."

What kind of choice was that?

Holly jumped into the front seat, slammed the door. "What are you waiting for? Drive!"

"Hang on." He drove up behind the black Cadillac, lowered his window, and shot out its rear tires with the Ruger, just as the other two came running out the door, weapons drawn. "Get down!"

BAM! BAM! BAM!

A bullet shattered the passenger-side mirror.

Another put a hole in the windshield.

"Shit!" Holly bent low and closed her eyes, the SUV's engine roaring as Nick tore out of the parking lot and bounced through a ditch and up onto the highway.

"Are you okay?" he asked a moment later.

Holly looked over her shoulder to see whether the Cadillac had followed them. "Have you changed your mind about killing me?"

"No."

"Then, yes, I'm okay." She sat back in the seat and drew in a breath, thinking aloud. "How did they find me?"

"I have an idea about that, but you're not going to like it."

"Really? And the day was going so well otherwise."

"I think they were sent after us by the only person who knew where we were."

Holly thought for a moment, tried to remember what he'd told her. "Your boss— you think *he* sent them?"

"He's the person who gave me the location of the cabin."

"Why would your boss collude with Dudaev's men?"

"I have a few ideas about that, too. We need to find a safe place to hole up until we can figure out what's really going on here."

"Oh, no! No, I'm not going with you." No way was she getting caught up in his mess. The longer she stayed with Nick, the greater the chance that she'd be compromised and considered a rogue officer, too. "Stop! Stop the vehicle! I want out!"

"Are you nuts, woman?"

"Javier is on his way to pick me up. I am *not* getting mixed up in your disaster."

He jerked the SUV to the side of the road and slammed on the brakes. "You're mixed up in this already. They want you *dead*, Holly. When they figure out Dudaev's men missed, they'll only send someone else. Don't you want to know why?"

"Of course I do, but I trust Javier to keep me safe. I trust my CO. I don't trust *you*. I can't even stand the sight of you." Holly reached for the handle, opened the door, started to climb out.

"I wonder what your friends would say if they knew the truth about you. You can't even be honest with them. What if one of them dies trying to protect you?"

She stopped, her foot inches from the ground, Nick's words giving shape to that terrible possibility. She would rather die ten times over in really painful ways than get Julian, Marc, Javier, or any of the others killed.

A sense of hopelessness washed over her. "I just want my life back."

"Too late for that. Our paths crossed for a reason. Someone put us together, pitted us against each other, set me up. If we work together, maybe we can figure out why and increase our chances of staying alive."

"The CIS team will protect me."

"Yeah? Well, they didn't protect you from me."

NICK DROVE THE minivan slowly down the streets of the town—"Los Ríos, Colorado, population 2,374," the sign said. He was willing to bet that about two thousand of those residents had moved away since the last time the sign was painted. Main Street was deserted, most of its shops boarded up or showing "Out of Business" signs. The high school was boarded up, too. Entire residential streets were abandoned, houses dark and empty.

Los Ríos was a modern ghost town.

They'd driven out of the mountains, careful to avoid the main highways, and had stopped in Boulder, where Nick had bought a blue 2009 Honda Odyssey with cash and one of his fake IDs. They'd ditched the SUV on a forest service access road after Nick had transferred all of the computers and other gear into the back of the minivan. Then he'd driven southeast, away from the mountains, where everyone from Dudaev's men to the local police were searching for them.

Nick knew Holly didn't trust him and didn't want to come with him. It was her concern for her friends that had made up her mind. He'd tried to win her confidence by answering her questions. It was only fair that she know as much about him as he knew about her. He'd told her about his background and where he'd been assigned, but she'd stopped him when he'd started to tell her about the Batumi op. She didn't want to know about it or the internal investigation or the files he'd cloned, certain that knowledge would put her career and life at greater risk.

In the end, it seemed to him they'd reached a truce. She'd made it clear she'd kill him if he so much as touched her again, and he'd promised to do all he could not to compromise her or get her tangled in his conflict with the Agency. Not that she wasn't tangled already, but she was in denial on that point.

He glanced over at her, felt a pang of regret. She'd been asleep since Castle Rock, her head resting against the window, one of her hands tucked beneath her chin. Proof of what he'd done was written all over her—the bruise on her forehead, her swollen lower lip, the deep purple bruises and torn skin that ringed her wrists, the dark circles beneath her eyes.

Way to go, Andris. Beat up on women often?

Fighting a gnawing sense of guilt, he shifted his gaze back to the road. He'd had a lot of time since they'd left Denver to think about what had happened, and no matter how many times he ran the details through his mind, he couldn't see how he could have figured out Holly was CIA sooner. She'd kept the secret well, and with Bauer misleading him at every turn, Nick hadn't even considered it.

Nick might have seriously hurt her. He might even have killed her.

Not that he'd never killed a woman. He'd once come face-to-face in a firefight with a Chechen terrorist, a woman, who'd been responsible for the deaths of a half dozen Russian and Georgian civilians. She'd drawn on him, and Nick had dropped her without hesitation. It hadn't bothered him—not the way this did.

Holly had only been doing her job, and she'd paid for it. Nick couldn't undo it. He couldn't make it better. He couldn't even be certain that he could get her out of this situation alive. Hell, he didn't even fully understand what the situation was—not yet. He needed to get settled somewhere and crack that damned password before this mess came crashing down around the two of them.

He made his way to the edge of town, turned down a dirt road, driving until he saw what looked like an abandoned farmhouse. There were no lights on in the house, and one of the upstairs windows was broken. Weeds grew in the fields instead of crops, the grass in the yard knee-high. A hand-painted sign that read "Fresh Eggs" hung upside down from a battered wooden fence at the corner of the driveway.

"We're here." He needed Holly to be awake in case an angry farmer suddenly appeared with a shotgun to protect the old homestead.

But Holly didn't budge.

He nudged her. "Holly, wake up."

She jolted upright, her wide eyes narrowing when she saw him. "What?"

"I'm going to clear the place."

She glanced out the windows. "Where are we—the Bates Motel?"

"We're just outside Los Ríos."

"Never heard of it."

"Yeah, well, there's a reason for that. The town is mostly deserted. I just want to make sure no one's home before we move in."

"Move in?" She stared out at the house. "I'm not staying there."

"Sorry, honey, but the Marriott is full. You're going to have to survive without room service for a while." He retrieved the Ruger from the center console, checked it. "Have you still got the flashlight and my SIG?"

"Don't call me honey. And it's *my* SIG now. I took it from you in a fair fight." She dug the flashlight out of the daypack and handed it to him. "Do you want me to come with you?"

He shook his head. "Get behind the wheel in case we need to leave in a hurry, and stay alert. I don't want to be shot because you fell asleep and were startled."

She fired him a scathing look, climbing into the driver's seat as he opened the door and stepped to the ground.

Outside the air-conditioned vehicle, the night was warm and

alive with the buzzing of cicadas and the chirping of crickets, the sky full of stars. Nick walked around the exterior of the house first, pushing his way through overgrown rosebushes to shine the flashlight through grimy windows. He found the ground floor deserted—no people, no furniture, just empty rooms.

A propane-fueled generator sat near the back porch, and from the amount of wear on the exterior he could tell it was only a few years old. If it still worked, they'd have electricity, which they needed for the computers if nothing else.

He forced entry through the back door and checked upstairs but found it deserted as well. A set of stairs off the kitchen led down to a basement. He descended into the darkness, the air hot and stuffy.

Something hissed.

Nick froze, pointed the flashlight at the floor ahead of him.

Snakes—at least a dozen of them. They twisted and writhed, dark shapes slithering across the pale concrete floor. Two of them coiled up into striking position, shook the tips of their tails. But there was no rattle on their tails, and their heads didn't have that telltale pit viper shape.

Bull snakes.

"Nice try, guys." Careful not to step on them, he searched the basement.

He located the control panels for the pump and water filtration systems that operated the farm's well, memorized the make and model of each. With any luck, the system still worked. The pipes seemed to be well insulated, so that was a good sign. There were also a couple of wooden workbenches that were well supplied with electrical outlets—a good place to set up the computers.

Apart from the snakes, the place had everything they needed.

Home, sweet home.

He'd bet his ass Holly wouldn't feel that way.

ALL HOLLY HAD to do was hit the gas. She could drive off and leave Nick here, stopping at the first truck stop or gas station she came across to call Javier again. She'd be back in Denver by dawn, and the computers, with whatever classified files he was trying to decrypt, would be back in Agency hands.

So why didn't she do it? Why was she sitting here in this freaking minivan like some kind of soccer-mom getaway driver?

She didn't owe Nick anything. The bastard! He'd lied to her, manipulated her, kidnapped her, hurt her, humiliated her. He'd put everything she loved about her life at risk—her job at the paper, her job at the Agency, her friendships, her life in Denver. She ought to toss his gear onto the grass and leave him to make his own way. Or, better yet, turn him in to the Agency and let justice take its course. Technically, that was her duty, her job as an officer. Anything less brought her perilously close to aiding and abetting a fugitive. And yet she couldn't bring herself to do it.

Damn it, Bradshaw!

What was her problem?

No, she didn't care about him. She detested him.

But she *did* care about the lives and safety of her friends.

And she cared about the truth.

If what he'd told her was true, and she'd been targeted for termination, she wouldn't be safe until she knew who was after her and why.

But could she trust him now after everything he'd done to her?

The part about his being recruited out of Delta Force was true—she was sure of that. That's why Javier hadn't been able to find out anything about his discharge. He'd said he was a paramilitary operator with the SAD. She believed that, too. He didn't have her HUMINT training. If he had, he'd have realized she was playing on his sympathy for her during the interrogation. As for the rest—the part about being set up as a fall guy—it was almost too absurd to consider. Except that . . .

Nick had warned her in his morphine stupor that his boss might send someone after them. Then Dudaev's men had showed up at that gas station, clearly on their way up to the cabin. If they knew where to find her and Nick, that meant someone at the Agency had tipped them off. And that meant Nick might be telling the truth.

She rubbed the bruise on her forehead, her thoughts too

confused, her emotions too ragged, her mind too exhausted to think through it right now.

She needed answers, answers only Nick could give her.

He stepped out of the back door, walked up to the vehicle.

Holly climbed back into the passenger seat, wincing at the pain in her ribs.

He opened the door and got behind the wheel again. "We won't have running water until I can get the well's pump system working again, but once we get some propane, we should have electricity."

She looked up at the darkened house, her dream of a hot shower and soft bed vanishing. "I bet the place is crawling with mice and spiders."

"I didn't see any mice but there's a nest of snakes in the basement."

"A nest of—of *snakes*?" Holly's skin crawled. "I am *not* sleeping in there."

She half expected him to make some smartass comment, but he didn't.

"I know you're hurting and tired. Give me a few minutes to unload the gear and move the vehicle to the side of the barn, and you can crash in the back."

Five minutes later, Nick disappeared inside with the last monitor and a fist full of power cords, the minivan now parked out of sight of the road, its windows open to let in the night breeze.

Holly crawled into the back, laid the rear bench seat flat, and curled up on her right side, the SIG P229 stowed beneath the seat where she could easily reach it. She tucked an arm beneath her head for a pillow—and was asleep in an instant.

She didn't hear Nick return. She didn't feel him lie down beside her. She didn't even dream.

CHAPTER 14

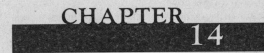

IT WAS SUNSHINE that woke her, the daylight stirring her from sleep. Holly opened her eyes and found herself curled up against Nick, who slept on his side facing her, one of his arms pillowing her head, the other wrapped lazily around her waist. For a moment, caught between sleep and wakefulness, she wondered where they were.

Then she remembered.

She jerked back, sat upright, pain lancing through her bruised ribs at the sudden movement. She clutched her side, breath hissing through her clenched teeth. "What the hell are you doing?"

"Hey, easy." Nick sat up, reached out to steady her. "I *was* sleeping."

"Couldn't you find somewhere else?" She took a backward step and sat in one of the bucket seats that made up the center row, the pain still sharp.

"And leave you out here alone?" His gaze dropped to her side. "Is it your ribs?"

"You ought to have been a doctor instead of an assassin."

His brows drew together in a frown, a muscle clenching in his jaw. He turned away from her and dug through his gear, then handed her an unopened bottle of water and a small packet containing two ibuprofen tablets. "You need something in your stomach before you take those."

At those words, her stomach growled, and she realized she was starving, thoughts of scrambled eggs, toast, and coffee filling her head. But that's not what Nick had in mind. He tossed her a brown plastic bag labeled "MRE Menu 17: Maple Sausage."

"Gee, thanks." She opened the bag, sorted the contents, and decided to eat the dehydrated granola with milk and blueberries and skip the rest. She opened the plastic spoon and the granola bag, poured in a little water, and stirred.

"I know you were probably hoping for breakfast and a latte at some café, but eating in public isn't a great idea right now, not when your face is likely all over the television. There's no way you won't attract attention with those bruises. Speaking of which, I should take a look at your wrists when you're done. You don't want those lacerations to get infected."

Holly shook her head. "I can take care of myself."

"Fine by me." He moved the bench seat back into its upright position, then held something up. "You forgot this."

The SIG P229.

She expected him to keep it or to criticize her for forgetting about it. After all, a firearm wouldn't do either of them any good if she didn't have it with her at all times. Instead, he reached over the seat and handed it to her without a word.

A peace gesture?

He'd have to try a hell of a lot harder than that.

"Thanks." She took it, tucked it in the back of her jeans, then started in on her granola. It wasn't as bad as she'd feared, but in truth she was so hungry she'd have eaten it even if it had tasted like cardboard. She finished it and found herself tearing into the cinnamon scone. It was dry as sawdust, but tasted good enough.

Nick climbed out of the back of the vehicle and closed the door, then came around to the side and got into the driver's seat. He turned to face her, pointed to the rest of the MRE. "If you're not going to eat those, I'll take them."

"Suit yourself." It almost hurt to sit here eating breakfast with him when what she wanted to do was rage at him.

Nick tore open the flameless heater, poured in a small amount of water, and propped the bag on the passenger seat. Then he opened the outer packaging for the maple sausage and stuck the inner packet into the heater bag. After a few minutes, he removed the packet, opened it, and began eating chunks of hot sausage with a spoon, the scents of pork and maple syrup filling the small space.

They finished breakfast in strained silence.

Outside, birds sang in the trees, a few crickets still chirping.

Holly found herself fighting a sense of unreality. For the past two days, she'd been chained to the ceiling, a victim of abduction. Today, she was on the run with the bastard rogue officer who'd abducted her. Well, she'd been right about one thing.

It hadn't been boring.

Holly? Are you okay? Where are you?

The sound of Javier's voice came back to her, making her throat tight. What had happened last night with him and his men? Had they arrived in time to take Dudaev's men into custody? Had shots been fired? Had anyone been hurt? They would have viewed the surveillance footage from the gas station by now. They would have watched her get into Nick's SUV. Did they still consider her a victim of abduction or were they starting to consider other possibilities?

Someone would have contacted her parents by now—the police, the FBI. Her mother would turn Holly's disappearance into a drama about herself. Holly had no idea how her father would react. Regardless, they wouldn't learn anything from the Agency. Even if Holly were killed, they would never know she'd been a CIA officer.

"What time is it?" Nick's voice cut through Holly's thoughts. He pointed toward the watch she still wore on her wrist.

"Almost eight." She hesitated a moment, then unfastened the watch and tossed it back to him. "Not really my style."

"Thanks." He strapped it on, glanced at the time. "Let's get supplies."

NICK STOPPED THE vehicle across from the hardware store. "See any cameras?"

Holly shook her head. "That doesn't mean the stores won't have them."

He crossed the highway into the parking lot. "I'll take the hardware store. You take the thrift shop. Keep your head down. Try not to let anyone see your face or wrists. And don't buy anything we don't truly need. I don't want to resort to robbing banks because you blew our cash buying shoes or some damned thing."

She tucked her hair beneath the baseball cap, then opened the door and stepped to the ground. "Go to hell."

Nick felt like he might already be in hell. He was on the run with a woman who despised him. The man he'd trusted and admired most had betrayed him, leaving both his job and his life on the line. His only hope lay in finding something in those files that would help him understand what was going on, perhaps even something he could barter for immunity. His world had turned upside down, and he didn't know why.

He needed Holly's help but she'd already made it clear she didn't want to be involved in decrypting the files. She didn't even want to know what they contained. How could he convince her that it was in her own best interests to help him?

He needed to prove to her she could trust him.

And how are you going to do that, Andris?

Hell, he didn't know.

He couldn't just apologize and expect her to get over it. He'd wounded her pride by beating her at her own game. But worse than that, he'd hurt *her.*

He'd used her loneliness against her and then betrayed her. That would have been bad enough. But he'd taken it a step further, calling her a whore, tearing into her, trying to break her. When he'd accused her father of having sexual desire for her, he'd seen anguish on her face, and he'd known that he had cut her to her core, laying bare a grief that she'd kept hidden from everyone.

He had exposed her, and she hated him for it.

He couldn't blame her.

Of course, the funny part of it was that Nick really liked her. The moment he'd realized she was a fellow Agency officer, all the reasons he'd had to despise her had vanished.

He'd come away from that interrogation with nothing but admiration for her mental toughness, her skill as an officer, her ability to think on her feet. And the desire he'd fought to subdue when he'd thought she was a criminal had come rushing back.

He wanted her—and she wanted him dead.

Perfect.

Somehow, he needed to reach her. If he could, he'd pick up the pieces of her he'd broken and give them back to her whole again. But that's not how life worked. He would have to show her trust if he wanted to win hers back. He would have to prove to her that he was sorry, make her see that they needed each other if they wanted to survive.

He headed into the hardware store, grabbed a cart, and began to fill it.

HOLLY WATCHED NICK enter the hardware store before passing the thrift store and walking a few shops down to Dot's Coffee Emporium and Internet Café. She'd noticed it when they'd pulled into the parking lot. Knowing she might not get another chance, she hurried inside and made her way to a bank of computers in the back.

The place was crowded, all the computers taken. Given the poverty they'd seen in this area, it was a good bet that many people didn't have home Internet access or even personal computers. But she didn't have time to wait for one of the stations to open up.

She walked up to a young teenage girl who was posting on Facebook, pulled a hundred out of her jeans pocket, and whispered, "I'll give you this if you let me use this computer for ten minutes. After that, you can have it back. I promise."

The girl stared at her and at the money, then smiled. "Sure."

She logged out, then gave Holly her seat.

Holly first logged on to the IP-blocking site she used. Given what was at stake here—her life—she didn't want anyone to know where she was right now, not even her CO.

When the blocker was up and running, she logged in to her public Twitter account.

She posted a Tweet.

I am craving a latte this morning! #NormalDay

It was just a way of letting her friends know she was okay.

Then she logged in to her secret account and sent a series of private ciphertext messages to her CO, using the last key he'd posted and hoping he'd think to use that to decipher them.

UNHURT. WAS ABDUCTED BY ANDRIS. HE KNOWS MY EMPLOYER. SAYS HE WAS ORDERED TO TERMINATE ME. SAYS HE HAS BEEN SET UP BY HIS CO. BELIEVE HE MIGHT BE TELLING THE TRUTH. DUDAEV'S MEN FOUND US AT REMOTE LOCATION. ANDRIS CLAIMS ONLY HIS BOSS KNEW WE WERE THERE. AT SAFE LOCATION WITH ANDRIS. NO INTERNET ACCESS. NO PHONE. HE POSES NO THREAT TO ME AT THIS TIME. PLEASE ADVISE.

She couldn't wait around for the reply. If Nick saw her in here . . .

Quickly, she logged out of Twitter, deleted her browsing history, then logged out of the IP blocker. It was time to go shopping.

NICK WORKED HIS way down the list. Filter for the water filtration system. A basic tool set. Bucket. Water pitcher. Well-disinfection kit. A few pairs of work gloves. Latex gloves. Extension cords. Lamp. Light bulbs. Bug spray. Cleaning supplies. Folding chairs. A queen-sized air mattress.

Nix that.

She did *not* want to sleep in the same bed with him.

Two twin-sized air mattresses. Air pump. Two sleeping bags. A double hot plate. A mini-fridge with a freezer box. Snake traps. Black weed cloth. Duct tape. Several tanks of liquid propane.

He paid with cash and made two trips to get it all out to

the minivan. He did his best to arrange things to save space. They still had to buy groceries.

Holly still wasn't back by the time he finished. He returned the shopping cart and walked across the parking lot to the thrift store. The asphalt was soft in the heat, weeds poking through in places where it had crumbled, the paint long since worn away.

Inside the thrift shop, Holly was making her way toward the door, pushing one cart and pulling another.

On top of a box piled high with pots and pans sat a baby's car seat.

He picked it up, looked at it. "Is there something you need to tell me?"

"They're looking for a couple, not a family of three."

"I don't follow."

She glared at him as if he were an idiot, pulled a large doll out from beneath a bag of towels. "Put the doll in the car seat, the car seat in the minivan, and to any law enforcement officer driving by, we now look like a family of three. I have a friend who straps a blow-up doll into the passenger seat of his car so that he can take the HOV lanes without being pulled over and fined."

"Devious." Nick found himself grinning. "I like it."

He put the car seat down, picked up the doll. It had blond hair in a shade similar to Holly's, pouty little lips, and blue eyes. "She takes after you, except for the eyes. What are we going to name her?"

Holly glared at him.

HOLLY BACKED AWAY as Nick emerged from the house carrying a plastic garbage bag full of snakes in one gloved hand. The bag writhed.

He grinned. "Twenty-three."

She shuddered. "How can you be sure you got them all?"

Maybe they should just burn the house down to the ground.

"I can't." He turned and walked toward the nearest field. "I'll set traps to catch any I missed. Hey, at least they kept the mice away."

She supposed that was something.

She glanced upward, the sun high in a cloudless blue sky. It was noon and already a hundred and five degrees according to the old thermometer attached to one of the porch posts. Sweat trickled between her breasts, beaded beneath the hair at her nape.

God, she couldn't wait for a shower!

She watched as Nick walked some distance into a weed-choked field and dropped the bag onto the ground, grateful she wasn't close enough to see anything slither out. She turned and walked up the porch steps and into the kitchen, prepared to wage war against filth. They had decided he would work on the generator and the water system, while she cleaned the bedrooms, bathroom, and kitchen. She had agreed to this arrangement in part because she knew nothing about generators or water systems and in part because it meant she wouldn't have to be anywhere near him—or the basement.

She slipped into a pair of rubber gloves, dropped bleach, a gallon bottle of water, some spray bathroom cleaner, and sponges into the bucket, then grabbed the broom, dustpan, and dust mop and lugged it all to the top of the stairs.

She claimed a bedroom at the back of the house as her own and started there. The room was stiflingly hot and stuffy in the midday heat. She tried to open the window, but it wouldn't budge.

"Want a hand?" Nick's voice came from behind her.

She jumped, startled. "I've got it."

But it was clear after a few minutes of struggling that she wasn't going to be able to make the window budge.

"Give up yet?"

"I think weather has made the wood swell." Holly stepped back.

Nick took over. "I'm sure that's it."

She tried not to notice his biceps or the way the muscles at his neck strained as he slowly forced the sash up. She was *not* attracted to him—not after what he'd done.

Fresh air carried the scents of summer into the room, a hot breeze offering some relief from the stuffiness, if not the heat.

"Thanks."

"I should have the generator running soon and then you can hook up one of the fans." He stood there for a moment as if there was something else he wanted to say, then turned and walked away. "I'll be outside if you need me."

She did not *need* him, even if his big Delta Force muscles sometimes came in handy. She hated him, could barely stand the sight of him. She'd be so much better off if she'd never met him. She did *not* need him.

She started in on the wood floor with a vengeance, stopping several times to shake the dust mop out the window.

Forget dust bunnies. This place had an army of dust orcs.

She opened the closet to sweep and found several big spiders. "Shit!"

She beat them to death with the broom, cursing all the while, then swept their grotesque corpses into the dustpan and dropped them out the open window, too. When the floor was reasonably dust free, she mopped it with bleach water, giving the room a clean, fresh smell. Finally, she went after the cobwebs in the corners and along the ceiling, her thoughts drifting back to Nick.

He'd been thoughtful and polite all morning. He'd let her keep the SIG. He'd pushed her to take care of the wounds on her wrists, given her ibuprofen for her bruised ribs. He'd tried to make sure she had what she needed from the store, even going back to buy a couple of electric fans when she complained of the heat. He was trying to make up for all he'd done—and it annoyed the hell out of her.

Did he really think a few kind gestures could atone for what he'd put her through? And how could she be certain he was sincere? He'd fooled her once already. Did he really care about her well-being, or was he trying to manipulate her again in hopes that she'd help him decrypt the stolen files?

She fumed about this while she dumped the dirty water down the bathtub drain, went downstairs for another gallon of bottled water, and moved the cleaning supplies to the bedroom across from hers, the room she intended Nick to use. She took a time-out from being angry to make sure that they would have the road to the house covered between the two of them—she looking north, he looking south—before she grabbed the dust mop and started in again, taking her rage out on the floor.

It was only after she'd started feeling sorry for herself, wondering whether their time in bed had meant anything to Nick, that she realized she'd let her big-girl pants fall off completely. She needed to set her hurt feelings aside and get back to thinking like an Agency officer again if she wanted to save her own butt.

From outside, she heard the generator kick on.

At least they would have electricity.

She tried to analyze Nick like she would any other target, but found that difficult, her own emotions getting in the way. But one thing stood out for her.

He didn't behave like a rogue officer, a CI threat.

For starters, he hadn't killed her. A rogue officer would almost certainly have done so if for no other reason than to keep her from double-crossing him or giving him away. But Nick seemed to trust her.

Second, he'd given her a chance to get out of the SUV and go back with Javier. He hadn't held a gun to her head and forced her to come with him that second time, though he could have easily done so. He'd also left her alone in the vehicle, keys in the ignition, more than once, giving her an opportunity to drive away, rather than keeping the keys with him at all times. He'd trusted her again this morning when they'd gone for supplies. Those were hardly the actions of a kidnapper.

Also, he wasn't planning a run for the border. Which meant he thought he had a reason to stay. He thought he had a future here. Any officer who betrayed the Agency would know that he was either going to end up dead or in federal prison and would use all of his tradecraft to get out of the country as quickly as possible.

More than that, he still had scruples and compassion, something an officer capable of betraying the Agency would have long since discarded.

And then there'd been Dudaev's men—the closest thing to proof she had that Nick was telling the truth. There was no way their presence at that gas station could have been a coincidence. They hadn't been in the mountains to sightsee.

They'd known right where they were going. If Nick hadn't found her, she'd have had to face them—three against one. She would have had to use the SIG. She would have had to kill—and she might well have been killed.

She finished the second bedroom, grabbed another gallon of water from downstairs, and carried it, with the other cleaning supplies, to the third bedroom. The door was mostly closed. She pushed it open, saw that the window looked out onto the fields to the east. One pane of glass was broken, what looked like dead bees on the floor near the sill.

She took the broom and dustpan and went to sweep them up. She was *so* done with bugs and spiders and snakes and dirt. When this was over, she was going to treat herself to a week in a luxury hotel somewhere on a beach and . . .

She heard a buzzing sound, felt a sharp stab of pain in her left arm. "Ouch!"

And then she saw.

In the half-opened closet was a nest of yellow jackets.

CHAPTER
15

NICK TIGHTENED THE wrench around the nut at the top of the well casing and tried again to turn it, putting his weight into it. The damned thing was rusted on tight. He needed to get it off so that he could drop disinfectant tablets into the well. It budged, moved a quarter turn.

A scream.

Holly had probably seen a spider.

Good grief.

But the screaming didn't stop.

He dropped the wrench and ran across the yard to the house, taking the porch steps two at a time, her screams now desperate.

He nearly collided with her as she ran out the back door, waving her arms to fend off a swarm of a dozen or so yellow jackets. She tripped on one of the stairs, fell onto the grass. He scooped her up and ran toward the barn where the mini-van was parked, ignoring the sharp bite of stings in his back and on his arm.

Son of a bitch!

He set Holly down on the grass near the back of the mini-van and smashed the remaining yellow jackets with his gloved hands.

Holly was whimpering, tears on her cheeks. "Damned things!"

"Are you allergic?"

"N-no. I don't think so."

He let out a relieved breath.

Still, yellow jacket stings hurt. The few he'd received burned like fire, and she'd been stung many times over. There were red welts on her arms, shoulders, and hands. They'd probably stung her through her tank top and jeans, too.

He opened the vehicle's back door, then climbed inside and lowered the bench seat to make a bed again. "Come here."

She climbed inside and sat on the edge of the seat, rubbing the stings on her arms.

"Try not to scratch or rub. It makes the venom penetrate deeper."

She squeezed her eyes shut, balled her hands into fists. "Damn, they hurt!"

"Hell, yeah, they do." Nick grabbed the medic kit, took out a bottle of liquid Benadryl and an EpiPen, tucking the EpiPen in his pocket just in case. "Was there a nest in one of the rooms?"

"A big nest. In the closet. The small bedroom. There's a hole in one of the window panes. Shit!"

Nick had checked the rooms but he'd done it at night when yellow jackets were less active. He'd been looking for people and hadn't seen the nest. He poured out a dose of Benadryl and handed her the little plastic cup. "This will help."

She shook her head. "Benadryl knocks me out."

"That's okay. I don't think you're going to feel like doing much for the rest of the day anyway." He found a packet of benzocaine swabs, took one out, then crushed the inner vial and passed it to her. "Rub this on the stings to numb them, starting with the ones that hurt the most. I'm going inside to get something that will help even more."

"The ones that hurt the most?" she called after him. "They *all* hurt the most!"

He hurried into the house and, ignoring the handful of yellow jackets that buzzed angrily around the door, grabbed the jug of vinegar they'd bought for cleaning, a roll of paper towels, and a half-filled bag of ice cubes, and jogged back to the vehicle.

Holly had stripped down to her panties, her tank top and

jeans discarded on the floor, her pretty face an image of misery as she rubbed the benzocaine swab on one sting after the next. "Vinegar?"

"You'll see." He took off his gloves and tossed them aside, then opened the bottle, soaked a folded paper towel sheet with vinegar, and pressed it to a welt on her shoulder.

She looked up at him through those big brown eyes. "That does help. Why?"

"Yellow jacket venom is alkaline. Vinegar helps neutralize it." He took on his father's heavy Georgian accent. "It is remedy from old country."

"Just dump it on me." She crawled out of the vehicle and stood there wearing only her panties. "Please!"

Nick climbed out, poured a thin stream of vinegar down her back, her left shoulder and arm, rubbing it over her bare skin with his free hand. "How's that?"

"Better. Pour it here!" She raised her arm so that he could trickle some down her left side. "Oh, huuuurrry!"

He saw the dark bruise on her ribs, tried not to hurt her as his hand passed over it and beneath her left breast. "How does that feel?"

"Here!" She turned toward him, lifted her chin so that he could pour it over the welts on her chest, breasts, and belly. She didn't object or push his hand away when he touched her, her breasts soft and yielding beneath his hand.

"Is it helping?"

"Yes." She opened her eyes, glared up at him. "You'd better not be enjoying this."

"I'm hating every second, I promise."

BOTTLE OF CHILLED water in hand, Nick walked out to the minivan to find Holly sound asleep, naked beneath a sheet, the scent of vinegar overwhelming. She hadn't been kidding. Benadryl really did knock her out. It was a Holly off-switch.

She'd slept through the afternoon while Nick had finished dealing with the well, the water pump, and the damned yellow jacket nest. He'd checked on her every half hour or so to make sure she wasn't getting hives or showing any other sign of distress.

Thirty-two stings.

It was a good thing she wasn't allergic to their venom. He wasn't sure an EpiPen would have been enough to save her life. Thirty-two stings was a lot—even for someone who wasn't allergic.

"Holly, honey, wake up." He leaned in, touched his hand to her forehead.

She felt warm, not cold or clammy.

She raised her head. "Thirsty."

He opened the bottle of water, held it out for her. "There's a bathtub of cool water waiting for you inside if you're interested."

She sat up, blinked sleepily. "You fixed the pump?"

"It's running just fine—as long as the power stays on. Those little propane canisters go fast. The water is okay for washing but not for drinking or brushing teeth. Use bottled water for that."

"What about the yellow jackets?"

"Dead. Every last one of them. I sprayed them and removed the nest." He'd gotten a couple more stings in the process, but it had been worth it for the satisfaction of obliterating the little fuckers. "I also cleaned the bathroom and sanitized it all with bleach. No spiders. No snakes. No yellow jackets."

If you don't square things with the Agency, Andris, maybe you have a future as an exterminator.

He reached for her. "Let's get you inside before the mosquitoes find you."

She took his hand, let him steady her as she climbed, naked, out of the minivan, clearly still drowsy from the two doses of antihistamine he'd given her. Though her skin was still covered with welts, they weren't as red and some of the swelling had gone.

He reached for the sheet, wrapped it around her, and scooped her up. "I don't want you stepping on a bee or a damned snake with your bare feet."

He also didn't want her falling on her face in a Benadryl stupor.

She smiled, let her head rest on his shoulder. He knew she was loopy from the drug, but he liked it just the same.

He carried her inside and up the stairs, setting her on her feet just outside the bathroom. "There's soap, a washcloth, and a towel. I put your shampoo and stuff in there, too. Let me know if you need anything."

She looked into the room. "Nice curtains."

"Like them?" He'd hung black weed cloth from all of the windows so that passersby wouldn't be able to see their lights at night. "It's a trick I learned from a Ukrainian agent. Weed fabric makes for cheap blackout curtains."

She stepped into the room. "Thanks."

He said what he ought to have said last night. "I'm sorry, Holly. I'm sorry for everything I put you through. I was acting on false information. If I could take it back, I would. If I'd had any idea you were an Agency officer, things would have gone differently. I never wanted to—"

She held up her hand for him to stop. "I appreciate the apology but I don't know that I will ever trust you again. I believed every word you said. You were the best time I'd ever had—until you became the worst time I've ever had. I thought you—" She stopped herself, looked away. "Excuse me."

Then she shut the door.

HOLLY SAT IN the cool water, soaking away the aches from thirty-six hours of interrogation. It felt so good to be clean again. She had shampooed and conditioned, shaved and scrubbed, until the grime of the past three days was gone.

If only she could wash away the memories as easily.

Your father never cared about you, did he?

No, her father didn't care, and chances were Nick didn't care, either.

Still, she appreciated the apology. She was also grateful for the way he'd saved her from the yellow jacket swarm, picking her up and carrying her to the minivan, smashing the little bastards with his hands. And for his help with treating the stings. And now the bath—yes, she was grateful for that, too.

Did any of his kind gestures mean he cared about her? No, they didn't. He just wanted her help decrypting the cloned files.

The thought left her feeling desolate.

She closed her eyes, remembered how it had felt to kiss him, to have his hands on her and his cock inside her. He'd been so good in bed, so much fun. But it had all just been a seduction game. At the same time he'd been having sex with her on the deck and in the shower, he'd been planning to drug her and abduct her.

I'm sorry for everything I put you through. I was acting on false information.

Acting under false information.

Did he think that was some kind of "Get Out of Jail Free" card? It wasn't. The intel might have been false, but his actions had been real. The hurt, the pain, the sense of betrayal were *real*.

What she'd given to him, she could never get back.

No, she couldn't trust him.

More than that, she couldn't trust herself around him.

She needed to get back to the Internet café so she could log on and see what her CO wanted her to do next.

What if he wants you to turn Nick in?

She'd have no choice but to do her duty, just as he'd done when he'd chained her to the iron bar at the cabin.

She opened her eyes, pulled the plug, and let the bath water drain away.

NICK INSTALLED THE last fluorescent light and hit the switch. The lights flickered on, casting an eerie glow over the basement.

He'd gotten the computers set up late last night and had spent the morning taking care of other things—removing a few stray snakes, plugging the computers into surge protectors, putting light bulbs in the few rooms he felt were safe to light.

Now finished, he went upstairs to check on Holly.

She'd moved her air mattress into his room in the middle of the night, calling it a "tactical decision."

"I don't want to get shot because I got up to use the bathroom."

"Right," he'd said. "Good call."

He was pretty sure it was the creaky, old house and the thought of spiders and snakes that was behind her decision, not strategic considerations, but he hadn't said so. It pleased him to know that she at least trusted him to protect her from things that crawled and slithered.

He found her asleep on her mattress, wearing a black tank dress she'd gotten from the thrift store, the stretchy, black cloth riding dangerously high on her thighs. A fan blew directly on her, giving her relief from the oppressive heat.

She didn't budge when he entered the room, knocked out from her most recent dose of antihistamine. Though the welts had begun to fade and were no longer painful, they itched. Nick's itched, too. He couldn't imagine how much worse it must be for her.

He knelt down beside her, saw she was almost out of water. The Benadryl was running low, too. They needed to make a trip into town.

Her eyes opened.

"How are you feeling?"

"The damned things itch like crazy." Her face was an adorable image of grumpiness and misery. "Even the Benadryl isn't stopping it completely."

Nick had an idea. "I'll be right back."

He went downstairs to the kitchen and filled a bowl with ice from the freezer, then grabbed another bottle of water for her and headed upstairs again.

"Ice?"

"It will help. Trust me." He sat beside her, held out the bowl. "Take a piece and rub it over a welt. It dulls the itch."

She took a piece of ice, rubbed it on a particularly red and swollen spot on her left arm, a place she'd been stung more than once. "You're full of tricks."

"With five sons, my mother was always having to deal with stings or sprains or fractures." He picked up a piece of ice and rubbed it over a welt high on her shoulder. "I learned from her."

"Five sons?"

"Five sons and one daughter."

"*Six* kids?"

Nick was used to that reaction. "My parents are Georgian

Orthodox. They defected in 1978 to get away from the Soviet Union and religious oppression."

"Can you get the ones on my back while I do my front?"

"Sure."

She turned away from him, pulled the dress down over her shoulders, exposing herself to the waist.

A glimpse of nipple. The rounded side of a breast.

The heat in the room seemed to rise.

Nick picked up a piece of ice, touched it to one of the welts on her back, heard her quick intake of breath.

"Mmm. That does feel better."

"Good." The sight of her scattered his thoughts, his gaze moving over the curve of her shoulder, the delicate groove of her spine, the flair of her hips.

"That must have been tough for your parents."

"Mmm-hmm." What were they talking about? Oh, yeah. "My mother was pregnant with me at the time and already had four little boys."

Nick told her how his family had been brought to the US by a Georgian Orthodox community in Philadelphia, how he'd been born only six weeks after his parents had arrived, making him the first US citizen in the family. The words came without conscious effort, his mind filled with the woman who sat before him—the sweet scent of her skin, the silky strands of her pale blond hair, the delicate shape of her body. She was so small compared to him. Water trickled from the melting ice cubes down her back as he treated one welt after the next, her body tensing slightly each time he pressed a fresh ice cube against her soft skin.

"Did you grow up speaking Georgian, or did your parents speak English before they came here?"

He almost missed the question. "Georgian and Russian. I learned English in school."

"I understand now why the Agency recruited you," she said in flawless Russian.

"Yeah," he said, stupidly, in English. "My maternal grandmother was Russian. That's why I'm named Nikolai instead of the Georgian Nikoloz. It honors my great-grandfather. My family calls me Nika."

God, he was just babbling now.

"Nika. I like that."

As yet another piece of ice slowly melted in his hand, Nick wanted for all the world to kiss her, to reach around and take her breasts into his hands, to tease those soft nipples into ripe points.

"Should I ice the stings on your back?" she asked when they had finished, pulling her dress up again.

"If you're okay with that."

What she ought to do is dump the bowl of ice down your pants, buddy.

"Of course I'm okay with that."

HOLLY WATCHED AS Nick slipped his T-shirt over his head and turned his back to her, the sight of his muscular torso bringing back memories of touching him, of lying beneath him, of feeling that hard body pressing against her.

She picked up an ice cube, rubbed it over one of three red blotches on his lower back. "How did you get that scar on your abdomen?"

"I was shot by one of Dudaev's men during the operation Derek Tower told you about—the one in Batumi that rolled up."

She had stopped him from giving her the details of that operation on the long drive from Denver, and she knew that his silence now was a way of respecting that request. Although she appreciated that, a part of her wanted to know more. It was impossible that anything that had happened there touched on her in any way, so how had she gotten caught up in the aftermath of it?

She picked up another piece of ice, worked it over the next welt. "How long did you serve in Delta Force before they recruited you?"

"A little more than three years. I was deployed for most of that time, mostly in Afghanistan."

"Chasing AQ and Taliban fighters from the Haqqani network, I'm guessing?"

He looked back over his shoulder at her. "Should we be sitting here talking about this? What's your security clearance?"

"Higher than yours."

"Oh, yeah?" He grinned. "I met an Agency officer while keeping Al-Zarqawi under surveillance in Baquba in 2006. We talked a bit. She asked about my background, my language skills. A year later, I was working for the SAD. How about you?"

"I was recruited out of Air Force ROTC in my freshman year of college and did my training during the summer months."

"Your freshman year? How old were you?"

"Eighteen."

He gave a low whistle. "That's awfully young for that kind of responsibility."

"Why do you say that? A person can join the military and be sent overseas to fight at that age. Why is my job different?"

"The men you deal with are dangerous."

"And armed insurgents and Taliban fighters aren't?"

"Asking a girl of eighteen to—"

"To be a whore?" She picked up another piece of ice, rubbed it over the last welt.

He turned to face her. "I wasn't going to say that."

"You already did. As I recall, your exact words were—"

"I don't need to hear my exact words. You're right—I said it. But at the time, I didn't know you were working for the Agency."

"So it's not the job description you take issue with, just the employer?"

"I don't know exactly what your job entails, but I know that whatever you do, you do it in the service of our country. That's good enough for me."

"I don't sleep with most of them. In fact, I try very hard *not* to sleep with them."

"You don't owe me any explanations, Holly."

Somehow, those words hurt.

He really didn't care about her at all, did he?

All at once, the rage and hurt she felt came spilling out, her voice cold with sarcasm. "Speaking of whores, how did a nice Georgian Orthodox boy from Delta Force end up having to *whore* for the SAD with the likes of me? How awful it must have been for you! Did they supply you with Viagra?"

In a single motion, he hauled her up against him, his

mouth coming down on hers—hard. She yielded to the sweet violence of his kiss, almost oblivious to the pain in her ribs, her anger melting into need as he punished her for her words with his lips and tongue. One big hand cupped her right breast through the cloth of her dress, his palm pressed against her nipple, the contact sending shards of heat to her belly.

He tore his lips from hers, his breathing rapid, his gaze hard as he looked down at her, still holding her tight. He nudged his hips forward just enough so that she could feel his erection. "I never needed Viagra with you. But, you're right, it *was* awful, not because I didn't want to fuck you, but because I *did*. It went against everything I believed in, but I wanted you—*you*, a woman willing to have sex with Dudaev to betray her country. Or so I'd been led to believe."

He released her, sat back, then stood, his dark brows furrowed, a troubled look on his face. "I'm sorry. I had no right to touch you like that."

Then he walked from the room, leaving Holly to stare after him, stunned.

CHAPTER 16

Nick connected the keyboard to the last CPU, started it, and waited for it to boot.

What the hell had he been thinking? He'd promised not to touch her again, and he'd broken that promise. Yeah, he'd been angry as hell, but that was no excuse.

He'd called her a whore during that interrogation, and he deserved to have the word thrown back in his face. She was right. He'd done the same thing—had sex with someone as part of his job.

He knew she must be thinking of turning him in. Any officer worth the title would be. He was surprised she hadn't tried to contact Langley already. He hoped he hadn't just pushed her over the edge.

It would serve you right, idiot.

The computer beeped, prompted him to log in.

He entered his password, launched the password-cracking program, cursing under his breath when the machine immediately crashed. This program was buggier than the others and he didn't know enough about computers to fix it.

He rebooted, waited, glancing around at his new office. The low-hanging fluorescent lights, exposed pipes, and lack of windows made it look like the hideout of a psychopath— or a spy. It was perfect.

They needed to make a run into town for supplies. If she was going to turn him in, that's when she'd make her move.

He ought to leave her here or find some kind of emotional leverage to restrain her. He didn't want to have to tie her up, to make her his prisoner again. Then he really would be one of the bad guys.

He had just gotten the last CPU up and running when he smelled something delicious from upstairs.

Holly appeared, carrying two plates. "I was hungry, so I scrambled some eggs with vegetables and cheddar. I thought you might want something to eat, too. There's salsa upstairs if you want it."

Surprised that she'd made food for him, Nick took the plate and fork from her. "Did you put rat poison in mine?"

"No. Darn! Why didn't I think of that?" Her eyes narrowed. "I believe the proper response is 'thank you.'"

"Thank you."

She glanced around the floor, and he thought he knew why.

"Relax. I haven't seen a snake all day." He stood and opened one of the folding chairs for her. "How are you feeling?"

She sat. "A little better. Still itchy."

"That should be gone in another twenty-four hours or so."

She didn't start eating, something clearly on her mind.

He had a good idea what that might be.

"I've thought a lot about my situation, our situation. I'm not saying that I'll help you. I don't want to ruin my position with the Agency or find myself on the most-wanted list. If you are what they say you are, if you are a CI threat, you're going to have to kill me or imprison me because I *will* turn you in."

Okay, that wasn't what he'd expected.

She went on. "If I believe you're being truthful, I won't turn you in, and I'll do what I can to help you, short of breaking the law or compromising myself. But I need to know where I fit into this—why you kept me under surveillance and why your boss ordered my termination. I also want to know why you took encrypted files."

He took a bite of the eggs and chewed, surprised by how hungry he was. "Where do you want me to start?"

"Why don't you start with that night in Batumi?"

Between bites, Nick told her how the unit to which he'd

been assigned had intercepted a shipment of firearms bound for a Chechen terrorist group. "The plan was to destroy the weapons—mostly old AKs. The Agency brass were under pressure from Washington to play nice and work with Georgian officials. I was chief of security and didn't want to involve the locals at all. Daniella Baranova, the officer in charge, agreed with me. Corruption is just a part of life there, and the Georgian Mafia has a lot of cops and military officers on its payroll."

"You worked with Dani?"

Nick found himself staring at Holly. "You knew her?"

Holly's lips curved in a smile. "We met during training. She helped me with my Russian and I helped her with cryptography. We stayed in touch until she went overseas."

Nick found his next words hard to say, regret and grief cutting through him. "We were going to get married."

"You were dating? Isn't that against the rules?"

Nick nodded. "It was kind of an open secret."

"I'm sorry. I know she was killed, but I never found out how she died."

"She was murdered that night in Batumi. Dudaev killed her—shot her fifteen times in the chest at point-blank range."

"Oh, God." Holly squeezed her eyes shut.

Nick realized it was the first time he'd talked about this with someone who'd known Dani personally. Somehow, that made it more difficult to control his emotions.

Holly's eyes opened, a sheen of tears making them glitter. "What went wrong?"

"I've asked myself that question for two long years." Nick walked over to the white board, which stood in one corner, and rolled it out so that she could see it. "I've tried to re-create everything about that night down to the smallest detail."

He gave her a quick overview of the map he'd drawn. It was too complicated to explain in detail now.

"In the end, Langley had the last word. We needed the support of the Georgian government in dealing with the threat from Chechnya, so we had to work with their military. The plan was to turn the weapons over to one of their intelligence units for destruction. We moved the crates to a secured warehouse on the docks, kept them under round-the-clock surveillance. My team was in position a good three hours before the turnover was supposed to take place. But it wasn't the military that showed up."

Holly set her empty plate on the workbench. "It was Dudaev's men."

"Somehow, they knew exactly where we were and how my team was deployed." He pointed on the board to where he'd placed snipers. "They took out my two snipers before I even knew they were there and claimed their positions. We became sitting ducks. I managed to redeploy my men, take a few of their guys out, but then I was shot and pinned down by sniper fire. Most of my men were seriously wounded in the first two minutes."

"That must have been terrifying."

"Yeah." Nick could see it all in his mind, hear it, smell it, as if it were happening now—gunfire, Dani lying dead on the floor, the coppery tang of blood in his mouth.

Nick stood, turned his back to Holly, fought to master his emotions. "Dani hadn't been hit. She'd managed to take cover behind a forklift during the firefight. Men in uniforms took the crates, loaded them onto a truck, drove away. Dudaev appeared out of nowhere. He walked over to Dani, passing several wounded officers on the way. He said something to her—I didn't hear what—then he drew his weapon and fired at point-blank range. I couldn't stop him. I was out of ammo and pinned down. I couldn't do anything but watch. Afterward, I crawled over to her, but . . . she was gone."

HOLLY KNEW DUDAEV had killed Agency officers. She hadn't known that one of those officers had been a friend. An image of Dani's smiling face flashed through her mind and she found herself blinking back tears. "I'm so sorry."

Some part of her wanted to go to Nick, to wrap her arms around him, to offer him some kind of comfort, but he was trying to be tough, trying to hide his emotions. She wasn't sure he would welcome her sympathy just now.

Nick turned around, a bleak expression on his face,

shadows in his eyes. "It was my job to protect her, to safe-guard the mission. I failed."

Holly certainly understood why the Agency had launched an internal investigation. Dudaev had been tipped off that night, possibly by an Agency officer, someone who was inti-mately acquainted with the details of the team's security plan. She understood, too, that Nick had a strong motivation for killing Dudaev. Taken together, these two facts would make Nick very interesting to investigators.

"This is all classified top secret, by the way," he added.

"I wasn't planning on writing an article about it or post-ing it on Twitter. But now tell me how I came into this."

He quickly filled in the gaps for her, telling her his side of the story from the day he'd landed in DC to the moment he'd driven off with her lying unconscious in the back of the SUV. "You know the rest."

She wanted to act like what had happened no longer mat-tered to her but listening to him talk so dispassionately about deceiving her resurrected the hurt and humiliation she'd been trying to bury. "So you spied on me for three weeks. That must have been deathly dull—like watching paint dry."

"Not all the time." He shrugged. "I learned a lot about the things women say to one another when they don't think a man is listening."

She tried to think of what she might have said. "Like what?"

He grinned. "'It's the clit, stupid.'"

She felt heat rush to her cheeks. "How educational that must have been for you. I suppose you used what you over-heard to your advantage to make yourself more interesting, more satisfying in bed."

He leaned forward, fixed his gaze on hers. "Believe it or not, I didn't learn about the clitoris from eavesdropping on you, and I've loved going down on women since I got my first taste in college. What you got is who I am."

Holly's pulse skipped, her mind flashing back to the way he'd kissed her this afternoon—the heat, the intensity, the near violence of it.

She changed the subject. "What did they believe you'd

overhear anyway? I'm not stupid. It's not like I chat with my CO on the phone or talk to myself about my missions. 'Today I think I'll get a mani-pedi, send a few ciphertext messages, and retrieve some stolen files from Dudaev.'"

"I told them you were clean—just a reporter with bad taste in men."

"That last part is certainly true." She scratched at the welts on her arm.

He refused to take the bait. "I felt like I was wasting my time but Bauer ordered me to stay with you. I figured he'd screwed up and didn't have the balls to admit he was wrong about you. I had no idea Bauer had some kind of personal agenda where you're concerned. When I saw you holding that image of me, I had to act. I'm sorry. And stop scratching."

She balled her hands into fists, pressed them into her lap. "I'm sorry, too."

"I know you hate my guts, Holly, and God knows you have good reason. But I need to know—do you believe me?"

Nick's gaze pierced her, tension rolling off him in waves.

Holly's mind swirled with events, names, dates.

Did she believe him?

She believed Nick's grief over Dani was genuine. He wouldn't have done anything to put her at risk, which meant he couldn't have been the one who'd sold out the Agency that night in Batumi. If he had nothing to cover up, then he probably wasn't behind the disappearances and deaths of the other agents, most of which had taken place when he was still in Georgia anyway. She knew he'd killed Dudaev without the Agency's approval—and he'd had a powerful motive to do so.

But whoever had betrayed the Agency to Dudaev and his men had an even more powerful motive for wanting Dudaev dead. What better way to get rid of him then to send the man they wanted to frame to do their dirty work?

As for what he'd done to her, he said he'd acted on false information. Given that he'd stopped hurting her the moment he'd realized she was with the Agency, she was inclined to believe he was telling the truth about this, too.

Then there was the fact that Dudaev's thugs had been sent

after them. Taken together with what she knew about Nick—his conscience, the way he'd watched over her these past couple of days, his faith that these files would clear his name—it indicated he was being truthful with her. She had her answer.

"I believe you." It almost hurt to say it.

"You believe me?" He repeated her words, surprise on his face.

"I believe you've been set up. I believe you didn't know I was with the Agency. That doesn't mean I've forgiven you. You've lied to me and used me, so it's hard for me to trust you. What you want from me requires a lot of trust. If I help you crack that password, I'll be held culpable for the theft and misuse of those files, too. I don't want to go to prison."

He nodded, as if he understood. "Those files may be the only chance I have of finding out what happened that night and proving my innocence. They may be your only chance of discovering why Bauer wants you dead."

"But won't the truth come out anyway once Langley sorts through the files? Why put yourself at risk like this? Why not trust that justice will take its course?"

"Langley has the files from the USB that you retrieved for them. I cloned Dudaev's entire hard drive, which I then gave to Bauer personally. I doubt the information on that drive made it beyond his office."

Holly hadn't realized that.

Nick glanced at his watch. "We should go, try to get supplies before the stores close. You need more Benadryl."

"Yeah. Okay." Holly was sure her CO would have responded by now but it wouldn't be easy to check her Twitter account. From what she remembered, the grocery store was on the other side of the highway from the Internet café. If she could convince Nick to drop her off and do the shopping without her, she could check her accounts and see what her CO wanted her to do.

And what if he wants you to turn Nick in?

The thought left her feeling uneasy.

"I've been craving a latte all day. Maybe there's a coffee shop nearby."

He muttered something about needing to find a liquor store instead.

She followed him upstairs, slipped into a pair of flip-flops, and grabbed the awful denim handbag she'd gotten at the thrift store. Outside, the sun had begun to set.

He grabbed the keys off the kitchen counter. "Don't forget Holly Junior."

"What?"

"The baby." He grinned, pointing. "You didn't want to help me name her, so Daddy had to do it himself."

Holly glared at him, grabbed the doll off the floor, and followed him out the door.

NICK DROVE DOWN the old dirt road that led to the highway, the sun low on the western horizon. Holly sat in the passenger's seat beside him, the doll buckled into its child seat. It struck him as funny. "Here we are—a modern family out for a drive."

Holly gave him a reluctant smile, then laughed, the sound warming him. "Don't judge. Families come in all shapes and sizes."

Did Holly really believe him?

There's no way Nick could be certain. If she was going to turn him in or run, it made sense for her to try to convince him that she believed him in order to win his trust. If that was her game, she'd make a move soon.

And what would he do if she *did* turn him in?

He didn't want to hurt her. He couldn't kill her.

They drove with the windows down, the cool evening air blowing through Holly's hair, the sunset reflected in the mirrored lenses of the cheap aviator-style sunglasses she'd bought at the grocery store. Somehow, despite the bruising on her forehead and wrists and the welts on her skin, she managed to look like a million bucks, frosty pink lip gloss making her lips look edible, that black sundress clinging to her curves.

"You probably should have worn something else."

If she walked into the store like that, she'd attract a lot of attention.

She glanced down at her wrists. "Is your jacket still in the back?"

"I think so."

She unbuckled the seat belt, planted one silky leg between her seat and the center console, and bent over to reach into the back seat, her motions giving him a glimpse of her panties and luscious ass.

Eyes on the road, Andris.

She turned and sat again, his jacket in one hand. "What about this Lee Nguyen you mentioned?"

"He's directly under Bauer. He was promoted a few months after the debacle in Batumi. He and I served together in Delta Force. He was recruited by the Agency a couple of years before I was. He put in a good word for me."

"Do you think he's involved?" Holly scratched at her welts again.

"He was in the room when Bauer handed me this assignment. He took part in the conversation. He even warned me about you, told me you were a pro. He was standing there when I handed Dudaev's laptop over to Bauer."

"I guess he has to be in on it, then."

"I suppose so." The thought left a bitter taste in Nick's mouth.

She looked over at him. "I'm sorry. It sucks to realize someone you believed in has betrayed you."

Was that a hint of sarcasm he heard in her voice, a reminder that he had betrayed her? She needed to get over that. They'd been intimate for just three days. True, he'd put her through hell after that, but he'd thought she was a traitor.

He and Nguyen, on the other hand, had trained together, fought together, bled together. They'd become brothers. They were supposed to have each other's backs.

"I wonder if Nguyen was promoted so that Bauer could keep an eye on him. What better way to watch over someone who has sensitive information about you than to put him in the office next door?"

"I hadn't thought of that." Nick turned onto the two-lane highway, heading south, the landscape on either side of the road nothing but dry-as-bones earth dotted with prickly pear cactus and yucca. "The Great American Desert."

"If you ask me, the pioneers were crazy."

That made Nick smile. For all her love of luxury and comfort, she hadn't wasted time complaining about their situation or the second-hand clothes she was wearing. She probably had more in common with the pioneers than she realized. "Yeah, there's nothing you hate like adventure."

She looked over the top of her sunglasses at him, a hint of a smile on her lips.

And for a while they drove in silence.

It was Holly who spoke first. "Why would a man in Bauer's position send thugs from the Georgian Mafia after us? Why not send someone from the Agency to carry out the hit, especially given your status as a fugitive?"

That seemed obvious. "Killing us wasn't authorized."

"Exactly. It was personal. If Bauer used Dudaev's men for his dirty business yesterday, then I have to believe he's done it before. That means he has ties with them, ties that perhaps date back to that night in Batumi."

"I've been thinking the exact same thing."

"It seems incredible to think that Bauer might have been the leak—Martin Bauer of all people. Why would he do that?"

"That's what I hope to find out."

"I met Bauer one night at an Agency event."

That was news to Nick.

"It was a long time ago. I doubt he remembers me, but I remember him. God, I was so in awe of him, almost afraid to shake his hand. To think that he's dirty, that he wants me dead. It doesn't feel real or even seem possible."

Nick didn't think any man who'd met Holly would forget her, but he didn't say that. "I know what you mean. He's been my supervisor for three years."

The lights of the shopping center appeared in the distance.

"When we get to the grocery store, you could head inside, while I drive to the coffee shop and pick you up on the way back. I think there's a coffee shop near the thrift store."

There was nothing about Holly's words or her voice that hinted she wanted to do anything other than satisfy her latte craving. He'd left her alone in the vehicle and let her go her own way before—when he'd cleared the house, when she'd gone to the thrift store, when they'd bought groceries. The fact that he was still a free man tended to support the idea that she hadn't turned him in yet.

Still, he couldn't risk having her take off with the vehicle. "How about I drop you off at the coffee shop and pick you up on my way back?"

"Okay. That works."

He turned left into the parking lot at the hardware store and saw the coffee shop. It was right next door to the thrift shop, and it wasn't just a coffee shop. It was also an Internet café. He pulled up in front, stopped the vehicle. "Grab a pound of coffee to take back with us while you're there."

She put on his jacket and climbed out, denim handbag slung over her shoulder. "See you in a bit."

Nick drove across the street, watched in the rearview mirror as she entered the coffee shop, then turned the vehicle around.

CHAPTER 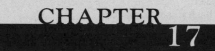17

HOLLY PROPPED HER sunglasses up on her head, sat at one of the computers, and logged in to her IP blocker, trying not to scratch.

Oh, these damned stings itch!

While the IP-blocking program booted up, she ordered a skinny no-whip mocha from a young blond woman in a Taylor Swift T-shirt and tight Levis, put a pound of ground beans on the counter, and paid, feeling strangely nervous.

What if her CO wanted her to turn Nick in? Once she'd received his orders and deciphered them, she'd be obligated to carry them out.

She'd taken a vow to the Agency. That had to come first, didn't it?

And yet as much as she trusted her CO, she didn't want to unleash a chain of events that got Nick thrown unjustly in prison or killed.

She carried her drink and the coffee back to her computer and logged in to her secret Twitter account. She had six private messages. She printed them, then went to her CO's secret Twitter account and printed the key. She would have to be quick if she was going to decode these and craft a response before Nick came for her.

She took a sip of her mocha, spread the printouts on the table, and was about to reach into her handbag for a pencil when a man's hand closed around her wrist.

"So you believe me, do you?" Nick whispered in her ear.
Her pulse skipped.

He'd doubled back to check on her.

"Yes, I do," she whispered back.

"You've got a damned peculiar way of showing it." His
gaze traveled over the screen, took in the string of ciphertext
messages, including the one she'd sent. "Print all of this—
with the keys."

"I just did."

"Print the one you sent, too."

"I can—"

"Do it!"

"Calm down or you're going to make a scene." She did as
he asked.

"And the key."

"That's in my head."

While he watched, she logged out and deleted her browsing history, then gathered the printed pages, folded them,
and tucked them in her handbag. She picked up her latte—
she wasn't leaving it behind—and stood.

Nick's arm went around her shoulders, turned her toward
the door.

She drew back. "We need to pay for the printing."

He tossed a five-dollar bill on the counter, smiled at the
woman behind the counter. "This is for the printing. Keep the
change."

The woman stared at him like she'd never seen a man
before. "Goodnight! Come back and see us again."

He pressed his lips to Holly's ear in what probably looked
like a kiss and whispered, "Move."

His arm still around her shoulders, he compelled her
toward the door, his body so close to hers that she could feel
steel in his jeans.

"Is that a pistol in your pocket or are you happy to see—"

"Just walk."

When they stepped outside, Nick took Holly's arm. "You
know, I almost bought your act. What a fucking idiot I am!"

"Yes, you certainly are, but not for the reasons you think."

He walked her to the passenger-side door, opened it,

crowding her, making it clear with his body language that he'd stop her if she tried to run. "Get in."

"That's 'Get in, please'—unless you're abducting me again."

He glared at her. "This isn't a game, Holly."

Holly spent a moment wondering how she could get out of this situation, and realized she probably couldn't, not without causing a scene that might have disastrous consequences for them both.

She climbed in and he locked the doors with the remote, walked around, and let himself in with the key. "Did you give away our location?"

She looked him straight in the eyes. "No. My life is at stake. Under the current circumstances, I don't trust my messages to reach my CO unobserved. I used a subscription IP blocker."

"You sent that first message yesterday morning when you were supposed to be in the thrift store."

"I saw my chance and took it." She knew he was wondering whether Langley would have had enough time to deploy a team to bring him in. "And, technically, it was three messages—a hundred forty characters each. I didn't tell them where we were. Do you want me to decode these?"

"Here? Now?"

"Of course." She pulled the pages out of her handbag, turned on the overhead light, and took a pencil from her purse. "I can tell you what mine says."

She wrote the plaintext of her message over the ciphertext, which was divided into standard blocks of four double-digit numbers, then jotted the key equation down in the margins and handed it to him.

He read the words aloud. "Unhurt. Was abducted by Andris. He knows my employer. Says he was ordered to terminate me. Says he has been set up by his CO. Believe he might be telling the truth. Dudaev's men found us at remote location. Andris claims only his boss knew we were there. At safe location with Andris. No Internet access. No phone. He poses no threat to me at this time. Please advise."

"See, you big bully? I didn't give you away."

Some of the anger left his face. "I'll want to double check this myself."

"Suit yourself. The key is right there." She studied the key to the new messages, memorized it, then began decoding.

Relief flooded her as words began to take shape before her eyes.

She saw Nick watching her. "What is it?"

"You can do that in your head?" He sounded impressed.

"I do have a brain, you know."

"Why didn't you go into cryptography?"

"Boooooring. Who wants to do that all day? God, no! Besides, there are a lot of people who are good at that, but very few who can do what I do."

She wrote the corresponding letters over each pair of numbers and read through the message again. "Are you sure you want to see this?"

"What do you think?" He jerked the pages out of her hands.

BELIEVE YOU ARE BOTH IN PERIL. ANDRIS STILL CONSID-
ERED A CI THREAT AND DANGEROUS. REMAIN WITH HIM
AS LONG AS YOU ARE SAFE. USE ANY MEANS TO LEARN
TRUTH OF HIS CLAIMS OR FACTS RELATED TO 'BATUMI OP.'
REPORT TO ME. TRUST NO ONE ELSE. URGE HIM TO SUR-
RENDER. WILL GUARANTEE HIS SAFETY.

Holly watched his expression change from anger to surprise to amusement.

He looked up, a lopsided grin on his face. "So you're spying on *me* now."

"You're not supposed to know that."

"I think it's better that I do." He glanced down at the decoded message. "Does this mean you're free to help me crack that password?"

Holly thought about that for a moment. Her CO didn't know Nick had cloned Dudaev's hard drive. Then again, he'd said she was to use any means. If there was information on that drive that could exonerate Nick and bring the truth to light, her CO would surely be in favor of her helping. "Yes. I'll help you."

"Stop scratching." Nick tucked the pages into the center

console, glanced at his watch, restarted the engine. "We need to get to the store. It's about to close."

They crossed the highway, Holly savoring a few more sips of her latte.

Nick parked, looked over at her. "What would you have done if he'd ordered you to turn me in?"

"I guess we'll never know."

AN HOUR LATER, Holly lay on her belly on her air mattress, drowsy from another dose of Benadryl, the maddening itching dulled but not gone. The room would have been stiflingly hot if not for the fan, which blew cool night air in through the window.

Nick sat on the floor beside her, rubbing ice cubes on her back.

It was a kind thing for him to do, and she had to concede that in addition to being an ass for betraying and humiliating her, he was also a good person.

"Thank you."

"For what?"

"For everything you've done to help me since I was stung." There was more. "And for not killing me. You disobeyed orders. That was kind of a big thing."

"You're welcome. Thanks for not turning me in. Thanks for believing me. That's kind of a big thing, too." His voice was deep, soft.

"I didn't want to believe you."

"No, I suppose you didn't."

"It would be so much easier just to hate you."

"Yeah, I guess it would be." He sounded amused.

"It's not funny. What you did to me—it wasn't funny."

"I know it wasn't. I'd take it back if I could. But isn't it what you do?"

"No!" It irritated her that he didn't understand. "Most of the time, my job is to set people up for surveillance—to plant GPS devices or listening devices. Sometimes I have no choice but to sleep with one of them, but I try hard to get my job done before their pants come off. I never pretend to have a relationship with them. I just act like I find them irresistible and fascinating."

In that respect, she supposed she'd had it coming.

"I underestimated you."

"Most men do."

His hands moved to massage her shoulders, which were still sore from hanging by her wrists. "Did any of them ever physically hurt you?"

She couldn't help but moan as he began to work away the knots. She let her eyes close. "Yes—but none as badly as you."

More than that, none of them had ever hurt her emotionally, where the damage was worse and the pain seemed to last.

"I really am sorry, Holly. If I could do it again . . ."

"You can't. I know that."

"What would you have done in my place?" he asked.

Holly thought about that. Twice her CO had set her up with US citizens, and she'd gone ahead with the missions without a second thought. If he had ordered her to move in next door to someone and pretend to become lovers, she supposed she'd have done it. "I don't know."

"I think you do. A loyal officer like you? You'd have carried out your mission."

So he'd seen through her.

Then she remembered what he'd said yesterday after he'd kissed her, that wonderful, brutal kiss.

I never needed Viagra with you. But, you're right, it was awful, not because I didn't want to fuck you, but because I did.

"What you said yesterday." It was getting hard to think, his soothing hands and the Benadryl making her so very sleepy. "Did you mean you wanted me but you didn't want to want me?"

"If I understand your question, the answer is yes."

Holly heard him, and with her next breath fell fast asleep.

NICK SAT BESIDE her for a time, watched Holly sleep.

Had he wanted her? Hell, yeah, he had, even when he'd thought she was a criminal. And now? He wanted her so badly it hurt.

He hadn't wanted a woman like this since . . .

Since Dani.

The realization took some of the breath from his lungs.

For so long, he'd felt little beyond anger, grief, and emptiness, his life shaped by his duty to his country, to the Agency, the past two years a blur of assignments. Now he was fighting for his career, fighting for his life. Yet somehow in the middle of this mess, Holly, with her big brown eyes and smart mouth, had made him feel again. She'd made him smile, made him laugh.

He'd misjudged her from the beginning. He'd known she was smart. What he hadn't realized is that she was smarter than he was. She was cool under pressure and able to think on her feet. She was a crack operative when it came to cryptography and HUMINT. She'd bested him twice—once in Dudaev's hotel room and once at the cabin. Hell, she'd been one step ahead of him when she'd sent those encrypted messages from the coffee shop, too.

He could see why she and Dani had been friends. Though Dani had been softer spoken and didn't care much for clothes or shoes, they were both smart, intuitive, and extremely stubborn, with insatiable appetites for life.

What was he thinking? Was he actually comparing Holly to Dani?

He had loved Dani. He still loved her. He'd been going to marry her. What he felt for Holly—it was nothing more than lust. Okay, it was lust on steroids. Besides, whatever chance he might have had with her was likely over, ruined by circumstance. He'd followed orders, and in the process he'd hurt her both physically and emotionally.

You were the best time I'd ever had—until you became the worst time I've ever had.

Well, hell. He'd be willing to be her best time again—if she'd let him. He didn't see how he could tell her that, not if he wanted to keep his nuts intact.

So, Holly, if you're done being hurt and pissed off, I think we should go back to fucking each other's brains out.

Yeah, he didn't see that going over well. She'd made it clear this afternoon that she still didn't trust him. Hadn't he promised he would never touch her again? Yes, he had, and he needed to keep that promise.

Still, she'd been attracted to him once. Yesterday, when he'd kissed her, she'd seemed to melt in his arms. Or maybe she'd just been surprised.

The tall one wouldn't bend, the short one wouldn't stretch, and the kiss was lost.

The words, part of an old Georgian proverb, came into his thoughts and stayed.

But he *had* bent. He'd apologized. He'd admitted wanting her.

What else could he do?

She stirred in her sleep, rolled onto her right side, the large bruise on her ribs a dark stain against her pale skin.

What was wrong with him? He shouldn't be thinking about getting between her legs. He should be doing his best to crack Dudaev's password and expose Bauer. His future and hers depended on it.

Dani's life had ended in five minutes of terror on a cold warehouse floor in Batumi. Now Holly's life was on the line, caught in the wake of that same terrible night. He owed it to her to get her out of this safely.

He pulled up the sheet to cover her, picked up the melting bowl of ice, and left her to sleep. He had work to do.

HOLLY AWOKE THE next morning feeling a little groggy from the Benadryl but much better overall. The welts had begun to fade and didn't itch nearly as bad. She got up, grabbed a towel, and walked across the hall to the bathroom for a shower, only to find the door closed, Nick already inside.

She heard the water shut off, followed by cursing.

"Shit!"

A moment later, the door opened, and he emerged dripping wet and furious, shaving cream covering half his face, a blue towel wrapped around his hips. "The generator must be out of propane."

The water pump didn't work without electricity and had apparently cut out on him mid-shave.

He headed down the stairs, the towel so low on his hips that she could see the rounded tops of his glutes.

Was he planning on going outside like that?

"Do you need help?" she called after him.

"Do you know how to hook a propane tank up to a generator?"

"No." She was sure she could figure it out.

"Then, no, I don't need help."

She heard the front door open and the screen door slam. Someone was grumpy this morning.

She went downstairs, took a strawberry yogurt out of the little fridge, found a spoon, and ate, watching out the window as Nick, still wearing just the towel, grabbed a propane tank, the muscles of his arms and chest shifting in response to the weight.

She felt a flutter in her belly.

He disappeared around the side of the house, ending the show.

She let her mind drift back to the few days when they'd been sexually involved. He'd been amazing, the first man who'd matched her libido, who'd anticipated her needs, who'd been willing to play with her, not just screw her. He'd made her scream, made her laugh, made her forget herself.

What you got is who I am.

More belly flutters.

She'd told him he repulsed her, that she couldn't stand the sight of him, but it wasn't true. It bothered her to realize how much she still wanted him. She was used to being able to walk away from men, hot men, wealthy men. So why couldn't she just forget about him and focus on her job?

Then it came back to her—what he'd said just before she'd fallen asleep.

If I understand your question, the answer is yes.

He'd wanted her.

Did he still want her? Did she want him?

Why couldn't she read him like she read other men?

You're too close to this emotionally. That's why.

She closed her eyes, remembered the feel of him on top of her, inside her.

Outside, the generator kicked on, and he walked through the door, abruptly ending her fantasy. There was a dark scowl on his face and grass stains on his bare knees from crawling around on the ground. Although he was clearly pissed off, it was hard to take his anger seriously when half of his face was covered in white foam.

"How did you sleep?" she asked, trying not to smile.

"Fine." He marched up the stairs, giving her the best view yet.

Oh, my.

Okay, so male genitals could look a little comical just bobbing around. But when he'd been hard and inside her, she hadn't been laughing.

CHAPTER 18

NICK REBOOTED THE computer, wondering if he should just delete the damned program and install one of the others on this CPU. He had five other computers running around the clock and none of them had yet cracked Dudaev's password. He couldn't afford to have this one crashing every half hour.

Holly—the other half of Nick's excuse for a bad mood—called down the stairs to him. "There's coffee if you want some."

He grabbed the pages he'd written up when she'd been asleep last night and headed upstairs. He stepped into the kitchen, saw her, stopped.

Holy hell.

Her hair was still damp, hanging to her shoulders in blond tendrils, the air carrying just a hint of her soft, feminine scent. This time, she was wearing a short pink slip dress that revealed the hot pink of her bra straps and the round tops of her breasts. To make matters worse, she'd put on that frosty pink lip gloss again, the stuff that made her mouth look irresistible, like candy.

How did she manage to look like *that* in secondhand clothes? Shouldn't she be wearing baggy sweats and T-shirts?

He'd gone to sleep feeling horny as hell last night, unable to take matters into his own hands, not with her sleeping in the same damned room. She wasn't making things any easier on him by walking around half naked.

She must have seen the scowl on his face. "Did the computer crash again?"

"Yeah. Are you any good at debugging?"

"No. Sorry." She poured coffee into a mug. "Do you take it black, or do you want—?"

"Black. Thanks." He held out the pages. "I want you to review and memorize these. They're security protocols."

"Security protocols?" She took the pages, glanced down at them.

He'd written up a few scenarios just to help her prepare mentally, giving her exit routes from the house and instructions on where to take shelter inside the house if they ended up in a firefight. He'd also put in a few reminders, basic stuff like having the information on her false ID memorized, knowing the number on the minivan's temporary plates, keeping her firearm loaded and ready.

He ought to have done this their first day here but she'd gotten stung by the yellow jackets and they'd been occupied with other things. Not that anyone was going to find them out here in the middle of nowhere. Still, they couldn't be too careful.

"We need to agree to certain things. For example, no more contact with Langley unless we both agree and are present."

She looked up at him. "You want veto power over my contact with my CO?"

"No." He'd known she was going to take it that way. "We didn't get off to the best start and—"

"That wasn't *my* fault."

"Regardless, we need to be able to trust each other, to work as a team, if we're going to get out of this alive."

"What have I done to make *you* lack trust in *me*?"

"You snuck off to the Internet café and sent that message."

She raised an eyebrow. "You abducted me. I had to check in and let people know I was okay. You ought to have anticipated that."

"How do you think I managed to catch you in the act yesterday? I anticipated!" Nick fought not to shout. "Your skills are cryptography and charm. Mine are tactical and security. If bullets start flying, you'll do what I tell you to do."

"Charm?" She glared up at him, standing almost toe-to-toe with him now, her cheeks red. "I've had firearms training, SERE, R2I. I am *not* some ditzy, helpless blond chick!"

He grabbed her shoulders, overwhelmed by the urge to shake some sense into her. Instead, he found himself kissing her, lust, anger, and regret getting tangled inside him, coalescing into some kind of insanity.

She kissed him back, her lips sweet against his, the security protocols slipping from her hands, falling to the floor.

With no warning, she pulled away, gave him a hard shove. "You bastard!" She glared up at him, her cheeks flushed pink. "That's the second time you've kissed me!"

He opened his mouth to point out that she'd damned well kissed him back that time, but he didn't get the chance. With a little jump she was in his arms again, her lips on his, her arms wrapped around his neck.

He caught her, crushed her against him, took what she offered, staggering across the kitchen like a drunk. Her tongue teased his, the two of them sparring for control of the kiss until they were both breathless.

He backed her up against the kitchen wall, the feel of her soft body making him hard. She began to grind herself against his erection, her motions telling him exactly what she wanted. God, he wanted it, too. He wanted to be inside her *now*, but he knew he wouldn't last two minutes like this.

He set her feet on the floor and dropped to his knees before her, yanking her panties down with one hand, lifting her dress out of the way with the other. Then he buried his face between her thighs and tasted her.

He heard her quick intake of breath, felt her fingers clench in his hair.

"*Yes!*" she whispered.

He ran his tongue over her smooth outer lips, then drew one inner lip into his mouth and sucked on it, tugging it free so he could see it. So much like a flower petal. He did the same thing with the other one, and felt her shiver. He took a moment to admire her beauty, then took the small bud of her clit into his mouth and suckled her.

She gasped, her belly tensing, her clit swelling in his mouth.

God, he'd missed her taste, missed her scent, missed the way she made him feel—lust-crazed and alive, his pulse pounding.

Some part of him wondered whether he was out of his mind to be doing this—doing *her*—when his life was a disaster. But then she moaned out his name, and it seemed to him that being with her like this was the only part of his life that made sense.

HOLLY LET HERSELF be carried away as Nick worked magic on her with his mouth, teasing her with velvet strokes of his tongue, tugging on her clit with his lips, drawing all of her into the heat of his mouth.

Why had she ever argued with him? They shouldn't waste time arguing. They shouldn't even talk. They should spend all of their time . . .

Just. Like. *This.*

Oh, God, what was *that*?

Some sweet trick with his lips and tongue.

She tried to ask him what he was doing and whether he was taking notes, because someone *ought* to be writing this down for the sake of all womankind. But her words unraveled, became moans, her legs trembling, her knees threatening to buckle.

Oh, it felt good, desire now a shimmering sexual ache deep in her belly. Her vagina contracted, longing to be filled. But he seemed to know. In the next instant, he slid two fingers deep inside her, stretching her, stroking her.

Oh, God, yes!

It was bliss, his mouth on her, his fingers inside her. And in no time at all she was there, floating along that golden crest that came right before an orgasm.

Then he did *that* again.

She came with a cry, grabbing onto his shoulders for balance as climax surged through her in radiant waves, his mouth keeping up its rhythm until the bliss had passed. And for a moment she stood there, breathless, her nails digging into his T-shirt, her legs weak, her body trembling.

He got to his feet, drew her against him, his mouth closing over hers in a deep kiss, his lips drenched in her scent, his tongue filling her mouth with her own taste. She heard the sound of a zipper and glanced down to see his beautiful erect cock jutting out of his jeans.

Her inner muscles clenched—hard.

She wanted him again.

She was about to drop to her knees and do for him what he'd done for her, but she never got the chance. He grasped her bare ass and lifted her off the floor, pinning her against the wall with his weight, the forcefulness of his actions making her pulse spike.

She'd always fantasized about having sex like this, but she'd never been with a man who was strong enough to pull it off. And, oh, how she liked it. It made her feel feminine and small—and extremely horny.

She wrapped her legs around his waist, opening herself to him, already anticipating the hard feel of him inside her.

His gaze met hers, the head of his cock nudging into her. "Are you sure you really want this?"

Something in her chest melted that he should think to ask. So few men did.

She kissed him, whispered, "*Fuck me.*"

He thrust his hips forward, burying his cock inch by inch inside her.

They moaned almost as one, Holly's eyes drifting shut at the exquisite feel of him, so hot and hard and thick.

"You feel *so* . . . good." His voice was strained, his body tense.

He began to move, slowly at first, then faster, his rhythm picking up until he was driving himself into her, fucking her hard and deep and fast. Each thrust felt sweeter than the last, until she was crying out for him, the slick glide of his cock sending her over that dazzling edge once again. But this time, she wasn't alone. She heard his breath break, felt his body shudder as orgasm claimed him, carrying them both away.

It was only after her pulse slowed and he'd set her on her feet that she realized they hadn't used a condom.

He realized it, too. "I don't know what I was thinking, Holly. I'm sorry."

She *never* had sex without a condom. "I don't think either of us was thinking of much of anything."

"I get tested as part of the Agency's annual physical, so I know I can't give you anything—well, except . . . you know." His gaze dropped to her belly.

She felt a little answering flutter.

No. Just no.

"I can't get pregnant. IUD. I get tested regularly, too." It went with her job.

"Okay, well, no harm done, then." He kissed her—slowly.

They shared a bath afterward, Holly leaning back against Nick's chest in the cooling water, his arm around her, the intimacy both strangely familiar and new.

"I want you to know that I truly am sorry for what I did to you." He kissed her hair. "I need you to believe that."

"I believe you." She knew, too, that he wanted her—sexually, anyway.

In that respect, he was no different from the other guys she'd slept with.

That was enough, wasn't it? Yes, it was. It had to be. Who knew how long they'd be together or where the two of them would end up when this was over. She would go back to her life, and he would probably end up leaving the Agency or serving overseas again. Now wasn't the time to start a relationship.

"About condoms—as incredible as it feels to be inside you without one, that's really your call. If you don't like the mess, I'll make sure to grab some next time we head into town for supplies."

"No, it's fine. It's kind of nice." She smiled, touched again by his thoughtfulness.

There *were* ways in which he was so very different from other guys.

Holly read through Nick's safety protocols, his stark words driving home how important it was to crack Dudaev's password and decrypt those files, the danger they both faced coming alive for her. She hadn't been afraid since they'd settled here—well, apart from the snakes, spiders, and yellow jackets. But now . . .

She glanced up at Nick. "Storm shelter?"

"There's a storm shelter about thirty feet off to the side of the house next to the field." He pointed. "I didn't see it when we first got here because the door is overgrown by weeds, but I checked it out. It's solid. We'll get some emergency supplies in there just in case—ammo, water."

"If the bad guys come, I'm supposed to hide in the shelter."

"That's one option. Obviously, you can't run out the door if they're outside. Just keep reading."

She turned her attention back to the page. He'd thought of everything—where to take cover, how to take on intruders without getting caught in a crossfire, where to meet if they got separated. It was all variations on a theme: He fought, while she hid.

"Okay. Done."

"Are we agreed?"

"Yes—except for the part where all I do is run and hide."

He got that broody frown on his face. "That's the important part."

"If our lives are in danger, I don't want to be skulking in a closet. I can shoot. I can reload mags for you. I can—"

He held up his hand to stop her. "Listen! It's not that I don't think you're capable. I know what it means to kill, Holly. I know what it's like to be in a real firefight. Chances are if anyone comes for us, it will be just a couple of guys—Dudaev's goons again or maybe someone from the Agency. The best way to help is to stay safe and out of the way while I get rid of them. That way you don't distract me, and you don't expose yourself to the legal and emotional fallout of taking a life."

It touched her to know he'd thought of that last part.

"What if something happens to you?"

"Then I guess you'll get to prove what a great shot you are."

"Wonderful."

He got to his feet, closed the space between them, and drew her into his arms, his strength comforting. "I don't want you getting hurt or killed because of me, and I don't want you landing in prison. Please, Holly, promise me you'll do what I tell you to do if it comes to a firefight. Let me do everything I can to keep you safe."

There was something in his voice, a vulnerability she wasn't used to hearing, and she knew that somewhere in his mind, he was thinking of Dani.

"Okay. I promise."

AFTER THEY'D GRABBED a bite to eat, Nick showed Holly which programs were running on which CPUs. He had two searching in Russian, one each in Code Page 855 and Code Page 866. He had two running the Georgian alphabet, and two programmed to run in English, one using English vocabulary, the other using Latin transliterations of Georgian and Russian words.

Holly listened, then paced the length of the room a few times, a look of concentration on her face. "Dudaev wouldn't use a Russian password. He was very proud of being Georgian. He only spoke Russian when he had to communicate with one of his Russian security guys. I just can't imagine he'd base his password on Russian. We'd make faster progress if you had all of the machines running Georgian."

Nick frowned. "Are you sure?"

"What language do you use for your passwords?" She sat across from him, seemed to study him. "You're proud of your Georgian heritage. You learned Georgian first, but you stopped speaking it outside the home after you learned English. Your parents were proud to have a US citizen in the family after you were born, and that matters to you. Your passwords are based on English."

She was dead-on, and from the smile on her pretty face, she knew it.

"Okay, we'll try it your way."

While he entered in the changes, she sat cross-legged on a chair, jotting down words for Nick to translate into Georgian and enter into the dictionary of the new password cracking program they'd just purchased and downloaded. They'd already run through the obvious ones—Dudaev's name, his aliases, his birthdate, his parents' names, the name of his hometown, his deceased wife, and so on.

The program took the words Nick entered and tried all possible variations of those words—capital letters, lowercase, a mix of numbers and letters, numbers used as letters, Latin alphabet transliterations—to guess the bastard's password.

"I know he had a dog as a kid, but he never told me the dog's name."

Nick looked up from the keyboard. "If it's the name of his favorite childhood pet, we're fucked."

"Most people choose passwords that represent themselves in some way—birthdays, family members, their jobs, their faith, how they see themselves. The South African banker I set up last year used versions of the phrase '1 percent.'"

"Seriously?" Wow. That was lame. "We haven't tried 'arms dealer,' 'smuggler,' 'murderer,' or 'asshole' yet."

Holly laughed. "The funny thing about jerks is that they never see themselves as jerks. Criminals work up narratives in their heads to excuse and glorify their actions. Many even see themselves as heroes in their own dramas. In his own mind, Dudaev was handsome, cultured, exciting, courageous. He thought of himself as a bold businessman, a patriot, a fantastic lover."

She got a look of revulsion on her face, stuck out her tongue.

Nick hated to admit it, but it bothered him to think of her naked with that son of a bitch. "I take it from the look on your face the latter assumption wasn't true?"

She shook her head. "Let's just say he was a terrible kisser—all tongue and no technique. I suppose I should thank you for preventing me from having to sleep with him—though you did almost kill me."

Nick's temper spiked. "Don't joke about that. It isn't funny."

"You're right. It isn't." Her gaze held his. "For a while, I thought you were the worst thing that had ever happened to me."

It hurt to hear her say that, but it was probably the truth. He'd drugged her, almost killing her. He'd left her in bed in a pool of blood beside a corpse. He'd misled and humiliated her. He'd assaulted her, abducted her, interrogated her.

Yeah, really, he couldn't argue with her there.

"What do you think now?"

She looked up, gave him an enigmatic smile. "I guess we have to wait and see how the story ends."

CHAPTER 19

HOLLY AWOKE TO find herself alone in the bedroom. She stretched, felt wetness and a slight soreness between her thighs, and smiled, last night fresh in her mind.

She had dropped ice down the back of Nick's T-shirt and Nick had chased her around the house and caught her, carrying her here as if she were a sack of potatoes. He'd peeled off her clothes and fucked her long and slow until she'd come twice, the pleasure of it so intense that she'd thought for a moment it might kill her. Now she knew why the French referred to orgasm as *la petite mort*—the little death.

Why are you so damned good in bed?

The same reason I'm good in combat—a detailed knowledge of human anatomy. But mostly, honey, I just want to make you feel good.

She realized with some surprise that she'd been with Nick longer than she'd been with any man in the past five years or so. They'd been together for three days before he'd kidnapped her, and now they'd been lovers again for almost a week.

Not that they were *together* together. They hadn't talked about the future or updated their relationship statuses on Facebook. Who knew where this would end or what would become of them? Even so, Holly felt closer to him than she had to any man.

Crazy talk, Bradshaw.

She showered, slipped into a T-shirt and shorts, brushed

her teeth, and went downstairs to make coffee. She found Nick where she knew she'd find him—sitting in front of the computers. He wore only a pair of jeans and had a cute case of bedhead, a shock of dark curls hanging down over his brow.

He really did need a haircut.

She bent down, kissed his bare shoulder, the sight of him bringing last night to her mind again. "Good morning."

"Morning." He smiled up at her, but she could see lines of worry on his face.

He was frustrated at their lack of progress. So was she.

They'd been at this together for five days now, Holly wracking her brain for words or concepts that Dudaev might have used in a password, the computers running twenty-four-seven. She was beginning to wonder whether she'd made a mistake, doubt gnawing at her during quiet moments. What if Dudaev had on some whim chosen to base his password on Russian or English?

She didn't want to steer Nick in the wrong direction or lose them precious time. Every hour that went by brought with it the possibility that they would be found and arrested or killed. If they couldn't find something in these files that Nick could use to bargain for immunity, he'd go to federal prison just for taking the files. If they couldn't prove that he'd been ordered to kill Dudaev, he would likely go to prison for life—if he wasn't murdered before his case got to court.

Holly had no idea what would happen to her. She would have to ask Javier for help or go into hiding until her CO assured her she was safe again.

She drew up the other chair and sat down beside him. He'd hacked into the city's wireless signal and was reading headlines. "Catching up on the news?"

"I've been keeping up with what they're saying about us." He scrolled up, and there on the page was a blurry shot of his face and Holly's staff-writer photo. "We're big news, at least in Colorado. Your paper has had us on the front page every day. We're going to have to be extra careful when we go into town for supplies. You might want to color your hair. I need to grow a beard."

Holly quickly read through the article, which Alex had written. It stated that Nick was wanted in connection both with the murder of Sasha Dudayev and her abduction. It mentioned the firefight at the gas station, stating that "sources close to the investigation"—she could guess who they were—believed she'd gone with Nick again simply to save her life. It also mentioned her single Tweet and speculation that she had been trying to reach out to tell her family and friends she was okay.

Nowhere did it mention the Agency.

There was a quote from her father.

"I'm a decorated veteran who served my country all my life, and I'm shocked by the inefficiency with which the search for my daughter is being conducted."

"How like my dad to bring up his military record even though it has nothing to do with the situation." She should be beyond the hurt. After all, he'd been her father for her entire life. And yet the hurt was there. "You were right about him, you know. He never really cared about me. If I'd been a son . . . Well, I wasn't, was I?"

There was also a quote from her mother.

"I haven't been able to sleep since I heard she was taken. I'm just torn apart and so stressed."

"How like my mom to make it about herself."

Neither of them had said anything about her well-being or pleaded for her release or offered her a message of encouragement or strength. Not that she really needed it, but they couldn't know that. For all they knew, she was dead in a ditch somewhere.

She felt Nick's hand come to rest on her shoulder.

Nick's parents had declined to comment, but one of his brothers—Peter Andris—had told reporters that the family was standing by him.

"My brother serves his country. We know that when the facts are in, there will be an explanation for all of this. Meanwhile, we're keeping both him and Ms. Bradshaw in our prayers."

"Hey, at least your family is representing." She smiled over her shoulder at him, rested her hand on his.

It couldn't be easy knowing the media had been bothering his parents and siblings—or knowing that they were living under scrutiny and suspicion because of him. But it was clear they loved him and believed in him.

Then, toward the bottom, there was a quote from Zach.

"As part of the Justice Department, the US Marshals Service takes seriously any threat against journalists and will continue to play a role in this investigation. Wherever she is, we want Ms. Bradshaw to know that we are concerned for her well-being and won't give up until she is safely home again. We would like proof that she is well and alive. We hope her captor will contact us so that we can negotiate her release."

Holly got a hard lump in her throat.

"It looks like your friends are standing by you."

She nodded, swallowed. "I should send another Tweet, give them proof I'm still okay or something. I don't want them to worry that I'm dead."

Nick drew her into his lap, kissed her cheek. "As your kidnapper, I agree."

They used one of the burner phones to snap a photo of Holly in front of a neutral background—a closet door. Then they emailed it to a new Gmail account they'd just created and downloaded it to the computer.

Nick studied the image of her on the screen. "This is good."

"Good? It's terrible. It's worse than my DMV photo. I should have done something with my hair, put on some makeup."

"No, it's good. The bruise on your forehead is still visible, and so are the ones on your wrists."

"Why is that good?" Holly didn't follow.

"I don't want them to think you're here of your own volition. I don't want you charged with aiding and abetting."

"Aw, that's sweet." He was thinking of her again.

"It's not a game." He moved aside, let her take the keyboard.

"So you keep telling me." She logged into her IP blocker

and her Twitter account and tweeted the photo to the US
Marshals Service with the message:

Proof of life. #ZachMcBride

She stared at the tweet for a moment, feeling an ache in
her chest.

She missed home. She missed the paper. But mostly, she
missed her friends.

There were no ciphertext messages from her CO and
nothing for Holly to report yet, beyond her amazing sex life.
She logged out and closed the page.

There on the screen in front of her was another browser
window showing a news article written in Georgian. There
was a map of Georgia, too.

Even though Holly couldn't read a word of it—Georgian
was Greek to her—something about it caught her eye.

"What is it?" Nick asked.

"I don't know. What is the article about?"

"Republic of Abkhazia has accused Georgia of commit-
ting acts of piracy on the Black Sea because the government
detained a few ships."

"Oh." Well, that didn't ring any bells.

But the Black Sea.

The Black Sea.

The phrase pricked at her memory. If only she could
remember why.

It wasn't until later, when she was making them sandwiches for lunch that it came back to her.

Star of the Black Sea.

Dudaev's yacht.

She felt an adrenaline rush. "Nick!"

She dropped the knife she was using to spread mayo and
ran for the stairs, shouting for him again. "Nick!"

He met her halfway to the top, pistol in his hand. "What
is it?"

She drew a deep breath, battled back the adrenaline.
"Dudaev's yacht. He was so proud of it that he carried pho-
tos. He talked about it all the time. Its name was *Star of the
Black Sea.*"

* * *

ZACH STEPPED OUT of the elevator into the headquarters
for Cobra International Solutions in downtown Denver and
showed his ID to the security guard. "Whoa."

A white marble floor stretched down a long, double-wide
hallway to a reception desk, walls of brushed steel reflecting
light from the white honeycomb-style lighting fixtures on the
ceiling. Two sets of gray sofas sat in the center of the hallway,
one facing left, the other right. The right side of the hallway
was lined by freestanding meeting rooms, their walls double
panes of bulletproof glass with blinds sealed in the middle.

So this is what it was like to run a private security
company.

Your DOD dollars at work.

Zach walked up to the receptionist, a young woman
wearing a trim pantsuit, a shoulder holster concealed beneath
her jacket. "Chief Deputy US Marshal Zach McBride here to
see Corbray and Tower."

She had him sign in, then pointed him toward one of the
meeting rooms. The blinds had been turned so that no one
could see inside.

He found Hunter and Darcangelo already there, seated
around a polished wooden table. "I got here as soon as I
could. A new Tweet went up on her account about an hour
ago. We've been analyzing it."

He opened the folder he'd brought with him and dropped
it onto the table. The color print of the image of Holly from
the Tweet sat on top. She looked tired, no make up on her
pretty face, her hair uncombed. And the bruises . . .

Seeing them had made Zach want to find and kill this
Andris bastard.

Darcangelo reached out, picked it up. "We're sure this
image is recent?"

Zach nodded. "Look at her wrists. Our medical guys said
the bruises there are consistent with her having been
restrained on or around the day she was abducted. Same with
the bruise on her forehead."

Darcangelo studied the image, his expression turning
dark. "He didn't just restrain her. He had to do more than

that to create those kinds of injuries on her wrists. I'd say he put them on too tight or dragged her or hanged her by her wrists. She looks exhausted."

"Our guys said the same thing."

Darcangelo handed the image to Hunter.

"I guess we know you have his attention, McBride," he said. "This Tweet must be in response to your quote in the paper. Any luck tracing the IP address?"

Zach shook his head, taking a seat across from them. "He used an IP blocker. The guy is CIA. He knows how to use the Internet without being found. We're analyzing the image to see if the background or the clothes she's wearing can tell us anything."

Hunter stared at the print. "What the hell does he want from her?"

"What do you think he wants?" A look of disgust came over Darcangelo's face. "We know for a fact that he manipulated her into having a sexual relationship with him. Why go on the run alone when you can have such attractive company?"

He shot Hunter a glance.

"Hey, why are you looking at me? That was different." Hunter put the photo in the center of the table. "Is the Agency still giving you a hard time?"

"They're stonewalling us at every turn. So far the brass in DC have stood by the Colorado office on this, even threatening the Agency with a hearing. Her father's ties in Washington are standing by us, as well."

Darcangelo took the photo again. "What did you make of her parents?"

"They are cold, unfeeling people. Meeting them made me wonder why Holly is as sweet as she is. Her father is a pretentious boor, and her mother vain and self-centered. When they weren't arguing with each other, they were talking about themselves. I found myself wanting to shout, 'Your daughter has been kidnapped!'"

Hunter shook his head. "You've got more self-control than I do."

"If we'd just gotten there a bit sooner." Darcangelo was talking about the gas station in Nederland.

"I hear you." That had been shitty luck. "The part I don't

get is how Dudaev's men knew where to look for her when we didn't."

"I think we may be able to shed some light on that." Corbray walked through the door, followed by Tower.

They sat down at the table, the gravity of Corbray's expression and the slight smile on Tower's face making Zach uneasy.

"What you're about to hear can't go out of this room. Got it?" Corbray looked at Zach and then the others. "You can't even share this with your wives. I know you're going to want to, but you can't. If you do, it will make its way through the 'You Go, Girl 'grapevine, and I'll hear it from Laura. If that happens . . . Busted."

"They're not all like that. If I tell Tessa to keep a secret, she does," Julian said.

Zach, Marc, and Javier shook their heads.

"We've got just one thing to say about that, Dorkangelo." Marc shared a conspiratorial glance with Zach and Javier.

Zach knew where this was going.

"Sucky-swirly," the three of them said in unison, grinning.

Darcangelo held up his hands in mock surrender. "Okay."

"Are you blushing, buddy?" Marc asked. "You are, aren't you?"

There was definitely some red on Darcangelo's face.

"No, I'm pissed off and planning to kick your ass."

"Guys. Do not repeat what we're about to tell you." Corbray was serious again. "We've been going back and forth with Tower's sources at the Agency, and they want us out of this. They say Holly's abduction is an internal matter and that we—"

Hunter interrupted. "An internal matter? What the hell does that mean? Are we supposed to let some rogue officer abduct and manhandle Holly while the Agency tries to pull its head out of its ass?"

"Sorry, but their 'internal matter' became our problem when that bastard manipulated and kidnapped one of our friends." Darcangelo looked *truly* pissed off now.

Zach had to agree. "The marshals service won't back down."

"You don't get it." Tower shook his head, grinning. "Holly is a CIA officer."

Silence.

Zach must have misunderstood. He looked over at Dar-cangelo and Hunter, who looked at each other, the confusion on their faces a match for what he was feeling. "Holly? She's CIA?"

Corbray nodded. "She's a non-cover officer—an NCO. She's been working for the Agency since she was a freshman in college. All information on her and her job are classified top secret. The fact that they shared this with Tower proves how desperate they are to get us off this case and out of their way."

Zach didn't know whether to laugh or lose his temper at Corbray and Tower for playing some kind of perverse game here.

"You're kidding, right?" Darcangelo took the words right out of Zach's mouth.

"Nah, man." Corbray leaned back in his chair. "Hey, I had the same reaction, but this is ironclad."

"Our Holly?" Hunter looked from Corbray to Tower and back again. "CIA?"

Corbray nodded. "Our Holly."

Tower was the only man in the room who didn't look like he'd just gotten kicked in the gut. In fact, he seemed to be enjoying this. "From what I've been able to piece together, her job is to carry out certain covert operations that can only be undertaken in up-close and intimate situations. She was probably working the night Andris showed up, drugged her, and popped Dudaev."

"Are you saying she sleeps with people—for the CIA?" Hunter asked.

That would certainly explain a few things.

"If that's what an operation requires, yes," Tower said. "Her job is to get close to men who pose a threat to national security—men like Dudaev that no one else can get close to. She was charged with recovering stolen Agency files from him that night. I have no idea whether she succeeded or whether Andris got there first. My sources believe Andris targeted Holly because he saw her there and figured out she was an Agency officer. They think he may be forcing her to help him."

But Zach was remembering the day he'd gone to Holly's

place to update her on Dudaev's murder. She'd seemed afraid, confused, innocent—and, well, kind of adorably dumb. But that must have been an act.

Tower glanced around the room at them. "Oh, come on, guys. Don't tell me your feelings are hurt. Yeah, I know she kept you all in the dark, but what was she supposed to do— pull you aside at a barbecue and say, 'Hey, by the way, I'm a CIA officer'? I'm not into helpless, dumb women, so, frankly, I feel relieved—and more than a little impressed."

For a moment, no one spoke.

Darcangelo cleared his throat. "It's a little different for those of us who've known her for a long time—or thought we knew her."

"I hear you, man," Corbray said.

Hunter rubbed the stubble on his chin. "I still can't quite believe it."

Zach found himself wanting a drink. "So what's the bottom line?"

"As far as we can tell, this internal investigation is tearing the Agency apart," Tower said. "It's devolving into a civil war inside the Special Activities Division, and thanks to this bastard, Andris, Holly has been dragged into the middle of it. Word is, Dudaev's goons were in Nederland because someone in the Agency told them where to find Holly. Someone wants to eliminate both of them."

"No way. No fucking way." Zach wasn't sure he gave a damn about Andris, but no one was going to get another chance at Holly—not on his watch. "So what's our plan? I don't care what Holly does for a living. I won't abandon her."

"No question. We stick with her," Corbray said. "At least we know now that she has some training and skills to help her stay alive."

CHAPTER 20

Nick watched as Holly reached for a piece of ice, her bare breasts swaying tantalizingly close to his mouth, her silky thighs straddling his hips. She ran the ice cube slowly down the side of his throat, tracing the line of his carotid, then moved it over his clavicle and down his chest to his right nipple. Her lips followed the trail of moisture left on his skin, the heat of her mouth a contrast to the cold as she nuzzled him beneath his ear, nipped his throat, flicked his nipple with her tongue.

A jolt of pleasure shot through him and he felt his nipple harden. "If this is your idea of cooling me off, I got to say I don't think it's going to work."

She smiled and reached for another piece of ice.

She touched the ice to his skin, a rivulet of water tickling his chest as she moved it to his left nipple, which she lavished with the same attention she'd given the other, kissing it, licking it, making it hard.

Another jolt of pleasure.

He hadn't thought of his nipples as being sensitive—but then he'd never had a woman do this to him before. Just watching her, seeing her naked body above his, her pink tongue on his skin, turned him on. He reached down, cupped one of her breasts, toyed with the sensitive tip.

"Uh-uh. Naughty boy." She shook her head. "This time is just for you, remember?"

Oh, he remembered all right. She had promised him the best blow job of his life if he would drive into town and get her a pint of strawberry ice cream. He knew that reading her parents' comments in the newspaper had left her feeling down, and since they were low on propane anyway . . .

He gave her breast a little squeeze. "Oh, honey, this *is* for me."

She looked at him through those big brown eyes, an expression of blatant female lust on her face, and reached for another piece of ice.

He watched as she trailed the ice cube down his sternum and over his abs to the sensitive skin below his obliques. His abs jerked, the ice and rivulets of melting water tickling his skin. Again, she followed the trail of moisture with kisses, licking his obliques, nipping the skin near his groin, making his abs tense again.

His cock, already hard, stood there, waiting for her attention.

She ignored it, moving to his inner thighs, teasing and kissing his skin until the ice had melted.

He understood now. She wanted to torture him.

"I think you missed something."

"This little thing?" She took his cock in her cold hand, stroked it.

He might have protested her use of the word "little" if his breath hadn't caught in his throat at the sheer pleasure of her touch.

She reached for another piece of ice, traced it along the underside of his cock, moving it in a circle beneath the rim then over the head, making the muscles of his ass contract and his balls draw tight.

He squeezed his eyes shut. "You know, cold doesn't do a lot for a man."

"What if it's followed by heat?" She took just the head of his cock into the warmth of her mouth, swirled it with her tongue.

"Holy hell." He opened his eyes, watched as she played with him, drawing his foreskin up over the head, licking him through that thick layer of skin, running her tongue beneath it, sucking on the ultrasensitive tip.

She was driving him crazy, the stimulation arousing as hell, making him ache for her. Just when he thought he couldn't stand all this damnable teasing any longer, she drew his foreskin back—and took him into her mouth.

He slid one hand into her silky hair, watching as she began to move her mouth up and down the full length of him. She was beautiful, so damned beautiful, the sight of her devouring him beyond erotic. *"Holly."*

God, it was good, and it just kept getting better and better. The wet heat of her mouth. The slick friction of her tongue. The tight pressure of her lips. Sensation overwhelmed him, driving him to the edge, the first hint of orgasm coiling inside him. He willed his body to relax, wanting to savor it, but then she went faster and increased the pressure, using her hand and mouth in tandem, stroking and licking him from the aching head to the base.

Ah, God, it was perfect. *She* was perfect.

He wanted more, needed more of this, more of *her*. Both of his hands were in her hair now, his fingers curling through the silken strands. He heard himself whisper her name, not once, but again and again.

Climax blasted through him, driving the breath from his lungs, his release intense and hot as she finished him with her mouth.

For a moment, he lay there, fighting to come down from whatever heaven she'd sent him to, his heart pounding. When he opened his eyes again, he found her watching him, a knowing smile on her face. Her lips were wet and swollen, her gaze soft. He smoothed the hair back from her face, felt an ache in his chest, tenderness for her stirring behind his breastbone.

He ran a knuckle down her cheek. "You sure know how to keep a promise."

She stretched out beside him, rested her head on his chest, and for a few minutes they lay there together in the dark, the fan blowing cool night air over them both.

Holly raised her head. "Do you hear that?"

Nick didn't hear anything. "Hear what?"

"It's a beeping sound." She got to her feet.

And then he heard it, too.

He jumped up. "It's one of the computers."

Still naked, they ran downstairs into the basement.

Nick sat, tapped the keyboard of the computer that was beeping to awaken the display. "It's about damned time."

"We cracked the password?" Holly let out a cheer, then looked over his shoulder. "What was it?"

"A variation on the name of his yacht combined with his birth date." Nick grinned, a feeling of warmth in his chest. "You are amazing."

Damned if she didn't blush.

And Nick wondered how often in her life Holly had been praised for something besides her appearance—or her skill in bed.

But her gaze was on the computer screen. "Now the real work begins."

NOT BOTHERING TO turn on the light, Holly grabbed one of her sundresses and a pair of jeans for Nick and hurried back down to the basement, pulling the dress over her head while he stepped into the jeans and zipped them.

He sat down again.

Holly pulled up a chair, excitement making her pulse skip. "I can't remember the last time I've had more fun."

Nick raised an eyebrow. "You need to work on your definition of fun."

Holly read over the folders on Dudaev's desktop and felt some of her enthusiasm slip away. "Most of this is in Georgian. I won't be much use to you, I'm afraid."

She saw an icon resembling a separate disc drive that bore the label of a popular brand of flash drives—SanDisk. "Those must be the Agency files from the USB drive."

"Right." He knew that.

She pointed to another. "That must be the key. Nice of him to keep it where we can find it."

Nick handed her the box of nitrile gloves. "Put these on before you accidentally touch something."

"Good idea." She slipped a pair of gloves onto her hands, watching as he opened the key and entered it at the prompt.

What appeared on the screen at first made no sense to her,

despite the fact that it was in English. "What are we looking at?"

"Oh, I'd say twenty-five to life."

"That's *not* funny." Okay, so it *was* funny, but there was a chance it was also true, especially in his case. "Is this all from the internal investigation?"

"I think so." He moved the cursor over the long list of files. "There's a folder with personnel files for everyone involved in the operation that night. The rest look like inter-agency memos, reports, and photos."

He opened one of the folders and clicked on a file. A document that was labeled "Top Secret" opened on the screen. Written on Agency letterhead, it appeared to be the official report about the operation in Batumi dated two years ago.

He clicked on another. It was a forensic report about the death of an officer named Robert Carver, complete with photos of his dead body and the crime scene.

Holly willed herself not to look away. "You know what we need now?"

"A printer," he said.

"And some way to organize all this stuff—folders, markers, labels."

It was after midnight, so there was no way to get supplies now.

Nick looked over at her. "You should get some sleep. I'll run into town to get what we need tomorrow morning first thing."

"Are you kidding? I couldn't sleep now." Holly glanced at the other CPUs. "Why don't you copy the Agency files to another computer? I can look through those while you look through Dudaev's emails. That way we can make faster progress."

He frowned, and she could tell something about that idea didn't appeal to him. "I'm not sure you'll understand what you're reading. All the people, the places, the events—you've only gotten an overview."

Didn't he trust her? Did he think she couldn't understand? The thought left her feeling more than a little irritated—and defensive. "I'm smarter than I look."

"I know you're smart." He turned toward her, reached

over, pulled her into his arms. "Okay, let's do it your way. I'm right here if you have questions. I wouldn't have come this far without you, Holly. Thank you."

And just like that her irritation was gone, replaced by a feeling of warmth.

She drew back. "I'm going to make coffee."

"Good idea."

HOLLY WAS GLAD that Nick had given her an account of what had happened on that terrible night in Batumi. Without that overview, it would have taken her much longer to make sense of what she was reading. But by three in the morning, she was too bleary-eyed to keep going.

She got up, kissed Nick on the cheek. "Goodnight."

He came to bed a short time later, his movements rousing her from sleep.

She reached for his hand in the dark.

"I didn't mean to wake you." He drew her into his arms.

She snuggled against him, resting her head on his chest. "That's okay."

He stared up at the ceiling, his body tense, his fingers trailing caresses down her bare arm. "What if we don't find anything? What if all of this gets us nowhere?"

Holly didn't even want to consider that possibility. "We can always turn to my CO. I know he would do everything he could to make certain you—"

"No. I don't trust anyone at the Agency right now with one exception—you." He kissed her hair.

"We could surrender to Zach and the US Marshals Service. I trust him with my life, and the marshals service is good at making people disappear."

"I'm guessing McBride would like to put a bullet in my brain right about now. Besides, I wouldn't qualify for WITSEC."

No, he probably wouldn't—unless he had evidence that could be used to convict Bauer in court. That's why it was so crucial to find something in these files to prove that Bauer, not Nick, had sold out the Agency in Batumi.

She pushed herself up, looked down at him. "It's going to be okay."

"What makes you so certain?" He tucked a strand of hair behind her ear.

"It just has to be. That's why." She kissed him.

They slept in each other's arms. By seven, they were both awake again. Holly made breakfast—scrambled eggs, toast, and some atomic-strength coffee—while Nick showered. Then she wrote a list of everything she thought they'd need to organize the thousands of pages of documents they would be sorting through.

Nick left just before nine, list in hand.

"Don't forget to get extra toner cartridges for the printer," she called after him.

"Yes, dear," he called back.

He stopped, looked down at the grass, a frown on his face. "Snakes?"

"Our driving over the grass has left tracks." He pointed. "Not good. One of the farmers around here might see this and report it to police."

The high grass was flattened where tires had driven over it repeatedly. She hadn't noticed it, but he was right. It wasn't good. "Should we mow it?"

He grinned. "Got a mower? Have you seen the size of this lawn? And who is this 'we' of whom you speak, because we both know it would end up being me."

After he drove off, Holly took a shower and then put together a spreadsheet that would enable them to organize the documents by metadata. By the time Nick had returned, the spreadsheet was completed and installed on both of their computers.

She explained it to him while he set up the printer. "For every document, list the date it was created, who it was from, who it was intended for, and any people, places, or events mentioned in the body of the document. That way we can cross-reference by any of those criteria. We'll keep one spreadsheet for the Agency files, and one for the Georgian files—but in English, please."

"I'm impressed." Nick started the printer. "Officer Bradshaw, you are hot shit."

She couldn't help but smile. "Actually, it was the journalist part of me that came up with this."

He grinned. "You're double trouble."

"And don't you forget it."

THEY WORKED IN silence through the morning and into the afternoon, Nick sorting through Dudaev's email and printing whatever might be relevant. Most of it was worthless. An email to his goons about their improving their English. Another wishing a cousin back in Georgia a happy birthday. Yet another asking one of his goons to set him up for a manicure, pedicure, and eyebrow waxing.

Nick had no idea the bastard had been such a metrosexual, and he pitied the esthetician who'd had to put her hands on him.

Some of it, however, was clearly related to his criminal activities. There were emails written in poor English about his good friend, Shavi, who would be arriving in town soon. Those were drug shipments, *shavi* meaning "black"—a Georgian slang term for heroin. There were also emails discussing how to find work for his poor nieces from the country—no doubt code for prostitution. These messages would all have to make their way to DEA and ICE.

He clicked on the next message—and felt his teeth grind. There on the screen were images of Holly. She'd been photographed, clearly without her knowledge, on her way to and from work, out at a club, and even in her home. There were several grainy images of her getting dressed in her bedroom, her breasts bare.

Nick looked at the date and guessed that Dudaev had sent someone to scope her out the moment she'd called about an interview. And clearly the son of a bitch had liked what he'd seen. He found five other emails like that one—all containing photos of Holly in her life before all of this began, her life before him.

His mood now sour, he printed them, then went to stand by the printer, hoping to retrieve them before she could see them. It was an absurd impulse. The photos wouldn't upset her. She knew the kind of man Dudaev had been.

But they might remind her of what you did, Andris.

As he waited for the pages to print, he found himself

watching her. She was reading something, nibbling on the end of her pen, her brow furrowed in concentration. She glanced up, smiled at him—and he felt a hitch in his chest.

Oh, no. He was not going there. He did *not* have feelings for her. Yes, he cared about her. She was a good officer—smart, resourceful, skilled. She'd been a great help to him. And if she was also beautiful, made him laugh, blew his mind in bed, and was pretty much the total package, that didn't mean he had to fall in love with her.

He didn't have time for that now. *She* didn't have time for that now. Besides, the last thing he wanted to do was get involved with another officer. If he fell in love again, it would be with a schoolteacher or a librarian or a nurse.

He picked up the pages, held them out for her. "You might want to see these."

She took them from him, glanced through them. "I guess I should close my bedroom curtains."

"That's all you have to say?" How could she be so calm about it when Nick wanted to resurrect Dudaev so he could kill him again?

"Believe it or not, I get spied on a lot. Weird, I know." She glanced up at him, a hint of a smile on her lips.

Feeling itchy and angry—maybe he'd had too much caffeine—he went back to scanning emails. He'd been reading for another hour or so when he found a subfolder that held emails written in English and dating back six months or so. He glanced over the first message and began filling in the spreadsheet with the metadata. He must have been distracted because it took him a moment or two to realize what he was reading.

He stopped filling in the spreadsheet and stared at the screen.

What the hell?

He went to the first email and quickly read all of the messages in order from the first to last, almost unable to believe what he was seeing. But there it was.

"You're not going to believe this," he said, hitting "Print."

Holly looked up. "Believe what?"

He stood, walked over to the printer. "It looks like Dudaev was trying to broker a deal with the Agency."

"What?" She gaped at him.

"He contacted the Director's office and offered to tell them everything he knew about the operation in Batumi, including who had leaked the intel about the arms transfer. They were interested, of course."

"Of course."

"Some of the conversation must have happened via an intermediary and over the phone, because it's not all here. There are time gaps and references to meetings." He retrieved the pages, handed them to Holly. "They made some kind of agreement. I think that's why he came to the US."

"Really?" She glanced down at the pages then up at him again. "I guess that explains why he wasn't stopped at the border."

"He decided the Agency was playing him, just trying to get information from him without having to deliver on their end."

"I'm sure he was right. He killed Dani—an Agency officer. There's no way they would honor an agreement with someone like him."

"He got angry, stole the USB drive, and killed the officer who was acting as his intermediary." Nick pointed at the documents in Holly's hands. "You weren't sent in just to retrieve stolen files. You were sent in to *steal* files Dudaev refused to deliver."

CHAPTER 21

HOLLY SPENT THE afternoon and evening reading through the emails Nick had found, matching them with documents from the Agency files Dudaev had stolen, the string of communications and intra-agency memos giving her a picture from both Dudaev's and the Agency's side of how things had come together.

She set the pages in chronological order on the other workbench, Nick walking along beside her, looking over her shoulder.

"He contacted them in January, offering to expose the officer who betrayed you all that night in Batumi. They considered detaining and interrogating him but decided they'd learn more about his network and any connections he had within the Agency if they played along. It looks like they had him under surveillance for a while, but his men found the listening devices and removed them. He felt betrayed. He accused his case officer of lying and killed him."

"That's rich—a murdering, thieving son of a bitch like Dudaev accusing anyone of playing dirty."

Holly checked the urge to turn over the crime scene photos from that officer's murder, not wanting to seem like a wimp. The poor man had been shot and then burned alive, the cruelty of it and the gruesomeness of the photos turning her stomach.

And to think she'd been alone with the monster who'd done this.

Averting her gaze, she went on. "It looks like the Agency had already planned to hook me up with him to re-establish surveillance, but after he killed his CO, they added retrieving the USB and taking his laptop to my assignment. And look at this."

She handed Nick another stack of papers. "They had an arrest warrant for him and several of his men. They planned to detain and question him."

It was further proof that Nick's termination of Dudaev couldn't have been authorized.

Nick looked through the documents. "Meanwhile, Bauer already had him under surveillance. He must have known all of this. He sent me to eliminate Dudaev and take the files and his laptop before anyone else from the Agency could get a hold of them. I'm guessing he wanted me to eliminate you to stop you from getting the information first."

"That's as good an explanation as any."

Nick tossed the pages on to the workbench, cold anger on his face. "Bauer used me. The son of a bitch. He knew about Dani and me. He knew I wouldn't hesitate to kill the bastard— or to take you down if I thought you were colluding with Dudaev."

"He was wrong about that last part."

"Was he?" Doubt clouded Nick's eyes. "I didn't kill you that night because I thought you were nothing more than a shallow blonde who wanted to land a wealthy man. If I had believed you were working for Dudaev . . ."

Holly made a mental note to knee Bauer in the balls if she met him face-to-face again. "Bauer is your CO. You trusted him. How could you have guessed his true motivations? It's even hard for *me* to believe he's capable of anything like this, and I don't work for him."

But Nick didn't seem to want her reassurance. "I made the perfect patsy."

"They can't pin this on you if they can't tie you to the murder scene. You're not an amateur. You didn't leave a trace of evidence in the room. As long as they don't find the Ruger with your prints or in your possession, how can they prove it was you? The way I see it, the only thing they can pin on you absolutely is my abduction."

"I suppose you're right." A look of realization came over his face, and he shook his head. *"Fuck!"*

"What is it?"

"I spoke to Dudaev. Before I killed him, I spoke to him. In Georgian. The audio feed would have picked it all up."

This was *not* good.

"What did you say?"

Nick closed his eyes. "Oh, nothing much. Just something like, 'Remember that night in Batumi? I'm here to even the score.' I called him a son of a whore. I saw his Makarov lying on the floor. I asked him if he wanted it, then picked it up and told him it was mine. Then I said Kramer's name and Dani's, and I pulled the trigger."

Holly's heart sank. "I take it back. You're screwed. You gave away your identity and handed them a motive *and* evidence of premeditation."

She could only imagine what he'd felt as he'd spoken those words, two years of grief over Dani's murder culminating in a single, sharp moment of justice. But she also knew how his words would sound to investigators.

Nick stared into space, a muscle tensing in his jaw. "I was a fucking idiot."

"That wasn't your best move."

An understatement.

Holly got up from her chair, walked over to him. "Stop beating yourself up. I'm sure Bauer has some plan to tie you to Dudaev's death without the audio feed."

Nick reached out, caught her hand, his fingers warm. "I don't regret killing him. I'm sorry my actions led to this mess, but I don't regret killing that bastard, if for no other reason than he never had a chance to hurt you. If I go to prison for that, well, that's all right by me. The man was a fucking murderer. But when I think how close I came to killing you—"

"Don't feel guilty for things you didn't do." She kissed his forehead. "We've done enough today. Let's go to bed."

Holly brushed her teeth and went to bed, not bothering with pajamas. It was so hot, the air strangely muggy for Colorado. Besides, Nick would only have to take them off anyway. He joined her a few minutes later, turning to her in the dark, taking her into his arms, and loving her slowly, the two of them falling asleep in each other's arms.

Holly couldn't say how long she'd been asleep when she realized she couldn't move. Her body was strangely heavy, her limbs sluggish. She opened her eyes, turned her head—and felt her blood turn cold.

Dudaev.

He was dead. Blood. Brains. Two bullet holes in his forehead.

Oh, my God!

There was blood on the bed, blood on her skin, and brains like curds of cottage cheese on the sheets.

She had to get off the bed, had to get away from him, but she couldn't move. She couldn't seem to scream, either, her heart tripping in her chest, horror washing through her in an icy wave. She fought hard, summoned all her strength—and screamed.

"Holly, honey, wake up!"

She opened her eyes, and Nick's face swam into view.

NICK HELD HOLLY close, stroked her hair. "It's okay. You're safe. I've got you."

She clung to him, her heart beating so hard he could feel it. "Wh-what . . . ?"

"It was just a bad dream."

Tears slid down her cheeks, her body beginning to tremble. "It seemed so real."

"They always do." He kissed her hair. "Do you want to talk about it?"

For a moment, he thought she would say no, but then the words began to spill out of her. "It was that morning all over again. I woke up covered in his blood, and he was lying there dead, blood and bits of his brains on the sheets. I tried to get out of the bed, to get away from him, but I couldn't move. I couldn't even scream."

"That sounds pretty terrifying."

She sat up. "I'm sorry I woke you. It was just a stupid dream."

Nick sat, too. He reached up, wiped the tears from her cheeks. "Hey, no worries. Besides, I think that nightmare was probably my fault. I shouldn't have let you see those crime-scene photos."

She frowned. "I'm not a wimp."

"I didn't say you were. You've been through a lot in the past few weeks. You wouldn't be human if you weren't showing some sign of trauma."

"Trauma?" She shook her head. "I am *not* a trauma victim."

"How many dead bodies have you seen?"

She looked away. "Not counting TV and the crime-scene and autopsy photos downstairs? Only the one. How about you?"

Nick wasn't certain that poking around in his mind would help her. She didn't need to know what he'd seen. He searched for an answer. "I don't know. I quit counting a long time ago. I've killed people, Holly."

"Have you ever had a nightmare like that?"

Just admit it, Andris.

"I still have nightmares about Dani's death. They feel real. When I wake up, it's like I just lost her again."

"That must be so hard." Her voice was soft with empathy.

"Yeah. It is." But this wasn't about him. "I don't think anyone could have gone through what you've been through without being traumatized on some level."

"I'm not just anyone. I'm a trained Agency officer."

"Yeah, but you weren't trained for this. Even Special Forces guys sometimes get pushed too far."

She flopped backward onto her air mattress. "My life sure has changed since I met you, Nick Andris, and not for the better."

He stretched out beside her, took her hand, kissed it. "We sure got off to one hell of a bad start, didn't we?"

She gave a little laugh, sniffed. "Yeah, we did."

For a moment, there was nothing but the whirring of the fan.

Her smile faded. "You must think I'm pathetic—just some weak chick."

"Where the hell did that come from?"

Her father, Nick realized.

That's how he'd treated her.

"I . . . I don't know. I . . . I just . . ." She looked away.

Nick had never seen her at such a loss for words.

"No, Holly, that's not at all what I think about you." He cupped her cheek, turned her face toward his, forcing her to meet his gaze. "Want to know what I think? I think you're incredibly strong. I think you're one of the smartest people I've ever met—male or female. I think you're one hell of an officer."

"Really?" There was a vulnerability in her eyes he'd never seen before.

"Really." He felt an impulse to kiss her, but squelched it. "Your father might not have appreciated you for who you are, but the rest of the world isn't as blind as he is."

"I don't know. Most men don't seem—"

Then he did kiss her—a soft brush of his lips over hers. "I'm not most men."

She gave him a shaky smile. "No, you're not. Thank God."

Her brow bent in a frown and she turned her face away from him again.

"I was telling the truth when I said my father never touched me. He wanted to. I could feel it. He would drink too much and say things." Her voice dropped an octave, imitating a man's. "'You are a hot piece of ass, baby girl. I bet there isn't a man on base who doesn't want to fuck you.' Or, 'You've got a mouth meant for sucking cock. That's what your husband is going to want, you know.' Or, 'One day those perfect tits of yours are going to make some man mighty happy.'"

Her voice quavered on those last words, dissolving into tears.

Nick had known something like this must have happened. He'd thrown it in her face when he'd interrogated her and had known he'd hit a sore spot. It bothered him to know that he'd dug this up. *He* had opened this wound inside her. "I'm sorry, Holly. No man should talk that way to a woman, let alone a child—his own daughter."

He found himself wanting to beat the shit out of the bastard.

What kind of sick son of a bitch openly lusted after his own child?

"My mother got angry—at *me*. She was jealous. I think that's why she had an affair—to try to prove to him how desirable she was."

That was every bit as disgusting as what her father had done.

"I'm sorry." *You sound like a broken record, Andris. Say something helpful.* "She ought to have protected you, put you first."

"It doesn't matter now. They're not really a part of my life." She turned her face toward him again, and he could see fresh tears on her cheeks. "You were right about me, though not in the way you think. I love my job in part because I get to bring down men who view women as nothing but mindless sexual toys—men like my father."

Not knowing what to say, Nick drew her into his arms and held her.

HOLLY STOOD IN the kitchen sipping a cup of coffee, a cool morning breeze blowing through the open doors and windows, fresh air and caffeine helping to smooth the rough edges off her emotions. She hadn't meant to dump her baggage at Nick's feet last night. She'd never told anyone about her father. Now she felt raw, exposed.

She'd lived so much of her life in boxes, moving from place to place as a child, taking out different personalities for different jobs as an officer, packing away her feelings as a woman and sealing them off until she had time to face them. Now it seemed all those boxes had come open, their contents strewn about for Nick to see. She just didn't know how to put it all away again.

It doesn't matter how you feel. All that matters today is what you do.

She'd put a pot of water on the hot plate to boil for instant oatmeal—they were out of eggs and yogurt—when she heard the crunch of tires on gravel. There were still operational farms nearby, so it wasn't unusual for diesel trucks and farm vehicles to pass by the house during the day. But Holly couldn't hear the engine, so this couldn't be a truck. More than that, she could tell it was moving slowly.

She glanced upstairs, where Nick had just gotten into the shower, then hurried over to the window and peeked outside, careful not to be seen.

Fan-freaking-tastic!

She drew back from the window, her pulse racing.

A blue-and-white SUV with the words "Ríos County Sheriff" painted on its side had pulled to a stop in the road across from the driveway. The officer had probably spotted the tire tracks the minivan had made through the high grass just like Nick had feared.

She set her coffee down and ran upstairs, not bothering to knock before she opened the bathroom door. "We've got company—the county sheriff."

"Fuck! Stick to the story. I'll be right down."

But Holly was already in the bedroom. Hoping to keep the officer's gaze off her face, she slipped into a short denim skirt and pink belly shirt, then grabbed the baseball cap out of Nick's gear bag and tucked her hair beneath it. Then she went back downstairs, willing her adrenaline to settle. An experienced law enforcement officer would be able to spot signs of fear.

She walked quietly up to the window, hoping he'd gone on his way, only to find that he had pulled into the driveway. He got out of the SUV, spoke into his hand mic, then turned toward the barn—and spotted the minivan.

There was no way out of this now.

The officer—a tall, muscular man with a handsome weathered face and a thick head of hair that must have once been red—walked to the back of the vehicle and spoke into his mic again, almost certainly calling in the number on the temporary plates.

Holly figured it was now or never. She picked up her coffee and stepped out the back door—and into the skin of Elise Bradley from Elizabethtown, Kentucky. "Good morning, officer. Can I help you, sir?"

If he was startled, he hid it well. "Good morning, ma'am. I was just driving by the property and noticed the tire tracks. Does this vehicle belong to you?"

"Yes, it does, sir. Well, it belongs to my fiancé. It's ours."

"I see. Excuse me." Someone spoke to him over his ear-piece, probably reporting back to clear the plates. He replied, speaking into his mic once more, then moved toward the porch, stopping at the bottom of the stairs, keeping a reactionary gap between the two of them and staying out of the line of fire from the doorway. "What's your name?"

"Elise. Elise Bradley."

"Can I ask what you're doing here, Ms. Bradley?"

"Josh and I needed a place to stay, and we found this place deserted." She hadn't heard a Kentucky drawl for years but it came back to her quickly. "We didn't hurt anything. We cleaned the place up real nice."

Okay, this was kind of fun—in an absolutely-nothing-can-go-wrong sort of way.

"Do you have an ID I can see?" His gaze was on hers, not her boobs or her belly.

"I do, sir. It's inside. Should I get it?"

"Yes, please." He was polite, but there was steel in his voice.

He meant business.

"Do you want to come in and have a cup of coffee?" She knew she was taking a risk inviting him in. If he searched the basement, he'd find the computers and a stack of documents labeled "Top Secret," and then they would be in deep trouble.

"Is your fiancé inside?" The man was smart, clearly trying to assess the danger that Nick, aka Josh, might pose. He didn't want to walk through the door and get assaulted or shot.

"He's in the shower, sir." She peered at his badge. "Deputy Davidson?"

"Sheriff Davidson."

"Come inside, Sheriff Davidson. Josh will be down in a minute."

The sheriff followed her inside.

CHAPTER 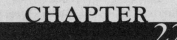22

"WE DON'T HAVE much—just some kitchen stuff we got from the secondhand store and our clothes upstairs in the bedroom." Holly poured the sheriff a cup of coffee. "Josh got the water system fixed up all by himself. He got the generator working, too."

"I noticed that."

"Do you take sugar or milk?"

"Oh, no thanks. No coffee for me."

She set the cup on the counter, grabbed her fugly denim handbag, and retrieved her false ID from her wallet. "Here you go, sir."

"Thank you." He scrutinized it but didn't hand it back.

"Good morning, sir." Nick appeared at the bottom of the stairs, wearing a pair of jeans and a T-shirt, his hair wet, his face unshaven.

It was about damned time!

He held out his hand, speaking with a Midwestern accent. "Josh Young. I know we're not supposed to be here, sir, but I'm between jobs right now, and we needed a place to stay. We haven't done anything to wreck the place."

"Have you got an ID?"

Nick reached into his pocket, handed the sheriff his fake driver's license.

"So you're from Kentucky, Ms. Bradley?"

"Yes, sir."

"Nice country there. Is that where you grew up?"

"Elizabethtown." Holly's father had been stationed in Kentucky for all of three months—long enough for her to know something about the area.

"I've got family on my mother's side from Kentucky." There was a smile on his face and his voice was friendly, but Holly wasn't fooled. This wasn't casual conversation. He was testing her. "Where did you go to school—North Hardin High?"

North Hardin High was in Radcliff.

"I went to Elizabethtown High." She raised invisible pom-poms. "Go Panthers!"

He smiled, looked down at Nick's ID. "So how did a fellow from Illinois meet up with a young lady from Kentucky?"

Nick explained what they'd rehearsed, telling the sheriff how he'd been between jobs and had met her when she'd been working tables at a diner. "It took me a couple of weeks to get up the nerve to ask her out."

He smiled at Holly, his gaze warm. She smiled back, tilting her head away, playing shy. They were just a happy couple reminiscing on their romance.

"What brought you two to Colorado?"

"I'm looking for work," Nick answered. "We thought Colorado sounded nice."

"How long have you been here?" Sheriff Davidson glanced around.

Holly looked over at Nick, counting on her fingers. "Almost two weeks. I got stung by some yellow jackets that had moved in upstairs, stung real bad, but Josh got rid of them. We're trying to take good care of the place, seeing that it isn't really ours. You could say it's our way of paying rent, I guess."

"I saw a child's car seat in the minivan. Is there a child here with you?"

Holly looked at Nick, her pulse skipping. They hadn't anticipated this and hadn't rehearsed an answer. "Well . . ."

NICK SAW THE spark of panic in Holly's eyes. He hadn't thought about the damned car seat when they'd crafted this scenario. There was only one way to handle it.

He walked up to stand behind her, slid his hand over her

lower belly. "The baby is right here—right where I planted it. We saw the car seat, and she had to have it."

He looked down, saw an adorable flush in Holly's cheeks. Either he'd embarrassed her, or she was pissed. He'd bet it was the latter.

"So you're pregnant, Ms. Bradley?"

"Yes, sir." She slid her hand over Nick's. "I'm almost three months along. We want to get married before the baby comes so it'll have Josh's name and all, but Josh needs work first."

"What kind of work do you do, Mr. Young?"

Nick shrugged. "A little of this and that—I'm a good mechanic—cars, boats, machinery. I can also do construction."

"If you'll give me a moment." Still holding their IDs, he walked outside and down the porch stairs, speaking into his mic.

Holly whirled on Nick, glared at him, but he could see the smile tugging at her lips. "You didn't tell me Josh was such a macho redneck. 'The baby is right here—right where I planted it.' Good grief!"

"You never told me how sexy you are as Daisy Duke. That accent turns me on." Nick kissed her on the nose, poured himself some coffee, lowered his voice to a whisper. "We need to go the minute he rolls out of here. I'll pack the computers. You handle the stuff upstairs. We'll have to steal some plates or a car, now that he's got the temp plate number for the minivan. It's only a matter of time before the BOLO on us catches his attention and he puts the pieces together."

"Okay. Sure. But can our next lair include air conditioning at least? Fewer yellow jackets, spiders, and snakes would be good, too."

They heard footfalls on the porch stairs. The screen door opened, and the sheriff stepped back inside.

He held out their IDs. "I understand that you're down on your luck at the moment. The family who lived here before you—good people—got down on their luck, too. They had farmed this land for three generations before a run of bad years forced them out. It's a real shame what happened to them."

"I'm sorry to hear that," Nick said.

"I'm real sorry," Holly echoed.

"If the bank wouldn't let them stay here, a family who'd been living on this land for a century, they certainly won't want you here. By law, you're trespassers, and I could have you arrested and removed."

"Arrested?" Holly edged closer to Nick, looked up at him with worry in her eyes.

He felt an answering tug of protectiveness.

Damn, she was convincing.

He wrapped his arm around her waist.

The sheriff held up his hand. "I'm not going to arrest you. I can understand how a young couple starting out might find themselves in need of a place to stay for a few days. There aren't any shelters for couples here, especially unmarried couples. There is a shelter in La Junta that would take you in, Ms. Bradley, given your condition."

"I want to be with Josh."

"In that case, your best hope is to head to Colorado Springs. There are some churches there that might be able to help you find work and get settled." He handed them a couple of business cards. "You can give these good folks a call when you get there. They ought to be able to set you up for a night and help you get started."

"Thank you, sir." Nick took the cards from him.

"If you need to stay a couple more nights, well, I understand. But be out of here by the next time I drive by on patrol."

"Yes, sir. Thank you, sir." Nick shook his hand.

Holly did the same. "Thank you, sir."

"I appreciate your understanding, sir." Nick walked the sheriff to the door, his gaze on the road beyond, searching for any sign that the man had recognized them and called for backup.

"Good luck with that baby." The sheriff's gaze warmed when it landed on Holly.

Holly smiled back, her hands pressed to her belly. "Thank you."

Nick watched as the sheriff climbed into his patrol vehicle, backed out of the driveway, and headed down the road. "He's gone. Let's go."

* * *

It was almost midnight when they rolled into the parking lot of the Big Chief Motel off Highway 50 north of Pueblo. The place looked like it hadn't been maintained in some time, grass and weeds growing up through the asphalt in the parking lot, the white lines that delineated parking spaces all but gone, the neon sign out front blinking "V can y" in hot pink.

Holly looked out the window of the minivan, feeling hopeful at the sight of the AC units in the windows. "Maybe it's nicer on the inside than it is on the outside."

Nick parked at a distance from the entrance. He was trying to avoid security cameras, Holly knew, though she seriously doubted this place had any. "Stay here. I'll be right back."

"Make sure to ask if they've had problems with bed bugs."

Nick shot her a look, then closed the door and strode off toward the entrance.

Holly rolled down the window, the buzzing of the hotel's neon lights like some kind of creepy soundtrack. How surreal this all seemed.

They'd left the farmhouse ten minutes after the sheriff had driven away, packing everything into the back of the minivan. Then they'd taken back roads toward Colorado Springs. Nick had stolen license plates off a car that was sitting in long-term parking at the airport. After that, they'd driven southeast, putting distance between themselves and the city, trying to stick with roads that didn't have traffic cameras. Now they needed a place to stay, a no-tell motel that would take cash.

Holly watched the hotel entrance, her gaze drawn to the highway every time a pair of headlights appeared. The sheriff had spent enough time with them to form a solid mental image of their faces. The moment he spotted a BOLO about them, he'd call in, and then federal agents would descend on this corner of the state—CIA officers, the marshals service, FBI. It was only a matter of time.

She pulled down the sun visor, turned on the lighted vanity mirror, and did her best to tame her hair, aware as she did it that she was only trying to soothe herself. The encounter with the sheriff had reminded her how much was at stake—and how quickly this could all come crashing down on them. They needed to find something on Dudacv's computer that would prove Bauer's guilt so Nick could negotiate his surrender and put Bauer behind bars.

And then . . .

She would be safe to return to her life, while Nick went to Langley to try to set things straight with the Agency. They would say good-bye and move on.

Why should that thought leave her feeling so desolate? They'd never talked about being together, never made any promises. They hadn't even had The Talk, the one where two people try to DTR—Define the Relationship. Did they even have a relationship? Or was this just about sex like it had been with every other man she'd known?

No. No, it wasn't just sex. Nick meant more to her than that.

He made her laugh. He made her feel appreciated. He understood her in a way no one else did, not even her friends.

Quit being ridiculous, Bradshaw.

He understood her better than her friends only because he knew about her real job. She was able to be herself with him in a way she couldn't be with the others. For the first time in a very long time, she didn't have to pretend. That didn't make him special. It made him well informed.

What was wrong with her? Why was she letting her emotions get caught up in this? She and Nick weren't dating. They were trying to bring a corrupt Agency officer to justice—and save their careers and their lives. There was nothing more to it.

She ignored the lump that formed in her throat, looked out the window, tried to get Nick out of her mind, only to find he wouldn't budge.

I'm not most men.

He'd said it, and it was true. He was unlike any man she'd known.

The scary truth was she didn't want this to end. Okay, she wanted the whole run-from-the-bad-guys part to end *yesterday*. But she didn't want to say good-bye to Nick.

* * *

NICK CLIMBED INTO the vehicle. "I got us a room with a kitchenette on the ground floor. Parking is around back. The proprietor doesn't speak much English."

"That's a bonus."

He started the minivan and drove it around to the back, parking it out of view of the road. Unless someone called in the plates they would have no idea they were stolen, but it didn't hurt to be careful.

He handed her the key card. "You take your stuff and get to the room as quickly as possible. I don't want to risk anyone seeing you. I'll carry everything else in."

He grabbed his gear bag and followed her down a long hallway to Room 134.

"The carpet looks like it's made from recycled circus tents," she whispered, swiping the key card.

"Is that your assessment as an Agency officer or an entertainment reporter?"

Her lips curved into a smile. "Both."

The air inside their room was stuffy and warm and smelled of cleaning products, but it would do. There was a small bathroom with a tub and shower to their left, a little kitchen with a small refrigerator, a sink, a hot plate, and microwave to their right. Two full-sized beds took up most of the space, a small table with two chairs sitting in one corner, a television mounted on the wall.

"It looks like the 1970s died in here," she said.

He could see what she meant. Goldenrod drapes. Royal blue carpeting with yellow and red swirls. Orange-and-green-striped bedspreads.

"As long as we don't do the same." He set his gear bag down and headed back out for the rest of it.

By the time he was finished carrying in their gear and supplies, she had the AC running and the food put away. He walked over to the window and checked to make sure it would open. Other than the door, it was the only way out.

"I think I'll wait till tomorrow to set up the computers. Might as well . . ." He turned around and his heart gave a thud, whatever he'd been saying forgotten.

Holy. Hell.

Holly was on the bed on all fours, her thighs parted, the short denim skirt that had driven Nick crazy all day pulled up to reveal that she'd taken off her panties. She'd taken off her bra, too, the rounded bottoms of her breasts visible beneath the belly shirt. She smiled at him over her shoulder, wiggled her bare ass.

"Cat got your tongue?" she said in that sweet Kentucky accent.

Nick got hard so fast he was surprised he didn't split his jeans. He walked over to the bed, cupped her, then slid a finger along her cleft. "Does the cat want my tongue? Or does she want my cock?"

He unzipped himself and freed his erection to give her a visual.

She squirmed. "Can't I have both?"

"Not without some serious rearranging of my anatomy."

"Your cock. *Now.*" She forgot the accent that time, but Nick didn't care.

He got up onto his knees on the bed behind her and nudged himself slowly inside her, a sensation of pure bliss shooting from his dick to his brain. She was already wet, her slick inner muscles gripping him hard as he began to move.

"Jesus." He bent over her, reaching with one hand to tease her nipples, putting the other to work between her legs.

"Nick." Her eyes were closed, her mouth open.

He kept up the pace, willing himself to take it easy, to make this last. But the tension inside her was already rising, her breath now coming in soft little moans. God, he loved this, loved being inside her, loved being with her. Was this nothing more than the excitement of being on the run, or was this just how they were together—the need, the urgency, this constant hunger?

Her breath broke and she arched her back, her inner muscles contracting around him as she came. He stayed with her until her peak had passed. Then he grasped her hips and drove into her again and again and again until climax carried him home.

BAUER JOGGED THROUGH Langley Fork Park, one of the few places he could talk without being overheard or recorded. He slipped the earpiece in his ear and dialed the number. "It's time to flush Andris out of hiding."

"Yeah, I'll say it is. You said he'd surface, that he would make contact with the Agency. He's too smart for that, isn't he? I told you he was too smart. We haven't seen a sign of either of them, and neither have those assholes from that private security firm."

"Have you always been this impatient?" The real question, Bauer realized, was whether he'd always been this stupid. "How did you ever make it through all those years of surveillance in the Middle East?"

"I'm hanging out here with these Georgian assholes in this shitty hotel while you're cozy at home. Don't talk to me about patience. I could leave, you know. I could dump this entire thing on you, let you handle it. I could get on a plane and be home free. I got what I wanted out of this. I'm only hanging here to try to help save *your* ass."

Heat rushed into Bauer's face. "If I thought you were truly threatening me, I'd have to pay your daughter a visit. How old is she now? In her late twenties, early thirties? She got married about a year ago, didn't she?"

"Listen to me, you son of a bitch! You stay away from my kid. She doesn't even know me. She didn't even grow up with me. She's not part of this."

"She won't be a part of this unless you make her a part of this. You know what happens to those who betray me. This isn't over until Andris and Bradshaw are dead."

"Hey, I was just mouthing off. I'm bored as fuck and sick of hanging with these bastards. I just want to be done with this so I can move on."

"That's what we both want."

Bauer had devoted his life to the Agency. He'd done his best to live up to his father's expectations, to make a name for himself, to get out from beneath his father's shadow. He'd pulled off a dozen schemes—drugs, intel, guns—and he'd never been caught. Now, when he was at the peak of his career and only a handful of years away from retirement, he was on the brink of losing everything because that dick-faced son of a bitch Dudaev had gone and whispered in the director's ear.

Well, Dudaev had gotten what he'd deserved.

Bauer jogged past a group of kids playing lacrosse. "I'm going to extend an olive branch to Andris, see if I can get him to come out of his hidey-hole."

Bauer filled him in on the details of the plan and the role each of them would play. "It's important to keep Andris alive until we've got everything we need from him. Don't terminate him if Bradshaw isn't with him. If you kill him, we'll have a damned hard time finding her. Got it?"

"Yeah, though I don't know if I can control our Georgian friends. They've got their own agenda."

"You tell them that if any one of them steps out of line or fires a shot without authorization, they'll end up just like their former boss."

"Any luck decrypting that hard drive?"

"Not yet. The bastard's password could be in Georgian, Russian, English. I've got a team working on it." It wasn't Bauer's main concern. "Now that we know the USB drive contained only Agency files, it no longer matters what's on his computer. Andris at least kept Bradshaw from getting her hands on that. All we need to do to wrap this up is get rid of the two of them. The rest is just cleanup."

"What do you have against Andris?"

"I don't have anything against him." No, he didn't have anything against Nick Andris. In fact, he liked him. But he wasn't about to spend his retirement in prison. He'd brought Andris into the Agency, and now Andris would repay that favor—with his life.

He thought about that for a moment, about the fairness of it. "When you do kill him, make it quick and clean. He deserves that much. You can do whatever you want with the girl."

CHAPTER 23

SOMETHING SKITTERED PAST Holly's feet.

"There's another one." *Damned roaches.* "That's the fifth one so far."

"You're keeping count? What is it with you and bugs?" Nick laughed. "How do you know it's not the same one? I haven't seen any."

"That's because your face is buried in naked women."

She had finished going through the Agency files and was now organizing documents using the bed they hadn't slept in as her surface. Nick, on the other hand, was looking through Dudaev's porn stash.

"If you think all of these crotch shots turn me on, you're wrong. Most of these women are probably underage, and I'll bet a lot of them didn't choose this."

A sickening thought.

He cocked his head sideways. "Hell, I don't even know what I'm looking at half the time. When you get that close up on the human body . . ."

Holly went to stand beside him and bent down to look at the screen. They both leaned their heads to the left and then the right, trying to make it out.

She pointed. "That has to be his—"

"No, that must be some other guy's. Different skin tone."

"You're right."

"I'm counting two sets of nuts—there and there."

"Oh, I see now. They're both . . ." The image began to make sense, and the moment it did, Holly wished it hadn't. "Ew! Good grief! Poor woman."

Where was the eye bleach?

Holly tapped a stack of documents on the table to straighten them, then set them down on the bed. "We might make faster progress if I looked through the porn and you went back to looking through his other files. I can't read Georgian, but I can see the photos just fine."

Nick shook his head. "I don't want you seeing this garbage."

"You don't want me looking at pictures of naked women having sex?" That was very protective of him. "You know, I live with a naked woman. In fact, I see her every day. I even sleep with her. Have I mentioned that I have sex with her, too?"

"Now *that* turns me on." Nick turned toward her, a grin on his handsome face. "Can I watch next time you two get together?"

She slid her hands into his thick, dark curls, gave them a playful tug. "That's fine with me, but I think she prefers having sex with *you*."

He chuckled, then turned back toward his computer screen. "Seriously, though, the bastard kept murder trophies—photos of people he and his goons killed. They're mixed in here. You don't need to see that."

An image of Dudaev lying dead on the bed, bullet holes in his forehead, flashed through her mind. Her stomach did a sick flip. "Okay. Have it your way."

She spoke the words in a light tone, but it touched her that he was trying to shelter her. How often in her life had that happened?

She glanced at the clock. It was almost one in the afternoon. It would be time for lunch soon. Day three of peanut butter sandwiches. Still, she supposed she shouldn't complain. Despite the roaches, the little room was much more comfortable than the farmhouse had been. The AC kept the place reasonably cool and it had been heaven to sleep in a real bed last night and not on an air mattress on the floor.

"I think I found something."

Holly turned to see an image of a document on Nick's screen. She went to stand beside him and looked closely at the screen. It was some kind of receipt. "Cayman National Bank."

"He transferred almost a million bucks from an account in Switzerland to the Cayman Islands. Look at the date." Nick touched his finger to the monitor. "This is less than a month after the Batumi op."

"Is there a name on the receipt?"

"No, but both account numbers are there. What do you want to bet that this money comes from selling the weapons Dudaev and his men stole?"

Holly's pulse picked up. "Dudaev probably had accounts all over the world. How can you be sure this has anything at all to do with our situation?"

"I guess I can't, but I found it in a folder that contains other things he didn't want people to see—dead bodies, for starters. He was trying to hide this. Given the date, it's hard for me to think it could be anything else. Why else would he hold on to a two-year-old receipt?"

"Even if the receipt is tied to this, we don't have investigative authority. We can't call the bank and ask them to give us the name on the account."

"No, we can't, but the Agency can." Nick looked up at her. "This could be the proof we need to tie Dudaev to Bauer and to expose Bauer's accomplice."

Holly knew he believed that person was Lee Nguyen. "I can contact my CO and update him, let him know what we—what *you*—found. Maybe you could offer to give him Dudaev's emails about the heroin shipments as a show of good faith."

"Not a bad idea. Ask if he's open to a phone call."

"I'll get started on the ciphertext." She sat at the table and wrote out a plaintext message, then held it out for Nick to see.

He took the piece of paper, caught her hand, kissed it. "I trust you."

She quickly encoded the message, wrote out the key, then sat at her computer and logged on to the hotel's Wi-Fi. It took her less than a minute to launch her IP-blocking program and log in to her Twitter account. She planned to post a Tweet to let her friends know she was still alive, but she saw she had a couple of messages. She clicked to view them and stared, adrenaline hitting her system in a rush.

"You're going to want to see this."

In her in-box was a message from Lee Nguyen.

NICK AND HOLLY left the hotel just after lunch and drove north to Colorado Springs, Holly behind the wheel this time. "I don't like this. My CO told me not to have contact with anyone at the Agency but him."

They had argued about this all afternoon.

Nick stuck to his decision. "You're not the one doing the contacting. If anything goes wrong, it's my head that will roll."

"But I like your head. I want it to stay where it is."

He reached over, ran his thumb down her cheek. "So do I."

"Remember to keep it short. Don't let Nguyen provoke you. He's going to want to draw this out so they can get a ping on our location."

Nick dug the burner phone out of his jeans pocket and activated it. "If I start to say anything stupid, stop me."

"During this call, or in general?" She smiled, but there was worry in her eyes.

"You're sweet." He dialed the number Nguyen had given them, surprised at how on edge he felt.

Nguyen answered on the first ring. "Andris, are you all right?"

The sound of his friend's familiar voice sent a surge of tangled emotions through Nick—hurt, doubt, rage. "I'm fine—no thanks to Bauer."

"Is Bradshaw safe?"

"Yes. She's in no danger from me."

"You know she's with the Agency, correct?"

"I wish you'd told me that a month ago. Bauer sent me to terminate her. Did you know that, buddy?"

Nguyen didn't answer him. "We need to meet in person, talk this through. There are things you need to know, and we need to work out the details of your surrender. It's time you turned yourself in."

"I'm happy where I am. Besides, I'm not sure I'd last long

in custody. Bauer intends to kill both me and Bradshaw. Are you helping him?"

"No. Nick, listen to me. There's more to this than I can explain now, but it's very important that we limit the Agency's potential exposure here. You need—"

"Fuck the Agency!" The rage Nick had carried inside him these past two weeks exploded. "Where was the Agency when Daly, Carver, and McGowen were murdered? Where was the Agency when Kramer was killed? Where was the Agency when Bauer sent me in to pop Dudaev without authorization?"

"You need to trust me, Nick.

Trust no one.

Kramer's words came back to him.

"Do I? I trusted Bauer. He betrayed me. He was my fucking supervisor, and he set me up. He wants me to take the fall for what happened that night in Batumi. He's trying to save his own ass. Were you his man on the ground, Lee? Were you the one who turned us all over to Dudaev and got Dani killed?"

"No! Damn it, Nick, listen. I had nothing to do with any of that. We can't talk about this now. I'm going to text you the place where I'll be staying in Colorado Springs. You and Bradshaw meet me there tomorrow afternoon at three. I want this to be over as much as you do."

Holly tapped the time display on the dashboard.

But then it hit Nick. "Colorado Springs?"

Why was Nguyen coming to Colorado Springs instead of Denver?

"We just got a call from the Ríos County sheriff. He says he ran in to the two of you in a farmhouse outside of Los Ríos. He didn't realize it was you until he caught the BOLO this morning. If you're still there, you're going to want to get the hell out."

"Thanks for the tip, buddy."

"You're like a brother to me, Nick. I've always had your back. Before this is over, you'll know I still do." Nguyen ended the call.

Nick waited for the text message, trying to rein in his temper. "He wants us to meet with him tomorrow afternoon at a hotel in Colorado Springs."

Holly glanced over at him. "I'm pretty sure they got a ping off that."

The phone buzzed, Nguyen's text message coming through.

"That's not our only problem." Nick memorized the contents of the message, then deactivated the phone and threw it out the window. "Nguyen said the sheriff made us."

"Are you sure we should go back to the hotel?"

It was a good couple of hours from the farmhouse to the hotel, but if the media announced they were in the area, no place in southeastern Colorado would be safe. Still, they had no choice but to go back.

"All the documents are there and the computers. Without those, I've got no leverage, no proof."

She turned the minivan around. "You know, everyone wants what we have—the intel on Dudaev's computer."

"You're right. We hold all the cards. Maybe it's time we went on the offensive."

* * *

ZACH PULLED OFF the road a few hundred feet from the farmhouse, patrol vehicles of all kinds parked along the shoulder.

"Looks like every LEO in the county is here," Javier said.

"You know how it is. Anything big happens and every officer within driving distance wants to be a part of it."

"The media, too."

Two television trucks sat parked nearby, reporters standing along the yellow crime scene tape that was stretched across the mouth of the driveway.

Zach had left Denver with Corbray as soon as they'd gotten word, flying by helo to the Ríos County Airport, where a rental had been waiting for them. Neither Darcangelo nor Hunter had been able to join them, as both had duty shifts today.

"Those must be feds." Corbray pointed with a jerk of his head to unmarked vehicles farther down the road.

"I wondered when the FBI was going to get into the game." Zach clipped his badge to his belt, handed another to

Javier. "Don't go waving this around. You aren't officially deputized. I just don't want you getting thrown out of the crime scene."

"Got it. Thanks, man."

"Don't thank me. Buy me a beer." He opened the door and climbed out into the heat, locking the vehicle behind him.

Sheriff's deputies milled about near the back porch, a few city police with them, while the sheriff stood on the porch talking with a couple of men in suits.

Corbray grinned. "Darcangelo is going to be bummed he missed this. He loves watching his former employer get dressed down by you marshals."

"I'm glad I provide him with entertainment." Zach didn't care much for the dick fight between his organization and the alphabet soup agencies, but there were days when the marshal's badge came in handy.

He ducked under the yellow tape, Corbray behind him, then made his way across the yard, up the steps, and onto the porch. He held his hand out to the man standing next to the sheriff. "Chief Deputy US Marshal Zach McBride. This is Deputy Marshal Corbray. The marshals service has claimed jurisdiction in the abduction of journalist Holly Bradshaw, as I'm sure you're all aware."

"I'm Special Agent Doug Meeker, and this is Special Agent Cal Lopez. You're hanging by a thread on that jurisdiction claim, marshal."

Zach grinned. "The point is, we're hanging on. Sheriff, can you fill us in?"

Sheriff Davidson told them how he'd been on a routine patrol when he'd seen tire tracks in the grass and had stopped to investigate. "We get vagrants sometimes. We've had people try to set up meth labs in some of the abandoned properties. You might have noticed that we have a lot of empty houses around here."

Zach nodded. "Yes, I saw that."

"I found a blue Honda Odyssey parked on the side of the barn. It had temp plates. I called it in, cleared the plates. At about that time, a young woman stepped out of the house. She had a cup of coffee in her hand and said hello. She invited me in and told me her fiancé was in the shower upstairs. I checked her ID, and we talked a little. She had a Kentucky driver's license and seemed to know the area. She spoke with a convincing accent, too. The man she said was her fiancé came downstairs. They told me how they met and how they were down on their luck. They said she was pregnant and they needed a place to stay. Their IDs came back valid and clear. I believed them."

"They told you she was pregnant?" Zach exchanged a glance with Javier.

If that was true, Andris was a dead man. He'd manipulated Holly into a sexual relationship to begin with. If he'd also gotten her pregnant . . .

"There was a car seat in the minivan. I asked if they had a child here with them. He said she was pregnant. She turned bright red."

"Ms. Bradshaw blushed?" Zach asked.

"That doesn't sound like Holly." Corbray said what Zach was thinking.

"Yes, sir—as if it embarrassed her to talk about it. When I asked if that was true, she said that, yes, she was about three months along."

Three months? In that case, Andris couldn't be the father, even if it were true.

Zach made a mental note to update the BOLO with regard to Holly's condition. She needed to be found so she could get prenatal care. "How did she look otherwise?"

"She seemed fine, though she was wearing a baseball cap and kept her face angled away from me. I guess she didn't want me to get a good look at her. But with a face like hers . . ." The sheriff's words trailed off. "I recognized her the moment I saw the BOLO. I'm sorry I didn't catch it until this morning. We don't get many fugitives down this way, and I don't read through the notices every day."

"I understand." Zach wished to hell the man had called it in immediately.

The sheriff went on. "I have to say it didn't look to me like she was being held against her will, though she did seem to defer to him."

"What do you mean?" Zach asked.

"There were a few times when she looked over at him,

waited for him to answer my questions. I got the sense that he was definitely the one in charge in the relationship. Still, there was a good five minutes or so when it was just the two of us. She had plenty of time to ask me for help or tell me her real name."

"That doesn't mean anything," said Special Agent Meeker. "Captivity does strange things to people. Some start to identify with their kidnappers. Maybe she was afraid he'd come down and pop both of you before backup could arrive. Maybe she thought she was protecting you."

"Some kidnapping victims all but forget their real names," said Corbray.

Zach knew he was thinking of Laura.

The sheriff looked troubled. "I'd hate to think that I failed her. She seemed like a sweet young woman."

"What kind of evidence did your CSI team find?" Zach asked.

"Fingerprints. That's it. They didn't leave anything behind, apart from several empty propane canisters on the side of the house near the generator."

Then Zach caught sight of a man in a tailored gray suit walking toward them. He was Asian, in his mid-forties, and wore fancy black shades.

"Don't look now, but I think the CIA is crashing the party," muttered Corbray.

"Yeah, I think you're right."

Shit.

The man approached them, flashed his badge. "Lee Nguyen, Central Intelligence Agency. You must be Chief Deputy Marshal Zach McBride. I'll need all evidence from this scene, including all reports and records, transferred into my custody."

Sheriff Davidson scowled. "You can't do that."

"I can." Nguyen took some folded pages out of his suit pocket and handed them to Zach. "I have a court order here transferring jurisdiction in this case to the Agency. We'll need all files pertaining to the case delivered to our office in Denver ASAP. That includes any records Cobra International Solutions might have, Mr. Corbray."

Zach handed the papers to Javier. "Looks authentic."

Javier read them, then shoved them back into Nguyen's hands. "You and your court order can kiss my ass. I'm not giving you access to any of our files."

Nguyen smiled. "I know the two of you care about Ms. Bradshaw. That's why you've been such a pain in the Agency's ass. But if you want her back, the best thing you can do is get out of our way."

CHAPTER 24

NICK SCROLLED THROUGH Dudaev's seemingly endless supply of porn, rage on a slow burn inside him. Nguyen had acted like nothing had changed between them. Did he think Nick was a fucking idiot?

Nguyen had been there. He *knew* Bauer had assigned Nick to take out Dudaev and run surveillance on Holly. He'd been there during the debriefing after Nick had terminated Dudaev, and he'd helped Bauer grill Nick over Kramer's death. He'd joked with Nick about his assignment with Holly and knew full well what Bauer had intended for her. And yet he'd had the nerve to call Nick "brother."

It sickened Nick.

Nguyen could have spoken out at any time to clear Nick's name. He could have reached out to Nick to warn him like Kramer had tried to do. He could have gone to investigators and blown the top off this thing. The fact that Nick was still being hunted and Bauer was still sitting at his desk at Langley proved that Nguyen hadn't said a damned thing. It didn't take a genius IQ to guess why.

Nguyen must have been the one who'd betrayed them all to Dudaev. He'd been Bauer's eyes and ears in Batumi.

Holly's voice cut through his thoughts. "Is something wrong?"

She was in the middle of scanning key documents and uploading them to an encrypted file-storage site. Only Nick and Holly had the password to this account or even knew it existed. When they were ready and Nick's surrender had been negotiated, they would send her CO the account information. Nick had already sent over Dudaev's emails pertaining to the heroin shipments as a good-faith gesture.

"Nothing's wrong." He could see that she didn't believe him. "Just thinking about Nguyen."

She stood, walked around behind him, and wrapped her arms around his neck. "It hurts to be betrayed by a friend."

Nick closed the image on his screen—a photo of a girl blowing two men simultaneously—not wanting Holly to see such filth. "He was more than a friend."

She sat on the bed nearby. "Why would he do this?"

Nick shrugged. "Hell, I don't know. Money?"

Nguyen had never seemed greedy, though he did have a big, extended family he supported—grandparents, parents, an elderly auntie or two. But that's one of the reasons he and Nick had connected. They both came from big families and were the sons of immigrants.

"I'm sorry."

"When I woke up in the hospital in Germany, he was there, sitting beside the bed. I was drugged out of my mind on morphine. It took a moment for me to remember why I was there, what had happened. When I remembered that Dani was dead . . ." Nick swallowed, his throat tight. "Lee held my hand. He held my hand, and there were tears in his eyes. It was all bullshit. The whole time he was with me, Dani's body was lying on a slab somewhere, and he was waiting for his cut of the money."

"God, Nick. That's terrible." She stood, wrapped her arms around him again, kissed his cheek. "I wouldn't blame you if you wanted to punch him right in the face—or, you know, do something worse."

Nick couldn't help but smile. What was it about Holly that made even the darkest moments seem lighter?

"They're talking about us on CNN." She reached for the TV remote and took the TV off mute.

"—County Sheriff's office reported this afternoon that kidnapping victim Holly Elise Bradshaw was sighted at an abandoned farmhouse outside Los Ríos, Colorado, yesterday with the man who is believed to be holding her captive, Nick Andris. Andris, a former Delta Force operator who was decorated for his service in Afghanistan and Iraq, is also being sought by authorities in connection with the murder of Denver art gallery owner Sasha Dudayev. Let's go to Rick Saunders, who's at the scene."

A man in a gray suit appeared on the screen. "I'm here at an abandoned farmhouse outside the small agricultural community of Los Ríos, Colorado, where investigators believe Nick Andris held Holly Elise Bradshaw for most of the past two weeks. You can see we have quite a law enforcement response . . ."

The camera cut to an image of sheriff's deputies and police milling about outside the farmhouse, talking with one another.

"FBI officials, who are present at the scene, declined to comment, saying only that they're close to apprehending Andris."

Holly gave a squeal and pointed to the television, a smile on her face. "There's Zach! And Javi, too! Look!"

The reporter droned on, while Holly's smile slowly faded.

"You miss them."

"They're out there looking for me. I feel terrible. I haven't been kidnapped. I'm with you by choice now. I hate that they're worried for me." Her gaze met his. "It's worse for you. Your family is worried about you, too, but the whole world thinks you're a murderer and a kidnapper. That must be so hard for them."

Nick had been trying not to think about that. "There's nothing we can do for them except bring this to an end. Like I said this afternoon, we hold all the cards. If we play them right . . ."

"A source close to the investigation says Ms. Bradshaw might be pregnant. Authorities are concerned about her well-being and hope to have her home soon."

"What?" Holly gaped at the television. "Oh, great. Fantastic."

"Well, that's what we told the sheriff."

She glared at him. "That's what *you* told the sheriff."

"I don't seem to remember you having a better idea."

She turned off the TV and dropped the remote onto the unmade bed. "What you said about going on the offensive— what did you have in mind?"

But Nick found himself staring at his computer screen. "What the fuck?"

"What is it?"

He scrolled through the next image and the next. "Photos of the warehouse."

"The warehouse in Batumi?" She bent down beside him.

"Yeah." There must have been a dozen shots taken from different vantage points. "Look at the date stamp. These were taken two days before the exchange. Someone on my team scoped it out for him, made certain he knew the plan."

"Are you sure they were taken by one of your guys? If Dudaev knew where the exchange was going to happen, couldn't he have sent one of his goons to do it?"

Nick shook his head. "My team had the warehouse under constant surveillance for two weeks. If anyone had gone near the place, I would have known. Someone on my team sent Dudaev these photos."

He scrolled back to the first photo. "These first two shots show where the sentries were posted down the block. The next three show the positions of the snipers. This one gives an overview of the interior of the warehouse."

There to one side was the forklift, exactly where it had been that night.

"Stay there!"

Rat-at-at-at-at!

"Dani! No!"

A hand touched Nick's shoulder, made him jump.

"It can't be easy to look at these."

"I can still remember the terror in her eyes. She knew I'd been hit. She was afraid for me. She tried to get to me, but . . . The last thing we had was that glance across the room." He swallowed, forced his grief aside. "Whoever took these photos knew the security plan. He was giving Dudaev everything he needed to prepare himself—the layout of the operation and the deployment of the men, the location of the firearms. It's all right here."

If he could remember who was on duty at the time the

photos were taken, he'd be able to confirm the identity of Bauer's accomplice. And if it was Nguyen . . .

Then God have mercy on him, because Nick sure as hell wouldn't.

"This isn't a plan. It's suicide!" Holly fought to keep from shouting, her toothbrush clutched in her hand.

Nick rested his hands on her shoulders. "I know what I'm doing. He won't kill me if he doesn't have you. Hopefully it will give me time to get some answers."

"He might not kill you, but a person can endure a lot of pain without dying. He's going to *hurt* you, Nick."

"It's a risk I'm willing to take."

"Well, I hate this plan." She turned, marched back into the bathroom, and began brushing her teeth with a fury.

He followed her. "If we stay here, it's only a matter of time before someone finds us. Once we're in custody, Bauer will send someone to take us both out. It won't matter if the Agency figures it all out later. We'll already be dead."

She spat toothpaste in the sink and glared up at him. "So the only alternative to our being murdered is for you to hand yourself over to Nguyen? It's probably a trap."

"I expect it is." He leaned against the doorjamb, crossed his arms over his bare chest. "It's the fastest way I can think of to end this and get you home. Dudaev's goons are probably in Colorado Springs now searching for us, and there's a chance they'll find us before we've got the proof we need to lock Bauer and Nguyen away. But, hey, if you've got a better idea, a viable alternative, I'm listening."

She rinsed her mouth, then reached for the towel, her mind racing. "We should keep working on the photos, keep trying to reconstruct the week before the exchange."

"We spent the past six hours doing that and it got us nowhere. Whoever took the shots wasn't stupid enough to photograph his own reflection, and it's been two years. I can't remember who was assigned surveillance duty that afternoon."

She pushed past him, sat on the edge of the bed. "Maybe the time stamp is enough. If you can remember where *you* were, give them a solid alibi, then at least they'll know *you* didn't give Dudaev the photos. We should contact my CO again, tell him what we found, send him—"

"I might be able to prove I didn't take the photos, but that won't keep me from frying for killing Dudaev. It won't put Bauer in prison. Until he, Nguyen, and their mafia buddies are in custody, you and I have great big targets on our foreheads."

"I could call Javier and Zach. We could show them the documents, explain things, prove to them that you're innocent. You could surrender to the marshals service. Between CIS and the marshals, I know they'd keep us safe."

"Can you be sure of that? Can you be sure there won't be a firefight that costs McBride or Corbray his life? Besides, that would mean divulging classified data and outing yourself. Is that what you want? Your career would be over."

"I don't care about my career! We're talking about your safety, your life." Why couldn't he understand? "We could upload the photos and key documents to a file-sharing site, email the password to my newspaper, and let Bauer and Nguyen know that if anything happens to us, the files will end up in print."

"What's to stop them from killing us and hacking the site or going after your editor?"

"They can't kill everybody."

He bent down, glared straight into her eyes. "I don't want them to kill *anybody*. I want to *bring them down*. That's why I'm doing this."

"At least let me call Zach so he's standing by and knows where you are."

"Not until we have what we need. If he knows where I am, he's going to move as soon as he and his team are in position. I'll never get to the bottom of this."

Tears blurred Holly's vision. "What if you're wrong and he *does* kill you?"

"You'll have everything you need to make sure he pays for it. But that's not going to happen."

"How can you be sure? If he realizes that you're recording him—"

"It's a chance I have to take."

"Well, it's a stupid plan. I veto it."

He laughed. "You *veto* it?"

"I couldn't stand it if anything were to happen to you."

He drew her into his arms. "It's going to be okay."

She wished she could be certain of that. "Why are you so set on this?"

"We have something Bauer and Nguyen want, but they have something I want—the truth."

She drew back, looked up at him. "This is about Dani, isn't it?"

"Yeah, in part. I want to know why Dudaev killed her. He could have killed all of us. Instead, he passed us by to kill *her*. Why?"

"Does the answer mean so much that you'd throw away your life to get it?"

"She was a member of my team, Holly. Yeah, I loved her. But beyond that, it was my job to keep her safe. I failed. I've learned to live with that, but, damn it, I have to know what happened."

Holly wiped the tears off her cheeks. "You can't bring her back, you know. Nothing you can do will bring her back. Punishing yourself—"

"I'm not punishing myself." He closed his eyes, clearly fighting to rein in his temper. "I'm taking a calculated risk to stop them and keep you safe. This isn't just about me. I know these past few weeks have been miserable for you. You want to go back to your life and your friends, and I'm trying to make that happen."

"Oh, great. So if they kill you, I get to live the rest of my life knowing that the man I lo—" She gaped up at him, astonished by what she'd almost said.

His gaze softened. "The man you . . . what?"

"Nothing." She turned away from him, walked to the window, her pulse tripping, a feeling like panic welling up inside her.

She couldn't love Nick. She just couldn't. She refused to love him.

He came up behind her, wrapped an arm around her waist, kissed her hair. "Are we going to argue all night, or are you going to let me make love to you?"

"I don't want you to meet with Nguyen tomorrow."

I don't want this to be our last night together.

"Shhh." Warm fingers brushed her hair away from her neck, his lips pressing butterfly kisses against the skin beneath her ear.

Heat skittered over her skin.

She let her eyes close, let herself sink back against him, his body so strong and hard, his touch quieting the confusion inside her. One big hand drew up the stretchy fabric of her black tank dress and slid beneath her panties to cup her. Oh, he knew her so well, knew just how to touch her, just what to do to turn her on.

Pressure right *there*. The glide of a finger. His teeth nipping her neck.

She turned in his arms, and they sank together to the bed, kissing. He sat up, undressed her, his hands sliding over her skin as he took off her dress, her bra, and then her panties. She watched as his gaze moved over her, as warm and gentle as a caress. Then he bent down, kissed her between her breasts, taking their weight in his hands, his thumbs teasing her nipples to erect points.

She slid her fingers into his thick curls, gasping as he drew one of her nipples into the heat of his mouth and sucked, little tugs that she felt deep in her belly. Pleasure shivered through her, leaving her wet and aching for him.

She reached down, tried to unzip his jeans, but he took over, pushing them down his hips and kicking them aside.

He rolled onto his back, grasped her hips, and guided her up his body until she straddled his face.

Holly grasped the top of the bed's rickety headboard and held on as his lips and tongue worked their magic on her. *"Oh, yes!"*

God, she loved him. Yes, she loved him. She didn't want to love him. She hadn't meant to love him. But she did.

NICK COULD STAY like this forever, his head filled with Holly's scent, his mouth alive with her taste. He'd heard what she hadn't said, what she'd stopped herself from saying. He'd heard it as clearly as if she'd shouted it to the world, her unspoken words setting something free inside him.

Well, this was his answer.

He drank in the sweet nectar of her body's response, wanting to give her all the pleasure she could take. He'd never known a woman as sensual and responsive as Holly. Uninhibited, fun, beautiful, graceful, sexy, sweet—words chased one another through his mind, a litany that somehow couldn't begin to describe her. He wanted nothing more than to venerate her, adore her, cherish her.

Soft little sighs tumbled out of her one after the other, her knuckles white where her hands gripped the headboard, her thighs trembling, her hips making little jerking motions. *"Oh, God . . . Nick."*

He knew how to read her, knew how to gauge her responses. She was hovering on the edge now. He slipped a hand between her thighs, slid two fingers inside her, stroked her. God, she was wet, her slick inner muscles gripping his fingers, making him ache to have his cock inside her.

Then her head fell back and she came with a cry, her vagina clenching around his fingers. He stayed with her until her climax had passed, then helped her settle herself on top of him, where she lay, limp as a rag doll.

Nick traced the delicate groove of her spine with his fingertips, savored the feel of her in his arms, her heartbeat gradually slowing. If only the world would disappear and leave them alone. And then it hit him.

How was he supposed to go back to living without her?

He couldn't.

She lifted her head from his chest, looked at him through dark eyes, then lowered her mouth to his in a slow, deep kiss, her fingers stroking his half-hard cock to fullness.

He flipped her onto her back, settled himself between her thighs, his gaze locked with hers as he entered her with a single, slow thrust.

There were so many things he wanted to tell her, so many things he wanted to say, but he kept them to himself, willing himself to focus only on loving her. Had he ever felt so connected to a woman? She was so much a part of him that he couldn't tell where his body ended and hers began. She was his home, his temple, his heaven.

Skin on sweat-slick skin. Moans mingling. Fingers twining.

He drew her hands above her head, pressed his forehead to hers, looked into those beautiful brown eyes. "Holly, honey, I . . ."

I love you.

Tears welled up in her eyes, spilled down her temples.

He fought to hold on, wanting her, wanting to make it good for her, his control hanging by a single thread. She felt good . . . so good . . . so perfect. Nothing was sweeter. Nothing was better. He was burning . . . God, he was burning up . . . Burning up inside her, his blood on fire for her.

Her eyes went wide and she cried out his name, a look of ecstasy lighting her sweet face as she came again, her inner muscles contracting around him, shattering what was left of his control. He exploded, orgasm scorching through him in an incandescent wave as he spilled his soul inside her.

Then in the stillness, he held her.

CHAPTER 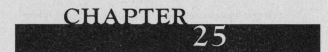 25

HOLLY ZIPPED THE fly of Nick's jeans, smoothed the denim with her fingers, then felt along his crotch. "You ought to be good for a pat down."

"Are you sure? Maybe you should check again."

He was being cute but she didn't have it in her to laugh. He was actually going through with this. If he wasn't careful, he was going to end up getting himself hurt or killed. "Hopefully, he won't run a metal detector over you, but if he does, he might believe it's just your zipper. I fooled people with the underwire in my bra lots of times."

Nick drew a shirt on over his head and tucked it into his jeans, then reached for his jacket. It was in the high nineties outside but he needed the extra layer to hide his shoulder holster and his SIG.

She put aside the little sewing kit they'd bought that morning and reached for the cheap cowboy hat they'd grabbed at the gas station. "I don't want you to do this, Nick. Please reconsider. If Nguyen is dirty, he obviously has no problem killing his own people—or watching them die. He could kill you, torture you, or remand you into custody and pay some stranger to shank you."

He laughed. "Would you stop worrying?"

"This isn't a game."

"Hey, isn't that my line? Come here." He pulled her into

his arms, held her. "You're right. I don't know what Nguyen has in mind, but I have the advantage here."

"You do?"

"Hell, yeah, I do." He drew back, cupped her face in his palms. "I have you."

He kissed her, a soft, slow kiss.

"Nick, I . . ." She needed to tell him. He was leaving. What if she never got another chance? "I . . . I can't lose you."

Oh, she was such a coward!

He gave her a lopsided grin, his gaze soft. "You won't."

And then it was time for them to move.

They quickly packed up the minivan, then Nick went to the motel office to check them out. They drove in silence up the highway toward Colorado Springs, exiting I-25 and heading into the business district.

"This looks good." He pulled into the entrance of a public parking garage, punched the button for the ticket, then drove up to the top floor. "It's going to get pretty hot in here. Have you got enough water?"

"Don't worry about me." Being hot was the least of Holly's worries. "If Nguyen turns you over to Dudaev's men, you'll have to get them to speak English or Russian, or I won't understand a word of it."

He nodded, pointed to the surveillance setup. "Are you confident you know how to run all this stuff?"

"Yes, of course."

"No matter what happens, no matter what Nguyen does or what you hear, you stay here. Do *not* come after me. Our lives depend on that. The moment they have both of us, we're dead. Promise you won't follow me."

"I'm not an idiot."

No, she wasn't an idiot, but if he could have a stupid plan, so could she.

He kissed her. "I'll be back as soon as I can."

"What if you can't get back? What if you never come back?"

"That's not going to happen." He stroked her cheek with his knuckles. "You mean the world to me, Holly."

He put on the cowboy hat, stepped out of the minivan, and walked away.

* * *

NICK WALKED THROUGH the side entrance of the Crest-wood Suites Hotel, the cowboy hat tilted to conceal his face. He glanced around the lobby for Dudaev's goons or anyone who resembled an Agency officer. A man reading today's paper, his luggage beside him. A family with two kids check-ing in. A young woman in a business pantsuit checking out. Two young men standing in uniforms at the concierge desk.

A bank of elevators stood in the center of the lobby. Not only would they be hard to reach without being seen, but the eleva-tors themselves were glass, which meant that anyone on any floor would be able to see him and observe where he stopped.

He sat in the back of the lobby until the two young men from the concierge desk were busy, then slipped into the staff elevator and took it to the eleventh floor, his mind shifting to yesterday's conversation with Nguyen. He'd denied helping Bauer, but apart from that, he hadn't answered Nick's questions.

There's more to this than I can explain right now.

Was Nick a fool to hope that there truly was some other explanation for the things Lee had done—and hadn't done?

You need to trust me, Nick.

Well, here he was, ready to trust or ready to shoot back, whichever it took.

The elevator stopped with a ping and the door opened. He followed the signs down the hall and around the corner to Suite 1120.

The door was ajar.

Nick drew the P229, pushed the door open, and saw feet in men's black dress shoes sticking out from behind a sofa. Someone was down.

He raised his weapon and moved in, keeping his back to the wall, his senses alert for any sound or movement. He did a quick sweep of the place, glancing down as he passed the sofa to see Nguyen lying in a pool of blood.

Son of a bitch!

He stopped at the desk, grabbed the hotel's phone, and dialed the concierge desk. "Call 911. A man has been shot in Suite 1120. I repeat—a man has been shot and is down in Suite 1120. We need police and an ambulance."

Leaving the handset off the hook, he hurried over to Nguyen, knelt down beside him, felt for a pulse.

It was weak and thready, but it was there.

"Lee, can you hear me?" Nick pushed aside Nguyen's sports jacket, tore open his shirt, saw a bullet wound in the right side of his chest. He took the handkerchief out of Nguyen's jacket pocket and pressed it hard against the wound.

Nguyen's eyes fluttered open, focused on Nick's face. "Go. Trap."

"You just hang on, and let me take care of me." Nick glanced around again, knowing he made an easy target. "Stay with me, buddy. Medical is on the way."

"It wasn't me . . ." Lee's words were cut off in a fit of strangled coughing, blood gathering at the corners of his mouth.

"Rest easy, buddy."

"It wasn't . . . me. Bauer . . ." Lee's eyes rolled back in his head, then drifted shut.

"No, damn it! Lee, come on, man!" Nick felt for a pulse again.

He was still alive.

Thank God.

Then Nick heard heavy footfalls in the hallway. His first thought was that it was staff coming in response to his call. But he hadn't heard the elevator open. He stood and moved back against the wall, out of the line of fire, his weapon raised.

Three of Dudaev's thugs stepped into the room, all of them armed.

Nick fired, dropping the first one with a double tap. He rolled to the side, came up finger on the trigger to fire at the second.

He heard a *pop* and the electric rattle of a Taser. Liquid agony flooded him, dropping him to the floor, making his entire body go limp.

And the world went dark.

HOLLY SAT IN the minivan, listening through headphones, hand pressed over her mouth, her pulse racing. She'd heard two gunshots, followed by the metallic rattle of the Taser. Was Nick down? Had he been shot or zapped or both?

Come on, Nick, say something!

A man groaned.

Someone spoke in a language she didn't understand. One of Dudaev's men. They must have shot Nguyen and been waiting nearby for Nick.

She drew a deep breath, fought to master her panic, her heart still thrumming.

Snap out of it, Bradshaw!

She listened, straining to hear.

Another groan.

More talk she couldn't understand.

"I don't speak . . . whatever that is."

Holly exhaled, a relieved sigh to hear Nick's voice.

"He killed Beso!"

So Nick had been the one to fire the shots. A savage satisfaction washed through her. Good for him!

"You killed Nguyen." That was Nick again.

So Nguyen was dead?

Oh, God!

"Your parents are Georgian, you piece of shit, but you don't know your mother tongue. Where is she? Where is the Bradshaw bitch?"

She's recording every word you say, you ass!

"I let her go."

"Liar. Get on your feet. She must be here somewhere. Where did you park?"

"I took a cab."

A muffled thud. A groan.

"Go fuck your mother!" Nick said—in Russian.

So he was provoking them. Great idea. Was he trying to distract them, hoping the police would arrive in time to help him?

Nick, you big idiot, be careful!

"Get up. You're going with us. If you say a word or try to run, we'll shoot."

They were taking him. They were abducting him.

Fan-freaking-tastic! Perfect. Absolutely perfect.

She heard the *ping* of the elevator, listened as they rode it down to the ground floor, the car stopping twice to let people on. Those people had no idea how close they stood to death at this moment. She was certain Dudaev's men must have a gun pressed to Nick's back. They wouldn't hesitate to kill anyone who got in their way.

People's voices. Footsteps on concrete. They must be outside now.

Traffic. The distant wail of sirens. Footsteps that echoed.

The parking garage?

A vehicle door opened.

"Where do you two think you're taking me?"

Two. There were two of them. He was letting her know there were two of them—and he had them speaking English.

Good job, baby.

The rasp of duct tape.

"Shut up, piece of shit."

They must have put duct tape over his mouth because he didn't answer. They were probably using it to bind his hands and ankles, too.

A thud.

Someone had struck him.

"Give us trouble, I slit your throat. You killed Beso, you whoreson!"

A heavy door closed. Or was that the trunk?

Two car doors opened and closed, the men's voices muffled and distant. The roar of a car engine. And then they were moving.

Her gaze was drawn to the computer screen and the GPS feed from the transmitter she'd sewn into Nick's jeans. The blip began to move.

Her heart constricted, panic sliding into her veins like ice. They'd gotten Nick. They were taking him away.

They headed east through the city, leaving downtown. Someone turned on music—Katy Perry?—and Holly saw they were headed for the interstate.

Well, to hell with this!

She moved the laptop to the front seat so she could see it, fished the keys out of her jeans pocket, and started the minivan. She wasn't going to get herself caught, but she wasn't going to let them drag Nick off to some remote place and kill him.

She grabbed a burner phone, dialed Javier's number. "Javi, it's Holly."

"Holly? Where are you? Are you safe?"

"I'm outside Colorado Springs. I'm okay, but I really need your help. Can you track this phone, get a GPS reading on my position?"

"Already working on it. Is Andris with you?"

"No." She fought back tears. "Dudaev's men took him. They'll kill him."

How was she going to explain the rest of it—the audio feed, the GPS transmitter?

She took a deep breath. "There's something I need to tell you."

"You're CIA."

"I'm CI— Wait. You know?"

"Yeah. Derek found out from some of his contacts. We've got a lot to talk about when you get back, but right now I just want to get you home safely."

Well, she hadn't expected that.

"I'm going after him, Javi. They're going to torture him, and when they don't get what they want, they'll kill him. I can't let them do that. I love him."

There. She'd said it. She'd told someone. "Will you help me?"

"You know we will."

OKAY, NOW *THIS* was torture.

Nick was hogtied in the trunk of a Cadillac listening to the asshole up front sing along to lyrics he didn't know or likely even understand.

"I got a eye of a tiger, fidduh, ants through a fire, cuz I mama champ on, you gonna see me row!"

Nick lay on his right side, his arms and legs bound behind his back, cords biting into his wrists, duct tape over his mouth. His muscles were sore from the Taser blast, his shoulders aching, his fingers numb.

Small holes near the tail lights told him this was the same Cadillac he'd fired at in Nederland. He tried to move closer, to look outside, but couldn't move.

Bastards.

They'd shot Nguyen and left him for dead, then hidden down the hall in another room or perhaps near the vending machines to wait for Nick and Holly. God, he hoped medical help reached Nguyen in time. The man had been hanging on by sheer guts.

"It wasn't me."

Nick believed him. He didn't think a man who'd been like a brother to him would lie to him with what might have been his last breath, no matter what he'd done. The fact that Dudaev's men had shot Nguyen didn't necessarily mean he hadn't been involved in this in some way. He knew something, and they wanted to silence him.

But if Bauer's accomplice wasn't Nguyen, who was it?

The car accelerated. They must be on the highway now, on their way to God only knew where. The GPS transmitter had better be working or today was going to suck.

It seemed to him they'd been on the interstate for about twenty minutes when they veered to the left and decelerated, but then, it was hard to judge the passage of time lying here in the dark. Still, it was clear that they'd just exited the highway.

He hoped to hell Holly wasn't following them. She was probably scared to death and angry as hell at him, and he couldn't blame her. So far, everything had gone according to her worst predictions. If he got out of this alive, she would glare at him and tell him that she'd told him so, and he would shut her up with a kiss.

An image of her sweet face came into his mind. He held onto it, tucked it inside his heart. He would make it out of this. They both would.

Stay strong, honey.

They went over a bump, the tires now spitting gravel onto the car's undercarriage, the washboard grade of the road shaking Nick's teeth in his skull. This went on until he was certain he was going to puke. Then the car slowed and headed down a steep hill. It leveled out, drove onto a smooth surface, and stopped.

Thankfully, so did the awful singing.

The car's doors opened, and he heard footsteps.

A key slipped into the lock, and light flooded in.

They'd taken his gun, and he didn't have a knife. They had firearms, and they had the Taser. There were two of them, and he was hogtied.

Yeah, he was going nowhere—not yet, anyway.

Besides, now that he was here, he hoped he got the chance to talk face-to-face with Bauer—or whoever was running this shit show.

They dragged him from the trunk and dropped him onto his gut on the concrete floor, knocking the breath from his lungs.

"Where's Beso? And where's the woman?"

Nick recognized the voice, felt his stomach sink, disappointment and anger washing through him.

No!

HOLLY PULLED TO the side of the road, then checked to make sure the audio feed was still recording and transmitting to her CO. Someone was there with Nick, someone other than Dudaev's men. Whoever he was, he'd just asked about her.

She compared the image on her GPS screen with a satellite image of the area. She'd stayed a mile or so behind the Cadillac, certain that Dudaev's men knew the make, model, and color of the minivan. If they saw her in their rearview mirror, they might kill Nick outright.

It looked like they'd taken him to an old gravel mine. There was some kind of a building—an old warehouse or garage—and then a series of pits and berms. She changed the image to street view and saw that the building was at the bottom of a steep hill.

She called Javier. "They've taken him to some kind of garage at what used to be a gravel mine. If we drive up, they'll see us. We're going to have to leave the vehicles some distance away from the place. They only way to approach is from the rear and on foot. If there are windows in the back of the building, we're going to have to wait until dark. There are some berms that might make good positions for snipers if you're bringing any. What's your ETA?"

"It took us forty minutes to get to the damned airport, so

we're a good hour out. We'll be landing at the airport in about ten, and we'll have to catch up with you from there."

"Do you have something I can wear—a vest, maybe some BDUs?"

"We've got a vest, but BDUs in a women's size four?" He chuckled. "Nah, sorry. And, Holly, you're not going in there."

That's what he thought.

"I'm going to do a bit of recon, find a good staging point. I'll call you back when I'm in position. You can meet me there."

She ended the call, kicked the van into drive, and headed down the gravel road.

"HE KILLED BESO, shot him dead in the hotel."

Kramer bent down, looked Nick in the eyes. "Surprised to see me?"

If Nick could have shouted in his face, he would have, but he couldn't say a damned thing with the duct tape on his mouth.

Go screw yourself.

"You're not stupid enough to take on all of us, are you? Yeah, you are." Kramer stood upright again. "Did you guys search him?"

"Yes. We found this." The taller of the two men held up Nick's SIG.

"Nothing else? Better search him again. You wearing a wire, Andris?"

They cut off his jacket, nicking his chest with the knife in the process, then yanked off his shoes and socks and felt beneath his shirt and his jeans, one of them even groping his balls—and not too gently.

"We find nothing."

"Untie him and take him to the back."

They cut the cords and jerked him to his feet, Nick's fingers and feet tingling as blood rushed back into them. They frog-marched him to the back wall of what looked like a garage for heavy equipment, walking past crates and boxes. He counted four other men along the way, sentries perhaps, each armed with an AK.

"String him up. And watch out, boys, because he's deadly."

"Yeah?" said one of the goons. "So are we."

They dragged Nick toward the center of the back wall. Two ropes lay on the floor, each of them running to pulleys that were fixed into the ceiling. He didn't need to ask what the ropes were for.

He glanced around the room, saw that, apart from Kramer, there were only the two men nearby. He was pretty sure he could take out at least one of them before they got the drop on him. But then they'd take him down with the Taser, and he'd be right back where he was now. Still, he needed to make this believable. There's no way he'd let them do this to him without one hell of a fight if his position weren't being monitored.

He broke free, whirled, his heel connecting with the tall one's jaw. The man fell with a thud and lay unconscious on the floor.

Nick backed away from Kramer and the other goon, ripped the duct tape off his mouth. "Kramer, you bastard. Why?"

At least he'd said the son of a bitch's name. Holly would have heard it, and it would have been recorded.

Pop.

The rattle of the stun gun.

A flood of agony.

And Nick was down again.

Kramer knelt down, felt the goon's neck for a pulse. "Why'd you do that? All you did was piss off Ilia here. Grigol is his brother."

The other goon, whose name was apparently Ilia, knelt down beside his brother, shouting expletives in Georgian.

Kramer shouted for help, and two men appeared in the doorway, Dudaev's army of thugs clearly answering to him now. "Help Ilia get Grigol out of here, then come back and help me with this son of a bitch. When I say he's deadly, I mean it. Watch it, or you'll be next."

The men approached Nick cautiously, tied the ropes around his wrists.

"We make the knots tight," said one of the new guys, grinning through gold teeth.

"Cocksuckers," Nick managed to say.

When they'd bound him fast, they pulled the ropes through the pulleys, hoisting him upward until he hung by his wrists from the ceiling, the muscles in his legs not quite recovered enough yet to hold his weight. It wasn't comfortable. But it wasn't himself he thought of when the ropes pulled tight. It was Holly.

He'd done something very much like this to her.

God, Holly, forgive me.

Kramer walked up to him, looked up into his face. "Here's how this is going to go. I'm going to—"

"Yeah, yeah." Nick got his feet beneath him, stood upright. "You're going to ask me questions, and I'm going to answer, or you're going to do bad things to me."

"You were always were a fast learner. If you tell me what I want to know with a minimum of bullshit, I'll kill you myself with a double-tap to the head, just like you did Dudaev. If you don't tell me what I want to know, this day is not only going to be the last day of your life, it's going to be the worst. Got that?"

Nick looked into the eyes of the man he'd once trusted. "Fuck you!"

CHAPTER 26

"Where is she?"

Nick raised his head, fighting to catch his breath, the pain in his right side excruciating. "Eat shit."

Kramer motioned for his thugs to hoist Nick up again. "Better soften him up some more, boys."

Nick staggered to his feet. It was less of a shock to the body if he was standing. The ropes bit into the raw, blistered skin on his wrists, his arms stretching tight over his head as he was slowly raised off the floor, his shoulders and ribs screaming in protest. He grabbed the ropes with his hands, tried to support himself with his strength, but was too exhausted to hold out for long.

While Kramer watched from an old wooden chair set back against the wall, Ilia moved in on Nick again, driving blows against his torso as if he were a human punching bag. It was impossible to hang by his wrists, keep his abdominal muscles tense, and still breathe, so every blow struck deep, driving whatever breath he had from his lungs, his abdomen and chest undefended.

An image of Holly wincing in pain as he'd pulled her arm over her head and chained her to the iron bar at the cabin flashed into his mind, the regret that washed through him more painful than the blows. He'd kept her that way for more than thirty-six hours, until she could no longer stand and her wrists were blistered and bleeding.

I'm so sorry, Holly. If I'd only known . . .

They lowered him to the ground again. He collapsed onto his back on the concrete, gasping for breath.

"There are seven of them and one of you," Kramer said. "You'll break before they do. Who should I give you to next?"

Nick inhaled as deeply as he could. "It's 'whom.'"

"What?"

"*Whom* should I give you to next."

Kramer's face flushed an angry red. "You were really good at that SERE and R2I shit, weren't you? I bet you think you're some kind of hero."

"No. Not a hero." Nick drew a breath, pain slicing through his ribcage, making him dizzy. "Just loyal to my friends . . . my country."

Kramer laughed. "What can I say? No one's perfect."

Ask him questions. Get him to talk.

Nick tried to focus, the pain in his ribs and belly unrelenting. "How much of the money Dudaev transferred . . . to that account in the Caymans was yours? Did you and Bauer split it evenly . . . or did he take more than his share?"

Kramer looked startled. "What do you know about that?"

"I cloned Dudaev's hard drive . . . found the transfer receipts to that account . . . and the photos of the warehouse you took. Turned all of it over . . . to the Agency."

Fear flashed through Kramer's eyes but disappeared behind a sneer. "They won't be looking for me. They think I'm dead. You've got to admit, I made it convincing. I spent six months getting my blood drawn every few weeks, saving it. Dump it on the sidewalk, toss out a few shell casings, throw my suitcase in a field, and I'm dead."

That's why he'd looked so pale and tired when they'd met for lunch.

And then it hit Nick. "You didn't meet with me to warn me. You met with me just to set me up . . . to make me look guilty."

Kramer nodded. "That was Bauer's idea."

As if that somehow made it less of a betrayal.

"In the end, it won't matter. Do you think Bauer . . . will take the fall alone? Investigators are onto him." They certainly would be after Holly gave them the recording of this audio feed. "He'll talk, work out a deal for himself . . . pin most of it on you."

Kramer's nostrils flared. "He'd better not. He's got family, too."

"Was this all his idea?"

"It was his idea to take the guns, but I'm the one who figured out how to do it." Kramer pointed at his own chest, grinned. "Hey, this is the land of opportunity, and I saw an opportunity."

Let him brag. Keep him talking.

"So *you* brought Dudaev in on it. I have to say . . . that was pretty damned clever. Make it look like he stole them . . . then sell the weapons and split the jack."

Kramer nodded. "If only Dudaev hadn't gotten greedy in the end. He tried to blackmail us—stupid bastard."

Another piece fell into place.

"When you wouldn't pay up, he went to the Agency . . . tried to broker a deal. That's why Bauer sent me in to kill him."

Nick had wanted Dudaev in his sights so badly, and they'd known that. He'd been the perfect tool.

"I always said you were smart." Kramer motioned for the goons to raise Nick up again. "Not smart enough to tell me what I want, though."

Ilia moved in again, working Nick over with crippling blows that left him blinded by pain and unable to breathe. The world turned to spots, went black.

He found himself on the concrete floor, gasping for breath, and staring up into Kramer's face, pain splitting his sides.

"He just passed out. That's all." Kramer sounded relieved. He turned to Ilia. "You gotta give him time to breathe. If he dies before I say so, you'll be hanging here."

"Why?" Nick coughed, tasted blood. "Why . . . did you do it?"

"One problem with nice, honest boys like you is that everyone knows you're a nice, honest boy, and no one trusts you."

Nick thought he must have been hit one too many times, because that made no fucking sense. "Wh-what?"

"Bauer's old man—back in *his* day, an officer could make

a killing by selling secrets to the KGB. Oh, nothing big, just little shit."

"Bauer's dad sold secrets . . . to the Soviets?"

"You're surprised?" Kramer laughed. "Why do you think he never got caught? He made a good living working both sides. You really think he could have gone into East Berlin that many times and gotten out alive if he didn't have friends there?"

The world really had turned upside down.

"Bauer wanted to follow in his daddy's footsteps, but the Cold War was over. The only way to make good side money these days is selling drugs or guns. Dealing with drug cartels is messy work, but running guns is even harder. Those old AKs were our chance to score big, and we took it."

A sense of sadness stole over Nick. So many good people dead, so many lives ruined, so much pain—all for money. "Was it worth . . . Dani's life?"

"Dani?" Kramer shrugged. "The stupid bitch was onto me, saw me open the door for some of Dudaev's men. I had to take her out."

Cold fury sent adrenaline surging through Nick's system, got him onto his feet. He took a step toward Kramer. "*You* had that bastard kill her?"

"I couldn't very well walk in and do it myself, now could I?" Kramer glared at him. "Where is she, Andris? Where is Bradshaw?"

"Why do you want her?" God, it hurt to breathe. "What does she have to do . . . with any of this?"

"The bitch was assigned to Dudaev for almost a month. Do you really think he could get in bed with her and not tell her anything? I hear she's good. But then you probably found that out for yourself, didn't you?"

Nick fought back a surge of anger, knowing that Kramer was just doing this to provoke him. "She didn't sleep with him . . . and she didn't know anything."

Kramer jerked his thumb toward the ceiling. "Take him up."

Nick gritted his teeth against the white-hot pain in his ribs and shoulders.

Hold it together, Andris. Hold it together.

If Holly was doing what he'd asked of her, the marshals service now knew where he was. All he had to do was hang on—and hope they got here before Holly was forced to listen to him die.

Kramer got closer. "Is she worth this, kid? Is she worth this pain and suffering?"

Nick struggled to inhale, hoping she would hear his answer. "*Yes!* She's worth anything."

God, yes, she was.

He loved her.

Kramer turned, gave a shrug. "I guess he wants more."

Ilia pounded Nick until he was on the brink of unconsciousness. He was lowered to the floor again, where he lay, struggling for breath. It felt like an elephant was sitting on the right side of his chest—probably a collapsed lung.

"This isn't working." Kramer's voice seemed to come from far away. He sounded angry. "He's protecting her. It makes him feel noble. We need a way to strip everything from him, make him forget her. Ideas?"

"Use my brother's blowtorch. Burn him bit by bit."

"Not bad. Anyone else?"

"I say we take turns to fuck his ass and then cut off his balls."

Nick drifted in and out, the conversation hovering just beyond his comprehension.

Kramer laughed. "Ilia, you're a fucking animal. Get the damned blowtorch."

And it hit Nick that they were talking about how best to break him. Fear snaked through his belly, coiled with rage. "This is how . . . you treat someone . . . you said was like a son to you?"

"I told you to trust no one. You should have listened."

"He *did* listen."

Nick thought he'd lost his mind. He'd just heard Holly's voice. But she was far from here. She was—

An AK opened up behind him.

Rat-at-at! Rat-at-at!

Ilia and one of the other goons fell to the floor, blood spatter on the wall behind them. The other one turned and ran but didn't make it ten feet. Kramer also ran, a spray of blood shooting up from his shoulder as he disappeared through the door.

The AK went silent, and there she was, looking beautiful and terrified and determined as hell.

"Holly?" Adrenaline shot through him—along with a dose of anger. "What the *hell* are you doing here?"

"Isn't that obvious?" Still holding the AK, Holly ran over to the two men she'd just freaking killed, took their weapons, and slid them across the floor to Nick. "The others are on their way. ETA about fifteen minutes. I'll cover you while you get the ropes off, but please hurry! I'm just making this up as I go and have no idea what I'm doing."

Heart thudding in her chest like a hammer, she backed up against the wall and looked for anyone who might be aiming a weapon their way, a man's angry shouts coming from the building's entrance.

"Get behind those crates over there. Do it!" Nick bit and tugged at the knots until his wrists were free, then grabbed the weapons and followed her.

He didn't stand upright, his right arm pressed to his side, his chest and abdomen a mass of contusions, red welts, and deep red blotches. She knew he must have broken ribs and maybe worse. He needed an ambulance.

Hurry, Javi! Hurry, Zach!

He sank down beside her, checked the weapons—an AK, a Makarov pistol, and a PP-2000. "You promised not to follow me."

"I mostly kept that promise until they threatened to burn you, rape you, and cut off your balls. Be angry with me if you want, but there was no way I could sit in the van and listen while they brutalized and maimed you."

"How did you . . . get in?"

Was he having trouble breathing?

"I parked the minivan on the other side of a berm behind the building, waited until the sentry on the roof was looking the other way, and then made for the back door. I had to shoot a guy. I shot him and took his weapon."

Nick stared at her. "You stormed this place alone . . . with a Ruger .22?"

"That's all I had." What else was she supposed to have done?

"You are fucking incredible. I wouldn't ask a Special Forces operator to do that."

"No Special Forces operator cares about you the way I do."

Nick's gaze went soft. He leaned over and kissed her. "I love you, Holly."

The breath rushed from her lungs, her heart knocking against her breast bone. "You . . . you do?"

He chuckled, winced in pain. "Don't act so surprised."

But she was. "I. . . ."

She didn't even know what to say.

Men's voices grew nearer.

"I think it's just the two of them," said a voice Holly recognized. *Kramer.* "Fan out, and stay alert. Andris used to be with Delta Force."

Nick's face turned serious. He lowered his voice to a whisper. "How many men did you see on your way in?"

"There were three sentries—two along the road and one on the rooftop—and the guy in the back."

"And you're sure he's dead?"

"Yes." An image of the man's sightless eyes, blood pouring from his temple, flashed through her mind, bringing on a wave of dizziness.

She would have to think about that later.

"Kramer said there were seven of them. You took out four. That leaves the three sentries from outside, plus Kramer, and you caught him in the shoulder."

"I wish I'd killed him." Holly's stomach churned at the thought of what Kramer had done—and what he'd been about to do.

"You might still get that chance."

A tremor of fear shot through her, the reality of what she'd set in motion catching up with her. "If we make it out of this, I'm going to need a hug—and a night of hot sex."

"It's a deal."

"What's the plan?"

"The plan is that you stay right here. I'll leave you with the pistol and the PP-2000. Do you still have the Ruger?"

"Yes."

"Only fire if you're discovered and have to defend yourself. Otherwise, stay down and stay quiet. Got it?"

She nodded. "Nick."

"What?"

Tell him you love him.

"Please be careful!"

You're pathetic, Bradshaw!

He smiled. "Always."

He got to his feet, the AK in hand, and disappeared on the other side of a pallet loaded with crates.

Holly checked both pistols, made sure each had a round in the chamber, then scooted back against the wall and listened. The only thing she could hear was her own heartbeat. She wouldn't be surprised if everyone else could hear it, too.

She drew a deep breath, tried to ratchet back on the adrenaline, to slow her pulse and clear her head. They'd made it this far. It was going to be okay.

All it takes is one bullet.

She quashed the thought, tried to lose the bad feeling she'd had all afternoon.

An explosion of AK fire made her jump.

The sound echoed through the building, making it impossible for her to tell which direction the shots had come from. Had that been Nick—or had someone fired at him?

And where were Javier and Zach? They'd been about fifteen minutes out when she'd last talked with them. They ought to be here by now.

More shots—pistol shots.

Answering AK fire. And then . . . footsteps.

Someone was walking toward her.

It couldn't be Nick. He was barefoot. This man was wearing boots.

Holly's mouth went dry, her heart thrumming in her chest. She steadied her grip on the Ruger, forced her fear aside.

A man in olive drab BDUs stepped into sight holding an AK. He hadn't seen her, but crept slowly in the direction

Nick had gone. He was only a few feet away from her now, his back toward her. He raised the weapon, sighted on something, his finger already on the trigger.

She aimed for center mass, hoped he wasn't wearing a vest, and fired.

Click.

A misfire?

Damned .22 subsonic ammo!

Shit!

But the man had heard. He whirled toward her.

She dropped the Ruger, picked up the Makarov, but it was too late, the muzzle of his weapon pressing against her chest. She set the Makarov down, raised her hands, looked up at him from beneath her eyelashes, doing her best to look helpless and terrified, which was really very easy.

He lowered the weapon, reached down, and grabbed her by her hair, yanking her painfully to her feet. His gaze raked over her, and he grinned, opening his mouth as if to speak. But then Nick was there.

He drove the butt of his AK into the side of the bastard's head. The man released Holly, stumbled sideways.

Holly sank back out of the way, grabbed the Makarov, ready to fire if she got a clear opportunity.

The man swung his AK at Nick, who was covered in sweat and clearly struggling to breathe. Nick parried, but the blow drove him back. He lunged forward, jabbed the bastard in the gut with the barrel of his weapon. The man doubled over, one hand sliding inside his jacket, his fingers closing around something—a knife or a pistol.

She shouted a warning to Nick. "He's got a weapon!"

Nick swung the AK up again, striking the man in the face. The man collapsed in a spray of blood. Then Nick brought the butt down on the man's head, crushing his skull.

Holly stared, the savageness of it taking the breath from her lungs.

Was the man dead?

Nick sank to one knee, fighting to catch his breath, sweat beaded on his forehead, his face pale. He felt the man for a pulse, shook his head. "Stay down. Got the other two . . . but

Kramer . . . still out there. He won't go . . . till we're dead. We're the only ones . . . who know . . . he's still alive."

She watched as he fought his way to his feet, obviously in pain, his jaw clenched.

"Holly!"

Zach!

"We're back here!" She started to get to her feet.

"Stay down!" Nick hissed, moving to stand across from her, his gaze traveling over the cavernous space, searching for any sign of Kramer.

It seemed to happen in an instant.

The red dot of a laser sight dancing on Nick's chest. A surge of adrenaline. Holly lunging to her feet, throwing herself against him, knocking him aside. The *crack* of the single rifle shot. Impact with the floor driving the breath from her lungs.

Nick rolled, aimed from a prone position, opened fire.

Rat-at-at-at!

Holly caught a glimpse of a man falling from scaffolding far in the back corner of the garage—and then she saw.

Blood spatter.

It was on the floor, on Nick's arm.

He'd been shot.

She pointed, tried to speak, but no words came. Then the pain hit, made it impossible to breathe. And she realized Nick hadn't been shot.

She had.

CHAPTER 27

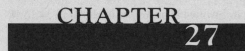

NICK WATCHED KRAMER fall and lie still. He let out the breath he'd been holding, sat up, clutching the pain in his right side.

It was finally over.

He turned toward Holly—and his blood went cold.

Oh, no. God, no.

She lay on her belly, blood soaking through her shirt, spilling onto the floor. She looked up at him, her sweet face a mask of pain. "This . . . sucks."

"Jesus, Holly, no." His own pain forgotten, he knelt beside her, turned her gently onto her back, then tore off her shirt and bra.

The round had caught her in the ribs beneath her left arm and passed through her at a sharp angle, exiting beneath her shoulder blade. From the heavy bleeding, he knew the bullet must have penetrated her lung. He needed to seal off both wounds, keep air from seeping into her chest. If he couldn't slow her bleeding . . .

Icy panic hit him, made his heart pound.

He couldn't lose Holly. God, no, not Holly, too.

Pull it together, Andris.

He ripped the cloth of her shirt in two and wadded it up, pressing half of it firmly into the exit wound and holding the other half on the entry wound in her side.

She whimpered in pain. "It's bad . . . isn't it?"

It *was* bad. But he couldn't tell her that.

"It's going to be okay, honey. Hang on." Then he remembered the bug in his fly. "If anyone can hear this, Holly's been shot. She needs medical help *now*."

Where the fuck were the marshals service and the CIS team?

She struggled for breath, her face pale, her skin cold, the cloth beneath his hands quickly soaking through. He had nothing else. If help didn't arrive soon, she was going to die right here on the cold concrete floor.

Just like Dani.

The thought made his heart constrict. "Stay with me, Holly."

Goddamn it! How the *fuck* had this happened?

She was too damned brave for her own good, too impulsive.

She reached over with her right hand, curled her slender fingers around his, her hands so cold. "Don't blame yourself . . . I saw . . . he was going . . . to shoot you."

Nick *did* blame himself. He had promised to protect her, to get her safely through this. "Save your energy, honey. Don't try to talk."

Tears spilled from the corners of her eyes. "I'm . . . I'm scared."

He was scared, too. Her blood had soaked completely through the cloth now.

He willed a smile onto his face, spoke with a confidence he didn't feel. "You're going to be okay. Just hang on."

She had to make it. She was so full of life and had so much still ahead of her. She'd brought laughter and happiness back into his world. He couldn't lose her.

"I'm not . . . so sure." She whimpered again, her pain tearing at him.

God, how he wished he had that auto-injector of morphine now—anything to ease her suffering. Then he heard the sound of boots.

"We're over here!" he shouted. "Get medical! She's been shot!"

A half-dozen men in tactical gear rushed up on them, weapons raised.

"Nick Andris?"

"That's him." One of the men tore off his helmet, and Nick recognized Zach McBride. He looked down at Holly and spoke into his mic, his expression hard. "Get Life Flight on the way. She's going to need air transport. Single GSW to the side. Tell Rossiter and the paramedics to get back here on the double."

Holly must have recognized his voice. "Zach?"

One of the other men removed his helmet—Javier Corbray. "We're all here, Holly—McBride, me, Hunter, Darcangelo. Rossiter is going to be here in a minute if he would just *hurry his ass up*."

Darcangelo removed his helmet, too, and knelt beside her. "Rest easy, Holly."

"Sorry . . . I couldn't . . . tell you . . . the truth . . . I never wanted . . . to mislead you."

"You have no reason to apologize." Darcangelo took her other hand, his gaze meeting Nick's, his eyes going cold.

Nick knew he and the other men wanted to kill him, but he didn't care what her friends did to him as long as they helped her.

She was trembling now, shock setting in. "Please . . . tell the others . . . I love them . . . If I don't make it . . . they can have my clothes . . . and shoes."

"Hey, don't talk like that." Darcangelo smiled. "You're going to be okay."

"Not Nick's fault. . . . He's hurt . . . Kramer was going . . . to shoot him."

He could almost hear the men's thoughts: *Better him than you.*

Didn't they understand he felt the same way?

"Shhh, honey. Just rest." Nick bent down, kissed her cold lips.

She gave him a weak smile, tears glittering in her eyes, spilling down her temples. "Don't be sad . . . I finally . . . found a man . . . who loves me . . . I couldn't . . . let you . . . die."

Pain seemed to split Nick's chest. "I won't let you go."

Not now. Not here. Not like this.

But her eyes had already drifted shut, her breathing erratic now. She was fading fast, bleeding out right in front of him.

"Stay with me, Holly." Nick closed his eyes and prayed,

tears blurring his vision. He didn't give a damn if the other men saw. He had no pride left, nothing to hide, no ego to protect. "She pushed me out of the line of fire . . . I would have done anything for her . . . I would have died for her."

God, please help her!

Marc Hunter's voice came from behind him. "We cleared the place. There's a man in back who's in pretty bad shape with a broken jaw, but everyone else is dead. Why is this piece of shit not in cuffs? Oh, God . . . *Holly.*"

Then a man with a prosthetic blade for a leg—Gabe Rossiter—appeared at Nick's side, medical kit slung over his shoulder, two uniformed paramedics right behind him. "Give me some room."

Everyone stepped back.

"Help her. Please!" Nick withdrew his fingers from Holly's cold hand, moved aside, barely aware of his own pain or how hard it had become to breathe.

While Rossiter started IV fluids in one arm, one of the other paramedics strapped a blood-pressure cuff to her other arm and clipped a pulse oximeter to her finger.

"Pulse is one-fifty-two. BP is . . . non-existent."

Her eyes fluttered open, and she called for him. "Nick?"

"I'm right here, honey." He moved around Rossiter, knelt near her head, stroked her pale, cold cheeks. "Your friends are here. It's going to be okay now."

"I thought I'd never find you . . . You're the best time . . . I ever had . . . I love you."

Nick looked into her beautiful brown eyes and saw the love she felt for him shining there, beyond pain, beyond fear, beyond mortality. "You are my heart, Holly. I love you so much."

She drew a shaky breath, whispered, "Kiss me."

He bent down, pressed his lips to hers again.

Then her eyes drifted shut, and she lay still, so still.

"No, Holly. No!"

"Shit! She's crashing. I'm going to intubate her. Get another IV going." Rossiter grabbed some gear out of his med kit, his gaze meeting Nick's. "I need you to move. *Now.*"

Nick stood—or tried to stand.

Black spots. Crushing pressure.

Blinding pain dropped him to his knees again. Strong arms grabbed him, drew him to his feet, pulled him back. When they released him, his legs gave out completely, and he fell, catching just a glimpse of Rossiter as he inserted a breathing tube into Holly's airway. Then the world around him faded to black.

Nick heard sirens and men's voices.

"We've got multiple broken ribs and a right pneumothorax."

"Get a chest tube ready."

"His BP is dropping. It looks like they beat the shit out of him."

"He could have internal bleeding. Open those fluids up wide."

Nick opened his eyes, found himself inside an ambulance, an IV in one arm, an oxygen mask over his face, electrodes stuck to his chest. McBride sat nearby watching him, still wearing tactical gear. The two paramedics who'd been helping Holly were now working on him.

But where was Holly?

"Holly?" He croaked out her name, the pressure on his chest unbearable.

"She's en route to the trauma center." McBride's face was lined with worry. "Rossiter, the other paramedic, is with her."

"Is she . . . ?"

"She was still alive when they took off a few minutes ago."

Thank God.

Nick closed his eyes, offered up a silent prayer for her. She was all that mattered, the only thing he cared about now. He couldn't lose her.

When he opened his eyes again, he found McBride still watching him. "Sorry about the cuffs. There's still a warrant out for you. I have no choice but to restrain you."

Nick hadn't noticed. He didn't care.

One of the paramedics looked down at him. "I need to insert a tube into your chest wall to let some of the trapped air out. Your lung has collapsed."

Nick nodded, gritting his teeth against the sharp pain of

the tube as it was thrust between two broken ribs and into his side.

Then he was out again.

He woke to the sound of someone shouting his name. He opened his eyes to find a woman in green scrubs looking down at him.

"Mr. Andris, the CT scan showed bruising on your spleen and liver. You're going to be staying here so that we can keep you under observation. We'll be taking you up to your room in a moment. We're giving you morphine for the pain. Let us know if you're not getting adequate relief."

"Holly?" His voice was muffled by an oxygen mask.

But the woman had already turned away. "Is he going to remain in restraints?"

"For the time being, yes, ma'am." That was McBride's voice. "We're posting security outside his door as well."

Nick drew as deep a breath as he could. "McBride!"

McBride's face swam into view. "What is it?"

"Holly . . . How is she?"

"She's still in surgery. We haven't heard anything."

"I want . . . to see her."

"That's not going to happen—at least not for a while. You're in Colorado Springs at Memorial Hospital, and it looks like you'll be here for a few days. She was flown to the level-one trauma center in Denver."

Nick squeezed his eyes shut, infuriated to feel so damned helpless. "I need to know. When you hear how she is . . . I need to know."

McBride nodded, a muscle working in his jaw. "I'll keep you informed. The CIA is taking over this case. They'll be handling your security detail. I expect someone is going to have a lot of questions for you."

Fuck the Agency. Fuck their questions.

"I would have done anything . . . to keep her safe."

McBride looked like he had a few things he'd like to say, but whatever they were, he kept them to himself. "I'll let you know when I hear anything."

As they wheeled him to his room, still cuffed to the railing, Nick closed his eyes and prayed.

God, please, not Holly.

* * *

ZACH ENTERED THE surgery waiting area and saw the
entire gang sitting together. Even Derek Tower and Alex
Carmichael were there. They took up most of the room, the
men standing, the women sitting together, some of them in
tears.

Natalie saw him and waddled over to him. He wrapped
his arms around her, held a hand against her pregnant belly,
the feel of her precious in his arms, a sadness he hadn't been
able to shake gripping his chest. "Any news?"

Natalie shook her head, tears in her eyes. "How did this
happen?"

"It's a long story. Let's see if we can get a private waiting
room." They were going to find out sooner or later. It was better that they hear it from him than read about it in the papers.

Reece went off to speak with one of the nursing staff, and
soon they found themselves crowded into a small room with
a table and six plastic chairs.

Zach ran a hand over the stubble on his face, feeling
drained. "God, I'm not even sure where to begin. There are
so many missing pieces."

"I think we can fill in a lot of them," Corbray said. "Tower
and I got our hands on the surveillance feed Holly set up in
the minivan and listened to the whole thing. I'll tell you right
now, Holly is a hero in my book."

"Hell, yeah, she is," Darcangelo said.

Zach figured he ought to dive in. "I guess I'll start by
saying that Holly is a CIA non-cover officer. She's been
working for the CIA since she was eighteen."

Surprised gasps, astonished glances.

"Holly is a CIA agent?" Kara gaped at him, wide-eyed.

"A CIA officer—with top-secret security clearance."

"Our Holly?" Tessa asked.

Zach nodded. "Our Holly."

"She's a damned good one, too," Corbray added, an edge
of emotion in his voice.

Zach knew he was beating himself up for not reaching
her sooner.

Zach told them everything he knew about Dudaev's

murder and Holly's subsequent abduction. Some of it he'd learned through his own investigation and some he'd heard from Nguyen, who was clinging to life in the ICU.

"Somehow Andris realized Holly was CIA, too. He refused to terminate her."

"Thank God for that!" Natalie exclaimed.

"Somehow she got away from him, but that's when she ran into Dudaev's men. Apparently, this Kramer guy knew where Nick had taken Holly and sent them up to the cabin to kill both of them."

Zach told them how Holly had then been assigned to remain with Andris. "Nguyen, who has been investigating Bauer for a couple of years now, says the Agency suspected Andris had been set up by his boss, but they didn't know who Bauer's accomplice was. They hoped the man would try to make a move on the two of them and that Andris and Holly would then be able to expose him."

"The CIA used them as bait," Laura said.

"It worked. Bauer told Kramer he was sending Nguyen to Colorado Springs to negotiate with Andris, and Kramer sent his men to kill Nguyen and ambush and kill Andris and Holly. Nick ruined that plan by not taking Holly with him, so Kramer tried to torture her location out of him."

"Remind me never to complain about my job," Matt said. "Never thought I'd say it, but there are worse people to work for than Tom Trent."

Corbray picked up the story. "Kramer tried to get Andris to tell him where Holly was, not knowing that Holly had put a GPS transmitter and micro listening device in Andris's jeans. The whole thing is recorded, from the moment they left the hotel where they'd been hiding to the moment we shut it off, and I'm telling you, it's some brutal stuff. Kramer and his guys were debating whether to burn Andris bit by bit with a blowtorch or to sodomize and castrate him. That's when Holly moved in on her own."

Corbray told them how Holly had been in touch with him, how she'd done recon and found a good place from which to stage a rescue. "I told her to wait, but she didn't. She went in and took out four men to get to him."

"She's hot *and* a badass," Alex said.

Derek glared at him. "If you want to talk about Ms. Bradshaw around me, you'd better show her respect. She's worth a helluva lot more to this country than one foul-mouthed journalist."

Corbray went on. "Andris hid Holly and took over after that."

"Wasn't he injured? How could he fight?" Kat asked.

"You'd be surprised what adrenaline can do in a combat situation. Andris took the rest of them out, but Kramer climbed some scaffolding at the rear of the building when Andris was engaged in close-quarters combat. When Holly saw the red dot from the laser sight on his chest, she pushed him out of the way and . . . she was hit in the side."

"The bullet entered at an angle," Rossiter said, lifting his arm. "It went in here, then exited beneath her scapula. If it had been an inch in the other direction, it would have been a graze. If it had gone an inch deeper, we would have lost her right then."

For a moment, no one spoke.

"Why was Holly with Dudaev that night?" Sophie asked.

Derek spoke up. "It's her job to do whatever it takes to get close to men like Dudaev and set them up for surveillance with listening devices and GPS transmitters. She's an expert at gathering intelligence through intimate interaction with people."

Zach watched while that revelation sank in, comprehension dawning.

"All those men she slept with—she was working?" Ramirez asked.

Corbray nodded. "You got it."

"Isn't all of this classified?" Sheridan asked.

"It is—or it was. Bauer was arrested trying to board an airplane about an hour ago. Before he left, he burned Holly and Andris in an email to some media contacts in Washington, outing them to the world, putting them in considerable peril. This is going to be big news by tonight."

Alex stood, notepad in hand. "If it's going to be big news, then I'm going to get on it. Someone has to tell the story right."

Darcangelo held up his hand to stop Alex. "There's

something she wanted me to tell all of you. Before she lost consciousness, she apologized for not being able to tell us the truth. She said she never meant to mislead us."

"She shouldn't apologize for that." Laura dabbed the corners of her eyes with a tissue. "She was serving her country."

Darcangelo took Tessa's hand. "That's what I told her. She also asked me to tell you . . . that she loves you all. She wants you women to have her clothes and shoes if she doesn't make it."

Tessa laughed through her tears. "That's our Holly—thinking of her shoes."

The other women laughed, too, all of them in tears.

"But she's going to make it," Sophie said. "She has to make it. Is she pregnant?"

"No." Zach's swallowed the hard lump in his throat. "I think you should know that she and Andris are involved. Holly loves him, and he seems to love her, too."

Corbray nodded. "Yeah, he does. I know we've all been hating on him, but after listening to what he went through, I've changed my mind. At one point when they were beating the hell out of him, Kramer asked him if Holly was worth his suffering. He could barely speak, but he said, 'Yes. She's worth anything.'"

Zach hadn't known this. "He wants to know how she's doing."

"I volunteer to keep him updated," Kara said.

"Count me in," Sophie said.

The door opened and a doctor in surgical scrubs walked in, mask hanging around his neck, the grave expression on his face putting a knot in Zach's stomach. "You're Holly Bradshaw's party? Are her next of kin here?"

Zach lied, motioned vaguely toward Tessa and Laura, both of whom had blond hair. "Yes—along with the officers investigating her case."

"How is she?" the women asked, almost as one.

"She made it through surgery, but her condition is extremely critical. We had to give her nineteen units of blood. The bullet shattered one rib, but that rib deflected the bullet away from her heart. She lost part of her lung. If she makes it through the next twenty-four hours, we'll have a much better idea. She's in the ICU now. We're doing our best to keep her stable and comfortable."

"Can we see her?" Kara asked.

"Who here is family?"

Laura cleared her throat. "We all are—well, except for Alex. He's a reporter."

Soft laughter from the women.

The doctor looked like he didn't believe them but was too damned tired to argue with them. "You can't all go in at once. Two at a time should be fine, but just for a few minutes. She's not conscious yet, and she needs rest."

The doctor left them alone.

Zach drew his wife into his arms again, kissed her hair. "Thank God."

They'd come this far, and right now it felt like a miracle.

CHAPTER  28

HOLLY ONLY KNEW that one moment there was nothing, and the next there was pain and confusion and noise. She couldn't seem to open her eyes or talk or move.

"You're on a ventilator, sweetie. Just lie still. We'll be getting you more pain medication in a moment."

Where was she? Why did she hurt so much? Who was talking to her?

Then the world faded again.

Warm fingers held hers. Hands stroked her cheeks. Soothing voices faded in and out. It sounded like some of them were crying.

"Holly, can you hear me? It's Kara. Reece and I are right here beside you. We love you, sweetie."

"Holly, it's me, Julian. How's my favorite superhero? Tessa and I are here for you, and we're not going anywhere."

"She looks so pale, Julian. When is she going to wake up?"

"I'm not sure you can hear me, *chula*, but you're gonna pull through this, and we're going to be with you all the way."

"It's Kat, Holly. Gabe and I are praying for you. We're holding an *inipi* ceremony for you tonight. Most of the gang will be there."

"Hey, Holly, it's Natalie. Never mind my crying. I can't seem to help it. I'm just so glad you're going to be okay. We're all proud of you, aren't we, Zach?"

"Yeah, we are. I heard that Andris—Nick—is stable. He's

going to be okay, thanks to you. I thought you'd want to know."

"It's Marc. Can you hear me? We've got you. Everything is going to be okay. You just rest and get strong again."

"Holly, your parents are here now. Isn't that wonderful? The other nurses and I have brought them up to date, and they'll be back here in a second to see you."

She heard the words. At times, she even understood them.

But then she was drifting again.

After that, the dreams began, dark dreams, terrible dreams. A man dead beside her, bullet holes in his head. Another man aiming a gun at her.

She tried to run, but couldn't.

Nick!

Where was he? They'd tortured him, hurt him.

She remembered the laser dot on his chest, blood on his skin.

Nick!

"Don't try to talk. You're still on the ventilator," said a kind voice. "We need more morphine."

Then she felt like she was falling, falling into silence, darkness, more dreams.

Sometime later, she opened her eyes, found herself in a semi-dark room surrounded by sounds. The soft murmur of voices. The beep of an IV pump that needed changing. The hiss of oxygen through a ventilator.

Slowly, it began to make sense. She was in the hospital. She'd been shot. She'd pushed Nick out of the line of fire and had caught a round in her side.

Well, that explained the pain.

But where was Nick? Was he okay?

A nurse injected something into her IV, and her thoughts unraveled again.

It was arguing that woke her next.

"I had to get up at six to catch a flight from Miami. I just want to get back to the hotel for some room service and a nap—and a glass of wine."

"You can sleep here. They have little fold-out beds. There's a cafeteria."

"You're not really suggesting I sleep on one of those

things. How can I be sure it's clean? What if there are bed bugs? Besides, their cafeteria doesn't have wine."

"I can't stay with her. I've got an important meeting with the marshals service and that penny-ante security company—Cobra, or whatever it's called. I want to find out why I wasn't kept up to date on the situation."

Her parents were fighting over who should have to stay with her. Couldn't they find it in themselves to care about her even now?

"An important meeting? You're retired, for God's sake! You haven't had an important meeting since the last time I took you to court. Besides, it sounds like Holly's work was classified above your pay grade."

While they continued to bicker, she opened her eyes, searched for the call button, hoping to get one of the nurses to send them away. But the nurses must have already heard, because one of them stepped into Holly's room.

"I'm going to have to ask the two of you to take your discussion into the hallway," she said. "This is the Intensive Care Unit, not family court."

"Do you know who I am?" her father asked.

"You could be the president or the king of Siam for all I care. I'm the head nurse, and that trumps everything else. If you don't leave, I'll have security escort you from the grounds."

Holly closed her eyes, a pain building in her chest that had nothing to do with being shot, tears spilling down her cheeks.

EVEN DRUGGED OUT of his mind on morphine, Nick found it hard to sleep. All he wanted was to see Holly, to be with her, to know that she was going to be okay. But he was still cuffed to his bed, unable to leave his room except for the repeated ultrasounds the doctor had ordered. Hell, he had to get one of the Agency guards outside his door to unlock him just to take a piss.

What Nick would have done without Holly's network of friends, he didn't know. Her girlfriends took turns calling several times a day to give him updates. He knew when her condition was downgraded to critical but stable, knew when she'd regained consciousness, knew that she'd asked about him, writing his name on a pad of paper because she was still on the ventilator and couldn't talk.

God, he hated being so far away from her, hated feeling this helpless.

His mom and dad and his brothers and sister all called and sent flowers, but he told them not to bother flying to Colorado. He couldn't have visitors, apart from law enforcement or investigators. He apologized for the hell he'd put them through—the media scrutiny, the doubt, the fear.

"Don't you apologize to us," his father said. "Wrong was done to you, and we were proud to bear the burden of it with you."

"We never once believed what the papers said about you," his mother said. "We knew you would never hurt that poor girl."

"I still might go to prison. I did some things to defend myself that crossed the line, things the Agency wishes I hadn't done."

"Whatever you did, you had a good reason," his father said.

Nick had no idea what he'd done to deserve the kind of faith his family had shown in him. He broke down, cried actual damned tears, telling them about Holly and what she'd done for him. "I love her. I want to spend the rest of my life with her."

They didn't know what to say about that. Holly wasn't Georgian Orthodox or even Russian Orthodox like Dani had been. She wasn't religious at all. They didn't know her or her family. She certainly wasn't the devout virgin and future stay-at-home mother they'd expected each of their sons to marry.

"Do you think she feels the same way about you?" his father asked after a moment of silence.

"Yeah, she does. She took a bullet for me and almost died. The last thing she said before she lost consciousness was 'I love you.'"

"I will light a candle for her and pray for her," his mother said—a big concession on her part. "Any woman who would give her life for you—this woman I want to meet."

McBride, Corbray, and Tower came to visit him a couple of times, bringing newspapers and giving him updates. He'd been relieved to hear that Lee was recovering and that Bauer was now in custody. But he was stunned by the news that the bastard had burned him and Holly, revealing their jobs and identities to reporters. Bauer's career was over and he'd apparently wanted to drag the two of them down with him. This had put all of Nick's assets in Eastern Europe in mortal danger, and he knew the Agency must be scrambling to provide them with new cover or safe travel to the US.

On the morning of the fifth day, he learned from a nurse that he was being discharged. His broken ribs still hurt like hell but his spleen and liver were healing and his doctor was certain he was beyond risk of internal bleeding or a rupture.

Nick was wondering what he was going to wear—he'd arrived wearing a pair of bloody jeans and nothing else—when someone he'd never met entered his room.

"I'm Jared Rensler. I've been retained to serve as your attorney."

"Retained by whom?"

"Someone who cares about your case." Rensler, a short man with birdlike features and a hairline that was in full retreat, was carrying a garment bag and a small suitcase with him. "I've brought clothes and personal care items. You'll need to shave. You're scheduled for an arraignment in Washington this afternoon."

That was news to Nick.

"This afternoon?" He shook his head. "I've got somewhere else I have to go before I leave Colorado."

He had to see Holly, had to see for himself that she was all right, had to tell her how much she meant to him. She'd taken a bullet for him. He ought to be at her side.

"I'm afraid that's impossible. We leave for the airport in an hour. We have a chartered flight ready to take us to Washington."

"Call someone. Change it. If it's a chartered flight, let's get a delay." Who the fuck did this guy think he was, anyway?

"You don't understand, Mr. Andris. You don't have the freedom to make that choice. You're under arrest for the murder of Sachino Dudaev and several other felonies. I fully expect most of the charges to be dropped given recent revelations, but you can't afford to be insubordinate or to contaminate Ms. Bradshaw's potential testimony by having contact with her prior to the conclusion of your case."

And Nick realized the fight wasn't over yet.

ONE WEEK TO the day after she was admitted, Holly was breathing on her own again. She was moved out of ICU to a private room where she was able to receive more visitors, two Agency paramilitary operators guarding her door twenty-four-seven. She was still extremely weak—walking up and down the hallway left her out of breath—but she was in less pain and able to stay awake for longer periods.

The world seemed to have changed during the time she'd been in the ICU. Bauer was locked up. She'd been outed as a CIA agent, her face in all the papers and on television, her career surely over. Nick was in custody in a federal facility in Washington, DC, awaiting a motions hearing to have all charges against him dropped.

As grateful as she was that she and Nick were both alive and whole, the fear of what might happen to Nick and concern about her own future with the Agency were clouds on her horizon. There wasn't much she could do lying in a hospital bed. She was accustomed to being able to take charge and act.

Not being able to talk with Nick made it all so much more difficult. She missed him so badly it hurt. She wasn't used to that—needing to be with a man to feel like everything was right with her world.

When it came down to it, being in love kind of sucked.

Her mother and father continued to visit, though they came separately now, staying for about an hour a day. Her time with them left her on edge. Both of them pressed her for details about her work and Nick—and accused her of betraying them by keeping the truth from them. She always felt relieved when they left.

Two days after she got out of ICU, her girlfriends held a little party to raise her spirits, bringing flowers, balloons, and, of course, cupcakes. Holly was able to eat only a few bites of her cupcake, but it was wonderful to spend time with all of them.

She told them the whole story, from the moment Nick had abducted her until she'd been shot. She even told them about her father and how he'd treated her. Like true friends, they listened, laughing when she laughed, tearing up when her eyes filled with tears, getting angry when she felt anger.

When she'd finished, she felt free—and extremely drained.

"When Zach told us that you were a CIA officer, I was floored," said Natalie, wiping frosting off her fingers with a napkin. "But then I thought about it, about all those super-wealthy and powerful men you've gone out with, and it made sense."

"That Saudi prince," said Sophie.

Holly smiled.

"And the South African banker," Tessa added.

Laura's eyes narrowed. "That Dutch woman you said was a *friend*."

Kat blinked. "You dated *women*?"

"When the job called for it." She didn't bother to explain it had only happened once. The stunned looks on their faces were too amusing.

They went on, speculating about the men she'd gone out with, trying to decide which ones had been part of an Agency assignment.

"You know, I'm not sure we should be discussing this," Holly said, her expression serious. "That's all classified top secret."

Silence.

They looked guiltily at one another and then at her.

"I guess we didn't think about that," Laura said at last.

Holly couldn't help but laugh, which hurt. "Ow! I'm just kidding. I'm kidding."

They laughed but she could tell she'd made them nervous. She hadn't meant to do that.

"There was a moment at the start of all of this when I worried that you would all hate me if you found out about my night job. But then I told myself that you would forgive me."

"Oh, Holly, there was never anything to forgive." Kara

stood, walked over to Holly, and gave her a gentle hug. "This was like finding out that my best friend is actually Xena: Warrior Princess."

Holly smiled, found herself blinking back tears. "You're my friends, the best friends I've ever had. I love you all so much."

They talked about little things after that—the latest gossip from the newsroom, the unrelenting heat, the colors Natalie wanted for her baby's bedroom.

But soon Holly was asleep again.

Her friends quietly cleaned up the mess, then tiptoed out the door.

HOLLY AWOKE THAT afternoon to find her CO sitting beside her. She sat up, startled. "I'm sorry, sir. I didn't realize you were here."

"Relax, Holly. It's okay. And please just call me Brian." Brian Graeber was dressed impeccably in a deep blue suit with a white shirt and blue tie. With dark hair and a Boromir beard, she'd always thought him a handsome man. "You have no idea how worried I've been."

Holly knew he would never have risked being seen with her under normal circumstances, but then, her situation was anything but normal. She knew why he'd come. "I'm out, aren't I?"

"If by that you mean you can't continue working in your current position, you're correct. I'm afraid Bauer brought that to an end. We're doing what we can to minimize the damage, trying to keep it out of the foreign press, but it wouldn't be safe for you to continue in your role as an NCO, and it wouldn't be effective for the Agency."

Holly had expected to feel crushed by this, but she didn't. Another door had opened in her life, one that mattered even more to her. "I guess it couldn't last forever."

"Indeed not." Brian smiled. "It might interest you to know you successfully held the position longer than anyone else in Agency history. It's going to be impossible to fill your shoes."

Holly smiled at his humor—and the compliment. "Thanks."

"Your actions during this crisis have won you respect all

the way to the top of the flag pole. I expect you'll be receiving some kind of commendation." He watched her. "That surprises you?"

"I'm not sure I did anything special, sir."

"You stood up to interrogation, escaped, won the trust of the man who'd abducted you, and worked with him to resolve the biggest crisis the Agency has faced in a couple of decades. As a result of your skill, you and Andris were able to obtain the evidence the Agency needed to complete our investigation of the disaster in Batumi. If that weren't enough, you rescued Andris from torture, despite having minimal training for that kind of action. What you did was absolutely reckless, but also incredibly brave. We couldn't have asked anyone to show more courage."

"I'm sure most officers would have done the same thing."

"Are you?" He raised an eyebrow, smiled. "I'm not."

She asked him the one question that truly mattered to her. "What's going to happen to Nick?"

"He's got a motions hearing in ten days. In light of the evidence the two of you uncovered, I expect the court will throw out most of the charges against him. We were able to trace the account in the Caymans and confirm that it was set up by Kramer."

Relief, sweet and warm, washed through her. "Can you help him—pull strings or influence people from the inside? None of this was his fault."

"We know the two of you are involved."

Of course they did. It wouldn't be the CIA if they didn't. Then again, the two of them hadn't exactly made it a secret.

"I love him."

Her CO frowned, something like disappointment in his eyes. "Danger has a way of creating bonds between people who ordinarily would never get together. We see it fairly frequently. The passion usually fades right along with the adrenaline."

A tiny spark of fear flared to life inside her.

Would time and distance make Nick's feelings for her change? When all of this was over and he was free again, would he no longer want her in his life?

"My feelings won't change." Annoyance made her words sharp.

How could he be so dismissive of her relationship with Nick?

What if he's right?

"Time will tell." He gave her what felt like a patronizing smile. "In the meantime, I wanted to let you know that the Agency is offering you your choice of position, either in cryptography or intelligence analysis. You'd have to relocate to the Langley area, but the Agency would cover your moving expenses, help you find a new home, and arrange to sell your old one. You'd see a marked increase in salary—we're talking low six figures. If you came in as an analyst, you and I would be working together."

Holly's stomach sank. Cryptography was boring. Working as an analyst might be fun. But living near Langley would mean pulling up the roots she'd managed to put down, leaving Denver, leaving her home, leaving her friends.

"You're going to love Virginia in springtime," he was saying.

She held up her hand to stop him, not wanting to think about it. "I need to think about it. I have a job here, a job I love, friends I love."

"You've got people at Langley who care about you, too." He smiled, his gaze soft.

He thought he was in love with her.

The realization hit her squarely between the eyes.

Why had she never noticed it before?

She fought to cover her surprise. "I suppose that's true. I need some time. I need to see how Nick's case ends and find out what he wants to do."

There was that disappointment again—or was it hurt?

Brian stood. "I should let you rest. I'm flying back this evening. I just wanted to deliver the news in person. I hope you'll join me at Langley. It's been a pleasure and an honor working with you, Holly. I hope this isn't the end."

He took her hand, bent down, kissed it.

"Thank you for all you've done for me. Working for you has been a great adventure. You kept me safe and got me out of more than one bad situation."

"We make a great team." He handed her his card, giving her something she'd never had—his direct phone number. "Think about it."

"Thank you, Brian. I will."

She watched him leave, feeling strangely sad.

THE DOOR TO Nick's cell opened with an electric buzz.

"Get off your ass, Andris. Your attorney's here."

Nick stood, wondering what Rensler had to tell him today. He held out his wrists and waited while the guards shackled him hand and foot, then stepped out of his cell and followed the guards down the hallway toward the meeting rooms, his chains clinking.

It was nice to get out of that damned cell. They'd put him in twenty-three-hour lockdown, both to protect him from potential harm at the hands of other detainees and because he was considered extremely dangerous. He was allowed out of his cell for only an hour of exercise and a shower—or for meetings with his attorney or investigators.

Rensler smiled when he saw Nick. Hopefully that meant he had good news. Nick needed to get out of this place and back to Colorado.

Holly needed him—and he needed her.

Nick walked into the little meeting room and sat.

"We've got a date for the motions hearing, and I'm hopeful it will go our way. Investigators confirmed that Kramer opened the account in the Caymans. The money was still there, so the Agency was able to confiscate the funds." Rensler drew some documents out of his briefcase and showed them to Nick.

One was the original document opening the account. There were a couple of deposit and withdrawal slips. One of them was an image taken from security footage that showed Kramer at the bank counter.

That son of a bitch.

"If that weren't enough, the recording you and Ms. Bradshaw made of Kramer during your interrogation, together with the documents you found on Dudaev's hard drive, prove conclusively that Bauer and Kramer were behind not only the unfortunate chain of events in Batumi, but also the deaths of several paramilitary operators here in the US and the unauthorized killing of Mr. Dudaev."

"That's good news." Nick had been confident they wouldn't stick him with those charges. "What about the cloned hard drive?"

"I believe we've got a convincing argument there. The files did not technically belong to the Agency when you cloned the drive, and you did so only because you believed correctly that your supervisor was dirty." Rensler was getting revved up, practicing what he would say in court. "Your actions helped solve the case. If you *hadn't* cloned the hard drive, Bauer would have destroyed that data and we would never have found out about the account in the Caymans or the photos that Kramer sent to Dudaev."

"Will that be enough for them to drop the charge altogether?"

Rensler looked uncertain. "If they *do* charge you, those mitigating circumstances will enable us to plead guilty to a lesser charge and avoid a lengthy prison sentence."

"What are you thinking—ten years, five years?"

Rensler shrugged. "Maybe two to five."

Nick's stomach sank. Two to five years before he could be with Holly again. It sounded like an eternity.

Would she wait for him?

"I went back through old deposition records. I was able to demonstrate that Kramer was on duty at the time the photos were taken, as were Daly and McGowen."

"He must have killed them so they couldn't speak up."

"That's what investigators believe. There's talk at the Agency of using the confiscated funds to set up scholarships for the children of the slain officers."

There was no way to give the kids what they'd lost, but that was something.

"Can't we get the hearing bumped up?" Ten days felt like ten years in this place.

"I'm sorry. The judge is on vacation until then." Rensler packed the documents back in his briefcase and closed it.

"Have you heard anything about Ms. Bradshaw?"

Rensler shook his head, glanced at his smartphone. "It

doesn't look like we'll require her testimony, so I haven't been in touch with her."

Nick wondered how McBride would react if he got a collect call from a federal detention center. "Thanks for the good news."

"Stay positive." Rensler clapped him on the shoulder. "In ten days, I expect you'll be a free man."

Nick followed Rensler out of the meeting room and was waiting for the guards to take him back to his cell when he heard the clinking of chains. He turned his head.

Bauer.

Blood pounded inside his skull. "You son of a—"

The guards grabbed Nick's arms, one on each side, holding him back.

"You look good in orange, Bauer. I guess you better get used to it."

Bauer's face flushed angry red, his gaze focused on his feet as he walked by.

"You have so much blood on your hands—Dani, Carver, Daly, McGowen." The guards were pulling Nick now, but he wasn't done. "You not only brought yourself down, you brought your old man down, too. You trashed the family legacy. How does that feel? You miserable son of a bitch!"

"Andris! That piece of shit isn't worth it. You want to get tazed?"

Heart still thrumming, Nick let himself be led away.

CHAPTER 29

HOLLY WAS DISCHARGED the following Monday. Because neither of her parents were around—a good thing, really—Kara drove her home, walking with her to her door and insisting on carrying the small plastic bag of belongings Holly had brought home with her from the hospital.

She unlocked the door and stepped inside her own home for the first time in almost a month. The place was immaculate. Her friends had come over during the weekend to clean it for her and remove any sign that the place had been a crime scene. They'd also stocked the refrigerator with easy-to-make meals so she wouldn't have to go grocery shopping for a while.

"Thanks, Kara." She gave her best friend a hug—or half a hug.

Her left side still hurt a lot, and it was hard to move her arm.

"You're welcome. Is there anything you need?"

Nick. She needed to be with Nick.

"No, thanks. You all have done so much for me."

"It's nothing you wouldn't have done for any of us." Kara kissed her on the cheek. "Get some rest, and call if you need anything."

And for the first time in what seemed forever, Holly was completely alone.

* * *

HOLLY SPENT THE first few days after her discharge sleeping, but by the fourth day, she was starting to go stir-crazy. She felt irritable, angry, out of sorts, her entire life up in the air. She wasn't strong enough to go back to work, which is where most of her friends were, and didn't want to spend another minute with her parents, who, thankfully, were flying out tonight anyway.

She called the paper to talk with Beth, but Beth was too busy. She went for a walk, but found herself out of breath before she reached the corner. She made herself some iced tea, and curled up on the sofa with one of her favorite romance novels, hoping to distract herself by reading, but she couldn't keep her gaze on the page.

No matter what she did, her thoughts kept returning to Nick.

What was he doing now? Did he miss her the way she missed him? Had his feelings for her begun to fade?

If she'd known how much worry came from loving someone, she might have sent herself a memo telling herself *not* to fall for the handsome next-door neighbor who kidnapped her, no matter how sexy he was or how good he was in bed or how much he seemed to understand her. Then again, she couldn't imagine a world in which she wouldn't love him.

Look at yourself! You're a wreck.

She was stuck on him, and she couldn't do anything about it.

She called Zach, begged him to contact the detention center. "Please, just tell him I love him. I miss him so badly."

"His motions hearing is tomorrow morning. Can you hold out for another twenty-four hours?"

"I suppose so. I don't know." She needed to get a grip, grow up. Instead, she dissolved into tears. "No."

"Okay, I'll see what I can do."

Now that the tears had started, the words came bubbling out. "What if he doesn't love me anymore? What if being away from me makes him realize that it was just the adrenaline? What if—"

"Holly." Zach chuckled. "I haven't seen many men as

desperately in love as he is. Trust me on this. But, hey, why don't I come by, pick you up, and bring you to the office. I'll make up a reason to call him, and you can listen on the line. How's that?"

Relief rushed through her, sweet and bright. "Zach, you're the greatest."

NICK WAS READING a biography about the Wright brothers and struggling to keep his attention on the narrative when one of the guards interrupted him.

"You've got a call, Andris."

Nick stood, waited for them to open the door and attach the restraints, then shuffled after them down the hall to one of the enclosed phone booths.

He sat and waited for them to transfer the call, wondering what news Rensler had for him now. He was surprised to hear McBride's voice. "Hey. What's up?"

"I have someone here who is desperate to know how you're doing. I've advised her not to say anything, but she is listening."

Nick's heart skipped a beat, then seemed to jump up and down.

Holly.

Holly was listening. She could hear him.

"I'm okay." Hell, in this moment, he was better than okay.

"Are they treating you well?" McBride asked.

"Yeah, no worries there. I'm in protective isolation, so the only real danger is dying of boredom."

"I'll bet."

"How is she?"

"She's good. She looks great. She looks fantastic, really. She's wearing . . . What? Okay . . . a blue sheath dress by Armani and a pair of black Jimmy Choo pumps."

Nick knew Holly had made Zach say that. He didn't know what any of that meant, but it sounded beautiful. "I'm wearing prison orange and five days of unshaved beard, but I'm getting a haircut before the hearing tomorrow."

"It's about time."

"How is she, really?"

"She's healing, but she really misses you."

Nick's mind filled with an image of Holly's sweet face. "I miss her, too. I miss her so damned much. I hate that I can't be with her now. She's been through such a rough time, and I think she needs me. As soon as I'm out of here, I'm coming to see her. If I don't get out . . . God, I hope she waits for me, no matter how long it takes. There will never be anyone else for me. She's all I think about. I love her."

There was a moment of awkward silence as Nick realized he'd just babbled a few Hallmark cards' worth of mushy stuff over the phone to a man he barely knew, a chief deputy US marshal at that.

"Um . . . Right." McBride cleared his throat. "She feels the same way."

There was so much more Nick wanted to say, but not with McBride listening. "Take care of her."

"You got it. And good luck tomorrow."

"Thanks. And, hey, McBride, I owe you."

"Yeah, you do—but not for this."

Nick shuffled back to his cell with a smile on his face.

THE ADRENALINE WAS gone, and Nick still loved her.

Holly was too happy, too excited—and frankly too nicely dressed—to go home and be alone right now. Zach dropped her off at the newspaper, which wasn't far from his office. She would have taken a cab, but he'd insisted.

The walk to the front door left her a little out of breath. Wearing a bra wasn't easy, either, the wing passing over her incision and hugging tightly against the rib the bullet had broken in her side, but she put the discomfort out of her mind.

Her heart still soaring, she stepped into the front lobby and waved to the security guard, "Hi, Cormac."

He gaped at her. "Ms. Bradshaw? Welcome back! You look . . . great."

She smiled, so filled with happiness she thought she might pop. "Thank you. What a sweet thing to say."

Aware that people were staring at her, she walked to the elevator and took it to the third floor, leaning against the wall to catch her breath. She stepped out and headed straight back to Entertainment, her three-inch heels clicking sweetly on the tile. The familiar scents of newsprint and coffee filled her head, made her feel at home. She had missed this place, missed her coworkers, missed writing.

She saw Beth in her office and waved, then walked toward her desk, thinking she would catch up on voice mails, maybe check her email. But when she reached her desk, she found it stripped clean, all of her personal belongings sitting on top in a cardboard box.

"What is this?"

Beth walked up behind her. "I think you should go talk to Tom."

Holly turned to face her. "Did you all give me up for dead?"

The answer was in Beth's eyes. "Go talk to Tom."

A knot of dread in her stomach, Holly cut through Sports, making her way toward the back corner of the newsroom that was reserved for the editor and the I-Team.

A new sports intern looked her up and down. "Who is that?"

"Holly Bradshaw, one of the entertainment writers," came a hushed reply. "Forget about her, bro. You'll never tap that. She's a fucking CIA officer."

The male attention barely registered with her, either to impress or to offend her. She was used to it. Besides, her mind was on what she'd seen in Beth's eyes.

"Holly?" Laura stood. "I didn't think you'd be back at work so soon."

"I'm not really back—not yet."

"Hey!" Sophie smiled, got to her feet. "Shouldn't you be resting?"

"I came in to check email and get caught up on phone messages, but all my stuff is in a box. Beth wouldn't say, but I think I've been fired."

Matt and Alex had joined them now.

"God, Holly, I'm so sorry," Matt said. "That doesn't seem right."

"It's not right." Alex looked toward Tom's office.

"You're looking kind of pale," Laura said, pulling out a chair. "Come here and sit down for a minute and catch your breath."

But Tom had heard them. He opened his door. "Bradshaw, get in here."

Holly had watched her friends put up with his verbal abuse for years. She'd never confronted him because she'd needed the job in order to do her work as an NCO—and because it hardly fit her persona to chew him up and spit him out.

But things were different now. She didn't need to hide who she was from her friends or the world.

"I'm not a dog, Tom. I don't come running when people shout my name. If you want me to come into your office, find a civil way of asking."

His face turned red. "Ms. Bradshaw, will you please come here?"

"Yes, Mr. Trent." She smiled to her friends, saw the hope and worry on their faces, their support precious to her. She stepped into Tom's cluttered, stuffy office and sat, her pulse picking up, butterflies in her stomach.

Why should she feel nervous around him? She'd faced spies, criminals, even murderers. He was just an editor with a bad temper to match his bad hair. If he fired her, she would bounce back.

If he fired her . . .

She loved this job. She didn't want to lose it.

Tom closed the door, walked around to the other side of his desk, and sat. "In light of revelations about your real job, I am terminating your employment with this newspaper effective today."

She'd expected this, and still his words left her stunned. "My work here has always been far above average. I've always met deadline, and I've won lots of state journalism awards. What about my job performance justifies termination?"

"While you were meeting deadline and winning those awards, you were actually working for the CIA and using *my* newsroom as cover."

"I was a non-cover officer, meaning I had no cover. This was my *real* job. Right now, it's my only job. I'm leaving the Agency. I planned to continue working here as my sole source of employment."

"Sounds like you need to make new plans. You were dishonest with us. For years, you misled us."

"I never lied to anyone. You never once asked me whether I had another job. Not once did I disclose anything I knew about activities or stories at the newspaper to anyone at the Agency. You have absolutely no reason—"

"In Colorado, I don't need a reason." He glared at her through unfeeling blue eyes. "You might be able to excuse what you did, but you *used* my paper."

"I never—"

"Did you or did you not write an article about Sachino Dudaev as a way to connect with him on behalf of the Central Intelligence Agency?"

Well, he had her there. "Yes—but Beth approved the article. It was a legitimate entertainment news story. I saw it as doing my job for both organizations."

He handed her an envelope. "Your last paycheck. We used your vacation time to cover the days you were away over the past month. I'll need your ID and keycard."

Holly reached into her handbag, drew out her ID and keycard and dropped them on his desk. "I'm sure you think people remember you for being a great journalist or an uncompromising editor, but what they remember about you is how you made them feel. They remember your lack of support when they asked for maternity leave or sick time. They remember how you yelled at them over trivial things just because you were in a bad mood. They remember how you belittled them."

His eyes narrowed. "Say what you want to say, and get out."

She would not let him see her cry.

She got to her feet, fought a wave of dizziness. "You're a dick, Tom. Eventually I'll find another job, but you'll still be a dick. Oh, and good luck with your karma."

She opened the door to find her friends standing outside, shock on their faces.

"No way." Sophie gaped at her.

"Yes way." Holly's vision blurred, and she felt suddenly out of breath.

Alex took her arm. "Come and sit down."

She pressed a hand against the pain in her side, drew in deep breaths.

Sophie had tears in her eyes. "I'll call Marc, see if he can give you a ride home."

"I can give her a ride. I'm quitting." Laura turned, walked to her desk, and started shoving things in her handbag. "If Holly goes, I go."

Holly stood, walked over to Laura, tried to talk sense into her. "I'm going to be all right. I don't want you to lose your job, too."

Laura lowered her voice to a whisper. "My old TV station in DC offered me the main news anchor position. Javier and I are moving there. I was going to give my notice at the end of the week anyway, but it's much more satisfying to do it this way."

Tom stepped out of his office. "Nilsson, what the hell are you doing?"

"I've seen how you treat your staff. I don't want to be a part of it." She shut down her computer, took her keycard and ID, walked over to him, and handed them to him. "I quit. Consider that my official notice."

"I don't feel very good," said Matt, logging out of his computer. "I think I've got that crud that's going around. Sorry, but I have to head home."

"Harker, sit your ass back down." Tom pointed to Matt's desk. "You've got tomorrow's lead story."

"I guess it will have to wait until I don't feel so sick." Matt grabbed his briefcase, turned to Laura. "I'll go get Holly's stuff and carry it down to your car."

Alex coughed, turned off his monitor. "Yeah, I'm feeling sick, too. Must be something in the air—a strong whiff of bullshit."

"You, too, Carmichael?" Tom glared at him. "You don't even like Bradshaw."

"That was back when I thought she was an airhead." Alex grabbed his backpack. "If it came to a smackdown between the two of you, my money would be on her."

Sophie hurried over to her desk and began grabbing her things. "I'm leaving, too. I can't work today."

Tom threw his hands up in the air, shouting now. "What the hell is wrong with everyone? She was a goddamn spook! You're not getting paid for today."

Surrounded by her friends, Holly strode past Tom. "I guess karma got here quicker than I thought."

Together, they walked out of the stunned and silent newsroom.

"THE MOTIONS HEARING tomorrow is canceled."

Nick gaped at Rensler "What? Why? When is it being rescheduled?"

"It's not being rescheduled. The prosecutor has dropped all the charges."

There was a buzzing in Nick's ears. "All of them?"

Rensler nodded. "As soon as we complete the paperwork, you'll be free to go."

"But how—?"

"I think you must have friends in very high places. Someone from the Agency spoke up on your behalf and lit a bonfire under the prosecutor's ass. I just got the call a half hour ago and drove straight over."

Nick sat. "When do I get these off?"

"Soon. We just need to process you out."

Nick thought he must be dreaming, but sure enough, the restraints were removed and he was led down the hallway to a room where his personal belongings were handed to him in a black garment bag—suit, shoes, watch, wallet, cell phone.

"Take care," Rensler called to him.

"You, too, and thank you." Nick stopped, turned back to him. "Are you ever going to tell me who hired you to represent me?"

Rensler shook his head. "That party would prefer to remain anonymous."

A guard pointed to a dressing room. "You can change in there, sir, and then you're free to go."

Nick walked in, stripped off the prison shoes, jumpsuit, T-shirt, underwear, and socks, shoved them into the laundry shoot, and put on the suit he'd worn the afternoon he'd flown out from Denver. He looked in the mirror.

God, he needed a haircut and a shave.

But he didn't care.

He was going home to Holly.

Home.

It had been a long time since he'd thought of any place as home, but that's what Holly was to him. She was his home.

He stepped out of the dressing room and found himself standing face-to-face with Nguyen. "Oh, man, are you a welcome sight."

They hugged, slapped each other on the back.

Lee grinned. "You need a haircut, man."

"How are you? The last time I saw you, I was afraid that was it."

"I'm alive, thanks to you."

"So you were behind getting me out of here?"

Lee shook his head. "I just got home yesterday. Believe it or not, Holly's former CO engineered it. He went straight to the Director. The Director personally reviewed all the evidence and called the prosecutors."

It was a day for surprises. "I wouldn't think Holly's CO cared much for me."

"He doesn't, but he's extremely fond of Holly."

"Are you going to tell me what the hell you were doing? I thought you were in on it all with Bauer."

Lee lowered his voice. "The Agency has been investigating what happened in Batumi ever since it happened. I was brought into Bauer's sphere to monitor him. It's not the first time the Agency has suspected him of wrongdoing. I've been putting together a case against him the entire time, pretending to be dirty. I wanted to warn you, but I couldn't risk it. I didn't have the proof I needed to tie him to Dudaev or the Batumi mess, and I couldn't be sure who his accomplice was. Some people on the investigating committee were certain it was *you*. I want you to know I never believed that."

There was regret in Lee's brown eyes, but Nick understood what it was to be torn between duty and friendship.

"Thanks, man."

"I came to Colorado Springs with Bauer's approval on the pretext of negotiating your surrender, but I had planned to explain it all then and try to find a way to save your life. Instead, you saved mine."

"How did you get Bauer to trust you?"

"The Agency set up a little operation that made me look

dirty. Bauer caught me, thought he had the means to keep me quiet."

"Clever."

"Enough shop talk. Are you ready to get the hell out of here?" Lee opened the door that led to the front lobby. "I'll drive you wherever you want to go and answer the rest of your questions on the way."

There was only one place Nick wanted to be.

CHAPTER 30

HOLLY SAT ON her sofa, propped up by pillows and surrounded by her friends, listening while Joaquin recounted what had happened in the newsroom for Marc and Julian, who'd just gotten off duty and come to join them all.

They'd wanted to go to a bar for drinks to celebrate the day's rebellion, but Holly had used up whatever strength she'd had in her confrontation with Tom and hadn't had the energy to go out. So while Laura had driven Holly home and helped her get comfortable, the rest of the gang had gone shopping for snacks, beer, and wine. And what had started as a walkout had become a party, with everyone crowded into her living room—everyone except Zach and Javier, who'd gone to the airport to pick someone up, and, of course, Nick.

Joaquin reached the end of the story. "So then she says, 'I guess karma got here quicker than I thought,' and we all walked out together."

"I would have loved to have seen his face," Julian said. "I wish you'd taped it."

Alex grinned. "If we put that shit on YouTube, it would go viral."

Marc turned to Holly. "Did you really call him a dick?"

"Yes, I did." Holly couldn't help but smile. "The only thing that worries me is what you all will face tomorrow. He's docking your pay."

Matt opened another Fat Tire. "I don't care. I'd have lit a

day's salary on fire just to watch that show. That son of a bitch had it coming."

"I'm sorry he fired you, Holly," said Natalie. "You didn't deserve that. You're a fantastic entertainment writer."

Reece raised his wineglass. "To Holly!"

There were general shouts of agreement, everyone raising a glass or a bottle—beer, wine, iced tea.

"Thank you." She raised her glass. "To friendship."

"To friendship!"

"It won't be the same in the newsroom without you," Kat said at last, looking first to Holly and then to Laura. "I'm going to miss both of you so much."

"I'm going to miss you, too." Holly felt tears prick her eyes, but blinked them back. "I loved hanging out with you every day. Work never felt like work to me."

"What are you going to do now?" Gabe asked.

"The Agency has offered me a job as a cryptographer or an analyst—my choice." She had to fight to keep her voice light. The thought of leaving them all was more than she could think about now. "I've got some money set aside. I don't have to decide right away."

But working at the paper had never been about money.

One of her CIA instructors had told her she was good at human intelligence because she loved connecting with people. It was the truth. She'd loved the challenge of entertainment journalism—learning about special people, finding a way to tell their stories, sharing their creativity through her articles. In some ways, it wasn't all that different from the work she'd done for the Agency—well, apart from the listening devices, GPS transmitters, and the risk of violence and death.

"Javi says you're a genius with cryptography," said Laura. "Can you show us how that works?"

Holly borrowed Matt's reporter notebook and wrote a message in plaintext, created a key, then wrote out the ciphertext, explaining what she was doing each step of the way. "Whoever has the key can simply take the ciphertext and decrypt the message."

"Whoa," Marc said.

"That went right over my head," Tessa said.

"Hot," Alex said.

Holly shrugged, set the notepad aside. "I find it really dull."

"Are you going to take the job?" Kara asked, the casual tone of her voice not quite enough to hide her worry.

She and Holly had been friends for more than ten years. The thought of living far away from her . . .

Don't think about it now.

"It depends in part on what happens at Nick's hearing tomorrow. If his case goes to trial and he goes to prison . . ." And then Holly couldn't help it. Tears filled her eyes. "I don't want to be away from him. I don't want to leave you all, either."

"It's going to be okay." Laura gave her hand a squeeze. "If you do end up at Langley, you'll be close to me and Javi. We'll get together a lot. I promise."

Holly reached for a tissue, wiped her tears away. "I'd like that."

"So tell us about this Andris guy who's got you tied in knots," said Joaquin. "I hear he was with Delta Force before he joined the CIA. Is he really all that?"

The women in the room exchanged glances, nodding.

"I'd like to kick his ass," Julian muttered under his breath.

"Get in line, buddy," said Marc.

Holly sighed. "I know you're just feeling concerned for me, but cut him a break. Yes, he did some rotten things, but it really wasn't his fault. If it weren't for Nick, I'd have been killed so many times—by Dudaev, by his men, by some other Agency officer with fewer scruples."

The doorbell rang.

Julian opened it. "Hey, McBride, Corbray . . . and, well, speak of the devil."

Zach and Javier stepped inside, wide grins on their faces.

"Looks like a party," Zach said.

And then . . .

"Nick?" Unable to believe her eyes, Holly stared at him, her pulse tripping.

In the span of a heartbeat, she was on her feet. She dashed through the crowded room and sank into his embrace, his arms enfolding her, his scent surrounding her.

He cupped her face between his palms, kissed her. "God, am I glad to see you. Are you okay? I don't want to hurt you."

"I'm healing. What are you doing here? Did your motions

hearing happen today, or did those two break you out? Are we on the run again?"

Everyone laughed.

"Apparently your CO went to bat for me with the Director. All the charges were dropped. The motions hearing was canceled."

Holly closed her eyes and sent a silent thank-you to the man who'd been a part of her life for so long—and yet not a part of it at all. "Then it's over?"

"It's really over."

"Oh, thank God."

He ran a knuckle over her cheek, sympathy on his handsome face. "I was told you got fired today. I'd like to hear about it."

It seemed so unimportant now. "For some reason, Tom didn't like the fact that I was moonlighting for the Agency."

"Holly is our hero," said Joaquin.

"She's my hero, too." Nick smiled, slid his fingers into her hair, and brought his lips to hers in a slow, deep kiss.

And in that instant, all became right with her world.

NICK SHOOK HANDS with Holly's friends and coworkers one by one, meeting most of them for the first time, though he already knew who they were. He held out his hand to Darcangelo. "Thanks for everything you did to help Holly."

Darcangelo hesitated for a moment, then shook Nick's hand, his crushing grip telling Nick that he wasn't forgiven. "Do you practice martial arts?"

Nick gave as good as he got. "Krav Maga. Tae kwon do. Aikido."

"We should spar sometime."

Nick grinned. "As soon as my ribs heal, you're on."

"Can't wait." Hunter held out his hand. "You should come shooting with us sometime, too."

Another crushing handshake.

"I'd like that."

But Nick's arrival seemed to be the secret signal for everyone to leave. Soon only Corbray and Laura remained.

"I'm glad I've got the two of you together," Corbray said. "I've got a proposition for you both."

Nick sat on the sofa beside Holly, her fingers laced through his. He couldn't seem to let go of her, and she didn't seem to want to let go of him, either. "Let's hear it."

"Despite this incident with you, Holly, Cobra International Solutions is growing faster than we'd imagined. As you know, I'll be heading the new DC office, while Tower stays in Denver. We need good people—people with the kind of proven skills that the two of you have."

"Brawn and brains," Nick said, liking where this was going.

"Now, Holly, I know you don't want to leave Colorado. If you two come to work for me, you can stay in Denver. You'd be sent abroad on assignment from time to time, but this would be your home base. And the two of you would be working together."

Nick looked at Holly. Holly looked at Nick. They both looked at Corbray.

"I have no idea what your salaries and benefits were with the Agency, but we're prepared to offer top compensation, plus a competitive benefits package that includes ground-floor stock options."

Nick nodded. "I like it."

"What kind of work?" Holly asked.

"Well, he's the brawn." Corbray pointed to Nick. "And you're the brains. We need help with everything from covert ops to intelligence analysis."

Nick glanced down at Holly. "I'd like to talk it over with Holly."

Holly nodded. "So much has happened."

"I understand." Corbray took a business card out of his wallet and handed it to Nick. "No need to decide tonight. Come down to the office when Holly's up to it and we can get into specifics."

"I told you everything was going to be okay." Laura gave Holly a bright smile. "I wanted to tell you more, but I couldn't ruin the surprise."

Corbray exchanged a glance with his wife. "Also, Laura and I have something we need to say to you, Holly."

Laura nodded, seemed to search for words. "I know what you did for us, for my little girl. Derek's source at the CIA told him about the role you played behind the scenes, helping Javi get the airplane that flew him and Klara out of Pakistan. I just wanted to say how deeply grateful I am, how grateful we both are. Klara means everything to us."

Holly looked surprised—and irritated. "I need to ferret out Derek's source. You weren't supposed to know."

"But I do know, and I'm glad I do." Tears filled Laura's eyes and she gave Holly a gentle hug. "You're an only child, and so am I. Now because of Klara, we're sisters."

Holly smiled, tears glittering in her eyes. "I like that."

Nick saw a sheen in Corbray's eyes and felt his throat grow tight. He hadn't known about this, but of course it made sense. Holly and her big heart.

There wasn't anything she wouldn't do for the people she loved.

HOLLY AND NICK ordered Chinese and ate at the table by candlelight, then curled up on the sofa together. Holly told him what had happened at the newspaper. He told her about his time in detention—and his confrontation with Bauer.

"He didn't say a word?"

"Nothing."

Then Nick told her about his conversation with Lee. "He offered me a teaching position at The Farm—tactical, firearms, that sort of thing. They're offering a pretty good salary, too. I was excited about it until Corbray made his offer."

And so they'd come to it—the discussion about the future.

"My CO offered me a job as an analyst or cryptographer—whichever I prefer."

"But you're not interested, are you?" His gaze was soft, warm.

How did he do that? How did he make her feel loved just by looking at her?

"I'd rather stay here, but I'll go where you want to go. I realize your family lives back east. You don't love Colorado the way I do, but I think you could learn to love it."

"Holly—"

"It's warm in January, and it snows in June, but people know how to drive in the snow. There's nothing like the aspens in autumn or a sunrise just after a snowfall. There's skiing and rafting and climbing. Do you really climb, or was that just part of your cover?"

"Holly—"

"It doesn't matter. Gabe could teach you. I know Julian and Marc aren't your biggest fans at the moment, but they'll get over it. There are lots—"

He pressed a finger to her lips, chuckled. "Holly, if you want to stay, we'll stay."

She stared up at him. "Really?"

"Let's go talk to Javier next week when you're a little stronger and see what he has in mind."

Holly couldn't keep the smile off her face. "Thank you."

"I do have a few conditions."

Holly arched an eyebrow. "Is that so?"

"I was raised in a traditional family, and I'm a pretty traditional guy. I can't help but want to take care of you."

She smiled at him from beneath her lashes, took on a sexy, sultry tone of voice. "Oh, there are *lots* of ways you can take care of me."

"I'm serious."

"So am I."

"I don't want you doing anything that could get you killed. When I saw that you'd been shot . . . When your eyes closed . . . God." He squeezed his eyes shut for a moment, shook his head. "I was so afraid I'd lost you, Holly. I can survive a lot of things, but not that. Not that."

An unfamiliar warmth spread through her and she realized this is what it was like to be with a man who truly cared for her. "Okay. Agreed. What else?"

"I don't want you doing the sort of work for Javier that you did for the Agency."

"You don't want me sleeping with other men for the sake of democracy?"

"No! Never."

She began to unbutton his shirt, her need for him taking a sexual turn. "Believe it or not, there's only one man I want—and that's you."

"Good." He helped her with his shirt, unbuttoning the cuffs, then shedding it, faint yellow bruises still visible on his skin where he'd been beaten. "I did promise you a night of hot sex if we got through that, didn't I?"

"Yes, you did, and I'm going to collect."

Chuckling, he lifted her into his arms and carried her to her bed, undressing her with a tenderness that put a lump in her throat—and set her on fire. He took off his pants and boxer briefs and stretched out naked on the bed beside her, his hands caressing the curve of her hip, the swells of her breasts, the red line of her scar. "There's one more thing."

"Go on." She reached for his erection, stroked him, her body aching for him.

"I never thought I could love again. I never thought I could feel what I feel for you. I loved Dani, but you, Holly, are the love of my life. Marry me."

"I love you, too, Nick, but if you're not inside me in the next ten seconds, I'm going to—" She gaped at him. "Marry you?"

"I don't have a ring. I should have waited to ask you, but—"

"No."

"No?"

"I mean, no, you shouldn't wait to ask me. Are you sure? What if it's just the adrenaline? What if a month from now you decide I'm boring and you want someone new or a younger woman or—"

"That is *not* going to happen."

"Are you sure?"

"Haven't you listened to anything I've said?"

"Yes!" She found herself laughing and crying at the same time, her heart so swollen with joy she was surprised her chest hadn't popped. "Yes!"

"Yes, you listened, or, yes, you'll marry me?"

"Yes, I'll marry you. Now, will you *please* make lo—"

He cut off her words with a kiss, then stopped, concern on his face. "Are you sure you're strong enough for this? I don't want to hurt you."

"Are you kidding?" She pushed him onto his back, straddled his hips, smiled down at him. "Never underestimate the strength of a woman in love."

EPILOGUE

Nick dialed Holly's extension. "I reserved conference room two. On my way."

He got up from his desk, walked down the long marble hallway of Cobra International Solutions toward the conference room, anticipation heating his blood.

How they were supposed to last another ten days to the wedding living apart, he didn't know. Why were they going along with this stupid charade anyway? His mom and dad knew that he and Holly lived together and had been living together since last summer. As far as he was concerned, they could stay in a hotel if that bothered them.

But Holly wanted so badly to get along with his parents and be accepted by his family. She had moved out of their new posh four-bedroom Cheesman Park condo and back into her old place the day before his parents had flown in from Philadelphia. Nick saw her each day at the office, and she joined him and his parents every night for the elaborate dinners his mother made.

But they hadn't slept together for more than a week.

The joke is on you, Andris. You're thirty-nine, about to marry the most beautiful woman in the world, and reduced to sleeping alone.

He turned the corner, saw Holly walking toward him wearing a tailored navy blue suit and twelve-hundred-dollar heels. Yeah, she looked all business, but he knew what she was wearing beneath that suit. She'd texted him a photo of those crotchless panties with the crazy laces in the back this morning when she'd put them on.

He'd spent all morning sitting across from her in a meeting with representatives of the nonprofit she was funding through the sale of the necklace Dudaev had given her. She'd gotten more than three million dollars for it at auction and was giving every cent of it to help the victims of human trafficking in the former Soviet states, including Georgia. And yet all Nick had been able to think about was those damned panties.

She opened the conference room door, walked inside, her gaze meeting his through the glass wall, a sultry smile on her face as she pressed the button that closed the blinds, giving them privacy.

Damn.

It took some serious self-control not to break into a run. He strode to the door, opened it, and locked it behind him. They didn't need anyone walking in on them.

"Ms. Bradshaw."

"Mr. Andris."

And then she was in his arms, and they were kissing. She felt sweet and soft and warm, her familiar scent both soothing and arousing. While she fought with his zipper, Nick yanked up that proper pencil skirt, ran his hands over those laces, then slipped a hand between her thighs to tease her clit.

Her hand closed around his erection, stroked him. "It's been so long. Please! I can't wait. This is all I've thought about all day."

They staggered together to the conference table, kissing as they went.

He set her on the edge of the table, took her hand, glanced down at the two-carat blue diamond engagement ring on her finger. "What will your fiancé say about this?"

"Who's going to tell him?" She lay on her back, her skirt up around her hips.

He caught her behind the knees, spread her legs wide apart, and took a long, hard look at paradise. Then he rested those expensive heels on his shoulders, took his cock in hand, and guided himself inside her. "*Jesus*, Holly."

She was slick, hot, tight, and he found himself pounding into her—no finesse, no restraint, no holding back. For a moment he was afraid he'd embarrass himself by coming right away. He took a deep breath and willed himself to relax, reaching down to caress her swollen clit, wanting her to enjoy this as much as he did.

Her eyes were closed now, her lips parted, little moans rolling from her throat with each thrust. She grabbed his wrist, her nails digging into his skin, her other hand bunched into a fist. "Oh . . . *yes* . . . Nika."

Thank God the conference rooms were soundproof.

He drove into her again and again, faster, harder, reaching up with one hand to open the buttons of her shirt and fondle her breasts.

Yes, *this* was the way to spend an afternoon at work.

JAVIER LOOKED AT the security monitor, moans and sighs coming in loud and clear through the audio feed. "No one told them conference room two has hidden cameras and listening devices?"

They took prospective clients to that room when they believed those parties were hiding something, let them spend some time there alone, and listened.

"No, sir." Ricardo Perez was one of the newer security guards. Like every other male at CIS, he was in love with Holly. He couldn't seem to take his eyes off the X-rated action on the monitor. "Should I go knock on the door?"

"Nah." Javier turned off the monitor for Holly's sake. "Leave the monitor off until they exit. I'll tell Andris myself. And, Perez, you're under strict orders not to mention this to anyone, especially not Ms. Bradshaw. Got me, man? I want that footage on my desk before the end of your shift today."

Javier would destroy it himself. He didn't need his two new employees starring in an Internet sex scandal. They'd had enough crazy publicity already.

Perez nodded. "Yes, sir. I understand, sir."

Chuckling to himself, Javier walked out of the security office and glanced at his watch. He and Laura had come back to Denver for the wedding, and Laura was chilling up at the Cimarron Ranch. Maybe he should give her a buzz and see how she felt about taking time for a little afternoon delight.

If anything was more contagious than a yawn, it was lust.

"ARE YOU SURE you don't want me to come with you?" Nick whispered.

"You can't come with me," Holly whispered back. "I don't want you to see my gown until the wedding."

"Right, but—"

"It's going to be okay. I've got it all worked out. Kara and Sophie are going to be there, and so is my mom. We have a plan. By the time we're done, she'll love my gown." She kissed his cheek. "Are you coming by tonight after supper?"

After learning that their office sexcapades had been filmed and recorded by security, they had changed tactics. Now Nick drove her home after dinner—and they had a quickie before he left.

It wasn't perfect, but it was better than sexual starvation.

"You bet I am." He gave her a smile that warmed her all over.

"See you later!" she called out, climbing into her car.

Ekaterine Natalia Mariami Tsiuri Andris sat in the passenger seat, a red, blue, and yellow scarf covering her black-and-silver hair, an enormous black handbag in her lap. She smiled at Holly, and Holly could tell she was nervous, too. Still beautiful at sixty-seven, she had a quiet grace and dignity that Holly admired. She was tall, too, taller than Holly, with an old-world elegance that made Holly think of vineyards and giant poplars.

"Are you ready?" Holly asked, putting on her seatbelt and starting the car.

"Yes, yes."

Holly put on some classical music, something soft to ease the silence. "I would love to see photos of your wedding."

"Next time you come to Pennsylvania, I will show you."

"When did you meet Papa Andris?"

"Oh, I was seventeen, and he was nineteen."

Holly drove through Denver, listening while Mama, as she insisted Holly call her, told her how she'd met her future husband one day when her bicycle had gotten a flat tire outside the grocery store that belonged to Papa Andris's family. He'd fixed the flat, then followed in his father's car to make sure she got home safely.

They'd seen each other at church after that, and her uncle was cousins with his father's sister-in-law—or something like that. Holly got lost in there somewhere. They hadn't dated, because respectable girls did not date, but were married two months later. She'd left school because the teachers felt uncomfortable with a wife—someone who was enjoying the benefits of marriage, as she put it—attending school alongside the unmarried girls. She'd given birth to her first son nine months later.

"Wow." Holly wanted to say something like, "That's so romantic," but it didn't sound even remotely romantic to her. Thrown out of school for having a sex life? Becoming a mother at the young age of eighteen? "You must have been so happy when Tomas was born."

Holly counted in her mind, hoping she'd gotten the birth order right.

Tomas, Peter, Michael, Jacob, Nick, and Katherine.

Their real names were Toma, Petre, Mikheil, Iacob, Nikolai, Ekaterine, but they all went by the Americanized versions.

Mama Andris smiled. "As will you be when your first child is born. You *do* plan to have children? You are—what, thirty-four now?"

Well you walked into that one, Bradshaw.

"Yes, we do want children, but not right away."

And certainly not six.

"Hmm," said Mama, like she always did when Holly said something of which she didn't quite approve.

Holly pulled into the parking lot behind the bridal shop and glanced at her watch. The others should be here at any minute.

"I can't wait to hear what you think of my gown." A frisson of excitement shot through Holly, the realization hitting her. "Two nights from tonight, I'm getting married!"

Mama smiled, her blue eyes warm. "Yes, you are."

They went inside and met Nora, the shop's owner, who greeted them with a smile. "We're so close to the big day. You must be so excited."

"I am. Nora, I'd like you to meet Nick's mother, Katherine Andris."

"A pleasure. Your son certainly chose well, didn't he?"

Mama smiled. "Yes, I think he did."

Nora took their coats and led them to the fitting area. "Make yourselves comfortable. We've got coffee, tea, white wine, bottled water. Can I get you anything?"

Holly asked for water, Mama coffee.

"I think your friends are here." Nora disappeared and returned a few minutes later with Kara and Sophie.

They'd already met Mama, and she welcomed them with a warm smile.

"Shall we begin?"

Holly's mother was late—again.

Holly quickly undressed until she was wearing only her panties, hanging her blouse and jeans on hooks. She turned to find Mama Andris standing behind her.

"Let me see that." Mama's brow was bent in a concerned frown.

Holly realized she wanted to see her scar. She lifted her left arm, slowly turning so that Mama could see the entire thing.

Mama's hands pressed against her ribs where the bullet had entered her. "This still causes you pain?"

"Sometimes."

Nora reappeared with the first of two dresses Holly was going to try on the pretext of it being her last chance to change her mind. "Here's the Badgley Mischka."

Operation Wedding Dress was underway.

Holly took the strapless bra and put it on, then accepted Nora's help getting into the gown. It was a body-hugging strapless gown with a corset-style bodice of shirred tulle and a dropped waist adorned with Swarovski crystals. The mermaid skirt was made of light, fluffy layers that trailed into a short train.

"That is so beautiful!" Kara said. "Oh, Holly, you look amazing!"

"You're the only woman I know who can wear that dress without worrying about her tummy sticking out," Sophie said. "Can I ask how much it is?"

Nora read off the price tag. "Six thousand seven hundred." Sophie gave a whistle. "Right."

"What do you think, Mama?" Holly turned, showing her the back.

"It is a lovely dress." The frown on her face told Holly that Mama wasn't happy with it. "But it looks like a dress for a party, not a bridal gown. A bride should be dignified, don't you think?"

"Let's try the Vera Wang." Nora winked at Holly as she helped her undress. She disappeared for a few minutes and returned with yards of lace draped over her arm. "Vera Wang is taking high fashion to new places when it comes to bridal gowns."

She helped Holly into the delicate garment, which wasn't much more than a sheath of transparent lace with a trumpet skirt. The deep V-neck showed off her cleavage, but the illusion lace showed everything else, including her breasts and panties.

"Isn't there more to this dress, something that goes on top?" Mama asked, staring at Holly's nipples. "I can see your boopsies."

"I've got to go with Mama Andris on this one," Kara said. "It's high fashion, but it looks like something you're supposed to wear *under* a wedding dress—or maybe on your wedding night."

"They have already had their wedding night," Mama Andris muttered.

Holly ignored the comment and studied her reflection, imagining the stir it would cause if she walked down the aisle dressed in nothing but air and lace.

"I don't know that Nick wants to share that much of you with your guests," said Sophie. "But it does look amazing on you."

It was time to stop shocking poor Mama Andris and try on her real gown.

"Nora, can I try on the one I picked?"

"These are not gowns you chose?" Mama asked.

"No, they're not." Holly could almost hear Mama sending

a silent prayer of thanksgiving skyward. But that had been the entire point of this exercise—to make sure she wasn't shocked by the gown Holly had chosen. It *did* have a low neckline. "I just wanted to try them. It's my last chance to change my mind."

Nora helped Holly out of the Vera Wang and disappeared, then returned with a large white garment bag that had Holly's name written on it. "Here it is."

Anticipation made it hard for Holly to breathe. "Oh, I can't wait to try it on!"

She'd been working with Nora's seamstress for weeks, getting the fit perfect, making tiny adjustments here and there.

Mama looked like she might need something stronger than coffee.

"Can I put this on in a dressing room and surprise them?" she asked Nora.

Neither Kara nor Sophie had seen the finished gown.

"Of course." Nora led her to a dressing room and helped her into it, then helped her put on the sheer blusher veil. "Oh, you look beautiful, Holly. Truly beautiful."

The gown had a sweetheart neckline and a tightly fitted bodice with delicate cap sleeves and a full princess skirt. There was no lace, no beading, no crystals, just clean white silk. Even the veil was simple—nothing but sheer fabric and a slender edge of white silk along its scalloped edges.

Holly stepped out of the dressing room, disappointed that her mother still hadn't arrived. She'd wanted her to be here for this moment. But the look on Mama Andris's face made her forget that.

Mama raised her hands to her face, her blue eyes wide. "Ah! There is a bride! Beautiful! This shows your lovely figure without giving it all away."

"Oh, God, Holly, it's gorgeous!" Kara stepped forward, helped Nora straighten out the short silk train.

Sophie smiled. "Mama Andris is right. It's perfect for you. You are going to be the most beautiful bride."

Holly turned and looked into the mirror—and the breath left her lungs. She looked like a princess, like a queen. In two days, she was going to walk down the aisle wearing this gown, and she was going to marry the man she loved.

"It's Carolina Herrera," Nora was saying.

Holly turned to face her future mother-in-law and her friends. "I decided I didn't want Nick to see my gown. I wanted him to see me."

"Oh, sweetie, you are going to blow him away," said Kara.

Mama laughed, a big hearty laugh, a smile on her face. "That was a funny trick to play on me. You show me shocking, half-naked gowns to make sure I will like this one. You didn't need to do that. It is beautiful."

Holly blinked.

"Oh, yes, I figured it out." Mama was still smiling and didn't seem offended. "I don't speak very good English, and I look like a silly old grandmama with a scarf on my head, but I was not born five minutes ago. I raised six children, you know. Oh, the lies those boys told me!"

Then Mama reached into her enormous handbag, got to her feet, and walked over to Holly, holding something in her hands. "In our church, a man and woman wear crowns during the ceremony. You are not getting married in the church, I know, but I thought you might agree to wear this. It is the crown I wore when Nika's father and I were wed."

She held out a circlet of delicate silver flowers and leaves held together by silver wire. It had recently been polished, and Holly could tell it was very old.

Holly took it into her hands, amazed by the detail and the quality of the silversmithing. "It's beautiful. Thank you. I would be honored to wear it."

Nora took it, lifted off the veil, settled the crown on Holly's hair. "Like this. We'll attach the veil like so. It will be perfect."

"Wonderful!" Holly couldn't stop smiling.

"You and I may be very different, but in one way we are the same. We both love Nika with our whole hearts. How do I know this?" She reached out, touched Holly's left side. "You offered up your life for his. There is no greater love than that."

Holly found herself blinking tears away. "Thank you."

"Hey, everyone!" Holly's mother breezed in, looked at Holly, but didn't say a word about the gown, that familiar glint of envy in her eyes. "Sorry I'm late. I felt like I needed a massage this morning, and then it took the coffee shop forever to get my latte right. Is my dress ready to try?"

She looked from Holly to Mama Andris. "Did I miss something?"

"You missed everything—including the point, I think," Mama replied.

"I'M TIPSY," HOLLY spoke in Nick's ear, her words a bit slurred. "Take me somewhere private and have your way with me."

Nick grinned down at his inebriated fiancée. "Not till tomorrow night."

Holly moaned. "Tomorrow night?"

Nick glanced around the club, but didn't see anywhere the two of them could be alone without security cameras. "Sorry, honey, but you're going to have to wait. We're both going to have to wait."

They'd rented the place out for a joint bachelor/bachelor-ette party and invited all their friends and family to join in. This way he and Holly had gotten to spend the evening together rather than apart trying to act amused by sex jokes and strippers.

"I better go say good-bye to Matt," she said. "It looks like he's leaving. Poor guy. It can't be fun to be here when you're in the middle of a divorce."

Nick's gaze followed her as she walked away.

Lee walked up to him, a glass of scotch in his hand. "This is kind of different for a bachelor party—no strippers, married guys hanging with their wives, single guys bringing dates, groom snuggling up to his bride."

Nick grinned at Lee's confusion. "Why would I want to watch some other woman take off her clothes when I have Holly?"

Lee glanced over at Holly, then back at Nick. "Yeah. I've got nothing."

Joaquin, Holly's friend from the newspaper, walked up to Nick, shook his hand. "Congratulations, man. I'm so happy for the two of you. I'm glad Holly found someone good, someone who really cares about her. She and I—we had a special friendship."

Nick frowned. "How special?"

Joaquin held up his hands in mock surrender. "Not that kind of special. We were just friends, man, but good friends, you know?"

"Shut your mouth!"

Nick heard Holly's shout, looked in time to see her slap her father across the face.

The room fell silent.

"Excuse me." Nick strode to her side, the crowd making way for him. "Is something wrong?"

Holly's face was flushed red, her body rigid and shaking. "My dad has had too much to drink. He was just leaving."

"What did he do, Holly?"

Tears gathered in her eyes, but she didn't answer.

Nick's father stepped closer to Holly, rage on his face, his gaze fixed on Holly's father. "He said things that no man should say to any woman, especially his own daughter."

"I overheard him." Nick's brother Mike repeated what her father had said, but spoke quietly and in Georgian so that others needn't hear. "He said, 'You made those pretty tits of yours pay off, didn't you? It's a pity you never let me touch them. You better let your husband do what he wants with them, or he'll go in search of new pussy.'"

Nick had to fight not to punch her father in his filthy mouth, his fists already clenched. Aware that everyone was watching, he kept his voice calm. "You are to leave the party this instant. You are disinvited from the wedding. If you show up tomorrow, you'll be escorted off the property. I don't want you around my wife. I don't want you around our children. Leave here now, and don't let either of us see your face again."

He felt the crowd shift, knew his brothers were behind him—and not only his brothers, but Lee, too, and Holly's friends.

Hunter walked up behind Holly's father. "Hey, Darcangelo, you want to help me take out the trash?"

"Yeah. Something stinks," Darcangelo said, coming to stand at Hunter's side.

Holly's father glared at Nick. "Don't think you can push me around. I outrank you in every way—military rank, money, social class. I have friends in Washington who could make your life very difficult."

"Really, dawg?" Javier stepped up. "I hang out at the Pentagon. Yeah, I go to meetings at the White House, too. I've never heard anyone mention your name. But I have heard them talk about your amazing daughter and her man. Now get a move on. Nobody wants you here."

Hunter gave the man a shove. "Move."

"Don't touch me, or I'll call the cops."

Darcangelo flashed his badge. "Dude, we are the cops."

Holly's father, surrounded by men who wanted to kick his ass, turned and stomped out the door.

Nick handed Lee a twenty. "Make sure he gets a cab."

Lee refused to take the money. "I got it."

Nick turned to his guests, his gaze passing over Holly's mother, who sat at the bar watching, indifference on her face. "Sorry for the interruption, everyone. It's over. Please just enjoy yourselves."

He looked down to see his mother standing beside Holly. "Don't you think about him," she was saying. "You have other family now."

"You have a *huge* family." Mike gave Holly a teasing smile. "You don't know the half of it."

Nick took Holly's hand, drew her into his arms. "I'm sorry for what he did, and I'm sorry for how I reacted. If you want him at the wedding—"

She looked up at him, pressed her fingertips to his lips. "No. I don't want him there. Thank you for doing what I should have done years ago."

"Do you want me to take you home?"

She wiped the tears from her cheeks, smiled. "Are you kidding? This is our party. I don't want to let him spoil it for us. I want to enjoy it."

*   *   *

NICK STOOD WITH his father, brothers, and Lee, his best man, on the eighteenth floor of Denver's Clock Tower. The place was full to capacity, most of their hundred or so guests already in their seats, the room illuminated by candles and by the lights that shone on the four giant clock faces that made up the center of each of the room's four walls. Flowers decorated the aisles, two large standing bouquets of roses marking the front where Nick and Holly would stand.

Nick turned to Lee. "Is my tie straight?"

"Chill." Lee adjusted it. "It's fine. You look good."

Of course, Holly had chosen the tux—Armani or something. Black shirt, black vest, black tie, black jacket and trousers.

"Why are you getting married inside a giant clock, brother?" Mike asked.

"It's part of the theme of the wedding," Reece answered when Nick didn't. "Time is precious. Carpe diem and all of that."

Reece was officiating—Holly's idea. She'd wanted someone who knew them well, someone who could handle public speaking, to be the one to marry them. Reece had been more than happy to do it, in part because it was Holly who'd brought Reece and Kara together.

"I remember when I married Marie," said Tomas. "I was afraid I was going to hyperventilate, I was so nervous."

Nick glared at his oldest brother. "I'm not nervous."

"You hear that?" Peter laughed. "Nick says he's not nervous."

"Quit teasing your brother," Papa said. "Of course he's nervous. Every man is nervous on his wedding day."

But Nick had no idea *why* he was nervous. He didn't have any doubts about his bride. Everything was handled and under control. He didn't have anything to do today besides say his lines—and they weren't difficult. But, yeah, he was nervous. Hell, he'd felt calmer before combat than he did at this moment.

"I want this to be perfect for Holly," he said, putting

words to his unease. "I want her to know how special she is to me."

"Yeah, because that rock she's wearing on her finger isn't enough," said Jacob.

"Ignore Jacob." His father patted him on the back. "It is a big responsibility becoming a husband. Your happiness depends for the rest of your life on her safety and her well-being and then that of children when they come along."

When his father put it that way . . .

"Just enjoy today. You have every day of the rest of your life to show her how much she means to you, Nika. Ah, look. Your mother is here. Your bride must be here, as well. I'd best take my seat."

Right on time.

"See you in a bit." Jacob shook his hand.

Tomas, Peter, and Mike did the same, then disappeared down the aisle, leaving Nick standing with Lee and Reece.

A hush fell over the room, and the harpist began to play.

The bridesmaids and groomsmen walked down the aisle in pairs, followed by his oldest nephew and godchild, Nicholas, who was the ring bearer. Then a troop of tiny flower girls appeared—his nieces, as well as Marc and Sophie's Addie and Tessa and Julian's Maire. They tossed petals every which way, drawing "awws" from the guests as they passed.

Then, there she was—Holly, his precious, beautiful Holly.

She took his breath away, made his mind go blank. God, he was so in love, his pulse pounding for her. Dressed in simple white, she was an angel, her veil floating around her face like gossamer, a sweet smile on her lips.

She walked herself down the aisle, came to stand beside him, her small hand sliding into his, the white roses of her bouquet giving off a heady scent.

"You are the most beautiful sight I've ever seen." He took her hand, raised it to his lips, kissed it. "I love you so much."

She reached up with one hand, cupped his jaw. "If your face had been the last thing I saw in this life, it would have been enough. You're everything to me."

Reece cleared his throat. "I also have a few things to say."

Soft laughter.

Reece welcomed everyone to the ceremony then began to

speak, but his words seemed to drift around Nick, whose gaze was fixed on Holly's. A light seemed to shine in her eyes, her face glowing with happiness.

"They chose this location for a reason. Love has taught them that time is precious. From one moment to the next, none of us know what might happen. Life can change in an instant . . . Time brought them together, and it very nearly tore them apart, a few seconds making the difference between death and life, an end and a beginning . . . The most meaning-ful part of our lives are the simple everyday moments we spend with the people we love . . . Tonight, we celebrate their love and witness their vows. This is their time, their special moment, but it's a special time for those of us who love them, too."

And then it was time to speak their vows.

Holly said, "I do," and Nick managed to do the same. She slid a platinum band onto his finger; he slid one onto hers.

"By the power vested in me by the State of Colorado, I pronounce you husband and wife."

Nick lifted the veil, lowered his lips to hers, drank in the taste of her.

"And the groom is already kissing the bride."

All around them, applause and cheers rang out. Then the clock bells chimed the hour, sounding across Denver. It was just one moment in time, one happy moment in what every-one there knew would be the happiest of happily ever afters.

FROM NATIONAL BESTSELLING AUTHOR
PAMELA CLARE

THE I-TEAM
NOVELS

SEDUCTION GAME

STRIKING DISTANCE

BREAKING POINT

NAKED EDGE

UNLAWFUL CONTACT

HARD EVIDENCE

EXTREME EXPOSURE

PRAISE FOR THE I-TEAM NOVELS

"Pamela Clare is a fabulous storyteller whose beautifully written, fast-paced tales will leave you breathless with anticipation."
—Leigh Greenwood, *USA Today* bestselling author

"Will grip your senses...You'll love this series."
—Romance Reviews Today

pamelaclare.com
penguin.com

BERKLEY SENSATION | Penguin Random House

M1327AS0915

When there's nowhere to turn
but toward each other…

FROM NATIONAL BESTSELLING AUTHOR
PAMELA CLARE

BREAKING POINT

An I-Team Novel

Denver journalist Natalie Benoit and Deputy U.S. Marshal
Zach McBride find themselves captives of a bloodthirsty
Mexican drug cartel. Working together, they escape
through the desert toward the border, the attraction between them flaring hotter than the Sonoran sun. They
fight to stay ahead of the danger that hunts them as forces
more powerful than they can imagine conspire to destroy
them both…

PRAISE FOR PAMELA CLARE'S NOVELS

"Romantic suspense at its best!"
—*The Romance Studio*

"Will keep you glued to the pages…Highly sensual."
—*Fresh Fiction*

pamelaclare.com
penguin.com

M1326T0613